aRos

african horse

By the same author

The Raining Tree War

african horse

DAVID POWNALL

Faber & Faber
3 Queen Square
London

First published in 1975
by Faber and Faber Limited
3 Queen Square London WC1
Printed in Great Britain at
The University Printing House, Cambridge
All rights reserved

ISBN 0 571 10712 5

for Jack, my father, who
was killed in Africa, and
my first son, Gareth, who
was born there.

A PROLOGUE WHICH BRINGS SOME OF THE LAST TO BE FIRST WHICH IS OFTEN THE AFRICAN WAY –

In a million years from now some life-form – maybe a highly developed hippopotamus or Anopheles mosquito – may unearth the skull of the hero of this book. Hopefully this super-being will have the sense and imagination to pause and give some time to guessing at what dreams busied themselves in that bucket of old bone. They may even raise the evil-smelling cranium to their ears and listen for the echoes of our lost age as our children listen to the sea in shells.

What they hear will be subject to their judgement, not ours. It may be deep music, it may be crashing discords and mass-hysteria. Fortunately for us, it will be those futuristic ear-drums that take the risk. Time may not be the great composer that he is generally cracked up to be. Sometimes the old bastard does not know a middle C from the hole in an ant-eater's arsehole.

Between the beginning and the end of this book there are only a few seconds – but they are long enough for the Consul's nicotine-stained thumb to play the scales on the electric door-bell.

Ding-dong-ding-dong-ding-dong.

Does this trite sequence of chimes spell the decline of the humanoid? Has manself crushed animalself into powerless, inarticulate jam?

You can ask Genesis.

You can try Darwin.

You can approach Leakey in his Tanzanian gorge.

You may not give a damn either way.

But the hero here will tell you anyway, as we hope he may tell the hippopotamus or Anopheles mosquito a million years hence.

The levelling process of democracy has done much good for manself in the world. It has helped him to realise freedom and equality of sorts and also it has dragged many autocrats screaming out of their airy perches. Yet it has done damage too. It has standardised our attitudes and interpretations of our animalselves. The myth of the common ancestor, this hidden ape-like creature, is rampant. Yet the manselves of Mankind may not have come from one root.

Just as our languages have evolved from many sources – the wind, the sea, the chink of rock on rock, the beating of the heart – so might our different beings. Our origins are various.

1

We are not all the same.

Except under the Law, which is fair enough.

We originate from separate life-forms.

For instance, I know an accountant with the morals of a microbe.

A boy with an empathy with elephants.

A slaughterman with eyes like a field-mouse.

A plain girl with a cast in one eye who can run like Grant's Gazelle.

In the Earth's great richness of life there are thousands upon thousands of options which we can entertain when trying to trace ourselves back to our *individual* animal fathers.

Look in the mirror for Christ's sake!

Cast a sideways glance at your wife, your husband, your friendly policeman, even the children of your body.

Our hero did.

And look where it got him.

ONE MUSHIKISHI AND THE GREAT MYSTERY OF THE BWANAS

The train arrived at Mufunsi at half past midnight. As the passengers got off and hurried away into the town, one young man remained behind. He was looking at the trees, at the station, at the porters asleep in the goods yards, at the African night sky which encapsulated the low white railway buildings in a black dome, relieved only by stars and a moon of immense light. He was where he had set out to be: the journey was over. He had managed to get half-way across the world to this mining-town in Zonkendawo, the jumping-off place for his search. Excited though he was, he could not help being nervous of facing the town with no money. He had nothing but what he stood up in. Beyond the station forecourt he could see white buildings, broad avenues lined with trees, some neon signs and the lights of vehicles moving through the half-darkness. Finding a hidey-hole to sleep unmolested was going to be a problem — but that could not sour his joy at having successfully arrived. With a final glance around him he walked out of the station and headed up the widest avenue he could see.

For an hour he wandered up and down the grid-pattern of streets. He was impressed by the number of bars and clubs still open and the volume of noise coming from them. This seemed to have a bearing on his hunt for a place to sleep because every time he found somewhere suitable it was already occupied, the air in the corner high with the smell of drink. All of the fellow-vagrants he found were Africans and they told him to go away with a curious humility.

In the main square he found a Christmas tree, its needles dried and fragile after many months in the sun. As he ducked under the still-sweet boughs, thinking that he had at last found his bed, he stumbled over yet another sleeper who had already staked a claim. From the ground rose a pale head of supreme ugliness which told him to *voetsak* with servile politeness.

At least comforted that he was not the only white person in such straits, the young man wandered off again. All he wanted now was to get his head down. His eyes were heavy. It did not matter where. He knew that outside the town was the bush – a wilderness that the train had travelled through for days on its climb to this upland country. He would go there. Did it not give him an early opportunity to experience the living conditions of his animal fathers?

At the edge of the town the road disappeared into the bush, unlit except by the moon, and unfathomable. He paused in the last artificial light, then hunched his shoulders and plodded forward, his big body slouched with fatigue. Without further hesitation he embraced the solitude of the trees and left the settlements of Man behind him. Even in his tiredness he could feel an affinity with the dark shapes around him. They were natural. Their time-scheme was that of Nature, not the clock on the wall. They were bed, peace, dreams. It was beyond belief that such a welcoming place could shelter any danger. He would lie down with the lion and not be afraid.

As he was scanning the silvered earth for a good spot to stretch out he saw a red glow in the trees ahead. Cautiously he walked towards it, intrigued. When he was close enough to see the fire and the figure sitting cross-legged by it, he heard himself addressed by a voice of firm and cheerful courtesy.

"Hello young bwana."

"Hello," the young man replied, eyeing the ragged, smiling old African warily.

"Come and warm yourself by the fire."

"Thanks."

The young man took the African's outstretched hand and shook it as he entered the firelight.

3

"Why have you come to visit Mushikishi, the impoverished charcoal-burner?" the old man's smoke-bleary eyes crinkled companionably. "The bush has claimed your motor vehicle?"

"I'm looking for a place to sleep. I've just got off the train and I'm broke."

Mushikishi frowned and fingered the holes in his filthy cotton vest.

"There are no hotels this side of Mufunsi young bwana."

"I told you, I'm broke. I have no money at all."

"What's your name young bwana?"

"Hurl Halfcock."

Mushikishi ran a finger along his front teeth and whistled softly.

"You have many problems. I too have no money and I am at the bottom of all the social hierarchies you can think of – but my name is bearable. It comes from the Bemba language and means white mahogany."

Hurl stared at the grey-headed, ash-covered, blackened black of the charcoal-burner's skinny self and doubted the appropriateness of his being called white mahogany.

"They also call me the Old Man Of The Woods."

Hurl squatted down opposite Mushikishi and they were silent for a while. On the outer fringe of the firelight Hurl could see smoking piles of earth.

"What are they for?" he asked.

"That's my living. My charcoal factory. But in my soul young bwana, I am a philosopher. That is why I choose to live here in this degrading fashion. It gives me freedom and time, though not a very strong constitution. Would you like to hear the story of my life?"

Hurl noticed that his weariness had left him. Somehow this chirpy, outlandishly dirty old man had raised his spirits and brought him into a fuller realisation of where he was. In Africa! He was squatting by a fire in the heart of the heart, the centre of it all. In the night walked the ghosts of the animal fathers, over the whole plateau scurried representatives of The Three Races of Man, each of them classifiable in Hurl Halfcock's unique theory of human types.

"Yes, I'd enjoy that," Hurl said while offering Mushikishi one of his last two cigarettes and lighting one for himself.

"*Sanju* young bwana. I was born in Lundazi, survived the early years in my father's village, and then went for my education to the house of my uncle in Solwezi. There I received my education from the beautiful, austere, serene, red-haired nuns of the Catholic mission,

4

each one of these fine ladies coming from Ireland. Without them and their patience I would be as ignorant as the day I was born and certainly not a practical philosopher.

"When I graduated with my standard 6 certificate – a happy, happy day for my father who was half-dead with sleeping-sickness, raspberry disease, tropical eating sores, swamp fever and strangulated hernias – the holy sisters, ah, I can see them now in my mind's eye in their dazzling robes, green eyes and flame-red tresses, they got me a job as a sanitation helper grade III at Mufunsi mine. With all the nations of the earth queuing at their door, the bwana managers gave that job to me! How was I to know that it was Sister Veronica O'Grady who gave the bwana employment officer three pounds and a short time in the private room at the Turk Club in order to get this valued post for me. You see how they loved us?

"For two years I worked on the great buckets of the *chimbusu*, humping the waste of my people and the bwanas in order to repay Sister Veronica O'Grady her three pounds – then I am free! No debts! And during those years I had married and had two children. Once again it was the bwanas who helped me – your people. It was the mighty *changa-changa* of the Personnel Department who lent me the Bedford lorry to bury my children who died in the subsidence at the North Shaft. Without his help we would never have transported all the mourners the twenty miles over the swamps to where the African cemetery lies."

Mushikishi paused in his story and fixed Hurl with an ingratiating smile.

"Young bwana, whatever advantages I have reaped in my thirty-five years have been through the efforts of the *musungu* on my behalf, you bighearted bwanas have been the pillars of my life."

"You're older than thirty-five!" Hurl said with some indignation. "Look at your hair!"

"Thirty-five planting seasons have I lived by the grace of the Great King Christ and the spirits of my ancestors. I am as grey as the elephant because my own people do not understand how to behave and contribute to the world the benefit of their unique African personality."

Taking a stick out of the fire Hurl stirred a half-dead pile of embers.

"Are you taking the piss out of me?" he asked calmly.

"Perish the thought!" Mushikishi grinned, widening his nostrils and blowing out smoke. "What an idea. I say bring back white rule

5

to Zonkendawo. Since independence we have only gone down-hill. Our President, Doctor Mulombe, is a cruel megalomaniac who has bank accounts in Zurich and St. Kitts; the price of mealie-meal has doubled . . ."

"Perhaps you're just a spineless old sycophant!" Hurl butted in with a trace of anger.

"That I am young bwana."

"If you don't support Doctor Mulombe who will? He needs your help? When the British got out of your country they didn't leave much behind except a hatred of centralised government."

"Dead right young bwana."

"Then why talk about bringing back white rule?"

"To please you young bwana."

"Why should you think that will please me?"

"Have you not come here to profit from the twilight of colonialism?"

Hurl gaped.

"No!"

"Then why?"

"It's a long story."

"We have all night."

So Hurl told the charcoal-burner about his search for the animal fathers and his wish to verify his Theory Of The Three Races Of Man in Africa, it having been completely vindicated in England.

When he had finished Mushikishi clapped his hands in delight.

"At last!" he said gleefully. "Oh at last! At last!"

"What are you so pleased about?"

"After all these years sitting here alone with my thoughts, along comes a colleague! A fellow philosopher! A real, honest-to-goodness, oldtime philosopher!"

Unable to restrain himself any further Mushikishi jumped to his feet with a crack of knee-bones and hopped round the fire in a delirium of joy.

"He has come! Oh he has come!" he sang. "A disciple has come to the master's feet!"

"I didn't say I was interested in being a disciple!" Hurl shouted. "I've got my own ideas."

"Of course you have! But I can teach you our way of thinking things out, young bwana!" Mushikishi squatted next to the big Englishman, one thin hand on his broad shoulder. "We have ways

6

you have never heard of!"

"What do you think of my theory?"

Mushikishi sat down again, this time much nearer to his companion. For a while he sucked at his teeth, chewed the lining of his mouth and wriggled his horny toes in the ashes. From under his grimy eyebrows and bush of frizzy grey hair he examined the features of his new-found friend. In the *musungu*'s green eyes he saw puzzlement and determination; in his sledgehammer chin all the manic passion of a Beethoven raging with inner deafness; in his squat, short-fingered hands, forearms, biceps, triceps, loins and legs a strength that was not entirely intellectual.

"Young bwana, you are an interesting person. Outwardly you have the appearance of a manual labourer used to digging ditches. But I can see through this exterior wall to your soul. You are a seeker after truth like myself. I think in your theory you may have found some of it, but not all. May I ask you some questions, just to clear my mind?"

"Fire away," Hurl nodded and smiled encouragingly. "The more the merrier."

"Now, can Race One be black?"

"They can be any colour."

"Aha, now I begin to see the history of my people in a new light!" Mushikishi clapped his hands with enthusiasm. "When the white man first came to the African continent and decided to explore our Zonkendawo they should have found a classical situation as far as your theory goes. Which is a long way young bwana, for your wisdom outstrips your years. What had happened was this. Stop me if I'm wrong. The great Race One empires of the Congo had driven many tribes south and east into this land, and the Race One Arab slavers had frightened all the people out of the east to come here. In fact we could say that Zonkendawo had become a haven of Race Twos. But no Race Ones."

"You sound like a liberated group of Race Twos," Hurl agreed.

"Ah, they were good times young bwana. All our disputes were settled with village democracy – the system still used by Doctor Mulombe and the Progress Party which we could express in this simple catch-phrase 'One Man One Vote Once' – and we had many kinship patterns and amusing religious rites. Tribal dancing was on the up and up, unlike today when the crewbosses go to ballroom-dancing classes in their monkey suits to learn the slow hyenatrot and the Dashing White Sergeant – what a world we live in young bwana. In those good old days the mealies grew to the height of three men and the lakes were full of *kapenta*, a small nutritious fish not unlike the Portugues sardine. The people, these Race Twos, were having a good time of it.

"And then came the bwanas.

"They took what grew in our fields, our cattle, our blankets, our bows and arrows, even the bones of our ancestors. All our rites were stopped, including the best ones which included a pubescent youth being allowed to *hlanganana* his aunties as much as he liked in order to learn the practical techniques of love. Were not these the actions of Race One?"

"No doubt about it!" Hurl averred strongly. "They crush everything really worth while."

"Then came the missionaries, the beautiful Irish sisters, Doctor Livingstone..."

"Spiritual espionage!" Hurl smacked his fist into his palm with the power of his conviction. "They were worse than the slavers! You couldn't see the chains they were putting round your necks."

"Right again young bwana," Mushikishi curtsied, his fire-tinted eyes bright. "You are opening many doors to me. I perceive a different pattern. Now what about the bwanas who were debwanad?"

There was a short silence round the fire as Hurl scrutinised the grimy philosopher's face.

"What are you talking about?" he asked eventually.

"What about the bwanas who came to live with us, ate our food, adopted our ways, loved our women. What about them?"

"Were there people who did this?" Hurl queried.

"Yes young bwana, a few."

"They were probably Race Three then, the Mad."

"They were mad? That fits in with what the other bwanas thought so you may be right. They said that any bwana who gave up being a bwana to become a kaffir must be insane. Many of my people agreed with them. But is it not true that these debwanad bwanas had originally come to Zonkendawo as pure Race Ones – the exploiting class? So they came here as Race Ones and changed to Race Threes? So what happened to Race Two in between? And why did they change? What happened? And while I'm at it young bwana, why do you talk such a load of shit about Mankind?"

Hurl straightened up, startled. Mushikishi, sensing that he might

8

have spurred the big, dumbfounded white man to a violent reaction, skipped away from the fire and stood behind a tree.

"Think about it young bwana. You are new to this country. You must approach it with a open heart. You will need help, I can see that. To understand our situation here will require some discipleship...will you learn?"

Hurt took a step towards the African but he skipped away again, nimbly mounting one of his smoking charcoal beds.

"Please don't go away," Hurl pleaded, "stay and talk to me. I'm not angry. You may be right, I don't know. Give me time."

"I cannot give you time young bwana. Time will give you time."

Mushikishi descended from the charcoal bed and sat down again opposite Hurl, his eyes watchful for any false move.

"I will help you if I can, but will you help me?" he said quietly. "We will be each other's student."

"Fine."

"Young bwana, I am nearing the end of my time. Our life expectation is thirty-four so I'm one year over already. Soon the charcoal-burner will be charcoal himself. Give me answers, insights, be a brother in thought. Ah, today philosophy is a discredited profession, put away in dark rooms in the bwana's breezeblock universities. Let us, for the brief time left to me, reaffirm the standards of the old school. Let us look and let us think. Let us bring back the days of the dedicated men who sought the Answer."

"With you heart and soul," Hurl blinked, strangely moved by Mushikishi's appeal.

"Young bwana, you see my condition. In rags. Near to despair. There is one reason for it, and one alone. I could have been a happy materialist like the miners of Mufunsi, but no. I had to tax my mind with the greatest of all philosophical questions. The bwanas. The bwanas have defeated my poor mind. The riddle remains. There are days when I have a little self-indulgent fantasy as I sit out here in the *bundu*. I dream that there are no bwanas and that we are back in those good old days I spoke of. But then I hear the cars on the road. I see the pylons stretching their wires this way and that. The aeroplanes fly overhead. I remember the *nyama* that once roamed here and see the empty land. Then I know that the bwanas are here and I must face reality and understand them before I die. That is my duty as a philosopher. I must unravel their ways and convince myself that they are human."

9

Mushikishi looked across at Hurl and noticed the deep clefts of the young man's frown. He was staring into the fire, hugging his knees. Mushikishi let the silence ride, waiting for a reply. Suddenly he stamped his feet in the ashes and laughed.

"Ah I feel ten times better since you came! Up until now no bwana has been prepared to lift a finger to help me. They drive me away. They behave like wild dogs with a bone..."

"Are you saying that I'm a bwana?"

"We must leave that question open young bwana, and see which way you jump. I only hope your quest for knowledge about the whole of Mankind does not reduce you to the state in which you find me after my years of trying to answer the question of one small group, namely the perplexing bwanas."

Hurl nodded as he examined the pitiable state of the ancient thinker: his smoke-reddened eyes, grizzled hair, coarsened skin, stringy arms poking through the arm-holes of the windowed vest, his knee-length shorts blackened and greasy from a thousand fires with stick-like legs emerging from their reeking bell-bottoms down to a pair of huge thick-skinned feet. Here was a terrible dream come true. Mushikishi was an example of what could happen to any man who turned his back on earning a living and complying with the standard requirements of a money-based society in order to seek truth. Would Hurl end up in such hapless poverty? This is what the question of bwanadom had done for Mushikishi. Would the Three Races of Man and the animal fathers do the same for him? Or had he been sent by some unknown agency, some guiding spirit of the last of the real philosophers of this world, to save Mushikishi from despair and the death that follows intellectual defeat?

"You are going to help me young bwana, aren't you?"

Hurl nodded.

"Thank you. How will we arrange our discussions?"

"I'll come and see you after I've been here a while. We'll just have to let things happen, then we can compare notes. I'll have to study the bwanas from inside first."

"That makes good sense young bwana. You'll come to see me soon I hope? I get lonely out here except for the occasional visitor, one or two, who comes to alleviate my anguish. Being a charcoal-burning philosopher isn't all fun I can tell you."

Mushikihi smiled again, then craned his neck forward and swivelled his eyes in a gesture to Hurl that he should look through the trees

10

towards the road. Hurl saw lights, then they went off. A slam followed.

"One of your visitors?"

"Almost certainly young bwana."

"Do you want me to leave?"

"No, stay here. This might help you."

They waited in silence, listening to the cracking of twigs and the crepitation of dead leaves underfoot as the person approached with an electric torch.

"Are you there Mushy?" twittered a mature female voice.

"Here my love!" Mushikishi shouted, waving a hand and drawing his lips back from his teeth in a wholehearted grin.

"Who is that with you?" the voice demanded nervously.

"A fellow-philosopher my love."

"Don't be silly," the voice said chidingly, "he's a European."

"That doesn't stop him being a philosopher."

"I thought you'd be by yourself."

The woman, a chubby blonde rapidly approaching early middle age, dressed in a flowered cotton short-hemmed skirt, a fur-jacket and gold sandals, stepped into the firelight, her eyes fixed on Hurl.

"Good evening," Hurl said.

"What's he doing here Mushy?" the woman asked rudely. "This is very embarrassing."

"He's my guest dear. He's staying the night."

"Staying the night?" the woman squealed. "He can't sleep in the bush! That's out of the question!"

"What question?"

"You know perfectly well what I mean!" the woman cried with displeasure. "God knows I take enough risks coming here already."

Then she turned on Hurl.

"Haven't you got any sense?"

"He is a philosopher dear. That means that he has much wisdom but no sense. That's the way he is made."

"Why are you thinking of sleeping here like some kaffir vagrant? Haven't you got a tent?"

"I'm broke."

The woman opened her handbag and took out some paper money.

"Here, take this and go back to Mufunsi."

Hurl was in two minds about taking the money. It was not pride that stopped him, but the prospect of being removed from interesting field-work. Here was an odd confrontation. It jarred his concept

11

of the ordinary. Not only that, it stuck wedges in some tiny cracks that were appearing in his Theory Of The Three Races Of Man. Mushikishi resolved the impasse by taking the woman's money and putting it in his pocket. Then he introduced her to Hurl.

"This is my girl friend, Mrs. Arabella Parkinson. This is my philosophical colleague, Mr. Hurl Halfcock."

Arabella sat down on a log, having first spread a handkerchief over it to keep off the dirt.

"I wish I hadn't come," she sighed exasperatedly.

"Look at the moon Arabella my love, the moon!"

"He can't stay here in the bush. It's not right. What kind of an animal are you?"

Hurl sat up, his eyes fierce.

"That's what I've come out here to find out."

Arabella shrugged dismissively and stood up.

"Well Mushy, I'm going home. It's a pity because I was looking forward to tonight. I think it's time you grew up and forgot all this philosophy business and stuck to what you know best."

Mushy took a hand of his beloved and planted a kiss in its moist palm.

"Sit down Arabella. You know you're not going anywhere."

"Well send him away."

Hurl glared at Arabella, his back up. He was not impressed by Mushikishi's taste in women. Her cosmetics and perfumes offended him. Her painted toenails put him right off. Her small, grim blue eyes, sharp and hungry as the points of twin stilettoes, scared him. Where he had come from there were hundreds of thousands of such bossy, mothering, bigbosomed creatures making their bids for power. He had not expected to find one in Africa. Or had he? Wasn't she an archetype Race Two mother?

"Tell him why he shouldn't sleep in the bush Mushy!" Arabella insisted winningly as her colour rose at the old charcoal-burner's lascivious games.

Mushikishi turned to Hurl and winked.

"Young bwana, it would be unthinkable for a bwana to spend a night in the bush with a kaffir. It would undermine the foundations of his society."

"What's she come out here for then?"

"Ah, that's different."

Arabella pursed her small mouth and looked at her nails.

12

"I'm doing charity work for him," she said defiantly, "on a voluntary basis. It's my project for the Lions Club."

"At this time of the morning?"

"I'm a very busy woman!"

Mushikishi stepped over and hustled Hurl to one side.

"Young bwana, will you do me a great favour? Go for a little distance for twenty minutes, and then return. This Arabella is the wife of the Dutch Deformed Predikant in Mufunsi and a very sensitive woman. She does not want your left hand to know what her right hand is doing. When you come back we can examine her position in bwanadom and compare notes. Another interesting side-issue is that she is the mistress of the underground manager of South Orebody and also sometimes entertains Mr. Viljoen who runs the crematorium and florist's shop on 14th Avenue. You see what I am prepared to go through for the sake of philosophy?"

Hurl looked as far into his newfound friend's eyes as he could, trying to reach the absolute end of the man.

"You're sure that you're not taking the piss out of me?"

"Be assured comrade."

Arabella watched Hurl leave and disappear into the trees, her eyes acid with distaste, her diamond-ringed hands clenched.

"It's people like him who have ruined Africa Mushy. It makes me so mad I could cry. When I think of what it was like in the old days. They're traitors to their own kind. Why can't they behave like civilised ... oh ... ah ... Mushy, your vest is caught on my tigers-eye brooch ... ooh..."

Twenty yards off in the bush Hurl sat with his back against a tree and looked at the white moon. He was trying to slot Arabella into his Theory Of The Three Races Of Man and failing. While he struggled with her mentally, Mushikishi struggled with her physically, once again enveloped in the white mystery, the answer to which had evaded him so long.

TWO **THE OPEN PIT**

Zonkendawo is part of the southern African plateau. Lying at about four thousand feet above sea-level, it has an undulating surface and almost continuous soil cover. The geological framework of the country consists of a raised basement of crystalline rocks in the east, flanked in the west by successively younger sedimentary and volcanic types which are intimately associated with gneisses and granitic eruptives. These rocks are the oldest in the country and lie over younger intrusives. Their base is not exposed.

Resting uncomfortably on the basement are sedimentary rocks which occupy much of the west. The oldest and most extensive is the Katanga system which is of pre-Cambrian age. The foundations of these ancient rocks runs from what was the Democratic Republic of the Congo, now Zaire – the Katanga province – in the north, into Zonkendawo, emerging at the surface at the town of Mufunsi.

There is copper in these rocks, oxide and sulphide ore. At the Open Pit in Mufunsi, Hammerkop, the Open Pit Manager, and his workers, have dug a chasm six hundred feet deep. Day by day they drill, blast, excavate, truck and trip the ore, sending it off to be concentrated, leached, smelted and refined. Inside the dusty chaos of the Open Pit work many gigantic machines, trucks that can carry a hundred tons at one go, power shovels that can bite off ten cubic yards of earth, a stacker that can spout stones and rubble in an arc fifty feet in the air, and the supreme technical achievement of the mining engineers of western Europe – the Bucket-Wheel Excavator.

Perhaps it was a pre-Cambrian instinct which made the Staff Officer of Mufunsi Open Pit, a woman of broad shoulders, splendid proportions and metallic eyes, peek over the screen while Hurl was having his medical examination.

"You'll do," she murmured appreciatively.

"Hold on a minute Staff Officer," the doctor said wearily, "he won't run away."

"You're a godsend. Just the man I've been looking for."

"Have you got a job for me? I'm broke. Anything will do." Hurl said.

"Is it true that you've been sleeping in the bush for two days?"

"Yes."

"Why didn't you come down to my place?"

"I didn't know you. I'm a stranger."

"It's bad form for Europeans to sleep in the bush. You're letting the side down."

"What side?"

"Our side."

The Staff Officer's steely eyes glinted over the top of the screen and she patted a beehive of dark, backbrushed hair.

"Anyway, let's put all that behind you. Into the office please."

It was a neat, clean room, cooled by an efficient air-refrigeration unit. While Hurl shivered in a pair of drill trousers and a thin shirt, the Staff Officer braced her lovely shoulders, smoothed out her eyebrows, crossed her strong legs and thrust her breasts at him through a starched white blouse.

"So you have a degree?"

"Yes."

"What in?"

"Anglo-Saxon."

"Just the man we're looking for."

Hurl stared at her.

"It must be fate. I've been looking for a European with your qualifications for weeks. Everything comes to those who wait."

"What kind of a job is it?" Hurl asked carefully, not wishing to upset a situation which, though unreal, seemed to be promising him a livelihood.

"A few questions first. Anything to hide? Police record?"

"No."

"What are you doing here then? Only dregs, scum, drifters, criminals and ne'er-do-wells come up here."

"I caught a train in Capetown. It was coming up here."

"Were you ever a mercenary in the Congo?"

"No."

"Are you wanted in South Africa?"

"I don't think I'm wanted anywhere."

The Staff Officer snatched a little breath and clasped her hands together on the blotter.

"I'm sure you're wrong. There must be someone who wants you – somewhere."

Taking off her blue-tinted spectacles, she allowed her metallic eyes to blaze at him again, two apertures of shaken aluminium foil.

"With new employees from overseas, especially educated men, I make a point of inviting them down to dinner at my place on the first night. We have a glass of wine or two, some soft music, get into something comfortable, you know the kind of thing..." she smiled at him boldly, exposing a perfect set of magnificent tombstone teeth.

"That's very kind of you," Hurl said in a low voice. "Could you tell me what this job is and how much I get paid please?"

"No, not until you've taken the oath."

Hurl bridled, flinging up his heavy chin.

"What oath?"

The Staff Officer opened a drawer and took out a book issued by Her Majesty's Stationery Office entitled, 'Mining Regulations', then laid it on the desk, keeping her hand over it.

"Place your hand on mine and say after me..."

Hurl did not move.

"I thought this country was independent now?" he said ill-humouredly, "if it is, why are you using a colonial publication?"

"The African government haven't got round to issuing a new one yet. Oh do come on, it's nothing serious. There's no need to get upset."

Hurl placed his hand on top of the Staff Officer's. It was cool and as steady as a rock beneath his.

"Mmmm!" she breathed, "you've got lovely body heat."

"What's this oath?" Hurl asked grumpily, "I didn't expect to be swearing oaths to get a bloody job."

"Big business needs human loyalty like any other organisation. Mines need people to die for them. The accident figures speak for themselves. Now, say after me..."

Stretching back her full length, the Staff Officer slowly undid the three top buttons of her blouse.

"Concentrate!" she snapped suddenly. "Keep your mind on what you're doing?"

"For Christ's sake!" Hurl protested, "let's get this mumbo-jumbo over shall we?"

"I, Hurl Halfcock..." she intoned.

"I, Hurl Halfcock..." he repeated surlily.

"Swear to uphold the disciplinary code, the joint consultative committees, the job evaluation points system and the existing wage differentials between skilled and unskilled workers. I will not crawl into the high-density townships at night searching for low women, nor will I enter into clandestine relationships with the wives and mistresses of officials senior to me. Under no circumstances will I use the Open Pit showers when the departmental head Mr. Frank Hammerkop is in there, nor will I encourage African employees to join the Dutch Reformed Church, the Mine Club or the British Empire Service League. Finally, I swear by God Almighty who is my judge on that great day when all Mankind shall be brought

16

to a reckoning, that I will never, no, not ever, make friends with the following Undesirables:

Matthias Mvula and The Bucket-Wheel Excavator Gang
John Pyper
George Crompton
Albert Lewis
David Pforzheim
Leonard Porthcawl."

Hurl had stopped repeating the Staff Officer at the phrase 'high-density townships'. As he listened to the remainder of the oath he experienced an unnerving vertigo. This was all going too far, leaving him behind. The journey northwards had been traumatic enough but Zonkendawo promised to be twice as bad. He could not take this oath. It was an insult and a limitation of his individual freedoms.

"Mr. Halfcock! Please finish off the oath. We haven't got all day!"

"I can't ...." Hurl said vaguely, groping for an expression of his inner rage. "What do you take me for?"

"You're unemployed. You're broke. You're white. That's what I take you for."

"That doesn't mean..."

"All right. Have it your own way. We'll terminate the interview. I don't make the rules Mr. Halfcock. Look at these – Mining Regulations, Disciplinary Code, Township Rules, Hospital Conditions... what's one little oath amongst this lot. I can't see why you're objecting. Just take the oath and forget it. You won't like any of the Undesirables anyway."

"Why can't I just do the job?"

"The company has to protect itself. These are dangerous times. This country could be in flames tomorrow. Do it for me Mr. Halfcock. Please. I don't want to lose you."

Hurl took the oath.

He knew that it was the worst thing he had ever done in his life.

Who were these men?

Would they ever forgive him?

But a man has to live. Even his animal fathers would appreciate that.

The Staff Officer drove him down to the Open Pit. The car bounced along a laterite road, then down a steep gradient into the yawning, red hole. It was terraced and on each level giant earthmoving trucks

17

and power-shovels clanked, roared, dug, toiled, smoked and thundered in the sun. The Staff Officer rumpled Hurl's hair appreciatively then drifted into a four-wheel skid round a hairpin bend full of soft sand and gravel, banking up a shower of small stones. A huge truck, primrose-yellow and high as a house, shot past them in the opposite direction, its klaxon blaring like an ocean liner.

"I'm sure you'll like it here," the Staff Officer assured the shaken passenger, "there's a splendid spirit of co-operation down here. There we are! Straight ahead! That's your new job!"

Hurl raised his dazed eyes and blinked through the harsh sunlight. Ahead of them, straddling a broad terrace on caterpillar tracks as broad as all six lanes of a motorway, was the biggest machine that he had ever seen in his life. A superstructure towered seventy feet in the air, booms, cat-walks, ladders, cabs, a church of criss-crossed steel and hawsers, belts and wheels bolted and prodded forward in every direction. The head of the monster was an enormous wheel fitted with toothed buckets which flailed and tore at a cliff of red earth, swallowing the loose material down a steel throat then on to a conveyor system where it was digested deep in the guts, then spewed out on to another conveyor that draped itself like the tail of a dinosaur, over the edge of the pit and away on to a distant dump where the stacker vomitted the overburden high onto a growing pile.

"I can't work that thing!" Hurl gulped, "what made you think I could?"

The Staff Officer smiled and pointed to a plate bolted on to the side of the machine. It read: WESSEX EARTHMOVERS INC. (Peterborough).

"It should be as easy as falling off a log for a man with a degree in Anglo-Saxon," she chided him sweetly, "don't be put off by its size. With an intellect like yours it should pose no problems. But," her tone changed to one of concern, "I thought it wasn't supposed to be working until I'd found a suitable driver."

Fascinated, Hurl gazed at the Bucket-Wheel Excavator as it continued its voracious gulping of the red ground, its buckets screaming. The whole framework shook as the crashing teeth tore through rock and earth. If it ever got out of control, a whole town could be destroyed, a civilisation devastated. It was a left-over, a reproduction in skeletal steel of the titans of the Mesozoic Age, seventy-five million years ago, when the giant reptiles gnashed at an unkind world in a fury of hunger and rage.

As the Staff Officer parked the Citroën next to the Bucket-Wheel

Excavator, a Land-Rover arrived in a flurry of red dust, driven by a grim-faced white man in a white mine helmet.

"Oh dear," sighed the Staff Officer, "I fear the worst. I think those awful men have been playing with it again."

Stopping his vehicle, the driver of the Land-Rover leapt out, scaled a steel ladderway, stormed along a catwalk, then flung open the door of the largest cab on the machine. Immediately, the buckets slowed down, the roaring died away. Then ten Africans in blue overalls shambled on to the catwalk, followed by the white official who was shouting and waving his arms about. Behind him came a fat African who was shrugging, glowering, arguing.

"They're not supposed to drive it," the Staff Officer explained to Hurl, "you'll have to be very careful not to allow any interference once you're in charge. Now they're independent they think they can do what they like – especially these men. They're well known for taking liberties."

"They seemed to be managing quite well," Hurl interposed. "It's working."

"With eleven of them in the cab. That's about the ratio you'd expect. But it's completely in breach of the agreement that the companies have with the European Mineworkers Union. The Bucket-Wheel Excavator is a designated job. Only a man with qualifications like yours can drive it."

Hurl was introduced to the mine-captain, who was the man in the white helmet. He gave Hurl a cursory briefing on the use of the machine, put a manual in his hand, showed him how to operate the two-way radio that connected the cab to the central control tower, warned him about the irresponsible, idle, shiftless gang of drunks, potheads and morons who filled the ranks of the Bucket-Wheel Excavator Gang (their job was to keep the machine in good order, to move the great-girthed electric cable when the machine had to be walked, and to blast rocks that were too big to be processed as the overburden was stripped from the cut), then he asked Hurl if he had any questions.

"Couldn't you give me a few elementary lessons and show me what all these levers and switches are for?"

"It's all in the manual."

With a curt nod, the mine-captain left the cab, shinned down the ladder and drove away, covering the blue-overalled Africans with dust as he left. The Staff Officer waved good-bye through the window of her old Citroën.

"Don't forget tonight. About nineish. Don't dress up."

Then she was gone, sweeping a broad cloud of pink dust over the Bucket-Wheel Excavator Gang who lay on the ground, their mine-helmets tipped over their faces, relaxing.

Hurl sat and gazed at the controls. He tried to make sense of the manual. It was incomprehensible to him. Poking his head out of the cab door-way he grinned shamefacedly down at the dozing Africans.

"Anyone know how to work this thing?" he shouted.

With a great clamour of joy the eleven Africans rose from the dust and mounted the ladderway. They crowded into the cab. Such was the power of their presence, enthusiasm and odour that Hurl recoiled, frightened. They leaned over him, gently pushed him out of the way, trod on his feet while they pulled levers and switched switches and issued strange commands into the radio transmitter in a weird language full of lo-los and lapa-lapas. Hurl listened to the replies nattering through the headphones that lay on the control panel, unheeded. The fat African with grey streaks in his hair and a careworn expression took the headphones and stuffed them through the flies of his overalls.

"Bwana," he addressed himself to Hurl, "now we are ready. We will teach you how to drive the Bucket-Wheel Excavator."

"Why have you put the headphones in there?" Hurl asked.

"What does the wise man do when he catches the elephant sleeping?" the fat African retorted seriously.

"I don't honestly know."

"He pisses in its ear."

"Why?" Hurl queried uneasily.

"Because it may be the only chance he will ever get."

Matthias, who was the supervisor of the Bucket-Wheel Excavator Gang, put a hand on Hurl's shoulder and adopted an avuncular stance, looking deeply into the novice's wary eyes.

"You've got a lot to learn."

"Yes, I suppose I have."

"Do you mind if I give you some bits of advice?"

"I'd be glad if you would. I'm completely in the dark up till now."

"Don't be tempted to enter any caves or tunnels which you might find out in the bush."

"Why not?"

20

"It could be an elephant's arsehole."

"Are you taking the piss out of me?"

"Never let it be said. Young fellow, we know you got this job on merit."

Hurl shrugged off Matthias's hand, his nerves shrivelling with humiliation.

There was an unproar in Matthias's flies, a bleeping, chattering, chirping from the headphones. Matthias took out the headphones and put them over Hurl's head.

"See what the shift-boss is saying bwana."

What the shift-boss was saying was that he had been watching the Bucket-Wheel Excavator cut through his binoculars and had noticed a rock the size of a bungalow immediately in front of the buckets. From his vantage-point, he guessed that it would only be a few seconds before the buckets came into contact with the rock and paralysed copper supplies to the Free World.

With a tremendous clanging and shattering, a devilish scream of tortured metal, the buckets struck the rock and flew off their base-nuts into the depths of the Open Pit. Showers of sparks shot into the air and the crane-jib buckled. Sighing, the Bucket-Wheel Excavator Gang headed for the door, leaving Hurl at the controls. By the time that Hammerkop, the Open Pit Manager, arrived with a long train of officials, the Bucket-Wheel Excavator Gang was hiding in the wasteland of the dumps.

"Where are they?" Hammerkop seethed, his long, osseous face burning with resentment, "where are those black bastards?"

"I'm really very sorry," Hurl began.

"Don't blame yourself sonny. You can't help it if those heathen kaffirs got the better of you. I'm the only man who can handle them. You just make a statement that it's their fault and I'll see that you're all right."

"I can't do that," Hurl said, "it was my fault. They were only trying to help."

Hammerkop leaned over the control panel, his shoulders shaking. From his mouth came a hoarse, clattering sound.

"You're really green aren't you Pommy? Look, if you swear that it was Matthias's fault and that the others were accomplices in an act of deliberate sabotage, I'll make you night-shift mine-captain. That gives you £220 a month and a very pleasant residence near the sporting amenities. What do you say?"

21

Hurl shook his head.

"That would be telling a lie."

"That's what I'm saying then. Tell the lie. You get me those saboteurs and I'll make you anything you want to be. The world is at your feet. Please, please..."

Hammerkop clasped his huge, bony hands together. Into his cold eyes there came a light of desperation. It hurt Hurl to refuse the man, but refuse him he did. To betray help that had been so readily and warm-heartedly given would have been an act of the most pernicious treachery.

The following morning, the Staff Officer had him into her office. From the expression on her face and the way she was banging files around on her desk, Hurl guessed that he was in trouble. Leaving him to stew for a while, the Staff Officer looked out of the window, her body arched hard against the wall. Tension was there, and indignation. She was a curved pillar of unspoken wrath.

"Why didn't you come to dinner last night? I sat up till half-past four in the morning."

Her metallic eyes flickered across the desk, belying the smiling exposure of her beautiful white teeth. A Bic Biro clicked in and out somewhere in the palm of her powerful hand.

"I was tired and a bit shaken-up by the accident," Hurl mumbled apologetically, "I'm sorry."

"You were in the Mine Club with Matthias!"

Hurl's mind reeled.

"Have you been spying on me? Haven't I got the right to any privacy at all?"

"You've broken your oath. That's not very good for one day's work is it? And you've got me into trouble with Hammerkop. He's always looking for a chance to blackmail me into his bed. God, I never have any peace. Anyway, he's sent you back. He says you're not suitable for the job."

"Oh," Hurl shrugged, "I expect he's right."

"He says you've got no mechanical aptitude. I've looked at your credentials anew and I think that your aptitude is in fact for human relations and humdrum administrative work. We have agreed that you'd make a first-class IRO."

"What's an IRO?"

"Promise you'll come to dinner and I'll tell you."

22

Once again, the Staff Officer drove him to the Open Pit. This time he was led to a large office with no air-conditioning. When they arrived it was full of Africans sitting on the floor. With a start Hurl recognised Matthias and the Bucket-Wheel Excavator Gang. They greeted him effusively, taking off their helmets.

"*Mwapoleni mukwai!*"

"I won't come in," the Staff Officer said, "not with these men at knee-level. That's your desk. You'll find everything you need."

"What am I supposed to do?" Hurl begged as she pushed him forward.

"Come to dinner."

She went, leaving him alone amidst the seated Africans. He walked carefully to the desk and sat down.

"Well," he smiled helplessly, "what am I supposed to do next?"

Matthias pointed to a pile of green cards on the desk. They were personal records and marked "Highly Confidential". The top one was for Matthias. It said that he was an Angoni by tribe, was 38, married with 11 children, had Health Science, Religious Knowledge and British Constitution at G.C.E. 'O' level. In a box marked 'RELIGION' there were many entries and crossings-out – 'Communist agitator', 'pinko-liberal', 'pan-African', 'white-hater', 'Boer-basher', 'sexual deviate', 'Mohammedan', then a further entry regarding a period of military service in the Territorial Army.

"It says here that you've got the Grand Order of the Fish Eagle with Copper Tail-Feathers," Hurl said genially. "What did you do to get that?"

"Ah, that is a story in itself bwana, "Matthias beamed. "One day I will tell you all about it."

Hurl read on. The next section was DISCIPLINARY RECORD. Matthias had stolen an oil-bottle, a waterproof cape, a 50-ton Haulpak, several cases of blasting-powder. He had been involved in a long list of fights and mêlées. He had attempted to blow up a PH 150 shovel while it was being driven by the South African Chairman of the board of directors for a publicity photograph. As Hurl read on, he realised that Matthias was a mass-murderer, a psychotic and an industrial maniac.

Matthias stood up and gently took the card out of Hurl's hand. He pointed with a stubby forefinger to a space next to yesterday's date.

"We are ready bwana," Matthias said with a deferential grin.

"Ready for what?"

"For discipline."

"For what?"

"For breaking up the Bucket-Wheel Excavator."

"But I did that!" Hurl protested loudly, "I was in charge!"

The enormity of the situation penetrated his spinning mind. The IRO was some kind of hatchet-man. He was being employed to punish the eleven men who had helped him most on his first day at work.

"There are many things you can do to us bwana," Matthias advised the new IRO, "you can give us, altogether now...

"A Verbal Warning.

A Written Warning (the rest of the gang now joined in),

A Severe Warning (chanting in a husky, musical chorus),

A Comprehensive Warning.

A Final Warning.

A Comprehensive Final Warning.

A Written Severe Comprehensive Final Warning.

An Indefinite Written Severe Comprehensive Final Warning.

An Ultimate Indefinite Written Severe Comprehensive Final Warning.

An Infinite Ultimate Indefinite Written Severe Comprehensive Final Warning.

An Eternal Infinite Ultimate Indefinite Written Severe Comprehensive Final Warning."

Hurl held up a hand. The gang hushed.

"I'm not doing anything of the kind."

Hurl looked sternly over the desk. The Africans were silent, playing with their hats by spinning them round on the tiles.

"And what the hell are you doing sat on the floor?"

Matthias struggled to his feet again, his mouth drawn to one side in a foolish grin.

"We always sit on the floor in the presence of the *changa-changa*."

"Who's the *changa-changa*?"

"You are."

"What's an IRO then?"

"A *changa-changa*."

"Why sit on the floor when there are chairs?"

"Why sit on the chairs when there is floor?"

Pushing back his chair, Hurl sat down on the floor and looked

24

through at the Bucket-Wheel Excavator Gang. At that level their strong body-odour of millet-beer was overwhelming. The Africans got to their feet in dismay.

"Sit down!" Hurl ordered.

"Bwana, we are not going to beat the system by breaking these minor regulations. We appreciate your sympathy but we have bigger fish to fry. We have adopted a policy whereby we make these old servilities in order to give the impression of obedience while we work ceaselessly for the downfall of Hammerkop, the burning of his mansion by the golf-course, the group-rape of his peaches and cream wife Gladys, the commandeering of his green Dodge and the destruction of capitalism in Zonkendawo. Right now you are making our lives very difficult. We implore you to punish us for the breaking of the Bucket-Wheel Excavator. It gives Hammerkop a false sense of security."

Loud exclamations of agreement greeted the end of Matthias's speech. Hurl stood up and sat down at the desk again, his expression hang-dog. He was being manoeuvred into committing an injustice. The only alternative would be to resign as an IRO. That would mean sleeping in the bush again. The Staff Officer would only give him a third chance if he went to dinner.

Step by step he explained his problem to the men now seated at his feet again. They listened carefully, nodded, ruminated and looked deeply sympathetic.

"Bwana," Matthias said after Hurl had finished, "there is an easy way out of your difficulties. Go to dinner with the Staff Officer. There is no shame attached. We of the Bucket-Wheel Excavator Gang visit her each Thursday at nine-thirty, eat the dinner which she so expertly and cunningly prepares, full as it is of inflammatory herbs and philtres, then we go with her to the famous lionskin in the bedroom. There we play with her until the sun rises, going to her fridge frequently in order to refresh and revitalise ourselves with the chilled beers and knick-knacks that she puts there for our delight. Apart from the sleep which we inevitably lose during these visits, we find them no great encumbrance. In fact we can say with our hands on our hearts that if they stopped we would indeed be the poorer."

Hurl rested his head in his hands and shuddered. The wedges placed by Mushikishi and Arabella in the cracks in his Theory Of The Three Races Of Man were being hammered home with thunder-

25

ous daemonic force. Great fissures were appearing! The roof was in danger! Central supporting pillars rocked and walls sundered from ground to eaves! Without mercy the battering-rams hammered at the gates, wielded by Hammerkop, the Staff Officer, and now these working men. Where would he have a home if his theory was destroyed? In the bush? Sharing Mushikishi's fire and despair?

He gave each member of the Bucket-Wheel Excavator Gang an Eternal Infinite Ultimate Indefinite Written Severe Comprehensive Final Warning and entered it on their cards as they showered him with thanks. Then he begged them to leave him alone. With a grateful smile and an oversize wink Matthias ordered his men to retreat, striking up a marching song for them as they strolled across the sunlit truck park towards the collar of the Open Pit:

> *"Tilitilili waa tiyeni*
> *Kaw Mcapi tamutema simbo!"*

he bellowed, clapping his hands. The Bucket-Wheel Excavator Gang started to shuffle forward in a strange little jogging dance as they repeated the words over and over again, working up a pink cloud of dust as they disappeared over the edge of the giant crater.

"What the hell does all that mean?" Hurl shouted sourly. "It doesn't sound like a mourning song to me."

Matthias stuck his thumb in the air and lumbered across the truck park, leaping sideways in his size 11 desert boots and cracking his heels together.

"An old Tumbuka song from the north east bwana. Great lyric. Good number. Top of the pops in the Open Pit! *Hamba!* Get up there!"

Once again he sprang into the air, his grin even wider.

"What does it mean?" Hurl demanded again as the chant boomed from the chasm into which the Bucket-Wheel Excavator Gang had trooped.

> "Let us go to Mcapi
> To be tattooed!"

Matthias chuckled as he pirouetted in the dust. "I'll teach it to you sometime, amongst other things."

"Who says I'll listen?" Hurl growled churlishly.

"You will listen because you want to learn. You have the wide-open look bwana. You are ready to be exploited."

"Shut those rowdy kaffirs up Halfcock!" Hammerkop roared

through his office window. "What do you think this is? Rhodes and Founders Day?"

"See, you're playing right into his hands!" Hurl shouted to the still-twirling and bobbing fat African who was now cavorting right on the lip of the Open Pit. "You give him all the opportunities he needs to persecute you!"

"Hammerkop!" Matthias howled from across the truck park. "Hammerkop! Come out of there and watch me dance on your grave!"

The Open Pit Manager threw open his door and appeared on the verandah, his cigar sticking out of his craggy face like a blunderbuss.

"Get back to work you kaffir bastard! What d'you think I pay you for? Dancing lessons?"

"We will get you one day Hammerkop, oh we will! It will go down in the history books! You will get your come-uppance! I swear it!"

"It will take more than you and that tribe of pox-ridden piss-artists to shift me, Matthias you coon idiot!" Hammerkop clanked, his rocky white face deadened in the sunlight. "Just wait and see who's here in five years, or ten! You hopeless *munts* can't do without us! Go on, get back to work before I get the IRO to *bulala* you all again!"

With a final bounce and a flourish of two black vee-signs, Matthias slid over the edge of the Open Pit to follow the Bucket-Wheel Excavator Gang. Hurl stood in the doorway of his office for a while, listening to the song as it trailed away into the depths of man-made crater.

Then he went back inside and phoned the Staff Officer to say that he would be coming to dinner that night.

Hammerkop did have something to moan about.

The accident figures were a disgrace.

100-tonners, Haulpaks, Euclids, tankers, Land-Rovers, all were seized with the mechanical falling-sickness of the Open Pit. They plunged over precipices, crashed into trains, each other, rocks and buildings, down old shafts, or simply disappeared into the surrounding bush. Every shift had its story of disaster and destruction; bulldozers and traxcavators tumbling off the terraces, power-shovels blown off their tracks by the absent-minded Drilling Gang, graders sliding down pebbly inclines and into side-walls, the Stacker firing its rocky projectiles on to passing vehicles and reducing them to a flattened pan of hammered metal.

A board-indicator had been erected by the Safety Officer. It showed the number of accidents per shift. The thick red line with its soaring, majestic peaks was a point of pride to the Open Pit workers. In this field they were the undoubted leaders. No other department on Mufunsi Mine could vie with them for the honours. If something moved, then an Open Pit man could crash it. Even the office cleaner had crashed his Hoover.

Outside the Engineering Workshops was a mountain of twisted metal. It represented a capital investment of hundreds of thousands. It was all irreparable, irredeemable. Hammerkop glared across at this sad monument as he racked his brains as to what he could do about his latest problem.

The crocodile in the sump.

Hurl sat in front of Hammerkop's desk, his spirits low. For the life of him he could not understand how an IRO could be responsible for removing crocodiles that had strayed into the wide drainage sump which carried away the Open Pit's surplus water when the rains came. Hurl had enquired about where the nearest river flowed and had been told that it was the Kafue, a major tributary of the Zambesi and its course brought it to a point only two miles from the town. Even with its short legs, a wandering, lost crocodile might smell the brackish water at the bottom of the Open Pit and mistake it for home. Only a zoologist could persuade it to leave now, or a bullet in the brain.

"I can't shoot the bastard!" Hammerkop raged, "it's contrary to the game preservation laws. That conniving kaffir Matthias would have me in gaol in five minutes. You'll have to get it out, you're the IRO."

"It's not my job, surely!" Hurl objected.

"Whose is it then, mine?" Hammerkop smashed his hairy hands down on the desk. "Am I the man? Have I got to do everything myself?"

"It's a job for an expert. I can't see why an IRO should be landed with it. I don't even know what an IRO's duties are but I'm damn sure that it doesn't include shifting crocodiles."

Hammerkop smiled savagely, his long granitic jaw thrust forward.

"It's in the job-description. I've seen it. That's one of your primary functions you slippy Pom shit-dodger! Now get out there and fish that fucking reptile out of my sump!"

28

Hurl did not move. Instead he stiffened his back and stared straight back into the garnet-black eyes of the Open Pit Manager in sturdy, independent defiance.

Hammerkop crashed his jaw shut on the chewed end of his cigar, then fell silent. He could approach this flagrant act of disobedience in two ways. He could ring up the rugby XV and get them to come down and pound the English lame-brained obstinate dog-fucker into a jelly, or he could reason with him. Although he preferred the more direct method, he was used to reasoning with Pom bastards. The General Manager of Mufunsi Mine Ltd was an Englishman and Hammerkop often reasoned with him. He followed this course because the General Manager had the power to dismiss Hammerkop from his post, and also because the mine's chief executive was tired of Gladys's retiring ways and needed to be humoured. This IRO, brimming with fire and ignorance, could certainly be manipulated. He was too big to fight single-handed but with skill, he could be used to advantage by a man who knew how to handle men.

"Look man, if I get disciplinary problems with the kaffirs, I call the IRO. If I want to give someone a raise, I call the IRO. If I want someone to pop back to my place and get my golf-clubs, I call the IRO. What's so different about extracting a crocodile from the sump? I call the IRO!"

Hurl turned his head away. Through the open door he could see the vehicle park. It was jammed with earthmoving trucks while the drivers sat in the shade and smoked cigarettes. Up on the terraces, the Bucket-Wheel Excavator was still, the Stacker was still, the shovels were still.

The Open Pit was on strike.

Matthias had been the spokesman for the African workers. He had laid it along the line. If Hammerkop was not going to lift his spell on the sump and take away the crocodile, then the workers would all go home.

"They think you've bewitched the sump," Hurl turned back to Hammerkop, anxious to elucidate the perfectly understandable impression which the Africans had received of the situation, "they think you've put it there deliberately."

"What?" Hammerkop roared, "do I need a younker like you to tell me the way the African mind works? I was brought up with kaffirs man. On the farm I lived on there was just me and the picca-nins. Until I went down to the Reef they were the only friends I

29

ever had. Don't try and tell me what the black bastards think! I know man, I know! Christ, what I have to put up with!"

"The crocodile has a special, symbolic significance to the African up here," Hurl persisted, "the spirits of the ancestral chiefs live in . . ."

But Hurl was not allowed to complete his anthropological analysis of the reasons behind the strike. Hammerkop, in a fit of apoplectic rage, had grabbed a heavy rock sample of malachite and was leaning across the desk, trying to crush Hurl's skull with it. With a nimble side-step for one so large, Hurl skipped out on to the verandah and dodged the green rock as it flew past him.

"Don't tell me about crocodiles!" Hammerkop thundered as he pursued the IRO along the verandah, a black and white surveying pole raised above his head like a spear, "I was fighting the scaly bastards in the Limpopo when your father was living off the Welfare State!"

THREE A QUICK GUIDE TO HURL HALFCOCK AND HIS THEORY OF THE THREE RACES OF MAN

As a babe at the breast Hurl had been a grabber, a goo-gooer, a laugher, a smiler, a hiccuper and a phenomenal shitter. These personality traits remained with him after he was weaned and formed part of his mature character. Hunger for warmth, affection and recognition was his to suffer, as was the craving for adoration, respect, swaddling and cosseting. He saw himself clearly, analysed the faults in his make-up, had often decided to change himself for the better, and had always failed. But he kept hoping.

In many ways Hurl had not shaken off all his infancy.

Yet he had got far enough for manhood.

He stood on his own two feet.

And he was very glad to be alive.

He often hoped for improvements in himself.

He hoped to die a wise old man who had lived much and done all he had ever set out to do.

In quiet moments he had often wondered about himself. Lacking in any objective sense, he did not have the introspective scholarship needed to discover the futility of his countless quests, or his boundless idiotic optimism. Pig-headed to the end, Hurl was under the impression that all the meaning there was to Life was within himself. Many people had tried to persuade him to settle down, accept his lot and shut up.

Poor Hurl. He was always a tryer, always a flogger.

He would not enjoy the thought that you were sorry for him.

So stow away your compassion.

About his early life we need to know virtually nothing, except perhaps that the Reverend R. F. Tillyard of Walton Parish Church refused to accept the name Hurl as a valid baptismal Christian prefix and Hurl's father walked out of the ceremony and took him home, never returning to any house of God again.

Hurl Halfcock was too much for God to swallow.

In later life he was often too much for Man to swallow.

At the time this story begins, he was twenty-five years old.

He had developed into a man. There was hair on his chest, on his chin, under his arms and round his genitals. Also his voice was deep, he had the vote, and he could drink with the best of them. His mother still claimed that he was lovable, but not with the same starry-eyed confidence as she had used of old. There was doubt in the old lady's mind. Her son had not lived up to all her expectations.

There are other things that you should know about Hurl.

He was simple.

That is not to say that he was unintelligent: his degree in Anglo-Saxon was adequate proof of the power of his mind.

However, he did tend to see things in a simple, clear light.

He was rudimentary.

In addition, he was a natural anarchist.

Throughout his boyhood he had been unmanageable, stroppy, a bloody nuisance, disobedient and truculent.

When he arrived at university, that was when he became an anarchist.

Many teachers had groped for that word and never found it. It would have made their lives easier when they wrote Hurl's end-of-term report. For 'Behaviour' they could have just entered 'Anarchist'. Instead they had written words to the effect that this boy was super-humanly obstinate, a coarse lout, and a dreamer.

Also, he was an intellectual hooligan.

Was short-sighted. Warm-hearted.

Often on the threshold of self-disgust.

31

Impractical. Trusting. Hopeless with money.

Enslaved by his baser passions.

Subject to strongly-coloured nightmares and apparitions.

His wife had called him an animal and left him.

He was genial, amenable, humble and bumble.

In the middle of October, 1964, this load of human vice and virtue had been discharged as supercargo from a great white ship and left standing on the dockside at Capetown, Africa.

Friendless, nearly moneyless, he had completed the first stage of his search for a new animalself, and a new home. Left far behind, way beyond the varying warm and cold currents of the vast Atlantic, was England and a life of mindless consumption which he had been forced to reject. He had been unemployable. A mis-fit. A thinker. A mess. He had been a burden on the tax-payer for two years, sitting around in flats, matinées and public parks working out his Theory Of The Three Races Of Man. He had wanted to journey to the beginning and live in the land where Nutcracker Man, Broken Hill Man and Homo Erectus had had their homes. He had bought a rail ticket to Mufunsi, a town in Zonkendawo. As the train pulled out of the station, Hurl had rejoiced that he was moving again. In the touchable future, up in the high lands, he might find some brothers in animalhood and confirmation of the truths which he hoped lay in his hard-won philosophy.

The Theory Of The Three Races Of Man

Race One were the Manipulators, the Accumulators, the Inheritors and the Plunderers. They sat inside a cast-iron crown and kicked their heels against the bony ramparts of the world's skull. You always knew that they were there, especially if you were Race Two. Race One could not exist without the mindless adulation of Race Two. The cream could never rise unless there was milk to rise through. Race One were the governors, the natural masters of consumer civilisation. They strolled along broad, tree-lined boulevards, rode horses, limousines, power-boats, each other, Race Two, the stock-market, the media. They were always in the saddle, their arses glued there with the fixative of history. Greedy, cruel, selfish, graceful, sophisticated, they all had grappling-hooks for finger-nails, a per-suasive Honest-Man's smile in front of cameras. They did not under-stand what Honesty meant. The women thought it was a plant with round, opaque seed-pods which made nice floral arrangements

32

with autumn blossoms and the men thought everyone in Race One was honest because they were honest about being snobs. Hurl hated Race One with a fervour that damaged his clarity of vision. If he could have gathered them all up into a giant bag, immersed them in water under a pile of bricks like a sackful of kittens, then he would have done so.

He was jealous of them.

They had made him jealous, deliberately. The envious aspirations of the lower races were the sweetest-tasting pleasure that Race One could ever experience.

Some countries had got rid of Race One. Good luck to them, Hurl said.

The Queen was not one of them.

Race One was the belly, while Race Two was the mouth.

Race Two was the dumb working-class with their banal, come-day-go-day routine and moronic courage. Without their vicarious enjoyment of Race One (when a Race One fell from power or was involved in a gory scandal, Race Two were overjoyed and shared in their superb unhappiness), the suicide rate amongst Race Two would have been uncontrollable and the factories, docks, warehouses, offices, sweat-shops and farms would have ground to a halt. They emitted a Race Two noise. A moan. It was this moaning sound that had alienated Hurl Halfcock and had made him shift places on buses when he was sitting next to Race Two going off to work. Even the sirens at the start and end of shifts emulated this noise. Fog-horns in anchorages and mighty river estuaries echoed it. Police-cars, ambulances and fire-warning devices imitated it. In pubs, clubs, cafés and places of public congress it was dominant. Popular singers tried to capture its essence in their soulful songs. Newscasters were trained to pitch their delivery at its resonance. Politicians droned to its accompaniment. This Race Two noise was powerfully amplified in the vocal chords of the womenfolk. They could drown the sound of natural catastrophes like earthquakes, tidal waves, volcanic eruptions when they made the noise in chorus. It was the womenfolk who kept Race Two together, but it was also the womenfolk who might start the revolution in England in five hundred years time. Hard, unimaginative, sharply critical of their husbands' inability to understand childbirth, the cost of living and Romance, one day they might man the barricades and fight for an active society.

33

The Queen was one of them.
Hurl had been born into them.
Race One aimed all their propaganda at them.
The Mouth.

Then there was *Race Three*.

They were the strange-eyed mental defectives, drunks, lost souls, beggars, seers and anchorites who shadowed Hurl Halfcock along pavements and tried to shake hands with him in the doorways of huge department stores. In white-tiled subways and bus stations they stamped their blistered feet and cried aloud that God was drunk or dead; they sat on public monuments late at night and shouted obscenities at policemen, or asked for a shilling for a cup of tea; they talked to gravestones through cemetery railings; they conversed with the inanimate and the unhearing. Hardly a day had gone past in Hurl's life without his being collared by one of these gifted mystics. They sought him out, hunted him down, checked bus queues to find his broad-shouldered, awkward form and questioning face, smiling to themselves as he turned away in fright and shyness. If one of these prophets was ambling along a busy street talking to himself or a zebra-crossing, then he would ignore the millions of Race Two which hurried hither and thither issuing their noise. He would be waiting for Hurl. There would be a heart-sinking moment as he fastened his crazy eyes on the big figure, an engaging laugh as he pushed his way through the crowds of Race Two: ha-ha! ho-ho! Look at this now! Good God Almighty, you're a fine lad for your mother! Lend me two pounds! Where d'you get that curly hair? The offered hand, the grin, the rags round their arses battering their brains out in the howling wind, oh who were Race Three? Where did they come from? Was there a country, a dark, magical, mad, phantom-crowded isle somewhere? When the women of Race Three tumbled out of old pubs doomed to be demolished in dockland areas, their voices shrill with Cassandrine warnings to the godless streets, they always excluded Hurl from the general curse, took his hand, cocked their white, blazing heads, and blew him feathery kisses.

Was there anything Race Three didn't know?

They were wise, anyone could see that. They knew the mysteries.

Race Three was the category in which Hurl had provisionally placed himself, having been assured by his ex-wife, his mother and father, and everyone closest to him that he was mad to set off on such a profitless adventure, travelling so far and using his savings to try and prove a patently ridiculous theory and to meet people who had been dead for a million years.

Hurl did not feel secure in Race Three.

He was scared of them.

He was no wizard and he knew that his ignorance was profound.

In the presence of Race Three he felt like a child.

They were a parent body.

Hurl had another problem to add to his quests. His name. As he lay in the bath before going to dinner with the Staff Officer, he considered alternatives. Halfcock would have to go. It had shamed him for long enough. Out of affection for his father he was prepared to keep the root, but the prefix would have to go.

In the past these options had crossed his mind:

Acecock	Firecock	Illustriouscock
Acumencock	Fatcock	Karatecock
Adamantinecock	Funcock	
Adorablecock	Feathercock	Lovablecock
Aestheticock	Fantasticock	Lightningcock
Alchemicock		Magnificock
Allcock	Grandcock	Multobuonocock
Almightycock	Goodcock	Merrycock
Approachablecock	Ghandicock	
	Gladcock	Olympicock
Ballcock	Gurucock	Proudcock
Biencock	Gastronomicock	Peacock
Boncock		
Bountycock	Happycock	Rapidcock
Bullcock	Holycock	Risorgimentocock
Banzaicock	Huntingcock	
	Hitchcock	Strongcock
Diabolicock	Hallocock	Strangecock
Darlingcock	Hirsutecock	Supercock
Dreamcock		Thundercock
Dreadcock	Joycock	Trombonecock
Dividendcock	Jollycock	Tusslecock
	Indestructiblecock	
Fortissimocock	Invinciblecock	Whatacock

Mournfully he cruised the wooden scrubbing-brush through

35

the bath-water until it docked against his recumbent organ of genera-
tion. Christ, Halfcock was no name for a young man adequately
equiped to offer himself in Love's tender sport. What about a Red
Indian name? He had long admired the courage of Chief Crazy
Horse, war chief of the Oglala Sioux. Crazycock? Crazy Bear?
Someone had once said he was ursine. Clearing his mind, he thought
of a Spanish name. His brother lived in Madrid at Ramon y Cajal
79–3rd. Ramon y Cajal was not only Spanish but Moorish and
mysterious. What did the *y* stand for? In time he might be able to
cut the name down to just *y* like the head of a secret service.

Lying back in the bath he endured a brief moment of depression
during which he faced the possibility that he deserved his name.
This created a rebellious reaction and he rose from the water like
Polyphemus, red-faced and streaming, catching a glimpse of himself
in the steamed-up mirror. In it his image was blurred, fuzzy and
distinguished.

Perhaps he should have a name to match?

What about George Robinson?

He wrote the name on the condensation, then rubbed it out. He
was well-made enough, big enough and awkward enough to have a
name that suggested something more colourful and original. There
were enough George Robinsons in the world already.

With the same finger he started to trace out a pattern. It was the
basic design for his pro forma which had been devised to record
analysis of personalities using the Three Races Of Man theory.
When he had sketched out the columns and boxes he attempted to
classify the Staff Officer as he towelled himself dry:

Behaviour	Environment	Motivation	Race
Supporting rep-ressive racial regime	*Position in hier-archy: part of management in neocolonialist org.*	*Security of tenure, pension rights, fear, just a groveller?*	2
Complaining about working class Race Twos	*Personnel admin.*	*Moaning for moaning's sake.*	2

Behaviour	Environment	Motivation	Race
Inviting me to dinner and direct sexual approach	*Cool, inhumanly efficient office furniture in grey steel*	*Wanton lust or slumming*	1
Giving me a job I cannot do	*Political situation*	*Sabotage?Stupidity?*	*1̶ 2̶ 3̶* ?
Regularly going to lionskin with 11 Africans who she says are Undesirable	*Sub-tropical clime*	*Nymphomania or may have terminal illness and not much time. Or trying to prove something?*	*3 or 1*

Result: $10 \div 5$? or $8 \div 5$, or is it 9? She's anything but a 2. Lapsed 1? Incipient 3? Where does this leave her? And me!

FOUR THE STAFF OFFICER'S DINNER PARTY

When he arrived at the Staff Officer's bungalow, his nostrils full of the night-scents of the town's fragrant avenues, his eyes reflecting the heavy silver stars and a big bright moon, he saw two cars parked in the drive. The Staff Officer was waiting on the verandah under a shaded golden light and talking to two seated men. One of them was paying attention to her; he was slender, girlishly slight in build, blond, and had strange eyes which burned with a blue ice-fire. He was dressed in chocolate cotton slacks, a cream shirt with lightning flashes embroidered across the breast, a pair of open-toed red Moroccan leather sandals, and wore a magenta scarf tied round his neck. The other man, who was taking no interest in the conversation because he was fast asleep, was a long, angular fellow with a short red beard, well-groomed red hair, a pair of heavy horn-rimmed glasses, and was wearing a light alpaca suit, modest Old Brightonians tie, and hand-cut Italian tan shoes. As Hurl walked along the drive through the hydrangea bushes and across the lawn, the fragile man with the astonishing eyes withdrew a delicately-boned hand from the Staff Officer's inner thigh and started kicking the sleeping man's shins.

"Looks like George has another attack of somnia old Staff Officer," he squawked sardonically in a harsh Antipodean accent. "You see the symptoms of the white man's sleeping-sickness. Poor bastard has been smitten down again."

"I wish I knew why he has to drink so much," the Staff Officer said with genuine perplexity, "what is he escaping from?"

"Old Hermione I reckon. She just uses him you know."

The Staff Officer then introduced Hurl. The two men on the verandah were John Pyper, a journalist on the Zonkendawo Times, and George Crompton, the red-haired Public Relations Officer and somnia-sufferer from the mine.

"I thought I wasn't supposed to talk to them," Hurl whispered to the Staff Officer as he sat down. "They're both on the list of Undesirables."

"That's not what the oath says," the Staff Officer glimmered her eyes, "what it said was you mustn't make friends with them. In other words you mustn't like them. It's quite easy I assure you."

The Staff Officer smiled. Already her mind was working out the permutations for the lionskin. With only four participating tonight things could be much more personal. That's if George recovered from his bout of somnia in time. Then there was the unknown quantity — the big curly-headed idiot she had posted down at the Open Pit in order to stop him getting out of her grasp and taking a job elsewhere. What would he be like?

"Well, before we get down to the real business of the evening old Staff Officer, let's get this Press Conference going," Pyper said, taking a pad and Biro out of his pocket. "Fill me in about this strike."

"No comment," Crompton drawled, then fell asleep again.

"Christ, what a PR man old George is. He's not even a reliable source. Look at the bastard. Pissed out of his mind by lunch-time every morning. Spends most of his time playing snooker down the Mine Club or screwing the arse off his secretary on the office carpet. What would you do with him? No wonder the mining companies have bad public relations. I'm surprised they have any relations at all." Pyper shook his head. "But I wish I had the bastard's salary."

The Staff Officer put a hand on Crompton's shoulder and lightly shook it. Crompton turned on her and savagely bit her hand, crying

38

out that he would murder the next man who touched him.

"It's his wife," she sighed, "she gives him a lot to worry about."

"Old Hermione? She's a talented woman," Pyper grinned impishly, "I reckon she's in the forefront of the old modern art."

"I suppose we might as well put him to bed," the Staff Officer stood up as she spoke, then went inside the bungalow and re-appeared pushing a wheeled hospital trolley. Running it alongside Crompton she helped Pyper to roll the comatose PR Man on to it, then pushed the trolley back into the bungalow, Pyper following behind. It looked to Hurl as though they had been through this routine on previous occasions.

"So you're the new IRO," Pyper said as he sat down again, "why don't you give me the story about the strike then since you're sitting here doing four-fifths of fuck all? You must know what makes the workers down there tick? Speak their language. Understand the old tribal lore. Any Communist influence from Bujumbura? African Democratic Congress making a come-back? I suppose there's a ringleader who can be blamed for inciting the rest?"

"Well, I think it's a little more complex than that," Hurl began.

"D'you mean to say that Matthias and the Bucket-Wheel Excavator Gang aren't behind it?" Pyper drew back, an expression of incredulity on his fair face.

"Of course they are," the Staff Officer joined in. "If I was Doctor Mulombe I'd deport him."

"He was born here," Hurl pointed out.

Hurl's observation was treated with light laughter. Doctor Mulombe, he was told, often deported citizens of Zonkendawo. They were put on aeroplanes flying north, south, east and west. Although none of them held citizenship of another country, they never returned.

"So don't think that would stop the old Doctor. If he wants to deport Matthias, he will, make no error," Pyper asserted cheerfully, "or he'll have the fat bastard's throat cut."

"The strike is over a question of faith," Hurl said, deciding to be explicit. "It's a serious issue."

"Faith?" Pyper breathed rapturously, "you mean religion? Black Mass? Hellfire Club? Human sacrifice? That kind of thing?"

"No, not that kind of thing at all," Hurl insisted, "It's about the Open Pit Manager putting a crocodile in the sump — which he denies by the way, he even denies that there is a crocodile in there —

39

and the Africans have taken this as an insult to the tabus. The spirits of the paramount chiefs live in the crocodiles."

"That sounds like one of Matthias's better ruses," Pyper chuckled, "Christ, that fat bastard has got an imagination like Edgar Allan Poe."

"There is something in the sump," Hurl continued, "I've seen it. It looks like a floating log. I don't see why you have to assume that Matthias has rigged the whole thing."

Pyper sat back and gave Hurl the benefit of the burning of his ice-fire eyes. A deep, elvish smile curled his rosy lips.

"You're as big a prick as you look, aren't you?" he sniggered. "You don't know what you're talking about you bald-faced dead-beat! Listen sport, old Matthias and me have been making the news around here for ages. We know why things happen. We make them happen. Christ, trying to get some sense out of you is like trying to poke butter up a porcupine's arse with a red-hot knitting needle. It's just not worth the trouble."

Hurl blinked, a jet of anger burning under his heart. The journalist smoothed his shirt out over his chest and grinned at the infuriated IRO, his feet poised on the balls, ready to jump out of the way should the offended creature try to charge him down.

"Back in New Zealand we'd have you as Prime Minister, you're so fucking stupid," Pyper giggled, "Christ, where do they get these IRO's from these days. They must be scouring the nut-houses and knocking-shops. I bet you crawled out of The Street Of A Thousand Arseholes."

"Since you seem to know so much about it," Hurl said levelly, "why don't you tell me what it's all about?"

"Why didn't you ask before, old IRO. What they're striking about is that they know Hammerkop *would like* to put a crocodile in the sump if it would upset the old en stroke ens."

"The old en stroke ens?"

"Jesus holy Christ!" Pyper exploded, "what did you bring this cretin down here for old Staff Officer? He's thicker than George here! The old Affs sport, the negritude, the nig-nogs. The Staff Officer said you were a graduate. What in? Wanking?"

Hurl got to his feet and entered the bungalow, his mind thunder-struck. Another minute and he would have slaughtered Pyper without mercy, torn the rasping nasal drawl out of his throat and strangled him with his own tongue. Outside he heard Pyper laugh again. The

Staff Officer followed him in.

"Don't let him see that he's upset you," she said, putting a hand on his arm. "He can't help it. He's the rudest man I know. One day someone will give him what for. But don't let it spoil my dinner-party. Come on, we'll eat now."

The Staff Officer's cooking was superb. The first course was an hors d'oeuvre of half an avocado pear on a bed of fresh green lettuce with a creamed prawn sauce heaped thickly in the hollow where the stone had been. Crompton had been sat in a straight-backed chair, still asleep, and bound upright with a clothes-line brought in from the garden.

"Oh dear, I hope he'll come round soon," the Staff Officer lamented, "I've made arrangements for four of us."

"George!" Pyper shrieked, hacking at the PR Man's shins under the table, "arise! They're hanging the General Manager from the shaft-head! The arse has dropped out of the London Metal Market! The company's been exposed as being a hidey-hole of racists, neo-colonialists and South African Nationalist Party spies!"

Crompton slumbered on.

"You see old IRO. He's exhausted. I know what a day he's had. He got up this morning at ten, went into the office, emptied his in-tray into his out-tray, went down the Mine Club, had five gin-'n-lemons, played a game of snooker with me, went back to his office, screwed his secretary standing up against the filing-cabinet, went to the British Empire Service League, drank a bottle of whisky, fell off his stool, was collected by his artistic wife, old Hermione, she took him home for lunch, did a bit of work on him, sent him out into the world again, back to the Mine Club where he started another bottle of whisky, half of which he took with him when he dodged over the wall of the General Manager's house, into the bedroom at the end of the hall where the G.M.'s wife was waiting for him. He works away there, telling her that she's got to help him get on in the world, then he's off, now weak at the knees, down to the Boxing Club, trying to pick up some of the crooked deals for Saturday's racing at the old corrupt Turf Club. He finishes his whisky, falls off his stool, I find him there, shovel him into the car and take him home. He wakes up while my old servant is cleaning the place up, tries to mount the poor old tribesman because he's as blind as a bat without his specs on, then shoots a tiger all over the carpet. I have to clean him up, give him a

41

cup of tea, and here we are bang on time for the old Press Conference and some dinner."

Crompton stirred, perhaps unconsciously rebelling against the account of his daily routine as rendered by the beautifully plumaged New Zealander.

"Don't admit anything," he muttered, "I'm the company spokesman."

"Ah, that's better," the Staff Officer brightened, her voice full of hope, "eat up George darling."

"What's this green thing?" Crompton said faintly, his gummed eyes gazing down at the avocado pear.

"It's a leprechaun's arse!" Pyper chortled, "dig in George."

"I'll kill you one day Pyper, you evil bastard!" Crompton grunted, his spoon poking ineffectually at the avocado pear, "and you're a bloody awful journalist. What do you care about this country? All this nonsense about crusading for an Undignified Society. You're a charlatan."

The Staff Officer had returned to the kitchen and was frying fillets of Kariba bream in garlic and olive oil. As she slid the fish around in the pan she checked her left tit for firmness, ripeness and skin-tone. Serving the fish-course naked to the waist had been a wow with the rugby XV and she could see no reason why it should not prove equally popular with her more sophisticated guests.

She was right. Pyper passed a number of colourful, complimentary remarks while Hurl Halfcock began to look across at her with dumb, bestial longing.

"I'll see you get a good write-up old Staff Officer," Pyper's cold blue eyes twinkled, "and the old IRO here. He's done his bit."

"Not yet he hasn't," the Staff Officer remarked under her breath.

As they ate the fish-course, Pyper explained what he was looking for in the story of the Open Pit strike.

"We need a frontal attack on Hammerkop. We've got to discredit him. If he'd any sense he'd have left Zonkendawo at Independence. What was the point of him staying up here when all he wanted was the old en stroke ens to make a balls-up of running the place? We all knew that the poor bastards were nearly as bad as the fucking dim Pom colonial government, and as corrupt, but Hammerkop wouldn't accept that. He tried to say that they were worse which is impossible. They're the most dignified pricks in the universe. Now old Staff Officer, why don't you use your influence — you know

42

Hammerkop would use your shit for toothpaste — and persuade him to hop it back to the old Transvaal?"

Pyper's closely-reasoned plea had no effect on the Staff Officer. Shaking her head she cast a worried eye at Crompton who was beginning to doze off again.

"No, no, what do you take me for? I wouldn't let him near me. The cleaner from the Open Pit showers has told me a few things about him. He's not my kind at all."

"Perhaps Hammerkop is only doing his job as he sees it?" Hurl ventured to say, his nerves bunched up in anticipation, "we all have to work through our prejudices. I've had some pretty silly ideas in my time."

"What?" Pyper commenced the onslaught, his eyes blazing with gentian flame, "d'you call putting reptiles in the sump doing his job? Giving soft numbers to bums like you who wander over the border when there's thousands of en stroke ens going mad for a nice job like that? Hammerkop's a racist! He lives in a white tower. He sees everything in racial terms!"

Hurl cringed inwardly, remembering Races One, Two and Three. What was he then?

"We'll get the bastard," Pyper finished his harangue with a strangely warm chuckle and grinned engagingly across at Hurl, "Matthias and I will fix him. Come on, eat up. What's for main course old Staff Officer? What are you taking off for that?"

After the cheese and biscuits, they carried Crompton through to the bedroom and laid him out on the lionskin. The Staff Officer untucked his shirt, then slowly pulled it up over his head. Blazoned across his back was a musical score, and when Hurl studied it closer he saw that it had been drawn with exquisite skill, in order to join up hundreds of moles.

"I told you his wife had talent," Pyper said admiringly, "look at that. Last week she did a tea-clipper in full sail. Bloody beautiful wasn't it old Staff Officer?"

"I like Hermione's insistence on detail. Look at these semiquavers here. Absolutely perfect. She's wasting her talents stuck out here in the *bundu* miles from anywhere."

The now-naked Staff Officer went across to a Welsh dresser and took out a flute, wetted her lips, leaned over Crompton's back and haltingly picked out the tune. It was Three Blind Mice and she played it with haunting grace, the melody echoing her sadness at the reduction of active lovers for the lionskin that night. All the regret and nostalgia of disappointed passion reigned in her piping, the lilting, pure cadences of unrequited love.

Hurl watched the Staff Officer, also catching the nonchalant, cruel smile on Pyper's beautiful face. Crompton snored on, unaware of the growing confidence of the flautist above him who was breathing passion and power into her reed, her metallic eyes shimmering, unaware of the moves of her imagination as she mentally hung the PR man over the window-sill or on the hooks behind the door in order to get him physically involved in the forthcoming liaison on the lionskin.

"She's pretty pissed off with old George," Pyper whispered as he stripped off his colourful clothes, "he's always dropping off like this. He's got no idea of responsibility."

The Staff Officer put away her flute, then flung herself on the lionskin, breast heaving, knees apart. Beneath her was Crompton, his head crushed by her splendid marble-white buttocks.

"Well old IRO, take your pick as you're a newcomer. You can have the top deck or the bottom deck. The old Staff Officer won't let you down. You saw how she handled that flute? She's the best gnawer of the old nana south of the equator. Or you can be the straight man, take your pick and hurry up about it before this thing runs away with a mind of its own."

Hurl closed his eyes. He knew that once on to the lionskin, he was committed, bolted on to the bold lunacy of the whole continent. His courage dwindled, then surged back again. He had to go forwards. The past was over. Clambering between the Staff Officer's knees he prayed hard inside himself for the strength to keep upright, whole and human, while ahead of him Pyper straddled the Staff Officer's breast. With one motion, the Staff Officer drew them both forward like two riders of a speeding machine.

Below her, Crompton slumbered on, making no comment.

FIVE DOWN BY THE RIVERSIDE

Hurl woke early. The sun was outside, pale and washed, and its light in the bedroom of the Staff Officer had a purity, a clean, unsullied

44

air. He looked around him, lying as he was in a tangle of arms, legs, mouths and easeful flesh, and remembered. Disgust mounted in his throat and he tore himself out of the pile and stood by the bedside, breathing hard. But the light held him, the pure light on the bodies. The Staff Officer, Pyper and Crompton lay together like the young of a beast, curled up, interlocked, trust exemplified. On their faces was the peace of sleep. They could have been in a nest or a cave, huddled together for warmth and protection while Time roared threateningly, unable to reach them because of their warm companionship. Hurl groaned and sat on the edge of the bed. For a moment he had a strong urge to get back in the pile and lie there, hooked up to these other animals, touching them, feeling them close, being one of the litter again.

Instead, he dressed and went out into the garden, saddened once again by his own vacillation and refusal to identify. They were all right. In their hearts was the knowledge that they were only as good or bad as each other. He still had some way to go before he could honestly say that he had met up with the leveller, the answer to his loneliness. Last night had inched open a door and he was peering round it. Perhaps next time the Staff Officer might allow him to come down with the Bucket-Wheel Excavator Gang.

Walking to the bottom of the garden he left a trail of footprints in the dew. He noticed how his feet were still at five to one like a duck's. Would he ever really be able to change? To wholeheartedly give himself to a new life of action? Wasn't he already formed, cast in a great brazen image? All the adjustments necessary to accept his animal past – wouldn't they be too much for his rudimentary engine of a mind to bear? Wasn't he a machine? Hadn't England done its work, the world's premier slaver, the country which had sailed its ships full of human cargo across the Atlantic and now sailed them up and down the housing-estates, the workshop aisles, the TV channels? Why should he think that he had escaped in one piece? Part of him was still chained up there, lying bound to a dockside ring in Liverpool.

He climbed over the low fence and into the bush. The dew hung on the brown leaves and shook on to his upturned face as he blundered through the small trees and bushes. He smelled the dawn scents and tasted the cool water on his lips and it made his agony of mind worse. He was here, surrounded by this great, free land where a man could cut off from the road and walk until he dropped dead without having

45

to account for himself, give an opinion, or fill in a form. Was his mind clear? Had he given himself over to this new experience? Having come to Africa to prove to himself that his prejudices were justified, and after having them robbed from him, he now did not have the courage to stand like the pauper he was and face the future. Was that kind of bravery beyond him? The bravery of the re-born?

He walked faster and faster, the twigs and leaves whipping his tall figure as he stormed through the wakening country. Insects burst up from clusters of dead leaves lying in forks, a flock of egrets passed over his head, white against the white of the morning, even the air stirred with the warmth of the massive orb pushing itself into the eastern sky. But he was not moved. Something was lodged across the gate of his soul, something heavy and padlocked. He was barred up inside and he knew what it was.

Pyper had seen it. His ice-fire eyes had burned through Hurl's flesh and espied the obstacle in the road.

It was Dignity.

Dignity, dignity, dignity. His feet scuffed through the red soil and leaves, pounding out the awful word. He had thought himself base, not proud, free-thinking, unconscious of status. But he had lied to himself. Faster and faster he walked, as if to escape from himself, tear his spirit out of the big body and gallop ahead crying – that's not me, that's not me! – oh, what a criminal piece of self-deception and arrogance! – what a man to fool himself so, then to expect this new world to believe him! Now he ran, he threshed at the trees, blindly pushing them out of his way. Faster and faster, his breath getting shorter, heavier, his head rolling on his neck. Like this he ran for an hour, crashing through the bush like a prehistoric creature, sightless, mad, driven mad by the wounds within itself.

His poor wife. Her tired face loomed through the leaves, the once-bright eyes now anxious, but fighting to hold on. He had loved her – had he? Was it her, or what he could make of her? He had wanted to pull her out of her soil like an onion, strip her down, layer by layer, then to consume her. He had used the poor, lovely child and made her hard, a gilt woman. She had survived his dragooning, his driving Dignity. Had he loved her? Had he? What was she now? Closing his eyes he fought forward into the trees, hacking, spitting and clawing at the man he was. He tripped and fell down on his face. With breath searing like hot acid in his lungs, his limbs twitching and trembling,

46

he got to his feet and ran on, the ghosts of his heart-broken love behind him.

He ran until he could run no more. Sweat streamed down his flesh like rain and his mouth tasted as though it was full of blood. When he spat, his saliva hung from his lip in skeins. His legs shook and there was no feeling in his knees any more. In this condition, taking one exhausted step at a time, he came into a clearing.

It was high-grassed and level, surrounded by trees, and at the far end he could see the shine of sun on water where a river bend shoved red earth up in a low cliff. It was the Kafue. Staggering across the *dambo* – the meadow-like flood plain – he found a rock near the river's edge and sat down, his heart still hammering painfully, his stomach sick.

"Oh I don't want to go on, I don't, I don't. . ." he sobbed quietly while his eyes ran with the river's swirl, "I'm getting nowhere."

Slowly, his body came back to rest. His blood stopped pounding and his head cleared. The sun warmed his skin through the chilled sweat. Slipping down the rock he nestled against its side and fell asleep.

And he dreamed a dream.

A dream of trees.

The ugly baobab tree, its girth huge, bloated and grey, stood by the river, its clawing branches thickened at the joints and tapered at the ends like witch's fingers. Repulsive to look upon, dropsical, diseased, it bore its great grey head proudly and glared at the sun.

"Hmmm! What a beautiful tree am I?" it hummed.

Once it had been. No tree on the earth could vie with the baobab. Its blossoms were rich and deep-dyed like a king's robe, its leaves were broad, delicately fretted with golden veins, and a green, such a green. That green has passed from the world now, it has been subtracted from the spectrum. The baobab remembered that green, and its former beauty. It had the picture of its glory firm in its grey head, for it had spent many years looking at itself in the Kafue. Now it was ugly – for it had been punished by the gods of Africa for its vanity and turned upside down so its roots kicked at the sky – it lived on the memory. The reflection which the baobab saw in the water was that of its heyday, the colours, the stature. Even though it knew that it was fooling itself, the baobab still thought that it was the most beautiful tree in the world.

What could the gods of Africa do? Turn it back the right way up?

47

Then it *would* be the most beautiful tree on earth again and the baobab would go unpunished for its cruel vanity. So the ugly tree stared at the ugly tree in the water and told itself that it was beautiful. The gods were happy because they knew the truth. The baobab was happy because it did not accept the truth.

"I'm gorgeous!" sighed the baobab, playing with the wind in its grotesque branches, "and nobody can tell me otherwise."

In full flower, the slave tree towered by the Kafue, its scarlet blood-like blossoms casting a warm light over the river bank. Beside it, the baobab was even uglier, its grey bark catching the reflections of the wind-stirred crimson, a colour contrast which heightened its horrible pallor.

"See how beautiful the baobab is," the slave tree sighed. "God, I wish I were so splendid."

"No, no," Hurl ground his teeth in his sleep, "please, don't say that!"

"I am so mediocre," the slave tree continued, its voice plaintive, "so uninspired, so lowly."

In its tall loveliness, the slave tree looked down at the squat baobab and arched its graceful neck, flowers tumbling down in a crimson cloud like a wild mane of blood. Its brilliant head shook, scattering leaves in the rain-wind which had blown up from the west.

"Help me, help me," it whimpered to the baobab, "show me how I can be like you."

"Certainly," the baobab bellowed in a loud voice, "bend lower and I'll tell you how."

The slave tree leaned over. Its magnificent trunk creaked. It was the sound of wooden yokes on lathered necks, of chains clinking, of ships groaning their timbers in the Atlantic swell. Lower and lower bent the slave tree, bringing down its radiant, red head. The baobab beckoned it to get closer, crooking its boughs, curling its twigs into grappling hooks.

"Come closer, closer!" it hissed.

"No! Get back!" Hurl shouted in his sleep, "get back!"

The slave tree strained lower, its spine arching, flesh creaking, bones cracking. Its beautiful flower-laden boughs swept the river, the dust, the lowly earth.

"I am coming," it gasped, "oh tell me, tell me your secret!"

"Just a bit more," said the baobab cunningly, "then I will tell you all you want to know."

Hurl shuddered and clung to his rock. Sweat started on his brow again and his mouth hung open in horror. The slave tree was going to break its back! It would die. Futile, ignorant, abject, the slave tree would abase itself to ugliness and pride, and pay the penalty. Over Hurl's head the lovely tree creaked lower. With a sickening crash a bough ripped off and fell to the ground. The slave tree screamed aloud but kept bending, prostrating itself to the grey belly of the hideous baobab. Blood poured from the gash and turned to petals which drifted away in the rain-wind.

"Stand up straight!"

It was the rock which had spoken. Hurl felt the reverberations going through his frame. The harsh surface broke and the clear voice sounded again.

"Get back up there! Get back in the air!"

The slave tree paused in its descent, weeping blood and flowers.

"Don't take any notice," the baobab barked, "it's only the rock. What does he know about beauty?"

"Get back up with the birds!" the rock commanded. "You're a tree! Be a tree! We've got enough creepers in the natural world. Get back in an upright position and do your job. Be seen from a mile away. Hold out your arms. Lift up your head and be beautiful." Hurl knew the stone in his bowel, the stiff rock in his heart. He had merged with the inanimate, gone back into the indestructible. It was his voice that the rock was using. He was the rock. As he saw the slave tree begin to unbend and lift its marvellous head to the sky again, he shouted a great shout of joy and clapped his unbreakable, gritty hands together like a crack of doom.

The baobab tree sank into the earth, sucked back into the underworld like a poisonous plant withdrawing from the sweet air.

In his sleep, he smiled, his fists clenched in happy triumph. Gradually the stone seeped back into the rock and his heart returned. Then his sleep became dreamless and he slumbered in complete tranquillity, satisfied.

When he awoke, there was a rain-wind on the river, blowing from the west. On the opposite bank of the river, throned on the cliff of red earth, stood a giant pod mahogany in full bloom, its crown sweeping the sky with crimson, its trunk as straight as a die. Hurl pushed himself up from the rock and as he did so touched the warm place where his body had lain. His fingers encountered an edge, a line, a groove, then a series of grooves. Brushing aside the weathered crust of the rock he saw the broad vales worn into the hard surface, each parallel to the other. They were not fissures, nor had the wind or water made them. Man had worked against the rock, grinding his weapons, sharpening his spear for the hunt.

They were here all right, the animal fathers.

And they had spoken for him.

SIX THE BATTLE IN THE SUMP

The headline in the Zonkendawo Times that morning read:

MUFUNSI OPEN PIT ON STRIKE
Manager appoints stateless alien to key post miners allege. Crocodile used as red herring in capitalist plot.

While Hurl was reading the front page in his office, the telephone rang. It was Pyper.

"What d'you think of the old story," he chirruped happily, "not bad is it?"

Hurl looked out of his window at a queue of workers waiting to see him to beg for cash advances, warnings, promotions and safety-bonuses. They smiled back at him with the knowing impudence of labouring men.

"Are you trying to get me fired?" Hurl said in an undertone.

"Christ, there's gratitude for you!" Pyper cackled at the other end of the line, "I get you a raise and all I get is suspicion, you grudging, perfidious Pom. Don't you know that Hammerkop would drink molten lead if he thought it would prove me wrong about something? I've done you a favour."

Matthias opened the door and crept over the tiles, holding out his hand for the telephone.

"Let me speak to him," he said quietly.

"You're not supposed to use the phone for personal calls!" Hurl reproved him, knocking away the meaty paw. "The call is for me, not you."

"All right then mighty bwana, but tell my *chamware* John Pyper, the Great Writer Of Lies, that the strike goes on today. The crocodile has not been removed from the sump, in fact it has been put in there for the first time. The floating log was a floating log, a decoy which we sailed in the sump to deceive Hammerkop. Now he has taken the bait and done exactly what we thought he would do. He has put a real crocodile in the sump in order to take it out again and end the strike. Tell my friend John Pyper that I suggest for tomorrow's headline: **OPEN PIT MANAGER BREAKS GAME CONSERVA-TION LAWS.**"

Hurl held the telephone away from his ear and looked at Matthias in wonderment.

"Who writes this paper? You or Pyper?"

"Me," Matthias replied modestly, "and you can tell the Great Writer Of Lies to get down here quick. Hammerkop has ordered shift-boss Swanepoel to walk one of the PH 150 power-shovels into the sump, supposedly to deepen it before the rains come, but in fact to kill the crocodile and take it out of the pit. If the crocodile, in whom rests the spirits of the great chiefs of my people, is injured in any way, there could be a rumpus."

"Did you catch all that?" Hurl asked down the telephone.

"I'm on my way old IRO. Tell Matthias he's a genius."

As Hurl put down the instrument, his intercom buzzed. It was Hammerkop. He wanted to see Hurl right away.

"That will be to tell you about your increase in salary for getting your name in the paper."

Matthias shouted out this witticism so the rest of the queue could hear. Laughing, they waved their copies of the Zonkendawo Times in the air and grimaced good-naturedly at the IRO.

Hammerkop held out his hand as Hurl walked through the door. A strange, eery light beamed from his garnet-black eyes and his craggy, chipped mouth was crumpled into a distorted line like sedimentary strata under igneous pressure.

With a start, Hurl realised that the man was smiling.

"What did I tell you?" he chuckled like a lorry-load of broken girders, "sheer bloody vindictiveness! It's that black bastard kaffir Matthias who's got you into trouble, but don't worry. I can run rings round that stupid coon any day of the week."

Then he officially informed Hurl of his raise.

While he was doing so, Hurl could hear the shift-boss in the PH 150 shovel talking to the day-shift mine-captain over the two-way radio, a receiver for which was in Hammerkop's office, always switched on so he could keep himself up to date with the working of the pit.

"The Public Relations Department have asked for a glance at your passport," Hammerkop said over the noise, "they've got a Pom bastard there who reckons he's got the Zonkendawo Times round his little finger. He's putting together a statement we can issue to the Press to contradict what that lying little fairy Pyper has written about you. I've got it all under control sonny. No need to get in a sweat. This feller Crompton is a foxy Pom man. He's a ball of fire when it comes to dealing with journalists."

Hurl nodded, refusing to be shaken. His new strength blocked the protest before it got to his lips. He would just take whatever came his way.

"Got a photograph? Crompton thought that it might look good if we put your *voorkome* on the front page, just to show you've got nothing to hide."

Hurl coloured slightly, then fought down the blush. The only photograph that he had was in a group. It had been taken by the Staff Officer last night with her Instamatic and flash-gun. It was not the kind of picture that would prove that he was not stateless.

"I'm afraid I haven't," Hurl said apologetically, "I'll get one taken if you like."

"No matter man. I'm like you. Never had my picture taken by any bastard. On my wedding photographs my wife asked me if she could have them all taken with just her on them. Go ahead, I said to her. This is a *mansmens* face, not a bastard ornament."

"I've heard she's quite a looker," Hurl enjoined, remembering the Bucket-Wheel Excavator Gang's plans for Gladys.

"Maybe she is sonny, but she's hard to live with. You don't know the problems I have at home."

Then, with this comment hanging in the air like a tormenting curtain over a mystery, Hammerkop cradled his jaw in his hands and listened to shift-boss Swanepoel walking the PH 150 shovel down into the sump from the ore-run. Having not been dismissed, and feeling an awkward, indefinable compassion for the Open Pit Manager at that point, Hurl stayed where he was, his ears straining to pick up the guttural dialogue.

"Okay Swanny, let's go *donder* that *krokodil* with the *skop* eh?"

"Right *kaptein*, let's *doodmaak* that bastard *wurm*!"

A jangling, clanking, chiming, rattling.

"They're off!" Hammerkop raised his eyes to the ceiling, "now Matthias you crafty kaffir! Just watch us go!"

As the great shovel rolled forward under his well-set hams, its boom raised, shovel gaping, shift-boss Swanepoel lifted his eyes to the collar of the Open Pit where the African drivers and their families had gathered to watch his manoeuvres. There they were, the kaffirs drawn up in their thousands, just like at Blood River, *impi* upon *impi*, regiment upon regiment – but they could not touch him, safe as he was in the jarring cab of the shovel, safe under the wing of Mr. Hammerkop. Mr. Hammerkop had not asked one of the boss-boys to drive the shovel, not even one of the Africans ear-marked for promotion as soon as the Zonkendawon government got interested in how manpower was used on the mines, no, it had been shift-boss Swanepoel he had looked to. Why? Because this job needed brains. To bring this complot to a successful conclusion needed plenty of brains, African hunting brains, white, sharp, shrewd, competent, unrelenting brains. Shift-boss Swanepoel had plenty of brains. That is why Mr. Hammerkop had chosen him to go and fish for a crocodile in the sump with the PH 150 power-shovel.

The late October day was overcast, heavy cloud having drifted in from the east where the Indian Ocean was brewing up the annual monsoons. At the bottom of the Open Pit the temperature was 100° Fahrenheit and the cab of the shovel was suffocatingly hot. At this time of year, the climate in Zonkendawo was moist and oppressive. 'Suicide Month' it was called, light-heartedly, but a few Africans, Indians and Europeans fulfilled the aptness of the name each year by blowing their brains out. The Africans usually conceded that they had no brains to blow out by going into the bush and quietly hanging themselves.

"What do you say Erik man?" Mr. Hammerkop had laid it along the line, no ifs or buts. If shift-boss Swanepoel would go to the Kafue, catch a live crocodile, bring it back to the Open Pit, put it into the sump, then fish it out under cover of appearing to be deepening the sump, he would be promoted. The job of night-shift mine-captain would be his.

"Leave it to me Mr. Hammerkop," shift-boss Swanepoel had said, his eyes misty with gratitude, "I won't let you down."

It was a pity that he would never be able to stand at the bar of the British Empire Service League and tell his mates the story of how he and his bonny wife Gretchen had spent the night cruising up and down the Kafue with a spotlight fixed to the bow of the motor-boat, trying to sight a crocodile. Even now he trembled at the recall of the

53

risk that Gretchen had taken by diving in and wrestling bare-handed with the fourteen-foot monster which they had found wallowing in a shallow outer bend. If ever a man knew that his wife truly loved him, it was shift-boss Swanepoel. During the long journey back to Mufunsi, she had sat in the back of the Land-Rover, her arms around the jaws of her catch, the lashing tail held tightly between her thighs. She had been forced to carry the tossing reptile in her arms over the last few hundred yards because the pit bottom was thick with dust and the Land-Rover could not traverse it. In the light of the head-lamps she had staggered through the dust, wading in it up to her knees, bearing the crocodile aloft, her pale body ripped and scratched by the flailing tail, then flung it into the sump. Relaxing over a brandy and orange at home, when the ordeal was over, Gretchen had con-fessed to her husband that there had been moments when she had wished herself at home and safely tucked up in bed.

The shovel clanked down off the ore-run, trundled along a ramp of broken stone and entered the deep dust of the pit bottom. Ahead of him, lying in the soupy green water, he could see the crocodile, its bumpy, malevolent eyes sunk in its armoured head. Above the reptile, cheering it on, were the Africans, urging their chief to *bulala* the *shifbas*. The rim of the pit was now packed ten deep, teeming with *piccanins*, *umfazis* and *madalas*, with more arriving from the township on the hill every moment, anxious to witness the contest. To the right, just below the offices, were the mine-captains and surveyors, geologists and planners, all gathered round Hammerkop and Hurl on the observation-platform. Sitting in the bush to the left of them, his aquamarine slacks brilliant in the sun, was Pyper, a jewelled grasshopper poised on the edge of the chasm. Around him squatted Matthias and the Bucket-Wheel Excavator Gang. As the shovel bulldozed through the dust towards the sump, they watched it in hopeful silence, praying for a useful conclusion. They were all indifferent to the fate of the horny reptile itself, some of them having lost brothers, sisters and children to its depredations over the years, and they liked nothing better than to see one laid out on the river bank, skinned, with its belly ripped open. But they preferred the crocodile to shift-boss Swanepoel. It did not sit in the Mine Club and go on about Africans having no brains. It did not say that kaffirs were a sub-species of homo sapiens. It did not ignore the truth about men.

Crocodiles just ate people.

That was a far more clear-cut issue.

The PH 150 entered the water and the clanking of the tracks was drowned in the sludge. Peering out of the cab, shift-boss Swanepoel held his breath. This was the critical moment. Would the bottom hold the great weight of the shovel? It did. It was good and hard. Jerking the levers, he flexed the huge toothed bucket and scooped up some water to check the mechanism. Everything was in working order. He was armed. Ahead of him the crocodile shifted its position, scudding through the green slime. Shift-boss Swanepoel grinned and lowered his head.

The hunt was on.

"You all right there Swanny?" the mine-captain grated over the two-way radio, "now you go and *slaan* that bastard!"

"He won't know what's hit him," shift-boss Swanepoel assured the mine-captain. "I'm going to *verbreek* his *nek*!"

The shovel turned, its bucket poised in the air. Moving forwards a few yards it paused above the crocodile, then down came the huge bucket, smashing on top of it. Shift-boss Swanepoel whooped with triumph. Hammerkop's roar could be heard all round the pit. The Africans went quiet. Then the crocodile surfaced behind the shovel, slipping through the stagnant filth with langorous ease, its tail waving slowly from side to side. A deep bellow of gladness rose from the Africans. Mine-helmets went spinning to the clouds. Women ululated. Small children threw rocks into the vast pit. Old men chewed their knuckles and whistled through few teeth. Relief was on every face.

The *ngandu* was as cunning as ever.

The shovel cranked round, searching for its quarry, the bucket drawn back like a snake's head, fangs exposed. Round and round the boom went, looking, prying, trying to keep up with the lazily swimming reptile. It came close again, flirted its great tail in a wall of frothy spray. The bucket roared down, hawsers screaming. Once again the crocodile disappeared and Hammerkop's cries of victory could be heard clattering through the moist air.

It did not re-appear.

The Africans crowded to the edge of the pit, their eyes straining for a knob, a ripple, a wave of the tail.

Nothing. Only the giant shovel, bucket sunk in the green muck, the driver bouncing up and down in his seat with jubilation.

A great sigh was already rising from the assembled Africans when the first people saw the long snout and the wide-open mouth, the enormous smile of the crocodile as it lay underneath the shovel, floating between the high caterpillar tracks. The perimeter of the pit erupted into gay confusion, dancing, singing, hand-clapping and gusty laughter. The sound was a source of bewilderment to shift-boss Swanepoel. What were the kaffirs so pleased about?

The mine-captain came on to the two-way radio.

"Swanny, you fucking *donkie*," he rasped, "that *krokodil* is making a fool of you. *Vermoor* him now before these kaffirs go on the rampage!"

"Where is he?" shift-boss Swanepoel demanded, "I can't see the bastard!"

"He's half-way up your arse, you dim *bobbejaan!*"

Shift-boss Swanepoel hastily engaged the clutch and the shovel lurched forward. Beneath it, the crocodile kept pace, cruising along between the caterpillar tracks. For half-an-hour the shovel staggered from one end of the sump to the other, round the circumference, across diameters, chords and in spirals, but it could not dislodge the huge scaly leech, apparently sticking to its underbelly. Up on the collar of the pit there was a full celebration. Plastic containers of millet-beer were brought from the beer-halls. Drums, thumb pianos and xylophones were tuned and ancient melodies rendered. Young men and women leaped and soared. The old *ngandu* was making bwana Swanepoel into the biggest cunt in creation.

Then the crocodile made a mistake. It moved out of the steel cave which had so effectively sheltered it. The shovel reversed, drew up its boom and dropped the bucket, catching the crocodile a glancing blow. The reptile reared up in the water, its roar of pain clearly audible. The dancing stopped. The drinking stopped. The songs of praise for the *ngandu* were cut short. The Africans crept closer, the hoarse shouts of Hammerkop sawing through their eardrums. As shift-boss Swanepoel flexed back the boom and prepared for the second blow, the Africans started climbing down the steep sides of the pit. The shovel struck, but it missed as the crocodile rolled over on its back, tail flogging the water into surf. Hammerkop saw the Africans climbing down towards the sump. He gave a shout of inarticulate rage and left the observation platform and slid down after them all, followed by all his officials. Shift-boss Swanepoel trundled the shovel backwards, trailing the bucket after him to try and trap the crocodile in the four steel teeth and pin it down. This way and that he dragged the gigantic comb, sifting the deep murk.

In the chaos, few people noticed the flashes of lightning and rumbles of thunder. They were a peripheral accompaniment to what was going on below them. By the time it had started to rain, both the Africans and Europeans were so incensed by the battle that all the external conditions that the world could throw at them did not matter a damn. What mattered was in the sump, the heroic conflict between the PH 150 and the snapping, enraged crocodile. Down and down the slopes they ran, heedless.

The storm caught them in two great blasts of rain, two buffets with a breath of the rain-wind in between. The skies emptied an ocean into the pit in a minute. Trapped in waves of silver fire, deluged by stunning blows of cataracts, spouts and gouts pouring and ejaculating from fissures in the rock, the people were battered step by step, slither by slither, into the bottom of the pit. There was no protection. The crowd screamed, tore at the streaming earth, tried to drag itself back up the cascading walls of red. But down it all went, earth, water, men and women, everything being swept towards the drainage centre of the great hole, the red boiling hell that was now the sump.

Forty minutes later, the storm subsided, the wind abated, the sun came back from behind the grey clouds. The Open Pit was a steaming shambles of mud. Caked, saturated figures, all of them red as the earth and indistinguishable one from the other, toiled back up the terraces to the collar to safety.

Few spared a glance behind them into the sump where shift-boss Swanepoel still sat at the controls of the PH 150 power-shovel beneath fifty feet of water. Even fewer, only Pyper in fact, his cruel smile carousing on his rosebud mouth, watched the slow progress of the limping crocodile, *ngandu*, chief, conqueror and champion of his people, as he dragged himself up the north slope towards the Kafue and his ancestral home.

SEVEN HAMMERKOP'S PREDIKAMENT

They sat in a booth in the main Mine Club Bar, an island of mournful calm amid the roar of one-armed bandits, torrents of dice-rattling and gale-like rifflings of pornographic photographs of Coloured and African women being passed from hand to hand of the hundreds of South African, Dutch, English, Scots, Irish, Jugoslavian, Greek, Canadian, Spanish and Portuguese miners gathered there. The bar was aswim with spilled beer and the air thick with the smoke of Van Rjin and Rembrandt cigars. The death of shift-boss Swanepoel was being waked in a manner he would have understood.

Only Hurl and Hammerkop were silent, each man alone with his thoughts. Hurl was seeing again the pathetic scene when Gretchen, the blonde, buxom widow of the deceased, had arrived at the collar of the Open Pit, summoned there by the Mine Police. She had stripped to her briefs, then tobogganed down the slippy red mud on her sturdy bum, straight down into the sump. From then on she had done a powerful crawl until she reached the spot where the shovel lay submerged, then duck-dived, re-appearing a minute later with her late husband gripped between her teeth like a bedraggled pup. On the way back to the shore of the sump she had performed a classic breast-stroke, forging through the red water until it curved into twin waves of pink foam on either side of her plunging head. Hurl had been struck dumb at this exhibition of devoted love. His heart had been sorely affected. There was no one in the world who would think of doing the same for him. Whatever politics or prejudices shift-boss Swanepoel stood for, they were as straws in the wind beside this picture of womanly grief. Hurl felt envious of the dead man.

"That black bastard Matthias pulled this one," Hammerkop ground through the ruminating motion of his iron jaw, "he got the *nyanga* to dance up that freak storm."

"What's a *nyanga*?" Hurl asked.

"The witchdoctor, you ignorant Pom *groentjie!*"

"What's a *groentjie*?"

"A greenhorn. What d'you want? A pint?"

Hurl nodded and Hammerkop went to the bar to order another two pints of Limosin brandy and orange. While he stood there, trying to attract the attention of the barman, Hurl noticed the slouch of his lumpy shoulders, the crick in his neck. The poor man had been hard hit by the loss of the PH 150 power-shovel. It had cost £80,000 new and would take four months to replace. The board of directors in Johannesburg would not be pleased. Hammerkop had confided to Hurl that at the last Staff Development Panel, the board

58

had granted him an A – provisionally. As Hammerkop returned with the lurid glasses of dark red fluid, Hurl asked him why the A had been provisional.

"Gladys," Hammerkop grunted as he sat down again.

"Your wife?"

Hammerkop nodded and sipped his drink.

"What's she got to do with it?"

"Haven't I told you about it? Christ, what a business. Have you ever reached that stage in your life when everything is a bloody mess? That's me right now. I don't know whether I'm coming or going. There's those fucking kaffirs I can't get rid of, this balls-up this afternoon, and Gladys."

"What has she done?"

"It's what she hasn't done."

"Well, what hasn't she done?"

"She's still a virgin. We've been married seven years and she's still a virgin. The board don't like it."

"Neither does she by the sound of it."

"It's not that you Pom comedian. She's worried about falling pregnant."

"Well put her on the Pill."

"She's a hypochondriac."

"French Letter, Dutch Cap..."

"She says they're unreliable."

"Why doesn't she want to fall pregnant?"

"It started off when she was made Rose Queen of Pofadder. She's never got over it. She says that if she has a *babetjie* it'll give her stretch-marks and pull her tits out of shape."

Hurl ceased his probing questions. Hammerkop's face had assumed the cast of a tragic mask, the mouth pulled down, the eyes half-closed. But there was yet one question that Hurl had to ask.

"I don't see what this has got to do with the board. Isn't it a very private matter?"

Hammerkop gave Hurl a contemptuous glance and shook his head.

"What an ignorant *aap* you are. Man, when you're at my level in the management hierarchy your wife is supposed to help out. If you're going to get to the top then the little woman can be a real social asset."

"I still don't see the connection," Hurl said, "are you saying your wife is an embarrassment to you as well as being a virgin?"

"No man, it's *because* she's a virgin. That's what upsets the board. She can cut a plate of tunny-fish *botterhammetjies* or talk shit till the cows come home at any cocktail party you take her to – that's not the problem. She's got all the graces man, she's very sophisticated."

Hurl had taught himself to control his facial reactions by this stage in his introduction to Zonkendawon society. He casually traced out a square on the side of his glass and shifted in his seat, trying to appear unmoved by the insanity of Hammerkop's predikament.

"Why don't you creep up on her when she's asleep?"

"She has her own room and keeps the door padlocked. One night I climbed through the outside window and tried to get into her but I found that she was wearing a pair of German leather trousers in bed."

"German leather trousers?" Hurl recoiled in amazement.

"That's what really upset the chairman. He was up here on a flying visit and stayed over at my place. He assumed that the usual conveniences were on hand and slipped after her into the bedroom for half-an-hour's frolic and ran up against this *hinderpaal* and nearly ruptured himself. He reduced my salary by 15 per cent, the bastard."

Hurl rubbed a thoughtful finger along the line of his jaw.

"What do you do for sex then?"

"I throw my self into my work. I've given up with Gladys. The only other women I really fancy is the Staff Officer but she's just as frigid I hear. She never hands out. What a fucking camp this is eh? It's you Poms started it, you and Prince Albert, that blockhead Kraut bastard."

Hurl relapsed into silence before his pity for Hammerkop had to be articulated. He knew that the tall, bony man with his long granitic head was in the depths of an agonising quandary. What could he do to help without giving offence, or appearing charitable? But Hammerkop's mind, rapid and mechanical as ever, was already far ahead of Hurl's whizzing round a racetrack of ideas and plans.

"Pommy, you're young. With the state England is in today, decadent, corrupt and venal, you must have had a cart-load of sexual experience. Why don't you see if Gladys will warm to you eh?"

Hurl gagged on his drink, and sat, eyes wide, with orange liquid running down his chin. He looked, and felt, very foolish.

"Me? With your wife?"

"Who else?"

"What about the Bucket-Wheel Excavator Gang? They'd be interested..."

Hammerkop went pale, his big nutty knuckles showing white on his hand. Into his garnet-black eyes came a livid flame.

"You talk like that again you *vark* and I'll break your back! I'm having no kaffir interfering with my wife! D'you think I've got no sense of fucking decency?"

Hurl stood up, brandy and orange coursing down his neck and chest. He could not stop the enraged spluttering in his gorge. Waving his arms around his head, spitting, crying, he made for the door.

"See you on Thursday for a *braaivleis* then IRO!" Hammerkop bellowed, peering through the tall potted rubberplants which surrounded the booth. "I'll be expecting great things of you."

Outside, sitting under a mango tree, was Matthias and the Bucket-Wheel Excavator Gang. When Hurl crashed through the outside door and stood with his head between his knees, heaving up the last of the four pints of brandy and orange which he had drunk with Hammerkop, they did not move to help or comfort him.

"We're disgusted with you," the Bucket-Wheel Excavator Gang chanted sadly, "on the night of our victory you elect to drink with the enemy of our race. Whose side are you on?"

Hurl heard their hoarse, melodious voices and looked up. He had never been more glad to hear any sound. Here was the real world. Something he could understand. Wiping his streaming eyes he joined them under the mango tree and told them of his conversation with Hammerkop.

"He speaks the truth. Gladys has resisted every attempt to *hlanganana* her. All the members of the board have tried it. The house-servant has tried it. The mine-captains have tried it. The rugby XV have tried it. She is like an ivory tower, this Gladys."

"He wants me to try," Hurl confessed.

"Then you should," Matthias said firmly, "it is your bounden duty."

"I should!" Hurl objected, "what the hell do you mean? I couldn't do that?"

"Why do you think Hammerkop is like he is? Because he cannot

61

be promoted. He will stay Open Pit Manager all his life unless Gladys is broken open and encouraged to accept the board. If you, with Hammerkop's permission, can get her interested in your *umtondo*, then she might extend this to other men, especially the board. They will be pleased. They will promote Hammerkop and send him down to work in South Africa in a senior job at head office. We will be rid of him."

"I don't think I could make her like me," Hurl protested. "I've had a lot of trouble with women in my time."

"Haven't we all?" Matthias said sagely. "That's what they're there for. But Gladys will love you IRO. I know it. She is longing for a man like you to turn her eyes away from her mirrors. She wants to be a whole woman and experience life at its best. You cannot screw your own image. Is that not so?"

"Thanks Matthias, you're being very helpful," Hurl said caustically. "Look, I've met women like her before. She sounds like a clitorosophist to me."

This long word drew a sigh from the Bucket-Wheel Excavator Gang who lapsed into fond dreams of just what it could mean.

"What do you mean IRO?"

"She's narcissistic."

"That's right."

"Why should she suddenly prefer me to herself?"

"Rape is the best approach!" shouted a member of the Bucket-Wheel Excavator Gang. "That way you don't have to buy her flowers."

"That's not my style," Hurl replied with a jaundiced air. "In fact I'm not even much good at seduction. I can only manage a direct approach."

"Oh, you are modest. The world is full of women dying to love you. Give Gladys a chance. It might be a perfect match."

"Hmm," Hurl grunted thoughtfully, "I doubt it. I don't think my luck goes that far. I've been in love so many times that I can't remember – but what I can remember is that I seemed to slowly drive them insane. I don't know what it is about me that gets their goat. For instance, I've never yet found one who has been interested in my Theory Of The Three Races Of Man or the animal fathers..."

"I don't think that kind of high-powered stuff would interest Gladys either," Matthias broke in hurriedly. "If I was you I'd stick to chit-chat and steer clear of intellectual subjects."

"You don't even know what I'm talking about, do you?"

"No," Matthias admitted honestly.

"You've never even thought about it, have you?"

"Look IRO, I've had enough trouble with two races of Man and my own father to have ever had enough time to work out any new ideas. Perhaps if you got through to Gladys and we got rid of Hammerkop, then I might be able to spare some time for philosophy. I could even do an Adult Education course."

Matthias paused, waiting for Hurl to indicate that he agreed with this indomitable pattern of logic. Hurl was silent. Matthias edged closer and sat shoulder to shoulder with the dispirited Englishman.

"Listen IRO, you have an opportunity here to prevent bloodshed. If things stay as they are, we will surely assassinate Hammerkop and group-rape Gladys anyway, chastity-belt or no chastity-belt. It's more than likely that a general racial war will follow on the Copperbelt. Thousands of innocent people will perish. Anarchy will roam the streets. Famine will follow. Zonkendawo will go under a tidal wave of violence. All that will be left afterwards will be ashes. You can prevent all this."

"He speaks wisdom," crooned the Bucket-Wheel Excavator Gang, "there is much *myanis* in what he says. You should *hlanganana* Gladys and free our country from the curse of Hammerkop."

"IRO," Matthias said consolingly, putting an arm round Hurl's shoulder, "come to the beer-hall with us. We will celebrate the death by drowning of *shifbas* Swanepoel, and we will work out tactics. When are you supposed to try and make Gladys see the joy of living?"

Hurl told them about the *braaivleis* on Thursday.

"That's long enough," Matthias crinkled up the corners of his eyes and hauled Hurl to his feet, "we will be ready for her."

On Thursday evening, as the tumbling darkness was descending on Mufunsi, Hurl left his flat over the Greek supermarket in Mulombe Square, opposite the brown Christmas tree, turned left into Mulombe Drive, then right into Mulombe Way, inclined right again into Mulombe Avenue, through an alley lined with mimosa trees called Mulombe Street, then into Mulombe Crescent which brought him to the management enclave on the western side of the golf-course. In Hurl's pockets were an assortment of aphrodisiacs which Matthias and the Bucket-Wheel Excavator Gang had collected for him from the surrounding bush, basing their searches on information passed

63

on to them by a Doctor James Russell who had worked at the mine hospital until the time when he disappeared during the Muntu uprising of January that year. In an envelope in his jacket pocket he had chips of the *muwambwangoma* tree's roots; in a phial in his left trouser pocket he had a colourless liquid made from the boiled roots of the *mawele* tree; in a plastic bag in his hip pocket the pulped fruits of the *mutimbwabusa* tree; and in his wallet the leaves of the *mupundukaina* tree.

Matthias had worked diligently and systematically to prepare the IRO for the seduction of Gladys. Hammerkop's house-servant, an ancient Lozi, was taken up to the waste-dumps and held over a disused shaft until he had provided all the intimate secrets of Hammerkop's household, especially those affecting the 35-year-old virgin. With this information, Matthias briefed Hurl on how to use the four aphrodisiac substances.

"She keeps a careful eye on her trim, youthful figure," he had said, reading from his scribbled notes, "and eats a lot of green salads. That's where you can put the *mupundukaina* leaves. She won't notice them in with all the other green stuff. Her favourite drink is gin and tonic. No problem there. The *mawele* philtre is colourless and she won't notice the taste, it's very mild. The old servant says that she's also partial to canned fruit and so is Hammerkop so there's likely to be a bowl at the *braaivleis*..."

"What is a *braaivleis*?" Hurl had asked, "hadn't I better know?"

"It's a barbecue IRO, an al fresco dinner. Then there's the *muwambwangoma* chips. Where can you put those?"

The Bucket-Wheel Excavator Gang had come forward with a number of suggestions, none of them practical. It was finally agreed to leave the use of the chips to Hurl.

"You might see an opportunity to get them down her throat that we can't imagine, sitting here like this and not facing the actual situation. I'm sure you've got enough resourcefulness to take a chance if it's offered to you," Matthias had smiled encouragingly, pushing the four aphrodisiacs across the table in the IRO's office. "I'm sure you didn't get your degree for nothing eh?"

There were coloured lights strung from tree to tree in Hammerkop's spacious garden and Hurl could hear music as he walked along the dusk-soft driveway, past all the parked Pontiacs, Chevrolets, Oldsmobiles and Fords. The mansion was a low-lying building, white, covered with fragrant creepers of Golden Glory and Jackomani clematis, all the windows wall-tall and left invitingly open. In the garden Hurl could see the glow of fires and hear the hum and tinkle of human conversation. He headed for the point where it was loudest and found Hammerkop talking to the Predikant of the Dutch Reformed Church and the scrum of the rugby XV. When he saw Hurl, his eyes flashed blackly, his mouth was jacked up at the corners, and he flung out a hard, hairy hand.

"Here he is! The man we've been waiting for! Our guest of honour! Hurl Halfcock!"

As Hammerkop pumped Hurl's hand, the scrum of the rugby XV, all crop-haired, burly, blond and blue-eyed, crowded round the IRO and pounded his shoulder.

"*Hemel!*" they cried in a bass chorus, "look at this *rooinek*! What a pair of *skouers*! Put him in the second row and we'd push a herd of *olifants* off the ball!"

The Predikant, a tall, stooped, dark man with a cast in one eye, bowed to Hurl but did not join in the welcome. Instead he gripped a small black book.

"Is this the fellow who has supped with the *Duiwel*?" he demanded in a gloomy, embittered tone, "is this the *kaffir-boetie*?"

"Don't be too hard on him Predikant!" Hammerkop beamed, "there's plenty of time. He'll see sense."

The Predikant sat down in a deck-chair next to a concrete barbecue-pit and studied a length of *boerwors* that was sizzling on the grille.

"This is the fate which awaits heretics like you!" he intoned, stabbing the fat sausage with a wire fork, "you'll roast in Hell if you have any kind of social intercourse with the children of Ham. It is written! It is all here! It is the word of God!"

He tapped the little black book with a finger-nail.

Hammerkop pressed a glass of brandy and orange into Hurl's hand and pulled him away.

"Don't take too much notice of the Predikant boy. He's in one of his fire-and-brimstone moods. He's not a bad sort when you get to know him. Come and meet Gladys."

Hurl allowed himself to be led across the garden, through the delicious aromas of steak, chops, black pudding and the perfumes of magnolia and jasmine. Ahead of him he could see another crowd of crop-haired, burly, blond, blue-eyed men gathered in a huddle beneath a spreading avocado pear tree. Hammerkop paused and drew Hurl aside.

65

"You haven't forgotten now, you Pom half-wit? If you can lay Gladys for me then I'll get you the Personnel Manager's job tomorrow. Anything you want. On the golf-club committee? A better flat? Anything. But before that, what's this I hear about you drinking in the beer-hall with the Bucket-Wheel Excavator Gang? Don't you know that's not expected of you? I'll want you to have a word with the Predikant before you actually get to work on Gladys..."

"What's he got to do with it?" Hurl enquired, "and I'll drink with who I like, when I like. Just because I'm willing to help you out it doesn't mean that I'm accepting your ideology wholesale."

"Never mind all this pseudo-liberal bullshit now Pom, we can talk about it later," Hammerkop said hastily, "don't get excited. Come on, I've told Gladys all about you."

Hammerkop squeezed through the huddle of men, introducing them to Hurl on the way through as the three-quarter line of the rugby XV, and then stopped at a white wicket-fence that encircled a wrought-iron chair and tablé, both painted white. In the chair sat a woman.

Hammerkop pulled Hurl to his side.

"Gladys."

"Yes Frank," the woman replied in a light, clear voice.

"This is Hurl Halfcock, the attractive young man I told you about."

Hurl inclined his head. The first thing that struck him about Gladys was her porcelain serenity. She sat very still, legs crossed, a discreet length of thigh exposed. She was wearing an oatmeal jersey and it hung on her breasts with all the symmetrical, bountiful elegance of a Marks & Spencers counter advertisement. Her hair was similarly perfect, tamed, golden, a turban of twisted gelt. Hurl watched the Blushing Pink rosebud move beneath the finely chiselled nose, saw the smallish but saucered pale blue eyes.

Here was Art in Nature, Design in Chaos.

"Good evening," he said huskily, "thank you for inviting me."

"May he come into the enclosure Gladys?" Hammerkop asked timorously.

"Will he behave himself?"

"He's not like the rest of us," Hammerkop assured her, "he's a cultured person. He's no barbarian."

Gladys nodded. Hammerkop opened a small gate and ushered Hurl into the enclosure, then shooed away the three-quarter line

66

of the rugby XV and left Hurl and Gladys together. Parting her
perfect lips, she allowed Hurl to catch a glimpse of her snow-white
teeth, then pointed at the ground at her feet.

"Please sit down Mr Halfcock. That's an unusual name, if I may
say so."

Hurl sat cross-legged at the vision's feet.

"I'm hoping to change it soon. It's always been a grave embarrassment to me," he said conversationally. "You know what people's
minds are like."

"I think it's a charming name," Gladys tugged down an inch of
her dark blue pleated skirt, conscious of Hurl's eye on her superb
thews.

"It is capable of many interpretations. I've heard many changes
rung on it," Hurl said with an engaging smile.

Gladys took a cigarette out of a packet and waited while Hurl
groped around on the wrought-iron table for the mother-of-pearl
ladies' lighter.

"I'm sure that I don't know what you're talking about," she sighed
as he held the flame up for her, "it's sounds like any other name to
me as far as interpretations go."

Hurl eyed the glass on the table. It was nearly empty.

"Would you like me to get you a drink?"

"In a minute."

"You've got a lovely garden here."

"Yes, it is nice, isn't it."

Hammerkop appeared at the wicket fence.

"Gladys dear, may I borrow Hurl Halfcock for a moment? There's
a little bit of business that I want to discuss with him."

Gladys nodded and blew a cloud of smoke into the cool air. Hurl
got to his feet.

"I'll bring you a fresh drink back with me," he promised.

"There's no need. I have a little bell here." She pointed to a brass
ornament. "Any one of the rugby XV will be glad to see to my needs.
Off you go now."

Hurl followed Hammerkop across the lawn until they reached the
bougainvillaea hedge around the swimming-pool.

"How did you make out with her?" Hammerkop asked urgently.
"All right? You haven't been too coarse in your approach eh? I
want you to use all that Pom old-world courtesy on her, understand?"

"What do you want to talk about?" Hurl asked irritably.

Hammerkop brought him round the corner of the swimming-pool. As soon as Hurl appeared on the concrete and tile surround, the scrum of the rugby XV grabbed him, pinioned his arms behind his back, then frog-marched him across to where the Predikant was standing on the steps of the pool, knee-deep in the shining water. A hand was firmly clamped over Hurl's mouth during this operation and he was held fast. He could not move, or call out. Hammerkop stood next to the Predikant and clasped his hands in prayer.

"Dear God," the Predikant said loudly, his eyes looking upwards at the bright moon, "we your unworthy servants ask for Thy help in the cleansing of this sinner. Whereas the water, blessed by Thy Holy Spirit, can wash the body of his heresy, only Thy mercy can grant him forgiveness for his crime. He has resorted unto the places of the heathen. He has drunk with the Devil. He has rubbed shoulders with the minions of Hell. As the water cleanses him of their filth, so let his heart be washed clean of their contaminating influence."

The Predikant nodded to the scrum of the rugby XV and Hurl was bundled down the steps and held waist-deep in the water, his head under the Predikant's hand.

"In the name of the Father, Son and Holy Ghost, amen!"

"Amen!" roared the scrum of the rugby XV.

"Amen!" said Hammerkop devoutly, "this'll teach the Pom bastard."

The Predikant pressed on Hurl's head and he went under.

When he emerged again, the rugby XV carried him up the steps and out of the pool, then across the lawn to the house. There, they undressed him and kitted him out in a dark suit, splendidly tailored to fit, a white silk shirt, snake skin shoes and dark green socks with a red stripe. As they busied themselves drying, combing, powdering, Hurl lay in a strange trance of iron-hard determination. No matter what happened to his physical self, no matter what indignities he was forced to suffer at Hammerkop's hands, his quest would remain supreme. It was all worth it. Only one thing worried him.

His assistants, the aphrodisiacs.

"Excuse me," Hurl murmured, pleasantly enough, as a stocky front-row forward buttoned up the silk shirt, "what's happened to my clothes, the ones I came in?"

"The kaffir servants is drying and ironing them man."

"There's a few things that I'd like out of the pockets."

"Everything is out on the dressing-table there man."

When they had finished dressing him, they allowed him to stand up, withdrawing to a safe distance, shoulders hunched, fists clenched. Hurl paused, then grinned to show that he had no ill-feelings. The rugby XV burst into chatters of relief and turned to Hammerkop and the Predikant who had entered the bedroom.

"I think it's worked Predikant! He's as gentle as a lamb."

"The Lord has wrought yet another miracle through baptism! Praise ye the name of the Lord," the Predikant declaimed. "Go! And suffer not the kaffirs to come unto thee again!"

Hurl adjusted the collar of the shirt and the too-tight knot in the Guards Brigade tie, wandering step by step over to the dressing-table. Of the phial, there was only a crushed heap of splintered glass. The plastic bag had burst. The chips had disappeared. All he was left with for the seduction of Gladys were the *mupundukaina* leaves still safe in his wallet. Slipping the sodden leather into his inside pocket, his brain already working on the problem of how to administer them to the barricaded virgin, he left the bedroom and accompanied Hammerkop back into the garden.

"Sorry about all that," Hammerkop murmured apologetically, "but I couldn't let you get involved with my wife in the state you were in. Those kaffirs are contagious man. If I was you I'd keep away from Matthias and that rabble of his in future. They can only bring down misery on your head."

"I understand," Hurl said bravely as he drifted through the trees with his mind still buckled on to the great cause which he had elected to serve. "You only did what you thought was right."

Hammerkop paused at the wicket fence and clapped Hurl on the elbow, gripping him with intense feeling.

"Christ, you're a civilised bastard Hurl Halfcock. If there were more people like you in Africa, it wouldn't be in the mess it's in now."

Hammerkop opened the gate and returned Hurl to Gladys, explaining as he did so that the new IRO had accidentally fallen into the swimming-pool while looking for the lavatory. Gladys allowed a trace of a smile to touch her flawless, dimpled cheek.

"Please don't use that word in front of me again Frank. You know I don't like vulgar language."

"Sorry my love, a slip of the tongue."

Then he was gone, leaving Hurl with the Golden Fleece of African Freedom, the glamorous, unirrigated Gladys.

"That was a silly thing to do, falling in the pool," the goddess observed laconically, "perhaps you were thinking about me?"

"I was," Hurl confessed.

"Yes, that's what I thought."

"If you don't mind me saying so, you made a terrific impact on me. I suppose I was dazzled."

"Hmm."

"You don't object to my frankness?"

"No, I understand."

"Would you like to dance?"

"I don't dance with people who react to my physical presence. No good can come of it. What's the point of starting something when I will only have to repulse you? Whenever I've danced with men who were looking at me like you are looking at me now, it's always ended up the same way. They won't be told. Being so attractive has its problems you know."

"I can guess."

"I've had them go mad, throwing themselves at my feet, threatening suicide, anything you can mention. I seem to have that effect on men. I make them desperate."

"That's not difficult to imagine."

"It's best to keep them at arm's length. They all want to get very close. They won't keep their hands off me. I've seen them go pale, even faint. Frank does that sometimes when I have to send him away. He just falls down in a strange fit and gnaws his fingers."

"That must be frightening for you."

"Well, what am I supposed to do? I can't help it if I'm so good-looking that men get affected in this way. I don't deliberately set out to drive them insane with desire. It just happens."

"How upsetting for you."

"Sometimes I look in the mirror and wonder if it's worth it. Life would be a lot easier if I wasn't as beautiful as I am. I could just be like all the other drab, overweight, ugly women whom I see everywhere."

"Yes, it must be a terrible responsibility. Anyone would want to be relieved of a burden like yours every now and then."

"Are you making fun of me?"

"Certainly not!" Hurl mumbled as he slipped a leaf into his mouth.

"A lot of people envy my appearance."

"Who wouldn't?" Hurl smiled warmly, "you're really lovely."

"The men want to possess me, the woman just get extremely

jealous. I suppose it's natural for other women to be a bit resentful of my figure but I know that deep down they just want to look exactly like I do."

"Mmmmmm! Mmmmmm! Yes! Mmmmmm!" Hurl sighed enthusiastically. "These are jolly good."

"What are you chewing?" Gladys frowned, the tiniest, most delicate frets appearing on her pellucid brow.

"Leaves!" Hurl smacked his lips, his jaws working. "What flavour!"

"Why are you eating leaves?"

"Oh, everybody is eating them in London these days," Hurl said airily, "all the models and fashion designers eat them. Quite a lot of top film people eat them. Members of the government, especially the right-wing Conservative landowners and members of the House of Lords, eat them."

"What kind of leaves?" Gladys leaned forward, puzzlement shadowing her lambently lovely features.

Hurl had prepared himself for this question during the desultory dialogue that had passed between them while he was thinking of a way to introduce the *mupundukaina* leaves.

"They keep the skin and complexion clear, prevent any distortion due to age, wipe out incipient wrinkles, revitalise tired hair-roots, keep down weight..."

"Give me one!" Gladys put out a slender, beautifully manicured hand.

Hurl gave her two.

With bated breath, Hurl watched Gladys open her delicious mouth and place the two leaves on her pink tongue. With tremors of anticipated pleasure throbbing through his loins, he watched her begin to chew.

Her exquisite rosebud mouth moved as if blown by a breeze.

Her china-blue eyes! Two perfect saucers! Blank and beautiful!

Soon the lovely figurine would come to life, to love! He sighed. The leaves were in her mouth. Her saliva was already fired with the magic property of desire. Soon it would travel to her belly, to her breasts. She would become inflamed with love. He would sit there at her feet, completely occupying her eyes. When the irresistible power surged through her beautiful blood, when her organs received the flaming shock of lust, he would be there, the sole instrument of satisfaction.

71

Together they chewed.

Together they sat in silence.

Round the barbecue-pits, the rugby XV were singing old Afrikans songs and their simple, heart-stirring rendering of these fine classics filled the African night with nostalgia. Hammerkop stood shoulder to shoulder with them, waving his pint of brandy and orange in time with the music, one eye on the couple in the enclosure beneath the avocado tree. Could this shambling, pig-headed English *idioot* be the key to a golden future? Was it possible that such a man could be a stepping-stone to higher things on the Witwatersrand?

> "*O bring my terug na die ou Transvaal,*
> *Daar waar my Sarie woon,*
> *Daar onder by die mielies en die groen doringboom,*
> *Daar woon my Sarie Marais.*"

He roared with the rugby XV, his garnet eyes reflecting the moon from their crystal facets, his heart lifted by the swing of the tune. By God, it would be grand to be back in Eloff Street, back in the Victoria Hotel, back in the Chamber of Mines Sports Club, and to drive home with the cyanide-yellow dumps of the gold-waste glimmering like hills around the suburban mansions.

"It's working," Matthias whispered to the Bucket-Wheel Excavator Gang who were hidden with him, up in the boughs of the spreading avocado pear tree, "look at her!"

Gladys was certainly losing her composure. Her eyes were shining with an unnatural brightness; her Blushing Pink lips were parted; her cheeks were burning; her complexion was dewy, filmed with perspiration. Under her oatmeal jersey her bosom rose and fell and she kept crossing and uncrossing her long legs. Into her eyes had crept a dumb, beseeching emotion, a longing, a craving. On her lap, her hands clenched and unclenched, her knuckles digging savagely into her stomach.

"Ooooh!" she moaned, "ooh! ooooh!"

"Ooooh!" Hurl replied, grovelling at her feet, "ooh! ooh!"

"Won't be long now," Matthias hissed, "he can do what he likes with her. The poor bastard deserves a good screw after what he's had to put up with tonight. If this wasn't so important to the future of Zonkendawo, I wouldn't have let him go through with it. As it is, we'll put that Predikant into number 2 position on the list behind Hammerkop. He's a religious pervert. How can he reconcile his views on race with Christianity..."

72

Matthias checked his whisper as Gladys doubled up in her wrought-iron chair as if she had been shot, her usually calm beauty disfigured by monstrous pain. The IRO stretched out a hand to help her but then pitched forward, groaning in agony.

"Who collected the *mupundukaina* leaves?" Matthias said wearily.

There was no answer from the Bucket-Wheel Excavator Gang as they stared down at Gladys and Hurl who were clutching their stomachs and rolling on the grass in the enclosure, retching, spitting and groaning.

"I said, who collected the *mupundukaina* leaves?"

One man, who was sitting astride a fork in the main trunk, scratched his head and looked thoughtful.

"Matthias, I did not collect the *mupundukaina* leaves, that I deny absolutely. You instructed me to go into the bush and find some of the leaves of the *mupundururu* tree, which I did..."

Matthias gripped his branch and tried not to cry out. His eyes closed and he experienced despair. Was there nothing that the Bucket-Wheel Excavator Gang could do properly? Was Hammerkop right after all?"

"You cretin!" he sighed, "the leaves of the *mupundururu* tree are used to bring about the onset of labour. Let's get out of here before the IRO has twins or Gladys has her womb blown inside-out."

So it was that Hammerkop saw Matthias and the Bucket-Wheel Excavator Gang shinning down the avocado pear tree as his wife's cries of agony, blended with the bawling of the new IRO, reached him across the cool night. Running across to the wicket-fence enclosure, he burst open the gate and stood, black eyes sunk into the rock of his face, watching Hurl and Gladys as they rolled from side to side, faces contorted with excruciating pain, pummelling their abdomens, pounding their pelvises against the grass and calling on Christ, God and Hellfire to deliver them from the unbearable turmoil in their bowels. Hammerkop champed his teeth into his lower lip. These two by now should have been joined together in the wondrous, illuminating and advancing act of love. There were several reasons why the plan had not worked, and all of them had come down out of the avocado pear tree and were now being pursued through the garden by the rugby XV. The juice of bitter regret was squeezed through Hammerkop's copper-encrusted soul and he saw again the awful doom that Fate had laid upon his battered spirit. No matter what he did, no matter where he went, no matter where he planted his garden or saw his future, there would always be kaffirs in his avocado pear tree.

EIGHT **IRONHEART**

In the bedroom of the flat over the Greek supermarket opposite the brown Christmas tree in Mulombe Square, Hurl lay and thought that he was dying. He was alone, having been dropped off by a disillusioned and disappointed Hammerkop. The only antidote that he had taken for the uproar in his alimentary system was a glass of Enos Fruit Salts and that had only served to exacerbate the tumult. His body was madly awake, screaming at nerve-ends, while his mind whirled in Technicolor fantasies. He tried to sleep, but each time he was on the verge of unconsciousness, his fear of death brought him back from the edge of the black pit. At the third attempt to creep up on himself and fall asleep without realising it, he cried out in mortal terror, howling for his mother. This was the point at which he gave up and decided to go out, find Pyper and stun the beast in his bowels with alcohol. There was no future in sleep. His mother was five thousand miles away. If he was going to die then he might as well do it standing up and in company.

While he was having a quick wash to freshen himself up before going to the Tonga Bar, he heard music coming from the other side of the front door. Leaving the bathroom, he peered down the short corridor. It was a song, being sung by an untrained but tuneful soprano, and it was coming through the letter-box. As this was situated at the bottom of the door and a frosted-glass panel gave him a blurred impression of the singer, he could tell that it was a girl, or willowy boy, who was kneeling down, head laid sideways against the ground, in order to serenade him.

> "I am Ironheart, mother of two,
> I am prepared to come and work for you!"

was the lyric being rendered past the aluminium flap of the letter-box. When Hurl opened the door he found an African girl on her hands and knees. From floor-level gazed two friendly, hesitant, brown eyes and a winning smile.

"Ha, oh, hem," she giggled, "you have caught me at it."

74

Hurl waited until the girl had got to her feet before replying. He noticed the combed design of squares on her small head, her long neck, the way she stood pigeon-toed on the front door-mat, her little jug-like ears, and the boyish strength of her slim body. From the tips of her big toes, looped through a pair of blue plastic Bata flatties, to the brief pig-tails at each corner of the squares on her head, she was uniquely attractive. When she clasped her small hands over her crotch, put her head to one side and sang the second verse of her song, Hurl was warmed to the lining of his jittery stomach.

> "I can cook and I can sew,
> I can come and I can go,
> I can scrub and make your bed
> And fill it if you are not wed."

"What is that song you're singing?" Hurl asked.

"That's my jingle."

"Your jingle?" Hurl studied her clear eyes, her faded print frock and her slightly knock-knees. "Did you make it up?"

"No, not me. The professional poet and scribe in the Wusikili township wrote it for me."

"How much did he charge you?"

"Fifty ngwee, ten bob."

"What do you want a jingle for?"

"To advertise."

Hurl brought her in and asked her to sit down.

"What are you advertising?"

"Me, Ironheart."

"What do you do?"

"You did not listen to my jingle. Perhaps the words are not clear when I sing in that difficult position. I live with people. It is better than having a house-boy."

Slowly Hurl was catching up with the situation, his malady sinking below the level of his conscious mind and being dissipated into the great ocean of the recent past, a mere stream into that huge reservoir of memories, signs and portents. Ever since arriving in Zonkendawo he had been waylaid, ambushed, importuned and hounded by job-seekers. Hundreds of African men with grubby letters and credentials forged by this township poet and scribe, had knocked on his door, collared him in the street, jumped out of doorways and barred his

75

way along pavements. All of them had promised Hurl a life of domestic bliss for the equivalent of five pounds a month. He had steadfastly refused, not wanting to participate in any relationship that
would put him in the position of being an exploiter of human need.

"Why did you sing through the letter-box? If you'd have knocked
on the door then you could have sung it standing up."

The girl grinned and rubbed her shiny, brown knees.

"You do not know the donnas in Mufunsi."

"Are they suspicious of your intentions?"

"Yes. Sometimes I find myself in trouble when I advertise to a
bwana who is having trouble with his wife. I have been shot at with
gas-pistols, bitten by Irish wolfhounds, and one donna squirted fly-
spray through the letter-box while I was singing. It had a *mubi* effect
on my voice and I could not advertise for two days."

"You have a hard life."

"Indeed I do. There is no dole forecast in Doctor Mulombe's
five-year plan, nor any allowance for unmarried mothers."

Hurl sat down opposite Ironheart, a broad, stupid smile on his
face. He suddenly found his breast full of an immense liking for his
visitor, an irrational, overwhelming affection that made him want
to pick the girl up in his arms and hug her.

"I was just going out for a drink. Would you like to come with me?"

"Are you going to take me on?" Ironheart enquired.

"Can't we talk about that while we're having a drink?"

"I am sorry, but if you cannot offer me employment I must carry
on and finish the two streets down from the square before I sleep
tonight."

"And you'd sing your song through every letter-box?"

"I hope it would not be necessary, but if need be, I would."

Hurl stood up and put out his hand. He was deeply, intoxicatedly
moved.

"I can't have you doing that. I'll give you a job. Come on, we'll
talk about the details at the Tonga Bar."

As they walked across the square, Hurl asked Ironheart about the
two children she had mentioned in her song. He said that it might be
difficult to keep them in the flat as there wasn't much room.

"That is all right. They are with my father and mother."

"Are you a widow?"

Ironheart covered her face with both hands and tried to stifle her
ironical laughter.

"Well, what I mean is, where's your husband?" Hurl explained, "where's their father?"

"They are *my* children," Ironheart hooted in the shadows cast by the streetlights shining on to the brown Christmas tree, "they come from *me*!"

"But they must have a father!" Hurl protested, "everybody has!"

"Aha! I see you are inquisitive," Ironheart smiled sharply.

"I think I should know," Hurl insisted, aware that he was being unchivalrous, but driven on by his passionate and spontaneous feeling for the African girl, "it helps to fill in your background."

"Friends!" Ironheart said with a suggestion of reproof, "just good friends."

All thoughts of death, nightmare and suffering long past, Hurl ambled along beside his new acquaintance, his mind firmly attached to the idea of having her permanently at the flat. The jingle had certainly done its job – engaged his interest, penetrated his subconscious, created a desire and finally made him accept the goods.

"Will you be able to cook, clean, do the laundry, all the housework? You're quite small."

Ironheart lengthened her easy stride.

"I am strong."

"I can be very difficult to live with, so I've been told."

"*Hau!* All you men think you are problems. It is easy when you know how."

"You sound very experienced for someone so young."

"I am a mother, I have been a wife several times. What else is there to know?"

Hurl pushed open the bat-wing doors of the Tonga Bar and held them wide for Ironheart to walk through. The bar was very busy, all the tables being taken. Hurl asked after Pyper and was told that he was upstairs with Margaret From The Tonga Bar. Hurl looked up the worn steps to the landing, his eyes stinging with the cigarette-smoke, his stomach beginning to recoil from the reek of beer, brandy and *bhang*.

"Will you tell him that I'm here," he said to the lugubrious barman who was blowing his nose on the drying-up towel.

"I would not interrupt the endless *hlanganana* of the Great Writer Of Lies for all the tea in China," the barman said dolefully, "he would expose me as a waterer of spirits, a fiddler, a fraud and a thief, none of which I am. The new Peugeot 404 that you have seen me driving around in was a gift from my maternal grandmother."

At that moment Pyper appeared at the head of the stairs, dressed in a pair of bell-bottomed white ducks, a turquoise satin shirt with flowing sleeves and a pair of Indian buffalo-hide sandals. Margaret From The Tonga Bar was behind him, her dark, handsome face composed and at peace as she tried to stuff her sumptuous black breasts into a flimsy brassière. Giving up the impossible struggle she made a makeshift cradle for the twin works of a generous God, kissed Pyper on the ear, then made her entrance down the stairs. The bar hushed, every customer rose to his or her feet. The atmosphere was charged with religious awe. And so it should have been.

They were witnessing a miracle.

In fact, a pair of miracles.

At one time Margaret From The Tonga Bar had been as flat as a bread-board. Such was the contrast between the true, steady, splendid contours of her unbeatable hip, thigh and loin and her unactivated mammary glands, that this conflict of physique had become the source of countless male jokes up and down the bars of the Copperbelt. The unfulfilled promise of the good-hearted whore's upper torso had become as denigrated, mocked and scorned as her lower regions had been celebrated. Often she wondered if the two halves of her body belonged to the same person. Was she the ultimate schizophrenic? Then she found faith in God, and He put her right. He put His Hands upon her, and she bloomed. Now she could outbreast any Greek goddess, lush star of the screen, or succubus in a life-term prisoner's dream. But it had not changed her personality. She remained as generous as the God who made her. All that had happened to alter her life-style as the most sought-after whore on the Copperbelt had been her decision to accept Pyper's often-offered love and to temporarily retire from her profession until their affair had run its course.

Up until that time she had entertained a protector, a brawny German rock-breaker with the strength of ten ordinary men. Ever since God had put His Hands upon Margaret From The Tonga Bar, Pyper had lusted after her with sincere friendliness and an open heart. He had desired her with an ardency that even surprised himself and for once in his life he had wanted a woman to call his own, just until the heavy-screwing phase had passed. When Margaret From The Tonga Bar had taken the German rock-breaker on as her steady lover, Pyper had been driven to extremes of romantic protestation. He had paid the township scribe to write her African love-poems in her own Lunda language. He had sent her exploding Valentine cards full of magnolia petals. He had sat at the foot of the stairs, a bottle of his beloved cane-for-pain in his lap, and called out her name a million times until the rock-breaker had stormed down the well-worn steps and beaten him. But he came back for more. Sang songs. Wrote lewd phrases on the walls of the bar with his biro, linking Margaret From The Tonga Bar's name with his in exploits of unimaginable licentiousness. Night after night, day after day, he had importuned the black whore until she could gainsay him no longer. A month ago she had accepted his suit, given the German rock-breaker notice of the end of their relationship, and agreed to be Pyper's woman.

The rock-breaker had not taken his dismissal badly, for his jealousy and indignation had already been eroded wafer-thin by the New Zealander's fanatical and fearless persistence. Instead, his heart heavy but crammed full of sensual memories that would keep his blood hot until the day of his death, the rock-breaker went on a bender, the like of which the town of Mufunsi had never seen before. As chance would have it, and the permutation of numbers, it was not long before he met up with Pyper in several of the 234 bars which the mining-town supported. On the first three occasions he had savagely attacked the flamboyant newsman, enraged by the taunts, jeers and unsubtle mockery of the bird-of-paradise journalist who was always as drunk as the rock-breaker because he was celebrating his break-through with Margaret From The Tonga Bar and the prospect of months of lascivious tenderness in her arms. Time after time Pyper went down under the mighty blows of the German until one night when they met up in the bar of the Mufunsi Theatre Co-operative. The rock-breaker had reached the depths of depression, and was lonely. Pyper had been the only customer in the bar who had recognised, or understood his misery. With a sudden and tearful gush of guttural complaints, sighs and moans, the rock-breaker had pillowed his head upon Pyper's fragile shoulder and wept his heart out. For three hours the journalist had not moved. His lilac Orlon shirt had been saturated with tears, his shoulder had ached until the cramp was almost unbearable, but he had stayed as steady as a rock under the sobbing weight of his rock-breaking rival. When he had recovered, the German had confessed to Pyper that he now felt a strong brotherhood between them and they had pushed on, teamed up in an orgy of manly triumph over Fate, Time and the untrust-

79

worthiness of Love. During the next few days they had often forgotten who was drowning whose sorrows and who was toasting whose success. The bender had reached its climax back at the Tonga Bar when Pyper, with Margaret From The Tonga Bar dark and dazzling with smiles on his dainty elbow, had led the customers on a wild Conga dance round and round the brown Christmas tree, singing at the top of his raucous registers that the Kraut Was Out. At the end of the long line of dancers had stamped and side-kicked the massive Teuton, his coarse Wagnerian baritone adding depth and texture to the refrain.

"Christ, it's the old IRO! I heard you were a bit crook sport. Matthias told me you'd been confined in the maternity ward."

Hurl tried to smile as Pyper's crack sundered the awed silence of the bar. Margaret From The Tonga Bar descended the stairs to floor-level, having paused in profile for a moment in order to make a striking contrast with a photograph of the Queen Mother. As she slowly turned to face her worshippers, they broke into rapturous applause, hammered the table-tops and crashed their boots on the floor-boards. Pyper grinned happily and shared in her popularity. With one milk-white arm round his love's dusky pillar of a neck and two fingers stroking the swelling cleavage of her Divine Gifts, he kicked open the half-door in the bar and invited Hurl to come into the back room.

"It's no use staying out here with these bastards," he said nonchalantly, "they'll just try and get the old girl-friend here to get back on the job and I'm not having that. Most of these ugly deadbeats have had the clap more times than they've had the common cold. They'd fuck a dead horse if it was fresh enough."

"I've got somebody with me."

Hurl cast his eyes downwards to the small head and diagrammatic hair-style of Ironheart. Pyper's ice-fire eyes followed their course and encountered two further eyes, large, critical, but full of encouragement to forgive and forget.

"Christ! It's old Ironheart! She walked out on me a few months ago!"

"That was your fault," Ironheart growled, her eyes narrowed, "you would not stop drinking when the doctor told you to. It was not my job to stay and watch you die. That was not in the contract."

Margaret From The Tonga Bar stood in the doorway of the back room and held it open for Ironheart and Hurl to pass through. As

80

he squeezed past the two domes of that holy, heavenly, ebony-black marble church to the munificence of an open-hearted God, Hurl's upper arm brushed them and he experienced a positive charge of sparkling, prick-stirring warmth which left him breathless. Margaret From The Tonga Bar smiled knowingly and shut the door behind them. She could see that the big *musungu* with the curly hair and faintly bewildered expression permanently on his face, was feeling the direct effect of her ball-aching beauty and she was sorry that the time had passed when she could help him to a fuller realisation of his dreams. When the liaison with Pyper was over and this lyre-bird lover had left her, then she would let the newcomer know that he was welcome. He seemed to be a simple soul and Margaret From The Tonga Bar felt sorry for him, also a little motherly. The way the IRO stood, and looked, and listened, his green eyes always moving from face to face, his big body always trying to find a corner where it could fit without too much hanging out into a dangerous world, affected the sweet-tempered and amenable whore. The time would come when she could help to show him what a wonderful place the world is, and teach him about the largesse of God.

"It's a good thing that you've got old Ironheart to take care of you Pom. She's a marvel round the house and screws like a ferret with a fire-cracker up its arse. Here."

Hurl took the glass of cane-for-pain from the hand of the radiant Pyper and stole a glance at Ironheart. She was smiling shyly and shrugging at Margaret From The Tonga Bar. The two women obviously knew each other and now that their common ground was the irrepressible crusader for the Indignity of Man, neither of them had it within their hearts to take umbrage at the bizarre nature of his comparisons. Ironheart refused a glass of cane-for-pain and watched disapprovingly while Hurl shot his down his throat, not wanting to trap the over-sweet taste on his palate.

"We certainly put old Hammerkop down the drain a few feet this week eh?" Pyper giggled, lying back in a basketwork armchair, "what with the fiasco at the *braaivleis* tonight, I reckon he must be starting to see the writing on the wall..."

The door opened and the mournful barman poked his head round the corner.

"The rugby XV are here, looking for Matthias and the Bucket-Wheel Excavator Gang," he sadly informed them. "They are going to break up the furniture, destroy the stock and hang me from the banisters by the belt that holds up my trousers. What should I do?"

Pyper pushed the barman out of the door, then beckoned Hurl to come out of the back room.

"Come on Pom, you've got to start sometime," he said resignedly, "I know you're not feeling your best but you can't sit on the fence too long or you'll get stabbing pains. Right, old Margaret From The Tonga Bar my love, hop out of the window and get round to the IRO's place. Give her the key now Pom, we don't want them standing in the street. This business will take an hour or so."

Hurl hesitated. He was not yet ready to commit himself to violence in defence of the Bucket-Wheel Excavator Gang, or the Tonga Bar. It wasn't his fight. Or was it? He watched Margaret From The Tonga Bar climbing out of the window. What would he do to possess such beauty? He looked at little Ironheart as she followed. Would he not be fighting for them? For their love?

"Why all the precautions?" he demanded, "Why does she have to be taken away from me? I've only just met her?"

"If the rugby XV get hold of old Margaret From The Tonga Bar and Ironheart they'll be up them like rats up a drain-pipe. You know what the Boers are like with their Calvinist repressions. They're almost as horny as the Bucket-Wheel Excavator Gang once they get steam up."

Dazed, his mind vertiginous with fear and grim forebodings, Hurl waited until the window had closed behind the two women before following Pyper into the bar. The rugby XV were lined up in formation at the entrance door, covering the full width of the room. When Hurl appeared they growled and bunched their fists, sank their cropped-heads into their shoulders and swore voluminously and foully. Pyper opened the half-door of the bar and sauntered out, his burning blue eyes checking out the allegiances of the customers who were cowering under the tables and benches or lying flat on the floor with their hands over their heads. There was no promise of allies there.

"Well, you hairyback bastards, it looks like the odds are on our side. Me and the old IRO here will leave you *voortrekers* not knowing whether you're punched, drawn or counter-sunk."

Then he leaned against the bar, his girlish frame relaxed.

"Where's that kaffir bastard Matthias?" the scrum roared suddenly, "we're going to tear him and his *broos* apart. You *skorriemorries* just keep out of the way."

82

Pyper executed a light, flitting step away from the bar and faced the rugby XV, feet apart, legs braced, puny fists raised like two balls of white wool.

"Come on then! Me and the old IRO are going to teach you *jaaps* a thing or two about the noble art of self-defence. No holds barred!"

Hurl gazed longingly back along the short corridor to the back room. All he had to do was run down it, open the door, cock a leg over the window-sill and he would be free. He would be able to walk round to Mulombe Square, up the stairs to his flat, collect Margaret From The Tonga Bar and Ironheart off the sofa and sweep them into bed with his masculine charms. The brief dream ended in a chill pause. They would have nothing but contempt for such a cowardly desertion. They would probably castrate him with the bread-knife.

"You see how the old IRO is built, like the side of a house? He's so strong that a waft of his arm will give you bastards pneumonia!"

The rugby XV glowered at the gaily-coloured, fluttering moth of a man who taunted them. They had taken enough. They were moving forward, still in formation, when Matthias and the Bucket-Wheel Excavator Gang came in through the emergency exit. Immediately they fanned out across the bar and Pyper pulled Hurl back to join them until the two sides faced each other. The customers lying on the floor dragged themselves to the walls and behind the bar. Tables and chairs were pushed aside. The two sides confronted each other, huffing and puffing in the lull before the battle broke. They glared. They growled deep in their throats. They thumbed their noses, stiffened their sinews and wound up their clockwork.

This was the line-up.

THE BUCKET-WHEEL EXCAVATOR XIII

Full Back

Right Wing   Washable Trinket Muzozo   *Left Wing*

Coronation Pork Mbaba   Salvation Tuba Mkana

2nd Centre

Rose Powder Makulu

1st Centre

Ginger Pencil Mulolo

Fly-Half

Rollyourown Mtine

Scrum-Half

Cumulus McCloud Molile

Lock Forward
Zoom Mzlhovu

2nd Row		*2nd Row*
Self-Raising Mnama		Honey Balls Mukambo
Prop	*Hooker*	*Prop*
Pyper	Matthias Mvula	Halfcock (the new IRO)

V

THE RUGBY XV

Prop	*Hooker*	*Prop*
A. Van der Merwe	B. Van der Merwe	C. Van der Merwe
2nd Row		*2nd Row*
D. Van der Merwe		E. Van der Merwe
Wing Forward	*Lock Forward*	*Wing Forward*
F. Van der Merwe	G.Van der Merwe	H. Van der Merwe

Scrum-Half
I. Van der Merwe
Fly-Half
J. Van der Merwe
1st Centre
K. Van der Merwe
2nd Centre
L. Van der Merwe

Left Wing		*Right Wing*
N. Vand der Merwe	*Full Back*	M. Van der Merwe
	O. Van der Merwe	

Salvation Tuba Mkana and Washable Trinket Muzozo were trying to leave the field by stealth when Matthias spotted them opening the emergency exit.

"Don't let them see you're afraid!" he shouted. "Come back here!"

"But I am afraid!" Salvation Tuba Mkana protested, his lips hardly able to frame the words due to the numbing effect of his terror. "If I am in the street outside then the rugby XV will not be able to see it. Surely that makes sense Matthias?"

Salvation Tuba Mkana was actually stepping through the door to safety when the match started.

The rugby XV Right Wing M. Van der Merwe galloped down the touch-line and crash-tackled the coward.

He was followed by Wing Forward H. Van der Merwe who grabbed

Washable Trinket Muzozo by the neck and ran the crown of his head into the wall.

Salvation Tuba Mkana, displaying a surprising turn of speed, fled down the open wing towards the main entrance after kicking his way free of M's tackle.

Full Back O was waiting for him. Salvation Tuba Mkana was pulled down with only inches to spare. Full Back O then grabbed the African by the throat and began to strangle him.

The whole scrum of the rugby XV charged.

Their impetus swept Pyper out of the way like a leaf before a gale.

Matthias lowered his bullet-head and stopped the Hooker B dead in full-stride, then booted him in the ear as he rolled over.

Hurl Halfcock moved away to the left, dodging a short-arm tackle from his opposite number Prop C. Hurl Halfcock was not yet ready to commit himself to this Armageddon. Prop C roared on and toppled Honey Balls Mukambo with a murderous jab to the heart.

"Remember Blood River!" he shouted.

As Hurl scrambled to the right to seek cover behind the bar he encountered Wing Forward F who had been described in many match write-ups as fast and dangerous in the loose. He ran at Hurl with his arm stiffly extended like one of Boadicea's chariot-wheel scythes.

It caught Hurl under the nose and bowled him over.

Wing Forward F was joined by 2nd Row D and together they started trying to kick in the Pom bastard's ribs. As 2nd Row D's boot was swinging downwards a sharp pain struck him in the rectum and he whirled round to find Pyper with the broken-off neck of a cane-for-pain bottle.

"Foul!" he screamed as blood ran down his trouser leg and pooled in his boots.

Hurl Halfcock veered away, scrambling on his hands and knees for the main entrance. He was mounted by Fly-Half J who grabbed hold of two handfulls of hair, then clapped his heels into Hurl's testicles. To Hurl's right lay Salvation Tuba Mkana with Right Wing M applying the final pressure to his throat. The black face was two shades blacker and the man's tongue was sticking out.

As hard-knuckled blows rained on to the nape of Hurl's neck, and steel-cleated heels hammered at his groin, Hurl suddenly felt a massive turning of his spirit. Anger burst out of his heart and he reared up, unseating Fly-Half J. While his ex-rider lay on the floor, Hurl grabbed a hand and a foot and threw him into an alcove.

Then he turned to Right Wing M.

The man's thumbs were half-way through Salvation Tuba's neck.

With all the passion and hatred of his attack, Right Wing M had unseamed the arm-pits of his shirt. Hurl seized hold of the under-arm hair and pulled with all his strength. Right Wing M's scream of agony rose above the din.

"I can stand anything but physical pain," Coronation Pork Mbaba whispered to Self-Raising Mnama who was hiding with him behind the giant refrigerator which stands behind the bar at the Tonga Bar.

As Matthias took the brunt of a pincer-movement by Lock Forward G and Scrum Half I, Coronation Pork Mbaba hauled open the fridge door and showed the two raging South Africans the hundreds of cold beers stocked on the shelves. Their attention was momentarily distracted from the able demolition work which they were doing on Matthias's spleen.

Their eyes glazed over.

Then they glazed over again.

And again.

For Rollyourown Mtine had snatched a frozen chicken carcase from the bottom of the fridge and was battering at the heads of G and L for all he was worth.

But Pyper had been captured.

The butterfly was about to be pinned and put in the collecting-box.

1st Centre K and Left Wing N were holding him down on the bar, having pulled up his shirt, while 2nd Row E made a guide-line scratch along his abdomen with a broken bottle preparatory to disembowell-ing him.

Rose Powder Makulu saved the life of the Great Writer Of Lies.

He broke three bottles of Zonkendawoan whisky over the heads of the amateur surgeons and then put his lighter to the shirt of 1st Centre K.

As the three men ran round in circles trying to beat out the flames, the match rose to a new pitch of competitive fury. Beneath the scrum lay Hurl Halfcock, admirer of the exploits of the North American Indian hero Chief Crazy Horse. Beside him lay Prop A and the man's teeth were sunk in Hurl's shoulder, their grinding edges working towards each other in the cud-chewing motion of an herbivore's molars. Hurl heaved up the fighting mass of the scrum, got a hand round to Prop A's face and rested two fingertips on the fellow's eyeballs.

"If you will stop chewing my shoulder, I will not gouge your eyes out."

Prop A paused in his cud-chewing motion.

"Did you hear what I said?" Hurl hissed.

"Grumff!"

Hurl pushed his fingers up against Prop A's eyeballs and stabbed once.

Prop A stopped chewing and bellowed.

"You dirty Pom bastard!"

Hurl struggled out of the pile of fighting men and staggered to the bar, blood streaming down his back. 2nd Centre L broke free and followed him.

"I'll teach you to be disrespectful to Gladys Hammerkop you *rooinek* kaffir-fucker. I love that woman! She's the best thing in this world!"

2nd Centre L's eyes glittered under his gore-smeared, bushy eyebrows. There was blood on his hands. His shirt was ripped open and Hurl could see the scars of a hundred battles on his mighty chest. In his right hand was the frozen chicken carcase, in his left a red and a white ivory ball from the bar-billards table. His plan was to crack Hurl's head between these assorted hard surfaces like a Brazil nut.

As Hurl, with the last of his strength, lashed out at 2nd Centre L, the night-shift from the Smelter arrived. The fastest man in the Bucket-Wheel Excavator XIII, Zoom Mzlhovu, had slipped out in the first stages of the fight, hared down Mulombe Avenue, and called on these men for help, Glad of any chance to escape from the fierce heat, they had grabbed their shovels and hammers and trotted up to town. When they poured through the main entrance of the Tonga Bar – some of them going straight up the well-worn stairs in search of God's Handiwork – the rugby XV swiftly re-grouped, collected their injured, made a strategic withdrawal, and thence to the British Empire Service League where they knew they would be safe.

Hurl lay in bed and listened to the Bucket-Wheel Excavator Gang pillaging his fridge and kitchen. Through the open door of the bedroom he could hear them telling stories about their exploits during the match at the Tonga Bar. Salvation Tuba Mkana's voice was loudest as he praised the courage of the new IRO for saving his life.

Margaret From The Tonga Bar smiled as she bathed Hurl's wound with antiseptic. Hurl closed his eyes and groaned.

It was not the pain that was giving him pain.

It was the closeness of God's Bounty.

Pyper entered the bedroom and pulled Margaret From The Tonga Bar's hand from under the bedclothes.

"Ironheart will take care of the old IRO now."

"He needs careful nursing," Margaret From The Tonga Bar complained gently as she was pushed towards the door. "That could become inflamed."

"By the look of the marquee the old IRO's pitched under there, he's become inflamed already. Now get back to work before the poor bastard blows a gasket."

The dark whore paused at the door and gave Hurl a regretful, warm smile.

"I hope you recover quickly. We must have a long chat one day when there is more time. I can see that you are a man of some standing. You are a person of substance, a friend worth having. I would like to thank you for the manly way you acquitted yourself tonight . . ."

"For Christ's sake woman, give it a rest. Go and clean up the mess those *jaaps* made."

When Margaret From The Tonga Bar had gone, Pyper sat by the bedside.

"Don't get agitated about old Margaret From The Tonga Bar fancying you Pom. She fancies lots of bastards because she's so open-hearted. Before she threw in her lot with me her pants were up and down more often than a lift in a skyscraper. When she's finished with me, then you'll be all right. You'll come into your own."

Hurl studied Pyper's smooth, unblemished cheeks, his rosebud mouth and burning ice-fire eyes. Here was a figure straight out of Victorian Romance talking about the Death of Love when he looked like the incarnation of Eternal Fidelity.

"You're better off with old Ironheart sport. You can graduate to Margaret From The Tonga Bar later. Ironheart's undignified, a nimble screw, very good natured. Think yourself lucky."

Pyper fingered the long scratch up his stomach which had been the marker for the first incision by 2nd Row E. Van der Merwe.

Hurl watched the journalist's finger as it delicately traced the red line. What would they have found in there? Did Pyper have organs like other men? Was his liver of polished silver, his kidneys of burnished brass? Was his heart a pump of tissues and gristle like other men's or was it hanging in his chest like a lamp of chased gold, fretted with jewels, suspended on wires?

"I think you should go now John. He is tired."

"All right Ironheart," Pyper drawled harshly, "keep your natural enthusiasm for your work in check for a minute. I've got to put the old IRO in the picture about the future. First thing is I'll have to run a front-page story tomorrow to say that the African Mineworkers Union have threatened another strike if any attempt is made to remove Hurl Halfcock from his job as IRO of the Open Pit. That'll give you some security sport. Hammerkop thinks a lot of the rugby XV and he won't be pleased when he hears about their crushing defeat at the Tonga Bar. They haven't been beaten in their last fifty-seven fixtures. Mufunsi is going to be a good place for the old IRO to get out of for the week-end so I've got him invited to a piss-up in Musangati tomorrow night, then I thought we might think about going to Elizabethville to see my old friend Reg, the Chef de Poste some time..."

"You are certainly not taking him to the Congo!" Ironheart said emphatically, "no! no! a thousand times no! Go away! You're spoiling everything!"

Ironheart vainly tried to push Pyper out of the door but he held on, his fair features in a devilish leer.

"Don't start getting bossy Ironheart. I'm going in a minute. I just want to give the old IRO some advice."

"He doesn't need your advice. He's all right with me!"

"I'm teaching him the ropes Ironheart! He's ignorant."

Pyper looked across at Hurl and grinned.

"See you tomorrow sport. I'll ring you and tell you how to get to Musangati. Now Ironheart is what I want to advise you about. She's a tough talker but not too heavily-set. If you climb on board the poor girl she'll go down like the Titanic. Try it with her in the saddle for a while, until you've had a chance to feed her up for a few weeks. She's been living off mealie-meal and beans for months you know..."

Pyper was not allowed to finish his counselling. Ironheart flew at him in a rage and drove the coruscating grasshopper away into the night, his scales flashing colour in the soft darkness. When he had gone, she was quiet for a while.

Then she sat on the side of the bed.

Hurl shifted his shoulder as Ironheart lowered her head on to his chest. He could feel her breath warm on his skin, and feel the agitation of her heart. Soon it had hammered out all its indignation, and quietened. The Bucket-Wheel Excavator Gang appeared to have gone home, leaving the fridge stripped to the plastic ice-tray and the kitchen ransacked. The flat was silent except for the two of them and the shy noises of linen upon linen. Hurl stroked Ironheart's neck, feeling along the shapely twin furrows up to the system of squares combed out on her wiry head.

"Thank you for taking me on," Ironheart whispered, "I was getting very tired tramping the streets and my voice was going."

"Thank you for taking *me* on," Hurl replied sincerely, "God knows what you've let yourself in for Ironheart. I hope I can be a perfect employer."

"You will not be perfect, but you may do. Any man who consorts with John Pyper and Matthias Mvula must be far from perfect. You are in for a lot of trouble Mr. Halfcock, and the best thing I can do is to keep this flat as a nice home for you to run to when times get bad."

Hurl was silent for a moment. Ironheart waited for his answer, holding her breath, anxious lest she should have offended.

"Ironheart," Hurl said eventually, "will you do me a favour?"

"Whatever you say."

"Don't call me Mr. Halfcock."

"I'm not going to call you bwana."

"I don't want to be called bwana. I have been debwanad."

"Then what must I call you? What is your first name?"

"Don't call me that."

"How can I when I do not know it?"

Hurl paused and cuddled the small head further up towards his face, mindful of the pain in his neck. Her very frailty and lightness seemed to exalt his arm and chest, lying against him like a black feather. Bending his head until the wound snatched at his nerves, he planted a firm kiss in the centre of one of the squares.

"Will you call me the IRO until I can find something more appropriate?"

"Make it soon then. What have I got to do with an Industrial

Relations Officer?" Ironheart giggled and grazed over his throat with warm lips.

"Is that what it means?" Hurl sank back into the pillow, another great question lifted from his mind. As Ironheart slipped out of his embrace and took off her frock, then slipped back by his side, under the sheet, Hurl was conscious of a strange happiness, a sense of having entered through a mysterious gate. He felt the girl by his side, the wound on his neck, the scrapes, scratches and bruises on his body. Outside was Africa, the brown Christmas tree, the Open Pit, danger, newness, and it was his. He belonged and no matter what happened, he was never going back through that gate.

The IRO, or something more appropriate, had arrived.

NINE SITUATION VACANT

That evening the Staff Officer had to work late. On Hammerkop's instructions she drew up a draft advertisement that was to be telexed to the Salisbury and Johannesburg offices of the mining corporation which controlled Mufunsi, with a request that every effort should be made to get the advertisement into the daily papers the next morning. When the telex operator received the draft she read it through, then sat very still looking at her machine.

"Are you sure you don't want to change it?"

The Staff Officer fixed the telex operator with a masterful glance from her shimmering eyes.

"Are you trying to teach me my job?" she said indignantly.

"No, but. . ."

"Get that message off! We're wasting time! You know what Frank Hammerkop is like if things don't happen the way he wants. I'll see you get the blame if this doesn't appear in the Rand Daily Mail and the Rhodesia Herald tomorrow!"

The telex operator shrugged and bowed over her machine. It was not her *indaba*. All she was doing was carrying out the Staff Officer's instructions. What did the telex operator care? It was only a job. The sooner she could get the message off, the sooner she could be back in the Tennis Club playing Crown and Anchor.

The next morning all the jobless of southern and central white Africa propped their newspapers up against their pots of Cape marmalade and read through the Situations Vacant. As they shovelled golden mealiepops into their mouths and sipped their morning coffee, their interests were arrested by this advertisement:

Mufunsi Mines Limited
Zonkendawo

A vacancy currently exists for an INDUSTRIAL RELATIONS OFFICER at the OPEN PIT section.

Salary and conditions negotiable

Candidates should be suitably qualified and be tall, broad-shouldered, narrow-waisted, well-hung, blond-haired, have frank blue eyes, a straight nose with small neat nostrils on either side, be well-hung, have eyebrows which meet in the middle and long lashes (dark preferrably for contrast), be well-hung, be interested in working with people, have regular white teeth, a supple smooth body, moderately hairy chest, be full of stamina and inventiveness, dynamic, thrustful, resourceful, tireless, play rugby, drink with the best of them, adroit, ambidexterous, be prepared to live under an inefficient and corrupt African government and to accept a fundamental alteration of their personal details, and be well-hung.

Applications should be sent to:

The Staff Officer
Box 57,
Mufunsi Mines Ltd,
Zonkendawo.

Please include curriculum vitae and *photostats* of all certificates and documents as return cannot be guaranteed due to declining standards in the local postal services.

TEN A SUGGESTION FOR A NEW NAME FOR THE NEW IRO

"Hey, *mvhu!*"

The albino African beggar shouted up to the balcony of the new IRO's flat from his pitch in the doorway of the Greek supermarket, his terrible pink eyes raised to the sun. In his baggy, knee-length shorts and tattered shirt, the colour-crippled boy was a disgusting sight. All day he begged at the door of the odorous shop, pushing his pasty hand under the noses of the customers, forcing them to look into his pink, raw face, at his pink-rimmed eyes, their rabbit-pink irises, his blond eye-lashes, his boxer's nose, smashed flat by his traumatic birth, his big lips, not purple or red but the colour of chewed gum. When he had saved up enough money from his begging his routine was to buy himself a bottle of Malawian Drambuie at the supermarket and lie under the brown Christmas tree, trying to forget what light was, what constituted shade, and shutting out the crazy horror of his body with draughts of the 100 proof elixir.

He was attached to the new IRO and considered him to be a neighbour, sleeping, as he did, under the brown Christmas tree in order to be close to his work and cut down travelling-time. When the new IRO went to the Open Pit on foot, the albino often left his pitch and followed him at a distance, shadowing him along tree-lined avenues, corridors, in and out of offices, mumbling that he was hungry and wanted a job. Once he had found a spoiled application-for-employment form in a waste-paper basket and had filled it in, slipping it through the new IRO's letter-box late at night.

Against the question — Race — he had left a blank.

"Hey, *mvhu!*"

Sticking out his long tongue, the boy reached up to the balcony with his skinny, stick-like arms.

"Give me twenty ngwee, O *mvhu*, then I can buy a miniature bottle of Malawian Drambuie for breakfast!"

The new IRO frowned. The albino had ruined his golden mood. Standing on the balcony with the cool morning resting in the square, he had been enjoying a deep-seated contentment. He could smell bacon frying as Ironheart made his breakfast. His mind was turning over the long, tender hours of coupling which he had enjoyed with his new manager. The bite on his neck had lost its fire, soothed by Ironheart's ointments. He was happy in this town and had been looking out over the roof-tops with a proprietary air, feeling himself a part of all he saw.

"What's that you are calling me?" he called down, leaning over the concrete balustrade.

"*Mvhu!*"

"Why? What does it mean?"

"That is now your name among the people."

"What people?"

"Us people."

The new IRO went back into the flat, slipped on trousers and shirt, then hurried down the stairs to the pavement.

"What does this name mean?" he asked urgently, slipping a twenty ngwee piece into the outstretched hand.

"Hippo!" the albino chuckled, showing his terrifying gums.

"Hippo? Why hippo?" The new IRO was flummoxed. "What's a hippo got to do with me?"

"On the grapevine it is said that you attacked the rugby XV with great courage last night. The Great Writer Of Lies, John Pyper, has picked up the name being used by the common folk of this tight-fisted town, and he has put it in his news report this morning. Here!"

The albino took a folded copy of the Zonkendawo Times from under his shirt and opened it up, then stabbed at the leader with a hideously-coloured fingernail.

"There we are... 'like an enraged hippopotamus'. Now the word in common usage in the north-western province is *mvhu*, which is onomatopoeic, deriving its music from the sound of the river-horse when it surfaces and blows air. Like this!"

Making a trumpet of his repulsive lips, the albino crouched on the pavement then slowly rose upwards, his arms pushing aside imaginary water. As he reached tip-toe he exhaled all the air in his tuberculosed lungs with a rush.

"Mvhu! Mvhu! Mvhu!"

The new IRO leaned against the sunny wall, his eyes closed. With a gentle, though nervous hand, the albino led him back up the stairs to the flat, rang the bell then ran down again on to the pavement. He knew Ironheart of old. She would have little mercy on any man who upset her employer, and even less on the albino.

The new IRO could not face his breakfast. Ironheart clucked, tutted and expressed her indignation by whipping the sheets off the bed while he was lying on it.

"What a thing to get upset about!" she chided him, pulling the pillows from under his head and stripping off the slips, "what does the beggar matter? If it hurts you so much I will go down and destroy the boy myself! Last night you said that all was going well with you. You are very unpredictable."

94

The new IRO did not reply, but stared gloomily at the ceiling. He had been lured to Africa by false hopes. Searching for an identity was all very well, providing there was an element of choice. He had not cut himself off from his past and his people in order to surrender his old name for something equally ludicrous. This continent had supplied anonymity to countless millions of primitive men, nameless animals who roamed the plateaux and valleys, slugging each other with the humerus-bones of antelopes, fighting over the bloody shreds of slaughtered carcases, berries, fruits, good shelter, clear water, and all without names. There had never been a Nutcracker Man called Frederick, nor a Homo Erectus called Bob, nor a Broken Hill Man called Julian. They were grunts and groans, nothing more. When Hurl adopted a new name it would be through the proper channels — a form from the British Consul, the existence of which he had checked before leaving England — and if he observed the statutory requirements, birth certificate, passport etc. he could have a new name in six months. Like the early men, taking a name would be a conscious, personal choice, an individual celebration of Life within oneself.

But the Africans had beaten him to it. They had called him Hippopotamus. A submarine muncher of weeds. A huge yawn.

There was only one course of action he could take. He would have to approach the Consul immediately and try to get his new name rushed through before Hippopotamus caught on and he was landed with it for the rest of his life. Dressing hurriedly he fended off Ironheart's questions and went to the District Officer, an administrator of the Zonkendawon government who was the liaison with all the citizenship and political status departments in Myakajunji. He explained his problem to an assistant in an outer office who advised him to see the British Consul directly and not to go through the Zonkendawon bureaucratic machine.

"If you do, then when there is a revolution — which is inevitable — the new régime will insist on you reverting to your old name because you altered it through the offices of the previous government. When the military take over to protect the country from anarchy and dissolution, they will force you to take back your new name because they will be sentimental about the first independent government and the honour of those who gave their lives in the Struggle. If the Chinese Reds, Rhodesian Whites or Insurgent Blacks take over, they will surely shoot you for being a man who is constantly changing his identity, probably suspecting you of being an espionage agent using

95

a cover-alias, which would be understandable. All in all you are better off dealing with your own Consul and not channelling anything through here."

The new IRO sat slumped in his straight-backed chair, his face dismal with worry. He could not ask for leave to go down to Myaka-junji to see the Consul. He had only been working at the Open Pit for a few days and such an absence would be frowned upon by the management. He explained this to the assistant who smiled.

"You have no need to fret. The Minister of Mines is opening a health clinic here this afternoon and I understand that the British Consul will be accompanying him as it is the British government that has provided all the equipment. You can approach him then."

The new IRO's face brightened. Only one question lurked at the back of his mind and he was unsure as to the advisability of asking it. He could leave the query aside and go home to Ironheart and try to forget all about any ramifications not central to the name-changing. However, his natural curiosity got the better of him.

"Why doesn't the Minister of Health open the health clinic. Wouldn't that be more appropriate?"

The assistant interlaced his fingers, gave the new IRO a pitying look and asked how the Minister of Health could open a health clinic when he was opening a mine? Could he be in two places at once? Was he a wizard?

Not having an answer to this, the new IRO left the building.

On his way back through Mufunsi he went into a bookshop and bought a small paperback book favoured by expectant parents which listed all the first names available for boys and girls. The new IRO was aware of the vast treasure-house of African names, but he shied away from them because no one seemed to take them seriously. When an African father named his new-born child, it was usually done in a flippant manner as the chances were 50-50 that the baby would die in the first three months of its life. The new IRO wanted no suggestion of light-heartedness in the manner of his taking a new name. It was a serious business and once accomplished would mark a turning-point in his existence on this earth.

When he returned to the flat, Ironheart had cleaned it from top to bottom. The pans in the kitchen shone like polished silver. The windows gleamed. The furniture smelled of perfumed wax. The bath had been scrubbed white. When the new IRO walked in through the front door he had been met by the sight of Ironheart skating over the wooden parquet-block floor, a yellow duster tied to each foot. As soon as he had settled down on the bed again, resting his bandaged neck against the crisp linen of the pillow, she brought him a cup of instant coffee and apologised for nagging at him.

"Ironheart, don't," the new IRO murmured as he flipped through the paperback, "don't say you're sorry for saying things that are true. I don't mind a bit of criticism now and then."

"It is my failing. I cannot help myself. When I see you making a fool of yourself, I have to speak up or try to make you see sense. I will stop it though because it displeases you."

He took her small hand and pressed it to his lips in a gesture of gallant affection. Ironheart took her cue and left, closing the door behind her. Taking her purse and a string-bag, she left the flat, went down the stairs and went into the Greek supermarket, pausing to kick the shins of the albino beggar who was sleeping off his breakfast curled up in a corner of the porch.

"If you call the new IRO names again, you nothing, you *nikis!* I'll douse you with petrol and make a human candle of your body. You are neither one thing or the other! You should keep quiet! *Nantsi!*"

Giving the albino a final kick, Ironheart swept into the supermarket, the string-bag trailing on the ground, her big leather purse clutched to her chest. Taking a wire trolley she began her hunt among the piles of cans, heaps of rotting vegetables and stacks of sweating packets which lay in jumbles in the malfunctioning deep-freezers.

Above her head, the new IRO was up to the Ds in his book.

The Consul sat on a tubular steel deck-chair two rows behind the Minister of Mines and looked around the cleared ground. The foundations of the new health clinic were already poured, even a portion of the wall facing the road had been built, but that was all. While the Minister of Mines droned on about the need for early vaccination against smallpox, the Consul allowed his eye to wander along the ragged barrier of bush. Perspiring, ill, chalk-white, chain-smoking, middle-aged, the Consul was at the height of his career in the Foreign Office. This was his sixth posting in ten years and it was not the first time that he had attended an opening ceremony of a building which had hardly got off the ground. When the Minister of Mines waved a hand towards an imagined roof, referred to a staff of nurses and orderlies that did not yet exist, and then cut a tape across a width of waste land and invited the Press corps to look around this symbol of international friendship, the Consul did not bat an eyelid. Instead he remained cool, unflustered and completely within the spirit of the occasion. He was sitting in a clinic, surrounded by shining medical equipment and women in starched aprons and little white caps. He was casting an approving eye around the décor, the gleaming tile floor, and the copper plaque set into the brickwork, commemorating the occasion. It was all there. If the Consul had not acted as if he gave credence to the make-believe, that gaudily-dressed journalist with the cold blue eyes would have given him a six-inch column of calumny in the paper the next morning. So he smiled, the expression belying the tedium in his drooping eyes and the rat-tat-tat of his nicotine-stained fingers on the cigarette-packet in his lap.

Zonkendawo was not the land of his choice. Paris was his dream, with Rome second, then Washington, perhaps Bonn, or Madrid, maybe Athens, he'd even give Peking a try, or Moscow, or the capital of Albania if they had a British Consul, even Pretoria, or Sydney... anywhere but Zonkendawo. Trying to persuade Doctor Mulombe to respect British capital, property and citizens was an impossible task. The old blackguard was beyond diplomacy. Things could not be worse. Every time he was confronted with one of Mulombe's ministers or minions he was humiliated and made to feel personally responsible for the whole colonial era. But he was wrong in thinking that things could not get worse. They could. A large European man proved this by appearing through the trees, leaves in his curly hair, dust and dirt all over his clothes. The man walked across the clearing and looked up and down the rows of dignitaries. The Consul knew who he was looking for. His expression was that of the Lost Englishman, a figure as familiar to myth, legend and reality as the Flying Dutchman. Wearily the Consul shifted back his chair and went along the row to where the man was standing.

"Are you looking for me?" he said dryly.

"Are you the British Consul?"

"Regrettably, yes."

"I was wondering if you had a form handy for changing my name?"

The Consul had faced some difficult situations in his diplomatic career. He had repatriated wrecked single-handed yachtsmen from islands near Cape Horn. He had rescued fifteen-year-old girls from the hands of Saudi Arabian night-club owners and sent them back to their mothers in Huddersfield and Chippenham. He had demanded compensation for riot damage off wild-eyed guerrillas and bandits who had seized power in bloody coups of atrocious cruelty. He had delivered, by hand, stern notes of protest to megalomaniacs and raving madmen. But he had never been asked for a name-changing form in the middle of a ceremony for the opening of a non-existent health-clinic. Suddenly it was all a bit too much. The Consul stuffed his hands in the side-pockets of his drill jacket to stop them shaking and tried to remember all his training.

"Do you honestly think this is the time and place?" he said in a low, steely whisper. "Your intrusion is fraught with possibilities of my being declared *persona non grata* and *de trop*."

"Of a what?" the man said vaguely.

"Never mind!"

"I don't mind! All I wanted was a form for changing my name!"

The Minister of Mines looked over his shoulder and glared at the Consul, then said something to his aide, a young lieutenant in the Zonkendawon Army. The young man snapped to attention and marched round the deck-chairs to where the Consul was waiting for him, bolt upright, features stiff.

"The worshipful Minister requests that you shut your damn face until he has finished his address!"

"Carry on Lieutenant!" the Consul bowed, "convey my apologies."

"He says that the British government are probably laughing up their sleeve at the unfinished condition of the health clinic, but let them remember the martyrs in the Struggle. If our country was not full of cripples and sick men, broken by the British MI5 and the Colonial Office, there might not be a need for a health clinic at all!"

"I take his point Lieutenant. Carry on."

The young man about-turned and marched back to his place by the Minister's side, whispered in his ear, then sat down.

"See what you've done?" the Consul hissed, "that's another fifteen thousand pounds worth of good-will thrown away. Christ Almighty, you people make me lose faith."

"What about the form?" the man insisted.

"I know of no such form!"

"There is one, I checked in U.K."

"Give me your name and address and go away! I'll send you the form!"

"Have you got a biro?"

"No I haven't got a biro. Keep your bloody voice down!"

The man went over to a pile of bricks, picked one up, then scratched an address on one side with a stone. When he had completed it, he held it out to the Consul.

"There you are."

"I'm not carrying that around with me!"

"Then I'll wait for you here."

Grudgingly, the Consul took the brick and put it in his pocket.

The man smiled, rubbed his hands, nodded to the Consul, then skipped back to the trees. He seemed to be ridiculously happy with the arrangement. The Consul sat through the remaining two and a quarter hours of the Minister's speech, then joined the official party on its tour of the foundations. As he followed the Minister at a respectful distance, a security man stopped him. He wanted to know why the Consul was carrying a house-brick around in his jacket-pocket. As the Consul tried to explain, the Press corps gathered round. In the front of the crowd was Pyper.

"Why do you want to assassinate the Minister of Mines?" was his first question. While his African photographer took a shot of the Consul holding the brick, he asked the second. "Why did you not choose a more sophisticated weapon?"

It took the Consul some days to talk his way out of the ensuing diplomatic furore. By the end of that time the address scratched on the rough red surface of that humble artefact was similarly inscribed on his brain, graven deep.

> The NEW IRO
> (ex-Hurl Halfcock),
> 14a, Mulombe Square,
> Mufunsi.

ELEVEN A CHRISTENING CAKE

As dusk was falling, the new IRO walked two miles out of Mufunsi to the corporation bus station. Ironheart had refused to go to the party because she knew how it would turn out. What was the point in contributing to a state of affairs which she deplored? There would be a lot of drunken behaviour, *maningi*, aimless fornication, much smoking of *dagga* and a great deal of stupid talk. None of this appealed to the new IRO's manager so she stayed at home, sewing buttons on his shirt, mending the holes in his pockets and socks, replacing dead light-bulbs, cleaning the oven and replanting the window-box with sunflowers.

The new IRO walked through a gap in the trees and found the bus station. It was in a patch of bare red ground, beneath the shade of several *munango* trees. In one corner stood an old prefabricated building with the words 'booking-office' daubed on one panel in red lead. On the cracked earth heaps of Africans slept and waited as the buses rumbled between them, carefully avoiding pot-bellied children, chickens, dug-out canoes and bundles. The new IRO stood by the office, very marked out by his whiteness, and looked at the bus indicators.

Every one said 'PRIVATE'.

"Excuse me," he said as he stopped a driver who was just getting out of the door of one dust-covered, battered vehicle, "where can I catch a bus to Musangati?"

"Who wants to go to a dump like Musangati?"

"I do."

"Why?"

"That's my business," the new IRO replied with some asperity.

The African driver bunched his fists and thrust them under his armpits.

"This mode of transport is not for bwanas," he said critically, "certainly not!"

"Why not for God's sake?"

"All God's bwanas got cars."

"Who said I am a bwana?"

"God."

Placing his hands behind his head, the driver began to twitch his biceps alternately in a mesmerising rhythm.

"No, no, no!" he sang, "we got no springs, no schedules, no organisation. Our tyres are bald. Our points are pitted. Our distributors are done for." A number of other drivers appeared out of the booking-office, or roused themselves from sleep under the *munango* trees. It was obviously the introductory verse of a popular song and there was soon a crowd of men standing round the new IRO and his informant, all clapping and singing.

No hooting is permitted at night!
Hayikona tshya lo huta ebusuku!
Where is your windscreen wiper?

101

Upi yinto yena sula lo glas?
No parking! No entry!
Hayikona yima lapa! Hayikona ngena!
Your lights are out! Cul-de-sac!
Malampu gawena ena file! Stalidi pela Pambili!
Oho! What a life! What an *indaba*!
This business is a One-Way Street to the Grave!
Munye stalidi kupela! Munye stalidi kupela!

The song died away and the chorus stood around, grinning at the lone white man. The new IRO watched the sinewy black muscles jumping along the first driver's upper arm and wondered whether this was a display of threat or a means of keeping up a rhythm.

"Is there a law against me using the bus?"

"Yes bwana, the Law of Nature."

The driver paused in his exhibition of dynamic tension and was suddenly sombre, deep in reflection.

"In the old days, if the police saw one of us *bantu* riding a bicycle, then he inevitably arrested us and threw us into gaol. That was the right thing to do because no African had enough money to afford a machine so it logically followed that it must be stolen. That was a natural law, and now there is another natural law. There is no bwana in Zonkendawo who does not have a car."

"What if a bwana *does not* have a car?" the new IRO said craftily, "what then?"

"Then he is breaking the natural law. He should have a car."

"But if he cannot afford a car?"

"Then it is doubtful whether he is a bwana at all."

Flexing his biceps for one last time, the driver gave an embarrassed smile. He noticed that the *musungu* had a quiet light of intellectual triumph in his green eyes.

"Then I cannot be a bwana. All I am is a private citizen without private transport. Got you, you side-stepping bastard!"

The crowd that had gathered around the disputants broke out into prolonged applause as the new IRO made his point. They could see what he was getting at and he appeard to have overturned the driver's major premise. But the driver was not beaten.

"However, we know that you are a bwana."

"How do you know that?"

"Because you are not black."

"You mean, because I'm white?"

102

"That's not what I said."

"Is everyone who is not black, a bwana?"

"No, but a bwana cannot be black. That is a different distinction."

"If I was yellow, would I be a bwana?"

"No, you would be a Chinaman."

"Is a Chinaman a bwana?"

"No, he is just a Chinaman."

"Then what else is it that makes me a bwana?"

"You are not black, and you are English."

"Are all Englishmen bwanas?"

"As long as they are not black Englishmen."

"Would an Englishman who was poor, mentally defective, spiritually abject, diseased and on the point of suicide, be a bwana?"

The crowd was silent for a moment, then it was decided that he must be a bwana, but only if he was in Africa.

"But not at home? In England?"

"There are no bwanas in England. When a white Englishman touches this continent with his foot, then he becomes a bwana."

"So it is Africa that makes bwanas bwanas?"

"It is Africa that makes kaffirs kaffirs."

"No, it is bwanas that make kaffirs kaffirs and kaffirs that make bwanas bwanas."

"You are tireless in your method of argument."

"That is because I am not a bwana and I want to go to Musangati."

"You have no private transport?"

"No."

The driver threw out his arm and pointed to all the bus indicators.

"Private transport? Look around you."

"That's all very well," the new IRO laboured on, patiently, "but I want to go to Musangati."

"Musangati! Musangati! All aboard for Musangati!" the driver shouted, re-boarding his vehicle. "What are we waiting for?"

Many of the crowd were galvanised by the driver's summons, gathering up rolls of chicken-wire, armchairs, paw-paws, copies of Playboy and blackened kitchen utensils and running over to the bus.

"Well done *mukwai*," one of them whispered as he passed the new IRO, "we've been trying to get one of these piss-artists to go to Musangati since six o'clock this morning. You must have awakened his conscience with your dumbfounding train of thought."

The new IRO offered his fare to the driver but it was refused.

103

"I would prefer to treat you as if you do not exist," the African explained. "I am not yet entirely convinced. You cannot expect an attitude of mind that has lasted a lifetime and formed part of a man's education and upbringing to be discarded in five minutes. So, as you do not exist, you cannot pay your fare. You are not a bwana, and you are a bwana. You are a perambulating question-mark."

The new IRO sat down next to a very old African woman who had a live chicken on her knee. Her dusty, tattered old wrap-around garment was covered with white feathers. After a moment sitting next to her, the new IRO discovered that the reason for all the loose feathers was that the crone was plucking the fowl alive. Also he could espy through the cloud of soft plumage, an old man who was sitting next to the window. He had produced several large pieces of dried cow-dung from an ancient overcoat and was lighting a fire on the floor with the help of a copy of the Zonkendawo Times and the wafting of the overcoat.

"Why don't you wring its neck first?" the new IRO suggested with as much calm as he could muster. "It would be more humane that way, wouldn't it?"

The crone yanked out a bunch of tail feathers and observed her accuser from one sunken eye which peered redly from the folds of her reeking head-turban.

"Why don't you go and multiply yourself?" she cackled hoarsely. "I don't tell you how to run your life do I?"

At the stage when the chicken, still alive but now bald, was cast on to the smouldering, evil-smelling fire under the seat, the driver guided the bus off the road, pulled up, turned off the engine and went into the bush with a schoolgirl with whom he had been engaged in animated chatter since leaving the bus station. All the passengers sighed and groaned, asking in loud voices why it was necessary for Central African Road Services only to employ the sexually depraved as drivers.

"Stop playing with your cassava-root and drive!" the crone shrieked out of the window.

"He is making us late for our appointment," the old man grumbled as he stamped the chicken down into the cow-dung, "if I was younger I would teach him a lesson with a *sjambok*."

The bus arrived in Musangati an hour later after a terrifying drive through the newly-fallen night. The interlude with the schoolgirl in the bush had inspired the driver with a masculine mania for speed as an additional expression of his virility. As the bus roared down the long, straight road, a slip-stream from the window acted as a bellows on the fire and it was soon a mound of glowing heat. The chicken roasted quickly, giving a new aroma to those already issued by the unique fuel.

"Want a piece?" the crone nudged the new IRO and pointed a bony finger at the charring carcase, "it's free-range."

"No thanks."

"Don't let his refusal offend you dear," the old man whispered comfortingly, "you know how peculiar the *musungus* are about what they eat."

Disembarking behind the crone and the old man, who had their fire secure in the overcoat, the new IRO set off to search the few streets for signs of a party. Outside one bungalow he saw a lot of cars parked, and heard the sound of music. The windows were open and he could see the curtains fluttering in the slight evening breeze. Entering the drive he paused momentarily under a tree to light a cigarette. He was nervous of meeting so many new people and unsure of his reception. The death of shift-boss Swanepoel had caused a stir in all the mining-towns of the Copperbelt, and the headlines in the paper referring to the new IRO had concentrated much unwanted attention on his part in the strike. He could be extremely unpopular. There was more than a chance that he would encounter animosity at the party and he had to be ready with some diversionary tactics.

"Who is that standing under the *mwanasamasaka* tree?" said a sharp female voice.

"No one," the new IRO replied uneasily.

"I can see you. So you must be someone."

A pale, red-haired woman with dangling silver earrings swayed towards him with a felt-pen between her teeth.

"Have you got any moles?"

The new IRO pulled his jacket together and did up the front three buttons.

"Is your name Hermione?"

The woman tinkled her left ear-ring thoughtfully.

"I bet you've got lots of moles. Come on, let's have a look."

"I've met your husband George."

"You've got the skin for moles. I should think your shoulders are covered, and your back, also your forearms."

The new IRO backed against the rough bark of the tree and kept

105

his eye on the point of the felt-pen as it approached the end of his nose. He could smell Hermione's perfume and see through the transparent shawl over her shoulders to a skin as clear and unblemished as driven snow.

"I haven't got any moles at all. I've got a birthmark on the inside of my right elbow and forceps-marks on my skull from my difficult birth, but that's all."

The conciliatory tone of his confession made Hermione waver. Into her slanted, wild emerald eyes came a gentle light and she smiled bewitchingly, tossing her red ringlets. Slowly she lowered the felt-pen, then seized the new IRO's hand and started pulling him towards the house.

"Come and see George. He's in top form tonight."

Once inside the front door, Hermione dragged him along to the kitchen. George Crompton was lying on top of a formica-covered draining-board and working-area, his shirt off. By his head stood a jam-jar full of felt-pens of different colours. George was fast asleep, a strong smell of whisky hanging in the sultry air around his head. Examining the picture on George's back was a small, podgy, bespectacled man with inky fingers and a round face.

"Hermy, why are you wasting your time in a backwater like this?" he mused. "You could be exhibiting at the Royal Academy with a talent like yours. Look at this!" He stretched out an inky palm. "Have you ever seen a mountain scene like this? Look at the cloud around the Matterhorn here. The skiers, two tiny figures but such realisation! Such detail! That hotel with the snow piled up around it. The horse pulling the sleigh, even the bell, even the arctic-fox fur round the female passenger's neck! God Hermy, if I could draw a tenth as well as you, I'd be a star in the art world by now. My work would sell for thousands of pounds."

"Thank you Albert," Hermione coiled an alabaster arm around the man's neck. "Now I'd like you to meet No One."

She put the new IRO's hand and Albert's together and watched approvingly as they said hello.

"This isn't No One Hermy," Albert Lewis smiled, "this is Mvhu."

"No," the new IRO said quickly, "I'm not. I'm No One."

"But I've seen you around. I know you by reputation. The town is full of talk about you. You're the man they call Mvhu. When the Bucket-Wheel Excavator Gang came down my printing-works to order their anti-Hammerkop leaflets, they told me all about you.

Why do you say you are No One?"

The printer banged his palms together then shook Vim on to them and held them under the hot tap.

"Is your name Albert Lewis?" the new IRO asked.

"The same."

"Why does the Staff Officer make new employees swear an oath not to make friends with you?"

"Because I'm a Creeping Republican."

"Do you ever go down to dinner?"

"No, I'm afraid not. My heart is elsewhere."

"Are you married?"

"No, but my emotions are not mine to play with. Hermy will tell you why. I'm going to get a drink."

Albert left the kitchen and Hermione explained that the tubby Jew was in love with an Irishwoman whose name he had forgotten. He abjured all other women and lived with his anonymous love hung round his neck like a stone. Until he could remember her name, her ghost could never be laid. She could never be laid because she had gone home to Kilkenny two years ago.

"It is always the same with Love and Albert. Every time he gets so far then — pouf! They leave him. I don't know what it is about him but he can't handle Love. I know he'd love to be loved, adored and never deserted, but he can't work out a system. Do you have a system?"

The new IRO said that he did not have a system, but he could remember all the names of the women he had really loved.

"You don't understand. If you are inferring criticism of poor Albert, then you're quite wrong. It is because he loved her so much when they were together that he had not time or energy to remember what her name was. As it was a clandestine relationship there was nobody else who could tell him afterwards. We didn't know who she was."

Hermione linked her arm in his and conducted him through to the room where the other guests had gathered. The french windows were open and the room led out to a patio surrounded by magnolia and flame-lily. Hermione took him outside and gave him a drink, then returned to the kitchen to add a bobsleigh run over the left kidney and a snow-owl in the branches of a Scots Fir just below the right scapular.

"Hello Hippo!"

"Christ, it's the old Mvhu himself!"

"Well, well. Len, I'd like you to meet Mr Hippopotamus!"

The new IRO flinched as the barrage of unwelcome greetings floated across to him, followed up by the appearance of Pyper, Matthias and the Bucket-Wheel Excavator Gang who had been sitting in the dark places under the trees. With them were two strangers, both young men in their middle twenties. One of them was dark, handsome, elegant and spoilt. His eyes were half-hooded, his nose aquiline and his mouth belonged to an age of sybaritic indulgence. Not only were his clothes beautifully cut, but they were atrociously expensive: a black silk shirt, a fawn suede jacket, 100 per cent wool black trousers creased like a knife, crocodile-skin casual shoes and a belt of tooled Spanish leather with a golden buckle. His Irish linen handkerchief was stuffed up his right hand sleeve and the right amount frothed on to his wrist, showing a monogram in embroidered black medieval illuminated capitals — D.P.

"Apt," the spoilt youth drawled as he poked the new IRO in the midriff with a manicured finger, "he looks the part."

"I shouldn't prod old Mvhu around too much Pforzheim. He's a terror when he gets going. He'd knock you into so many pieces your Dad would never be able to put you back together again, not even with all his money."

David Pforzheim examined the new IRO from under his hooded lids, his rich lip curled.

"Want me to beat you senseless? I'm the golf-club Indian wrestling champion. I can beat all these bastards at billiards. Give me a cricket-bat and I'll clout six sixes off one over. I can run a 100 yards in 10 seconds. I can drink any man under the table and fuck my way from Shanghai to San Francisco without pausing for breath or refreshment. Come outside you big dope and I'll show you who's top dog! You bloody has-been Hippopotamax!"

The new IRO did not move a muscle.

"We are outside."

"Don't split hairs."

"If you don't stop calling me Hippopotamax, I'll split more than hairs you spoilt, supercilious bastard!" the new IRO said heatedly.

The man called Len, who had acid burns on his shirt, asked how the new IRO knew that Pforzheim was spoilt.

"You're dead right of course. He's unbearable, arrogant and childish. Being the only son of a wealthy, indulgent and brainless

108

father has been the undoing of him. But, getting back to you Hippo, what else can we call you? You have placed us, Mr. H., in a difficult position. We could use some kind of abbreviation like Mr. Hip, or just Hi, or even Po. Then there's Ipo or Pot..."

"I know a lot
       about pot," interjected a member of the Bucket-Wheel Excavator Gang who was standing at the back of the group.

"Or we can call you Amus. How about that? Do you like Amus?" Leonard Porthcawl, a chemist from the Analytical Laboratory, went on, his eyes meeting the new IRO's on the same level for he was the same size, even bulkier.

"No, I don't fancy Amus."

"What do you want us to call you then?" Leonard asked jovially, "we could manage Sumatopoppih."

The other guests at the party began to look over to the rowdy corner of the patio where the new IRO was being tormented and persecuted by people whom he had sworn not to make friends with. At that moment, the keeping of his oath was an easy matter. He weighed Leonard up, then David Pforzheim, and wondered whether he could take them both on. Pyper intervened when the new IRO's face had darkened to a choleric shade and he was crouching low, big fists raised.

"Come upstairs old IRO. Forget these dissipated drangos. They're not worth half a bucket of horseshit. They don't know your quality like I do. I've got a piece of confectionery in the big bedroom. Baked it myself. You didn't know I was a dab hand with the old flour and margerine eh? Christ man, I can make puff pastry, apple strudel and chicken vol-au-vents with the best. I can put a crust on a pie that would withstand more pressure per foot than the roof of the Sydney Opera House."

Leonard and Pforzheim linked arms with the new IRO as they mounted the few stairs to the upper half of the split-level bungalow. They grinned, laughed, patted his back, assured him that they were in no wise as bad as they were painted. They had heard reports of the new IRO's character, strength, and had been given a résumé of his principles by the Bucket-Wheel Excavator Gang. At no time did they mention the semi-aquatic herbivore which was beginning to haunt the new IRO. They kept off the subject. Pyper winked over the heads of the rest of the crowd.

"You'll get along with these deadbeats old IRO. They're just like you. If you exchanged their brain and their arsehole no one would notice the difference. They didn't mean any harm. Just a bit of the old piss-taking."

"I can take a joke," the new IRO said with a shrug.

"Of course you can!" Leonard squeezed his elbow. "What a state of affairs it would be if we had to take life seriously for twenty-four hours a day."

"I don't trust morose people," Pforzheim added. "Give me a man who can laugh at himself now and then."

"If you couldn't see the funny side of things when things get tough you'd feel like cutting your throat with a rusty razor blade," said a wise member of the Bucket-Wheel Excavator Gang. "Take for example the 6-furlong race run by our friend here David Pforzheim's half a racehorse some weeks back. If I had lost my sense of humour I would have felt like kickings its balls off as it staggered in stone-last with ten kwacha of my money on it. Instead I went to the ablutions, cried for a while, then came out and faced the world with a smile on my face for the whole human race."

"Why has he only got half a racehorse?" the new IRO asked, pausing on the landing outside the bedroom door.

"Pforzheim's Dad kept the other half for himself. He wanted father and son to share a human experience together. He paid four thousand kwacha for the pleasure, didn't he Dave?" Pyper jeered. "I reckon that crippled quadruped wouldn't break into a gallop even if its arse was wreathed in flames."

"Maybe it's suffering from a crisis of identity?" Leonard suggested. "How is it divided? From nose to tail or across the middle?"

Pforzheim raised his arm, flashing a pair of gold monogrammed cuff-links which his Dad had bought him for his eleventh birthday. Pyper flinched and leaned against the wall, his hands shielding his fair face.

"Christ Dave, don't take it to heart. If you work me over I'll do a few lines on how you slip down to the paddock and prod that knacker's-yard throw-out with your polony when the moon is full."

Pforzheim smiled savagely, his rich underlip thrust out at the colourful newsman. Slowly he lowered his arm, gritting his teeth.

"You're an envious little shit Pyper. Just because you piss your salary up against the wall every month it doesn't mean that I have to do the same with the interest on my mining shares. Dad and I are where we are because of hard work and intelligence. He worked his

110

way up from nothing."

The new IRO heard the shout of laughter from the crowd on the landing and felt more at home now the attention had been switched from him to the spoilt son of the legal eagle. Pushing open the bedroom he entered, his mind engaged on his childhood when every family disaster had been followed by his mother, father, grandad, grandma, aunts and uncles sitting around in the parlour assuring each other that you had to laugh sometimes didn't you? It was reassuring to find that it was a trait common to all sorts and conditions of men, a truly universal quality in Man's spirit. It was his ultimate strength, laughing in the face of impossible odds, grinning while poised in the foetid jaws of Death.

The new IRO joined the crowd around a small mahogany occasional table. He noted the silence of their appreciation and the smiles of approval on every face. Standing on a tray which was ingeniously worked into a creditable representation of a reed-banked African river, was a cake covered in grey icing. It was in the shape of a bull hippopotamus.

Unfortunately the new IRO did not laugh. He refrained from holding on to his neighbour and roaring with mirth, holding his ribs, wiping away tears of merriment, gasping, shrieking, calling out ooohs, aaahs and Jesus Christs with the rest of the hilarious crowd around the cake. Instead he regarded the amphibious mammal with black disfavour and forgot how enjoyable a good joke could be. While a pandemonium of hysterical laughter surrounded him, he could not muster up a smile. Instead he leaned forward and picked up the knife that was lying by the side of the cake.

"Old IRO," Pyper panted, ice-blue eyes melting with salt tears, "it's a thank-you from all of us for helping to strike a blow against Hammerkop! Now, now! Steady on! Christ, I haven't seen a face like yours since Grandad pissed on the generator at McMurdo's sheep-station!"

The Bucket-Wheel Excavator Gang jumped on the new IRO and disarmed him, returning the knife to the cake-stand. While they sat on his chest and legs to hold him down, George Crompton entered with Hermione and Albert and the laughter was re-doubled. Hermione let it be known that she had advised Pyper on the sculpturing of the fruit-and-nut mix.

"Hippopotamix!" Pyper screamed, struggling for air, bubbles seeping from his maiden's mouth, "Oh what a beaut!"

George Crompton, being the culinary columnist for the Zonken-dawo Times and an acknowledged master of kitchencraft, was given the honour of dissecting the bull hippopotamus. His butchery was excellent, slice after slice falling evenly into the icing river and reeds. When the cutting was over, George took the first mouthful and gave his verdict. Pyper waited the judgement with an eye on the new IRO who was still struggling to free himself in order to do a similar carving job on the peacock newsman.

"Oh yes, well up to standard," George Crompton said approvingly, "you may not be the world's second Rodin John, but you make a better cake than any other person I know. This is jolly good."

"Thanks George, it's nice to get compliments from a connoisseur."

Hermione took the cake-stand round the crowd in the bedroom until everyone had a piece. Pyper insisted that the tail and extreme end of the rump be kept for the new IRO.

"I don't think he will eat it," Matthias said sadly, "he is still breathing heavily and his muscles are straining to cracking point."

"He'll forgive me," Pyper mumbled through a mouthful of cake, "let the poor bastard up."

"I wouldn't advise it."

"I'll take the risk. If he fucks me up I'll put his name in the paper again. This time I'll say he's a Rhodesian spy and they'll shoot him. Hear that old IRO? You wouldn't try and kill me would you? Old Margaret From The Tonga Bar wouldn't like that, would she?"

Pyper smiled at the beautiful black whore who was licking her fingers after consuming the right front hoof. She had helped to make the cake, especially the extra ingredient. For an hour she had ground a cob of compressed *dagga* leaves through a baby food-mixer, and then stirred the fine flour into the mixture. She knew that the best antidote to the anger of the IRO was to get him to eat his portion. Once he did that, he would feel better about the thank-you cake. Taking the tail and extreme end of the rump in her hand, she knelt down by the new IRO and looked deep into his eyes.

"You and I have a long way to go in our friendship O Mvhu. We have much knowledge to acquire about each other. At the moment we are apart but in time we will get closer. It is what I want, and what you want if I read your eyes well. If you will eat this cake, swallow it with your pride and forgive my present lover, then you may rest assured in your heart of hearts that one day I will be yours and you will wake the next morning a better man."

112

With a titanic effort the new IRO sat up, shrugged off the Bucket-Wheel Excavator Gang, snatched Margaret From The Tonga Bar's hand and licked the cake off her palm, the groaning of his terrible rage outshouted by the grunting of a prodigious lust.

The hostess was standing near the front door, anxiously waiting for the arrival of the caterer. She had arranged for a new company – Peripatetic Barbecues Ltd. of Mufunsi – to provide the food for the party, and they were already an hour late. She was satisfied that her party was going with a swing but knew that her guests were getting hungry. Soon they would start roaming through the kitchen, burgling the fridge and plundering the vegetable garden. Walking down the drive she came upon two old African people sitting on the grass verge. They were huddled round a fire which smelled of Turkish cigarettes.

"Good evening *madala*. Have you seen a van which looks as though it might be lost?" she asked politely.

The crone looked up at the *musungu* woman, at her peroxide hair swept up round her temples like a tidal wave of egg-flip, at her mascarad Mickey-Mouse eyes, at her short taffeta skirt. With a sniff the old woman prodded the fire.

"The only thing we have seen which is lost, is us," she croaked.

"Where are you looking for?" the amiable, overdressed blonde asked helpfully.

"We are looking for Mrs. W. T. Franks."

"I am Mrs. W. T. Franks. Why are you looking for me?"

"We have got a job to do for you."

"I don't think so. I've got a garden-boy."

"You rang up and asked us to do the catering for your party tonight, but you gave no address..."

The hostess stepped back in involuntary horror as the crone got to her feet and opened her tattered wrap-around cloak. Inside, hanging on sewed tabs, were a number of live chickens.

"Thank the great king Christ we have found you Madam," the old man said gladly, "we were getting worried. Just show us to a suitable position and we will start cooking."

The hostess clutched at her throat as if a demon had leaped out of the dark and was trying to throttle her.

"Are you Peripatetic Barbecues Ltd?" she managed to squawk.

"At your service!"

With a flourish, the old man swept the cow-dung fire up into his overcoat, shouldered it and walked down the drive, smoke billowing from the sleeves. The crone followed on, already starting to pluck a white chicken, scattering clouds of feathers through the night. Behind them stumbled the hostess, a grotesque social nightmare climbing into her brain. This was what came of trying to identify with the aspirations of the independent Zonkendawo government. This is what happened when you gave your valuable custom to one of the new African-run companies which President Mulombe was always urging everyone to support.

When the aged catering contractors entered the patio area they shooed a parcel of guests away from the spot which they selected as a good site for their fire, then squatted down to prepare the chickens. White feathers flew in all directions as the crone and the old man plucked furiously at the protesting birds.

"Look, I'll pay you the sum we agreed," the hostess begged, "but please go away. There's been a frightful mistake. It's my fault and I apologise but please, please pack up your things and leave."

From out of the cloud of feathers came the crones' thin piping.

"It's just because we're black isn't it? It would be all right if we were Europeans!"

"No!" the hostess declared, terrified of the implication. "It's not that at all. It's just that I didn't imagine the barbecue as being. . . like this," she added lamely. "Not at all like this."

"Look madam," the old man quavered, "we all have to start somewhere. We had very little capital to start this company. The government gave us a ten kwacha loan and that was that. All we ask is that you give us a chance to prove what we can do. Our contract will be honoured to the letter, rest assured of that."

The hostess knelt on the concrete by the old man's side. She pleaded with him. Offered to double the agreed fee. Run them home in her car. But Peripatetic Barbecues Ltd. were adamant. They would supply the goods.

"Madam, don't you understand? This is our first break-through, our first really substantial project. If we fail this time, what confidence can we have in the future? Now, if you will return to your guests and leave us to get on with the preparation of the food, I think it will be better for all."

The hostess crawled away as the old man's voice faded in the snowstorm of feathers. Ignoring her sympathetic friends, she went

114

and sat in an armchair by the telephone, trying to summon up the courage to ring the police and have the old couple removed. She never made the call. Politics had caught Mrs. W. T. Franks unawares and she was trapped. Whether she liked it or not, she would remain a contributor to the cause of Zonkendawo's fight for economic survival and be a supporter of home industries.

Cumulus McCloud Molile was the member of the Bucket-Wheel Excavator Gang who knew a lot
about pot.

   He did not know much about the *mupundukaina* tree and had been the person responsible for the débâcle at Hammerkop's *braaivleis*. However, on his chosen subject, the holy healing herb, he was an authority. He had recognised the flavour of the ground dried leaves in the hippopotamus-cake and when he did so, the whole evening took on a more serious complexion. In his own elementary way, Cumulus McCloud Molile was a psychologist. For many years he had studied the effect of the benevolent green magic on his own nervous system and had taken much pleasure out of smoking, eating, drinking the tall-growing, finely-fretted leaf which was to be found growing wild in the bush. Then he had developed a pastime which brought about a change of character in the Open Pit worker. The British Sunday newspapers. His brother worked as a house-servant for an Englishman who had these journalistic paradigms sent out to him every week by his mother. When he had finished with them, he gave them to Cumulus McCloud Molile's brother with an encouragement to read them as, he confidently claimed, all the accumulated wisdom of Mankind was pressed between their endless pages. As the brothers shared a one-roomed shanty in the squatter township, it was natural that Cumulus McCloud should read these papers. From them he learned that, instead of liking the delicious dream-making weed, the bwanas in their island fastness actually considered it a threat to their security, sanity and civilisation. Cumulus McCloud had set himself the task of resolving the apparent contradiction – how did the happiness in the hemp become the curse in the cannabis? If he could analyse this dichotomous state of affairs he might be able to help the English to a better realisation of their potential as human beings and take an unnecessary load off all the judges, policemen, columnists, social-workers and song-writers who appeared to be solely employed in arguing the toss about the rights and wrongs of this verdant emperor of the vegetable kingdom. Now, at last, he had his chance to study a number of *musungus* under test-conditions. All of them had consumed a slice of the spiked hippopotamus-cake. With his own mind on the upsurge, familiar as he was with the golden zooming of the spirit under the impetus of the happy herb, he followed the new IRO when he stomped off into the garden, still in a rage after the humiliation of Pyper's practical joke.

Taking a dog-eared note-book out of his overalls' pocket, the dusky psychologist crept up behind the Englishman and listened with bated breath.

"Who does that little bastard think he is? I'm not asking for anything but a bit of common respect," the new IRO muttered savagely. "He'll come a cropper one day when there's no one around to stick up for him like Margaret From The Tonga Bar."

The flow of angry soliloquy halted as the big man thought about the promise made to him by the dark, lustrous whore. Sitting down on a low wall, a screen of trees between him and the patio, he looked up at the star-nailed sky and a dented-saucer moon.

"Ooooh God," he groaned, rubbing the insides of his thighs.

Cumulus McCloud Molile smiled. His experimental material was obviously feeling better for an erotic foray into the imagination. In that condition he might react affirmatively when the cake had been digested and the drug had entered his bloodstream. Looking at his watch he saw that it had been twenty minutes since the new IRO had taken his portion off Margaret From The Tonga Bar. The time was about right.

"Think about it some more Mvhu," Cumulus McCloud whispered, "it will make you more receptive."

The new IRO whirled round and saw the dark figure crouched under the wall.

"Who's that?" he cried.

"A friend."

"I haven't got any friends!"

Cumulus McCloud Molile stood up and patted the new IRO on the shoulder.

"We are all your friends, even if we call you Mvhu to your face instead of behind your back."

"What a name to be saddled with," the new IRO complained bitterly, "of all the names to choose from."

"It is a much-admired creature," the psychologist said gently.

116

"Why fight against it? Why not relax, go with the tide, enjoy it? To you it may be an insult but to the people it is a compliment. They do not look down their noses at the *mvhu*."

The new IRO closed his eyes, his mouth drooping sadly. What an idea. For him to accept it, just like that. To agree to be four tons of blubber and fishy flesh. To concur in the adoption of a round, hairless body and four short legs. To sign on the dotted line that he was an even-toed ungulate, a member of the Order Artiodactylae whose head weighed a ton, whose eyes bulged, who could hold his breath for half-an-hour, run faster than a man, chastise crocodiles with sickle-like, sharp-edged teeth, beat the hell out of motor-boats, lions, anything that trespassed on its feeding-grounds. Did he undertake to be such a beast? Why should he adopt such a carcase? But wasn't it true that hippopotami were common in England during the interglacial period of the Pliocene Epoch? Like him they had drifted away to Africa, got lost in the great rivers, bound by the ancient crazy continent to browse and blow. Isn't that what he was? Wasn't he an even-toed ungulate at heart? Wasn't it true that these men of daring insight had penetrated a secret cave in his heart of hearts and seen a hippopotamus standing there, chin-deep in the green waters of the Kafue, or the Zambesi, or the Limpopo?

He was an *mvhu*!

They had given him the name that went with his actual nature and their unerring perception of the state of his soul!

"Mvhu!"

Cumulus McCloud Molile smiled uncertainly as the new IRO got down on his hands and knees and started nibbling the bark off the trees.

"Mvhu! Umph! Grumff!"

"What are you trying to say to me?" Cumulus McCloud Molile ventured, one hand on top of the wall to facilitate a quick escape.

"Call me Mvhu!"

"You want me to call you the name you hate?"

"I don't hate it! I love it! It's my name! It's the best name I've ever had! Now call me Mvhu or I'll bite you in half!"

Mvhu opened his mouth, the biggest mouth in the world barring the whales of the ocean, and showed Cumulus McCloud Molile all his fillings. But there was no need to threaten the psychologist. With a beating heart and a happy grin, the man was writing in his note-book that the sweet herb had done its work and conquered

117

yet another truculent and paradoxical spirit. One minute the *musungu* had been ready to shed blood because of a word, and now he embraced it as if it was a crown. Was there any other substance known to Man that could work such miracles, wreak such lightning changes for the better? His suspicions were correct. If the *musungus* took the herb in the right mood, forgetting all their *mulandu*, all their tyrannical obsessions with respect, then they became one of the joyous brotherhood of African Hemp.

Cumulus McCloud Molile was not a man to forgo an opportunity for doing good. Beckoning Mvhu to follow him, he crossed to a garden shed, unhooked a hose-pipe, fixed it to a garden-tap, propped its nozzle in the fork of a tree and provided the four-ton herbivore with the conditions it loved most of all. When he looked round during his walk back to the bungalow, he saw Mvhu lying on his back, even-toed hooves in the air, enjoying the cool moonlit water of his natural domain.

"Go well Mvhu!" the jubilant scientist called.

"Umph-umph! Cherloaaa! Sprunt miff! Ooooh-gaaaplooms-tumpboom!" the massive barrel of blubber, sickle-teeth, bulging eyes and even toes bellowed, "this is the life!"

"Are you at peace in the world now, O great doubter?"

"Never felt better! I'm just getting this mud really thick so I can roll in it properly and cover my hairless skin with a protective layer of cooling slime against the sun's rays. Whushlooofume! Bumf-bumf! Oh happy day! This is terrific fun!"

Cumulus McCloud paused before he walked on. Should he leave Mvhu in this state? Was he sure that the inspired *musungu* would come to no harm? There was no deep water in which he could immerse himself for ten minutes, nor any crocodiles to fight, or dambo-grass to eat. Also Mvhu would have that strongly developed instinct of all living creatures – survival. But being forty times his previous mass he should have forty times more instinct. He had no worries about Mvhu. The Englishman would not harm himself and when the effects of the cake had worn off, he would feel much better for his journey into the animal kingdom. He would be one with those gods who could become animals, birds and fishes, and yet remain gods; gifted with the power of change, which is the most wonderful power in the world.

Arabella Parkinson was at the party. At the moment when Cumulus

McCloud Molile left Mvhu by the hosepipe, she was confiding in a small group of intimate girl-friends about the Predikant. He had lost interest in any physical union, and after Hammerkop's *braaivleis*, now only sought union with God.

"It's enough to make a girl think about going off to look for this legendary Old Man Of The Woods I keep hearing about," Arabella laughed.

"Who says he's so legendary?" one of Arabella's friends said slyly.

"What d'you mean?" Arabella bridled.

"Think of the number of women who've disappeared for a couple of days lately. Moira. Valerie. Janice. Hennie Thing, you know who I mean. Gwen. Celia..."

The rest of the group then started listing women of their acquaintance who had left home and, on their return, been unable to account for their whereabouts. The list took several minutes to compile and when re-checked and counted was well into three figures.

"And they always find them in the same condition! Wandering along the road with a stupid smile on their faces covered with dirty finger-marks!"

"I believe he exists!"

"So do I!"

"I wouldn't mind paying him a visit myself!"

At the back of the giggling crowd, Arabella looked across the garden to the moon, her hungry, sharp eyes suddenly dulled with fond memories. She could smell wood-smoke, feel the rough texture of his unshaven chin, smell the bush on his body.

"Well Arabella, we've decided to organise an outing to see the Old Man Of The Woods," one of her friends joked, "he sounds interesting."

"Only one at a time. He says only one at a time," Arabella whispered. "He's out there now."

"What are you talking about?"

Arabella snapped out of her day-dream and smiled thinly.

"Sorry. Too many gins. I think I'll have a stroll in the garden."

Leaving her friends, Arabella stepped into the darkness. Right now she would have given what was left of her soul to go and see the wild Old Man Of The Woods and lie between his smoking charcoal-beds. Then she heard water playing on the ground and started away in case her dress got wet.

119

"Archentroolsomph?" Mvhu grunted, his legs in the air.

Arabella looked down. The moon illuminated the face of a nightmare.

"You!" she said with a shudder. "What do you want? Money? Are you trying to blackmail me?"

"Bububudrusuffle!"

"He's not a kaffir! He's not. It's his job makes him that colour! He's as white as you or me!"

Mvhu pointed at his muddy features with a tremendous hoof and grinned daemonically.

"The Predikant would never believe you anyway. Not now you've shown which side you're on. You're vile! You're mad! Get away from me!"

Arabella ran back to the house, her cold soul cracking like desert rocks in the frost of her fear. Mvhu lay on his side and chuckled. Oh sloomdrong de muffkong drerch, he thought to himself, what a grumfy joom.

While searching for more *musungus* to observe, Cumulus McCloud Molile found Albert Lewis in tears. The psychologist did not hesitate. He walked straight past the blubbering Jew, swatting away his ink-stained, outstretched hand. As he hurried away, Cumulus McCloud Molile had no qualms of conscience. Running away from Albert was like running away from a road-accident – a course of action officially recommended by the Zonkendawon Police – because if you did not, then you stood in peril.

Albert was treated with wary respect by all his friends in case he might try to unload some of his headed note-paper or visiting-cards on them. Where his friends were concerned, Albert did not bother to ask for orders. He presumed their needs. Men with a total income of £17 a month had embossed writing paper with their hut numbers picked out in a cheerful red italic script in the top right hand corner. Unemployed vagrants with hardly a stitch to cover their nakedness had breast-pockets full of white cards giving their names and "no fixed address" in a fine copperplate.

Sober, he could be argued out of these imagined orders: but under the influence of any stimulant he would not be gainsaid. So Cumulus hurried on in search of another *musungu* who had eaten of the christening-cake.

As a jobbing-printer Albert had a power much akin to Pyper's

120

and he never hesitated to use it when he felt an injustice had been committed or the public weal threatened. At the time of his love for the dark-haired Irishwoman whose name he had forgotten, Albert had printed ten thousand leaflets attacking her husband's business methods in an attempt to drive a wedge between husband and wife. They were distributed throughout the Copperbelt by *piccanins* on Albert's pay-roll and posted to all government offices, factories, shops, warehouses, institutions for the deaf, blind, mentally ill, and leprosariums.

In the leaflet Albert alleged that the Irishwoman's husband had been in cahoots with a Lieutenant-Colonel who had an administrative post in the Ministry of Works and how this had been why he had been tipped off about the lowest tender that had been put in for the Mushishima Bridge project so he could send one in himself suitably undercutting it. He pointed out that the Lieutenant-Colonel had been to an English public school, was a bachelor and was interested in the Scout movement while the dark-haired Irishwoman's husband had a collection of nude male photographs. Was this the kind of foreign investment Zonkendawo really wanted? Albert asked.

The leaflet caused a stir. The Lieutenant-Colonel shot himself after his wife left him and Albert immediately printed another ten thousand leaflets carrying his declaration of eternal love for the dark-haired Irishwoman, saying that he worshipped her, would be willing to embrace the Roman Catholic faith, and wanted her for his own. But he was too late. The husband, completely ignorant of the storm around his head and the designs of the love-lorn printer on his wife, had left Zonkendawo to return to Kilkenny and open a garage with his expatriation cash. The leaflets were delivered to an empty house to be reduced to pulp by the October rains.

So it was not for nothing that Albert sat at the end of the stairs and cried.

"Is it too much to expect?" he wept. "One reply to ten thousand declarations of eternal fidelity! What do you have to do for them? Is it any wonder I'm cynical about the bitches? No, I'm not cynical. I'm not! If I could find her name I'd track her down. I'd give all my money to the IRA if she asked me to! I'd throw myself at her feet and beg for her love!"

Beating his temples on his ink-stained knees, Albert sobbed on.

Outside in the garden, Cumulus McCloud Molile was sitting at Leonard Porthcawl's elbow as the Welshman explained the working

121

parts of the gecko lizard to the peroxide hostess.

"There are twenty families of lizards. Iguanidae, agamidae, chamel-eontidae, geckonidea, lacertidea, teiidae..."

"Oh God in Heaven, when are those two awful old Africans going to leave?" Mrs W.T. Franks muttered tearfully, her mascara running. "They've ruined my party. It's not going the way I wanted it to."

"Most of the families are nocturnal," Leonard continued, stroking the gecko's head, "they are characterised by large eyes and expanded tips on the digits, see?"

Cumulus McCloud Molile shuffled closer to Leonard and imparted one of his secrets to the couple, talking from behind a raised hand.

"Did you know that in the report of the Hemp Drugs Commission of 1894 it was made public that Major R. Cobb, Civil Surgeon and Superintendent of the British Army Lunatic Asylum, had confessed that hemp had been widely used in the relief of mental strain and neuroses and that there were no grounds for suspecting that any moral, physical or mental degeneration had taken place as a result?"

Leonard Porthcawl put his nose to the gecko lizard's.

"So what Cumulus? How does it help this little chap?"

"It might help his expanded digits."

"So it might."

"Why are you talking in this strange way?" the hostess said wildly, struggling to her feet. "Everything has gone wrong! Oh I wish every-body would go home. I don't like it! I don't care for what's going on here! It's those dreadful Africans and their wretched chickens! Oh I can't stand it! Go away all of you!"

As Mrs. W. T. Franks was abandoning herself to a bout of hysterics, the Staff Officer drove up to the front of the bungalow in her Citroën. Her red shantung cocktail dress was cut low, her hair glittered with rhinestones, her white body was redolent with desire-inducing per-fumes, her heart was cast in an ingot of flaming pure silver, a star re-poured, and the fire shone in her eyes. She heard the voices raised, the crying, the laughter, the hum of men talking in herds, the rutting murmur of bull and stag. Here was a harvest to be reaped!

With purposeful strides she stalked down the drive, the lionskin over her broad snowy shoulder, and kicked open the front door. Albert looked up and saw her. He shrank back, terror in his eyes.

"No!" he gabbled, "oh no! Not me! Please! Take somebody else! My heart belongs to another!"

His cries went unheeded. Scooping him up, the Staff Officer bundled the lachrymose printer into the nearest bedroom and tied him to the bed-rail. Then she went in search of more prey.

She was spotted.

The lionskin was flung back, ready for the attack.

"Look out! The Staff Officer's here!" a man yelled in panic, hurdling the flame-lily bushes and fleeing through the dark.

"The Staff Officer's arrived!"

"Run for it!"

"Every man for himself!"

The next minute saw scenes of hysterical confusion. The house emptied. The men ran into the garden, trampled on flower-beds, vaulted over walls, borders and rose-bushes, started cars, switched on headlights, gunned engines, shouted incoherent cries of dread.

"Come back!" shouted the Staff Officer, yanking at car-door handles, waving her lionskin, "don't run away! The fun's not started yet!"

They ignored her pleas, drove over lawns, seedlings, through shrubs, knocked aside garden ornaments, bird-baths and deck-chairs, heedlessly heading for the great darkness of the road and escape.

They deserted her.

By the light of a gibbous moon, the Staff Officer stood in the middle of the road and watched the red tail-lights dwindle into the night. The lionskin was draped over one heroic shoulder, her strong pale thighs shone through the hip-high split in her shantung dress; Diana, Mistress of the Chase, sad and silver in the growing moon, the ardent huntress of love and purity in a spoiled world, defeated by fear and misunderstanding, cowardice and small-mindedness.

"Her parties don't usually finish this early," the Staff Officer said to herself disconsolately as she returned to the bungalow, "I'd better arrive sooner next time."

But there was Albert.

The Staff Officer smiled down on the tubby Jewish printer, her tombstone teeth newly-brushed and dazzling. He had managed to gnaw half-way through the nylon dressing-gown cord which had been used to bind his wrists together. The Staff Officer had returned in the nick of time.

With a swirl, the Staff Officer spread the lionskin over the bed, picked Albert up off the floor and threw him on to the mattress, snapping the last of the nylon cord as the printer arched through the air.

This was going to be a night for Albert to remember.

123

He would never forget the name of this lady of love.

TWELVE **THE SLEEPDRIVERS**

Mvhu joined in the stampede, obeying the powerful herd-instinct.
As the human animals ran hither and thither, the bulky, round-ribbed
giant of the river heaved himself into a sitting position, shook off
the excess mud, looked around him with bulging high-set eyes, then
set off at a lumbering 30 m.p.h. for the nearest car. As he hoisted
his moist, soiled mass into the back-seat the vehicle set off, tyres
screeching, doors waving. Mvhu caught a glimpse of the Staff Officer
standing in the road, holding up a hand against the mad rush of cars,
brilliantly illuminated, then the driver swerved round her and accele-
rated, clocking up a tremendous, spine-jarring surge of speed along
the dark road.

"Good God Pforzheim!" George Crompton muttered dazedly,
"you'll kill us all. Slow down!"

"Why is your friend naked and covered in mud?" asked Mrs.
W.T. Franks of Leonard who still held the gecko lizard in the palm
of his hand. "He smells!"

"Is Hermione in another car?"

The last voice belonged to the wife of the metallurgist who was the
mistress of both Pforzheim and Crompton in equal parts. She had
been biding her time at the party to see who would end up taking
her home and showing her what a big world it was outside. She was
frightened of Hermione because the red-haired creator of living
frescos had visited her the previous week carrying an O.K. Bazaars
plastic shopping bag containing several large stones. With this
weapon she had smashed a glass door, all the windows in the kitchen
and narrowly missed murdering the wife of the metallurgist herself.
When she was being shown what a big world it was outside, the wife
of the metallurgist liked to be as far away from Hermione as possible.

"George darling," she whispered into the PR Man's ear as Pforzheim pushed his 3.8 litre white Jaguar past 100 m.p.h., "you're
much better than David is in bed. He's got so much to learn."

Crompton groped for her cool hand and squeezed it, her mouth
strained into a smile as the big car bowled through the night, slashing
through blackness with its battery of lights. Here was comfort indeed.

Leaning over the back of the driver's seat, the wife of the metallurgist drew Pforzheim's dark, well-barbered hair away from his ear and applied her sweet lips to its entrance.

"David darling," she sighed, "you could teach George a thing or two about love. He can be incredibly amateur."

The needle on the speedometer trembled as Pforzheim's foot trod on the accelerator pedal and the Jaguar's engine whined into a frenzy. Up and up, past 115, 120, 125.

Pforzheim had always known he was the better man.

He could fuck George Crompton off the board.

"You're in a terrible mess," Mrs W.T. Franks remarked to Mvhu who was trying to squash his 4 tons into one corner and not be noticed. "Have you had an accident?"

"Most of this family are nocturnal," Leonard crooned while stroking the gecko's head.

"That one certainly is," the wife of the metallurgist giggled, "it's half-past twelve."

"Grumff!" Mvhu grunted warningly as the lizard looked his way.

Like the elephant is afeared of the mouse, so the hippopotamus is scared of the gecko. It might scramble up through one nostril and enter the brain, doing untold damage. Mvhu closed his waterproof nose-holes. Here was a threat!

"Who is this person?" Mrs. W.T. Franks demanded as Mvhu chomped at the gecko, crashing his sickle-shaped 4 lb teeth together inches away from Leonard's hand.

"Will you stop the car please?"

It was Leonard who spoke, one arm protectively encircling the little lizard.

"What for?" Pforzheim demanded irritably, "I have to get back. It's my turn tonight according to the schedule."

Leonard held the gecko forward so its marble eyes rolled towards the driver, terrifying the stinking mountain of blubber in the back seat. The analytical chemist rubbed the tip of his thumb over the lizard's head.

"I think this little fellow wants to get off. You're going too fast for him."

"You think I'm going to knuckle under to a gecko?" Pforzheim sneered. "Do you think I've got no mind of my own just because I accept an allowance of £150 a month off my father?"

"Smarthenlooblooh!" roared Mvhu, pounding the car body with

his even-toed front hooves as the gecko got ready to attack, swivelling its terrible eyes like a fire-breathing dragon, "aaarchentraaafen-grumph!"

With a hideous yowl the Jaguar braked, slinging its occupants forward against gravity, tyres smouldering. Mvhu saw the gecko leap closer and balance on the edge of the humid basin of his left nostril.

"Halakaaphroooo!" he sneezed, pawing at his thunderous muzzle as it streamed with phlegm and mucus.

"Do you mind!" shrieked Mrs W.T. Franks, reeling in the blast.

Pforzheim got out of the car, then opened the door on Leonard's side. The analytical chemist leaned down, his hand held out, and shuffled the little lizard on to the grass.

"Go well," he whispered gently, "goodbye *chamware*."

"Kaboom!" sighed Mvhu with relief.

Pforzheim flung himself back into the car, gunned the engine and shot the Jaguar off into the night again, his mind racing ahead to Mufunsi and a night between his crimson silk sheets with the wife of the metallurgist.

For ten minutes they tore through the darkness.

Then Pforzheim started leaning forward and staring through the windscreen.

He slowed down.

"Are you sure this is the road to Mufunsi?" he said worriedly to no one in particular, "I don't remember any hills this steep."

Mrs. W.T. Franks asked why he thought he was going to Mufunsi because all she wanted to do was go home.

"We're all going to Mufunsi, up this hill!" Pforzheim replied sharply.

"But I don't want to go to Mufunsi!"

"Where do you want to go then?"

"Home, to bed!"

"Where's that?"

"Musangati."

"I don't remember going down any hills this steep to Musangati."

Mrs. W.T. Franks started crying. She didn't know what she was doing in this car with all these people. When the Staff Officer had appeared she had made a run for it, welcoming the opportunity to escape from Peripatetic Barbecues Ltd. Now she was in a worse situation. These people were acting in a strange way. Their conversa-

126

tion and behaviour were abnormal. Also she knew that there had never been any hills on this road and there were none now. She was in the hands of a madman.

Pforzheim changed down to third gear. The Jaguar was beginning to labour as the incline got steeper and steeper. Ahead of him rose the road in a sharp gradient, a black mountain which ended up on the edge of the moon. The car would never make it. He stopped the car.

Seizing her chance, Mrs. W.T. Franks got out.

"Careful you don't fall down the slope!" Pforzheim yelled.

"I'm walking back!" she screamed tearfully, shaking her fist through the window. "You'll never be invited to one of my get-togethers again! If I get assaulted or raped then it will all be your fault!"

They watched her stumble off down the near-vertical mountain-side, her peroxide hair tinged by the moon.

"You'd think she was an experienced mountaineer to watch her, wouldn't you?" Pforzheim reflected, "strange how some people have inner strengths you've never suspected."

"That's true," George Crompton agreed, "I'd have put her down as a typical white African, lazy, seldom taking exercise, driving every-where, but just look at her running down that slope! She's certainly sure-footed!"

Pforzheim shifted in the deep leather of the driving-seat.

"I'm really sorry about the car. It's powerful enough for most hills but not this one. I'll have to leave it here then get a crane or something."

"What are you talking about, David darling?" the wife of the metallurgist asked nervously.

"You can see for yourself can't you?" George Crompton snapped, secretly upset because the roster had worked against him, "for Christ's sake woman, look around you! What do you think you're in, a bloody cable-car?"

The wife of the metallurgist looked round her in an attempt to gain support. She was about to argue with both her lovers about the topography. As far as she could see the car was standing on a perfectly flat road. The only other ally she could think of was the large, mud-covered, naked man who was huddled up in one corner of the back seat, breathing heavily through nostrils which he kept opening and closing.

"Will you talk to them please?" she said in an undertone.

"Troof-troof! Mlaargh!" Mvhu grunted aggressively, opening the enormous cave of his mouth.

"Oh Christ, I'm going to be murdered," the wife of the metall-urgist whimpered.

"I reckon you could give it a try," George Crompton said sourly, "if you've a driver's arse you should be able to get her up to the top. Are you scared? If you are then I'll drive. Come on..."

Pforzheim pushed the red-headed PR Man back into his seat.

"Don't give me all that bullshit George. I can drive you off the road any day of the week."

The Jaguar crept forward, inching along the road in bottom gear. The wife of the metallurgist stared out of the window on to the moon-lit bush, thinking that it was probably her last sight of the earth, of the big world which was out there. As the speedometer mounted to 5 m.p.h., George Crompton had another bout of somnia, Leonard was collected into the arms of Morpheus and Mvhu slipped away into a land of herbivorous dreams. Pforzheim was not far behind them, his dark, handsome features unruffled as he thought about the fun he was going to have with the wife of the metallurgist when he got her back to Mufunsi in four hours time at this rate of travel.

The car nosed its way off the road and ploughed slowly into the bush. For several minutes it bounced along, headlights carving a bright path through the trees. The wife of the metallurgist tried to take the steering-wheel off the sleeping Pforzheim but his grip was secure. The car went over an ant-hill and his foot was dislodged from its timid pressure on the accelerator and the gear was jolted out of position, returning to neutral.

The Jaguar stopped.

Opening the door, the wife of the metallurgist looked behind. The car's path was visible, written over the disturbed bush. She ran back towards the road and civilisation, hoping to stop a passing vehicle.

Then all was quiet, the only sound being that of the big engine ticking over, drinking up the petrol, the barrage of lamps assisting the moon in illuminating the Dark Continent and running the battery flat.

Four dreams floated in four brains in the steel shell of the car, all stimulated by the golden glee-maker, the smiling spice, the happy hemp herb. Around them slumbered the Earth, the source of all the merriment they had swallowed, the giver of goodness and poisons, the rich and bountiful mother. Like four chicks in an incubator, the four young white men slumbered, the cold of the night kept at bay by a quarter-inch of steel and plastic, the warmth of the day yellow as the yolk of the egg they were hatching from. Oh what dreams wended from that steely womb!

Leonard was a traveller.

He dreamed a travelling dream.

With leaps like rainbows he sprang from his house-boat on a lake in Kashmir, to the first A-Bomb test on Christmas Island, to a fruit-farm in California, to Bahrein where he had been a chemist with an oil company, to the British South Africa Police barracks in Salisbury where he had been a trooper. He was alone in his hop-step-jump, hurdling Mankind, skimming over their ant-heads. If he ever tumbled from the sky they would tie him down like Gulliver and light bonfires in the inflammable acres of his crutch.

They would hurt him.

Men hurt him. Women had hurt him. He was a crypto-fascist and in his dream he strode through the clouds with a black flag honouring himself. Yet he was a man of warm heart! Had boundless enthusiasm! His mind bubbled with invention! He could be socialist, democrat, humanist, republican, fascist, don't-know, changing his political complexion as he strode from country to country, legging it round the globe. He was a chameleon now, a fire lizard in the sky, hedge-hopping Iron Curtains, Walls of China, oceans, mountain ranges! O sky-lizard, came the cries from below as the ants waited for the sticky lash of his tongue and death in his digestion, the world is thy leaf!

In Russia the chameleon is red, the ants sang.

In Britain it is blue.

In Ireland it is green and orange.

In Scotland it is tartan.

In America it is striped.

The chameleon is all things to all man.

It is a believer in survival.

But in Africa, here where it is feared, the chameleon is known as the *hamba-gashli*, the go-slowly. It creeps, rocks to and fro, speed one inch a day.

Go-slowly Leonard. *Hamba-gashli* Leonard.

This many-coloured Welshman was one of the creatures of God, a Methodist tool of the Almighty. His pigments came and went with eve and morn. There in his dreams he sat, scuttled and sunned himself between God's toes. Around him gambolled all the fowls of the air and the beasts of the field and forest, strutting, pecking, grunting.

"It is time to call in all Men for the washing of their skins!" God announced from thousands of feet in the air. "Here, in the Pond of Musungu!"

Leonard *Hamba-Gashli* the Chameleon quivered down to the end of his tail with anticipation. God was going to make use of him. He was going to be a divine instrument!

"*Ingwe*, the Cheetah, go to the Men of the North-West in their cloudy islands, to the Men of Europe, and tell them to come here to be washed. *Hamba!*"

The Cheetah sprang away from the feet of God and raced across the world.

"*Kalulu*, the Hare, go to the Men of the Orient in their jungles and green hills, to the Men of Asia, and tell them to come here to be washed. *Hamba!*"

The Hare leaped in the air and was gone, his feet thudding like a thousand drums.

"*Nayati*, the Buffalo, go to the Men of the West on their plains and in their river valleys, to the Indians of America, and tell them to come here to be washed. *Hamba!*"

The Buffalo heaved himself up and lumbered off towards the horizon.

A pause. God was silent. Then came the thunder and the white smoke from his beard of clouds.

"Leonard, the *Hamba-Gashli*, the Chameleon, go to the Men of Africa who live here, not far from the Pond of Musungu, and tell them to come and be washed. *Hamba!*"

With joy in his heart, Leonard started to rock and shift forward, hairsbreadth by hairsbreadth, changing colour to a beautiful gold to show how pleased he was that God had noticed him.

On the first day he travelled the length of a man's foot.

In a week he had travelled the length of a man lying on the ground.

In a year he had covered the distance a man can walk in an hour.

Ingwe, the Cheetah was the fastest, and he returned with all the Men of the North-West, the Men of Europe. At that time they were black, straight out of the sun's furnace. God washed them white. Each man stood in the Pond of Musungu and the darkness was cleansed from his skin. God did a good job, rubbing and scrubbing. The level of the Pond went down, and the water became slightly dirty.

Kalulu, the Hare was the second fastest, and he returned with all the Men of the Orient. God washed them from their blackness as well, but was a bit more sparing with the water, which was already discoloured. So the Men of the Orient came out yellow.

Nayati, the Buffalo was the third fastest, and he returned with the Men of the West, with all the Indians of America. When God washed them the water was only up to their waists, and very dirty. He could only use a few handfuls for each man. So the Men of the Americas came out red.

Then God waited beside the black, low pool. For years he waited. The sun shone down on the water and evaporated it. God became tired of waiting.

After a hundred years, Leonard, the *Hamba-Gashli*, the Chameleon, came back with the Men of Africa. He found God in a poor temper and the Pool of Musungu dry.

"Where have you been Leonard?" God demanded.

"About your business God," Leonard replied, very humbly.

"You've taken your time about it!" God thundered angrily. "These men cannot be washed now. They must stay like they are, black as the day I first made them!"

Then the Men of Africa turned and beat Leonard for being so slow in the execution of his duty. They snatched up sticks and flogged his scales until he was changing colours like a kaleidoscope.

"Black bastards!" Leonard muttered in his sleep. "Don't take it out on me!"

In his dream he thought God had done it deliberately, sent him to the Men of Africa so they would be last at the Pool of Musungu.

God was a swindler.

Leonard was a scapegoat.

The black waters of the Kashmir lake.

The white cloudy beard of God on Christmas Island, the face-fungus.

The blackened rotten fruit of the Californian fruit-farm.

The black oil of Bahrein, spouting like blood, or semen.

The white horses of the British South Africa Police.

Leonard, the *Hamba-Gashli*, the only Chameleon who could change from pure white to pure black.

A chequered reptile.

Crompton was a public school boy.

His education had been of the best.

In his dream he was back at school with an enormous *umfazi* who was naked and handcuffed to him. The woman adored her gaoler and linked his arm as the tall, red-headed PR Man walked down those familiar cold corridors to the Headmaster's study. Crompton was thirty-five now but he quaked in his expensive hand-cut Italian shoes as he heard the Headmaster shouting "Come!" What would he think of Crompton's companion? Would he approve? Returning after the hols to join 3B was all very well but would matron object to his eighteen stone bedmate? What would the chaps do when they saw her?

"Well Crompton?" the Head asked dryly as the PR Man stood before him. "How are your mother and father?"

"Both dead sir," replied the red-haired scholar, conscious of the tugging at his wrist as the black woman bent over and presented her bare arse to the Head.

"Brother George and Sister Florence?"

"Died in infancy sir."

"How far are you going to throw the javelin this sports day Crompton?"

"This is a friend of mine sir."

"No keeping squirrels in the airing-cupboard this term eh boy? Don't want to have to flog you again."

"This is Hyacinth sir, my wife."

The Head reached over and drove a pair of compasses into Hyacinth's left buttock and she went down like a balloon.

By the time Crompton got outside he was trailing a black skin at his side which was all that was left of Hyacinth. He saw the green cricket square, roped off and sacred. He saw the rugby posts pointing at the heavens. Then he dropped to his knees on the lawn and started saying his prayers. The Head's window opened.

"Don't kneel on the grass or I will have to flog you Crompton."

The PR Man got to his feet, then noticed that the handcuffs had turned black, then his hand, then his forearm.

"Have you been masturbating again Crompton?" the Head demanded to know, swishing his cane. "Have you been demonstrating to the younger boys again?"

"I never do that sir," Crompton replied stoutly as his shoulder turned ink-black. "I have my dreams instead."

132

When Crompton was black from head to foot the Head climbed over his window-sill and took him to the meteorological enclosure where he bent the mature student over the rainfall tank and beat him.

As each stroke fell across Crompton's buttocks the welt was white.

Steadily the Head beat Crompton all over from head to toe.

Then he was white again but burning with pain.

He was a pale pillar of suffering.

He cried out.

He ground his teeth.

The Head went into the centre of the cricket square, tucked up his gown and knelt down to pray. As he prayed a black cloud issued from his ears and ascended into the air. It became Hyacinth and she was standing on the Head's shoulders. When he stood up she sat on him piggy-back.

"This is the new matron Crompton," the Head said as he cantered past.

Crompton wept and the tears ran down his chin.

As they ran they washed away the whiteness.

George Crompton was black underneath.

He was infra dig.

Infra red.

Infra hard time.

Pforzheim was spoilt.

He had always had his own way.

Except in his dreams.

His father could never find a way to buy him dreams.

So he had an unbuyable morepreciousthangold dream.

His half of the racehorse was in the ring ten minutes before the off. The rear-quarters of the animal had been curry-combed until they shone and the tail was bobbed. The two hooves had been taped with white. The front half — which belonged to someone else — was Pforzheim's father. Dressed in his usual light-grey suit, dark hair brushed away from his highly polished temples, smoking a meerschaum pipe, his Dad was the front of a new centaur. As the centaur walked round the ring a queue of bookmakers approached its anus and whispered questions.

"How will Scots Canadian like drawing number 4?"

"What's that tobacco you're smoking?"

"Would you accept a kaffir jockey?"

"Every horse in this race is being pulled. How will the race ever finish then?"

The centaur answered each question with a puff of tobacco-smoke which swirled into a reply in a strange incomprehensible language. The bookies reached up and snatched their smoky answers out of the air and put them in their satchels, then returned to their stands.

The centaur became favourite at 4-5 on.

Pforzheim took a bundle of notes out of his pocket and went and punted his Dad to win his half of a racehorse second. He was on to a sure thing. His half of a racehorse was 12-1, nearly an outsider. Dad was sure to win because he always won. If he was first at the tape then the half of a racehorse had to be second.

He watched the centaur trot up the field to the starting-gates. Dad's tie streaming in the breeze. The loudspeaker crackled into life.

"David Pforzheim to saddle his father!" it boomed.

He was driven up to the starting-gates. Dad had already saddled himself and was patting the leather.

"Jump up son and let's get on with it," he said smilingly, "it's nice for us to actually spend our leisure time together."

From the anus of his half of a racehorse came a raspberry.

The gates flew open and Pforzheim's Dad was first out, the bit hanging on his bottom lip. David Pforzheim was afraid to hurt his father's mouth.

"Ride me!" Dad yelled as he rounded the first bend, "don't give me my head! Ride me like I've never ridden you! Giddiap!"

Round and round the track they galloped, the bit still dangling, the reins slack. David Pforzheim hung on his father's neck and asked him to stop. Nothing could halt the old man. With a toss of his dark hair he thrust his neck forward. The winning-post was in sight.

On the final straight David Pforzheim looked over his shoulder and saw his half of a racehorse disengaging itself from his father. When it was free of the parent body it swerved to the outside, white-taped hooves drumming the hard earth, then high-stepped past in a burst of power to win, its bobbed tail bumping over its oracle anus.

He had lost a fortune.

His Dad would not pay his gambling debts this time.

His half of a racehorse did a victory lap singing:

> "Doo-da, doo-da,
> I'll bet mah money on de bob-tailed nag
> Somebody bet on de bay!"

Mvhu's dream was an action dream. It was not mindless.

He stood in all his hippopotamorphic grandeur atop a hill, the sun basting his round-ribbed sides, front hooves firmly planted on a rock, sniffing the desert breeze through his cavernous nostrils. On his back, riding with no saddle or rein, was Chief Crazy Horse, war chief of the Oglala Sioux. The red man carried a rifle and had one fish-eagle feather in his hair.

Below them toiled the waggon-train.

Ox-waggons.

Voortrekers.

Gaunt, buff herbivorous brothers heaving under the sting of the *sjambocks*, lashed to the *disselbooms*, only with prickly desert melons for water. The Boers sat in the driving seats, broad-brimmed hats over their eyes, reading bibles four feet square. When they spoke to Mvhu's brothers, the straining oxen who could only do 4 m.p.h., they only used curses and foul language. On the sides of the waggons were painted gigantic words.

The first waggon said CRUMPLEDCOCK

The second said CANARYCOCK

The third said SADCOCK

The fourth said KAFFIRCOCK

And so it went on, all along the line.

The dust of the column stretched back for miles.

Mvhu stamped his front hooves and Chief Crazy Horse patted his restless, fiery steed. He felt the strength vibrating through the great barrel of his mount and thoughtfully sucked the muzzle of his rifle.

The waggons made a *laager*, a giant O.

Then they broke up and made a word in the desert.

HIPPOPOTACOCK.

Mvhu broke into a gallop, his rider clinging hold of his little piggy ears. As they charged the laagered waggons in their HIPPOPOTACOCK the Boers started firing their guns. Mvhu felt the bullets going into his body then going out the other side. He knew no pain nor lost a drop of blood. The slugs merely tickled.

"Hopo-hook-ahay!" shouted Chief Crazy Horse, "let's go!"

"Jooslbrawnlaff!" roared Mvhu through his Mersey Tunnel of a mouth.

"Christ almighty, a red kaffir!" Hammerkop shrieked from behind a wheel of a waggon in the second P.

135

As Mvhu smashed into the first waggon it turned into dirty water and Mvhu sank with his master. Chief Crazy Horse put his tongue down the muzzle of his rifle to keep it dry. Slowly he consumed the gun, inch by inch, while Mvhu grazed on the thick green weed on the bed of the river. Chief Crazy Horse dismounted and sat on his haunches looking up at the light on the surface.

He liked Mvhu's home.

Even his fish-eagle feather kept its perkiness.

The Boers were lying on their bellies drinking from the pool and looking down into the depths.

Hammerkop saw Chief Crazy Horse in the slowly-waving weeds and the way the light transmogrified the North American hero.

"Fuck me!" he gasped in astonishment. "A green kaffir."

Mvhu continued with his massive subaquatic salad.

Chief Crazy Horse just smiled.

They had won the day.

THIRTEEN PETIT DÉJEUNER SUR L'HERBE

"Dad! Dad!" screamed Pforzheim as he woke up with his head jammed in the steering-wheel, "save me!"

"Get out!" Crompton snarled, lashing out as he always did when suddenly roused from slumber. "I'll kill the next intruder!"

"Oof!" groaned Leonard as Crompton's kick twanged his early-morning erection and ruined his second dream of the night, an erotic fantasy about Esquimaux, "that's lost that one."

Mvhu opened the car door on his side and eased himself down into the long, dew-freshened grass. In the echoing amphitheatre of his hippopotamind the cries of his frightened friends did not register. While they ran about in the clearing, Mvhu rolled in the high pasture and snuffled the moisture off the seed-heads of the grasses. But slowly his manself was returning and by the time a pale-faced Pforzheim sat down next to Mvhu, rubbing his stiff neck and chattering hysterically, the man and his beast were co-existent.

"Leonard must have been driving my car," he chuckled, "I'd never make a mistake like this. It's a good job it's not damaged because if it had been my Dad would have sued you for every penny you've got."

"We're lost," Crompton said, "we're lost."

"We can follow our trail," Leonard shouted from across the clearing where he had drifted to nurse his gyrating gonads which had been building up to a spectacular conclusion to his Arctic dream.

But there was no trail.

All the bushes had sprung back, the grass had raised itself in the dew.

Pforzheim sulked at the foot of a tree, remembering how he'd lost a night in the schedule with the wife of the metallurgist.

"The sun roses in the east."

Mvhu looked closely at George Crompton. The PR Man was staring at the sky and waving towards the dawn. Again and again he sawed his hand through the air declaring that the sun roses in the east.

"Well? What are we going to do?" Mvhu asked. "We can't sit here all day."

"Christ, I'm hungry," Pforzheim murmured beating at his stomach, "even though I've got a lousy taste in my mouth. Tell you what. We'll drive back."

He got in the car and tried the ignition.

The starter did not attempt to turn the engine.

"The sun roses in the east," Crompton repeated in a religious drone.

"George, we don't even know what side of the road we left on. We could be anywhere. We've got no bearings. If we make a mistake we could walk for a thousand miles without finding civilisation."

Leonard's reasoning had no effect on Crompton. Getting down on his hands and knees he worshipped the sun as it continued to roses in the east. He would follow it wheresoe'er it went.

There was a long pause as they thought.

Mvhu was so happy in his new animalself that he was certain they would be able to find their way back to the brown Christmas tree by scent.

Pforzheim started crying.

Then they heard the singing.

"We could die here!" Pforzheim blubbered, "and I'll never make up for last night. She'll be asking someone else to show her that big world out there and George and I will lose out."

The singing came from the bush and through the trees Mvhu could see a flash of white, pink, gold, then a fluttering. The song was plaintive but it had a fine peasant boisterousness beneath the melancholy.

Nakumanye nshimu,
Kumutenge mushitwililia,
Mwenda nakapula enda nkape,
Naangeni ibala.

were the words, and they were rendered with an affectionate candour which cannot be found in many trained voices. As the crone and the old man came through the trees, Mvhu could see that another chicken was being plucked and the cow-dung fire was still alight in the old man's overcoat. Between them, a pale arm over each of their shoulders, was the wife of the metallurgist. She was singing an English translation of the ancient Bemba lyric. The crone had thought that it would help the double-helping courtesan to keep going over the rough country.

I have seen bees
On the roof where I work.
A beggar carries a
Container. Show me the field.

As the trio swung into the clearing Pforzheim flung himself on to the old man's shoulder, crying out with relief. The old man patted the spoilt son of the successful solicitor and carefully put his smouldering overcoat on the ground.

"There, there now," crooned the crone as Pforzheim clasped her withered hand and pressed it to his lips, "did you poor *musungu* children think that you were done for?"

"Yes Mother," Pforzheim gabbled, "oh I'm so glad you came by."

"You see how much notice he takes of me!" sniffed the wife of the metallurgist as she sat down next to the cow-dung fire and warmed her hands. "I spend a night in the bush, easy prey to lions or black spiders, and what kind of a reception do I get? I might as well have died for all he cares."

The crone cradled Pforzheim's head in her lap and rocked to and fro while plucking the white chicken over his dark head so soft feathers drifted on to his weeping handsomeness.

"He's a bit highly-strung my dear. The wealthy interbreed too much as you know. He'll be all right in a minute or two."

Crompton saw his love, the gold-haired nymph of wood and water. Strolling over to where the wife of the metallurgist was sitting he informed her that the sun roses in the east.

"Leave me alone!" she answered with hostility. "I'm disgusted with the way you and David have treated me recently. Hermione can have you and next time she does a bit of art-work along your spine I hope she uses a pneumatic drill."

Only Mvhu was happy among the four young white men gathered round the cow-dung fire. When the chicken was thrown on to the glowing lumps of ordure he smiled and remembered the great journey he had made during the hours of darkness. His mouth never stopped smiling and his heart was filled with peace.

The crone's red eye latched on to Mvhu from beneath her head-turban.

"Funny place to park," she said mildly.

"We fell asleep on the way back from Musangati," Mvhu explained.

"We lost a lot of business last night," the old man grumbled. "When you all ran off we were just getting ready to serve up the first batch of Doctor Sanders' Original Recipe Kentucky Fried Chicken. We had to eat it all ourselves. If the Staff Officer of Mufunsi Mine hadn't stopped by we would never have finished it. She's got a wonderful appetite."

Leonard blanched as the first leg was torn off the chicken and thrust under his nose. He remembered the gecko of last night, and the fact that birds are only reptiles that have evolved into airspace.

"Come on sonny!" piped the crone cantankerously, "Hammerkop isn't the only one who knows how to run a *braaivleis*."

The old man nodded and put a long arm round Crompton's shoulders.

"You'll feel better once you get some breakfast inside you," he said, giving the PR Man a comradely hug.

"It was a good job you came along Mother," Pforzheim sighed with relief as the crone wiped away his tears with the tattered sleeve of her reeking wrap-around cloak. "God knows what would have happened to us if we'd been left out here. We could have died of exposure, gone mad...anything. Now you can direct us home. You know the way."

The crone screwed up her one red eye until it burned like Mars in the battered night of her face.

"Yes, we can show you the way. We know where we're going which is more than can be said for you poor white children. We can guide you past the terrible hairs of the buffalo-bean, over the sleeping snake in the sun. We can rest you in the shade of the *mufundwelamba* tree, or put you in the eye of '*Nkwazi*, the fish-eagle, our national bird. Where hunger begins and hunger ends, that's where you find

139

'*Nkwazi*, not sailing around in the sky looking for mindless entertainment. Yes, we will help you *musungu* babies back to what you call civilisation where you imagine yourself to be safe. In fact you would be safer here, sitting in the bush and trying to learn a few things, but I don't expect you to believe that, pig-ignorant as most of you are. You won't listen to reason from us old ones. When it comes to self-knowledge you Europeans are at the bottom of the league. Now eat up your breakfast and we'll be on our way. By the great king Christ you lot make me wonder sometimes.''

Mvhu accepted a leg of chicken and munched it thoughtfully. As the blood and grease ran down his chin and his molars ground away at the half-cooked meat, he considered the old lady's words.

There was a lot in what she had said.

But he thought that the crone had deferred slightly to him – just a nod of the head, a red twinkle of her eye. She had not included him with the others.

FOURTEEN SQUASH

After a four-hour trek through the bush they arrived on the outskirts of Mufunsi and said good-bye to Peripatetic Barbecues Ltd. As Pforzheim's house was in a nearby suburb they headed in that direction and arrived in the early afternoon, footsore, hot and weary. Pforzheim's father had provided him with an Olympic-size swimming pool and cocktail-bar and by early evening they were all pleasantly drunk, especially Pforzheim. On his return he had discovered that his wife had left him for the third time that month. She had gone over to Mulongobeba to protest to his father about the affair with the wife of the metallurgist and to cadge some new dresses. Pforzheim knew that he had two days on his own before his wife came back. This was the average time that she stayed away. When she came back she would want to find the house in a terrible state, dirty dishes everywhere, signs of riot and all the living proof that Pforzheim could not live without her.

With the help of Crompton, Leonard, Mvhu and the wife of the metallurgist, also Matthias and the Bucket-Wheel Excavator Gang who came over at the end of their afternoon-shift, Pforzheim set about giving his wife what she wanted. They drank through evening, night and into the early hours, behaving like children, pulling down curtains, throwing Jacobean furniture of recent manufacture into the swimming-pool, setting fire to the kitchen and driving Moses, Pforzheim's house-servant, wild with grief. At half-past four George Crompton had a strong fit of somnia and curled up on the gravel drive. Seeing his rival unconscious, Pforzheim took the wife of the metallurgist into the master bedroom. One by one the Undesirables fell asleep, leaving Moses in tears beside his blackened four-plate and eye-level grill electric stove.

When Mvhu awoke he found himself lying on a sheepskin rug in Pforzheim's living-room, having his face licked by a pedigree Springer spaniel and a Basset hound which Pforzheim's father had had sent out for his son from England. Pushing the animals away, Mvhu got groggily to his feet, noticing how his brain still sang with alcohol. In an imitation Queen Anne commode across the room snored Pyper, his notebook hanging open with a scribbled account of how Pforzheim's wife had broken the Zonkendawon record by leaving her husband 57 times in two years. Beneath a bougainvillaea bush which encroached on the stoep, rumbled Matthias, his hand down his overalls. The whole of the Bucket-Wheel Excavator Gang were in the *kaya* at the back where the nanny for Pforzheim's children lived, and Leonard slept in a narrow gap between the filtration tank and a pile of beer crates. The patch of gravel where Crompton had fallen after his attack of somnia was now empty. As Mvhu walked over the lawn he thought he understood why as voices reached him from the open windows of the master bedroom.

"But he told me that you had said he was the best..."

"I never said any such thing..."

"And he told me that you had said I wasn't bad but that he was much better..."

"That's not true. I've always said you were about the same."

"The same!"

"Christ! Be reasonable! The same!"

"Look, I don't want to start any kind of disagreement. What the hell does it matter? We're all here aren't we?"

"Well, I'm not sure about this kind of arrangement. It's not exactly what I visualised."

"It's the logical solution isn't it? What else can we do?"

"Has he been telling you things about me?"

"No..."

141

"Are you sure. Hasn't he suggested that I've got bad breath?"

"Oh shut up and stop being ridiculous. If you've got bad breath you've got bad breath. If I objected to something like that I'd say so...no David, wait until this is sorted out...George! Stop that at once!"

"He puts me off."

"Stop looking at me like that."

"God, will you sort yourselves out!"

"Can't you move your feet over?"

"Get your elbow out of my ear!"

"What's that on your back George?"

Giggles and manly laughter. Groans from George Crompton. The sound of a door slamming, then a shower.

"I liked that dove with the olive branch in its beak."

"The heifer was good. She's not up to much on hands though. Did you notice St. Francis' hands. They were out of proportion."

"I don't think this is fair David. George is at a disadvantage."

Silence.

"You know we have an agreement."

More silence.

"You know, you are better than George but don't tell him I said so will you?" Then the wife of the metallurgist sighed and yelled, and yelled and sighed, punctuating her cries with shouts of "There's a big world out there and I want some of it!"

Mvhu walked down to the edge of the garden. The house was on the first fringes of the bush and looked down a short slope to a stream. Light mist hovered over the surface and a group of African children roamed through the long grasses and reeds. He could hear their chatter as though they were a flock of birds. They saw him standing in the garden and waved. He waved back, his head spining. Suddenly he became conscious of the fact that he was ruining his health, deliberately running himself into the ground through boozing. For what? Insights? Secrets? What would he see if he was always blind-drunk?

Standing stiff-backed he started doing deep-breathing exercises and then touched his toes, driving the stink of beer and brandy out of his lungs like a draught from bellows.

"Trying to get fit?"

It was Pforzheim in a silk dressing-gown that was covered in green and gold dragons.

"Just a bit shaky this morning."

Pforzheim cocked a leg over the window-sill and stepped out on to the lawn.

"You've got a weight problem. Do you play squash?"

"I have played."

"We'll have a game this morning. I'll beat you. I'm the best player in Mufunsi."

The wife of the metallurgist appeared in the window, her large grey eyes bold with the morning light. Although she was a little wan, yawning and stretching her slender girl's body, there was enough in her womanliness to convince Mvhu that she was the kind of person that agreements, treaties and contracts needed to be drawn up about. She smiled at the dazed, bewildered man who was relishing her fine pointed breasts with his green eyes.

"Good morning."

"Good morning."

"I think we might arrange a tripartite pact to include you," she mused while putting a hand on a roundly curved hip.

Hurriedly Pforzheim steered Mvhu towards a guava tree and forced him to disengage his eyes from the vision in the window and her deep smile.

"Wouldn't be practical at all. It's bad enough with two of us. Look, have a swim, we'll get some breakfast down us, then we'll go down to the squash club and I'll beat you to pulp. Okay?"

"All right," Mvhu replied slowly while casting a furtive glance over his shoulder to the solemnly voluptuous nymph in the window who was just being dragged away by a pair of RP Man's soft, un-blistered hands.

They all breakfasted together on the stoep after Moses had been dragged out of the pantry where he had locked himself upon hearing screams and laughter coming from the garden. Thinking that it was the Youth Brigade of the Progress Party come to take him to another tedious meeting, or the beginning of the revolution promised by the southern rebels, the old servant had taken steps to assure the safety of the bwana's food and was working his way through a sugar and salad cream doorstep sandwich when Pforzheim found him and told him not to worry as what he had heard was only the Bucket-Wheel Excavator Gang waking up with the traditional pressure of blood in the genital organs and taking it out on the nanny.

After breakfast everyone sat down for a while and waited for the eleven o'clock horrors. Once they had passed away the Undesirables drove into Mufunsi and made their way to the squash club. The idea of Mvhu playing squash was amusing in itself – a hippopotamus playing a game designed for whippets – and there was a bar to steady shrinking and dehydrated nerve ends. But at the club the party of red-eyed, reeking men encountered an obstacle. The bar was full of European mineworkers, and as Matthias puffed up, on these men there fell an icy silence. They stared at the African as if he had just crept out of the nearest dustbin.

"Is he a member?" someone said from the other end of the bar.

Mvhu ignored the question and chose a racquet to hire from the rack.

"I'm on the committee here. I said is he a member?"

Pforzheim looked down the bar at the tall, broad-shouldered, narrow-waisted, blond, frank blue-eyed young man with the accent of the English Dominant Hundred Thousand in his clear bray.

"Who's he? I'm a he, he's a he. So who's he?"

"The chap in the dirty overalls."

"He's my guest," Pforzheim said coolly. "I'm a member."

"What about the others?"

"They're all my guests."

"You can only have one guest at a time, it says so in the rules."

"Fuck the rules," Pforzheim drawled, "and fuck you too you chinless wonder."

Sweeping the visitor's book up off the counter Pforzheim began signing everyone in.

The young man with a straight nose and small neat nostrils on either side whose eyebrows met in the middle, made a grab for the book but drew back his hand as Pforzheim aimed a savage karate chop at his wrist.

"You can't sign that many in!"

"Report me to the committee."

"I will. And another thing. There's no provision in the constitution for non-Europeans to be members or guests. We're still talking about it I understand. Nothing's been decided."

"Christ, what a tribe of lame-brained wankers you bastards must be! The country's been independent for long enough! You can't still keep the old en stroke ens out of here! What is this? A Durban knocking-shop or a squash-club? I reckon you bastards are so

144

slow-witted it takes you a week and a half to decide whether to shit yourselves or not!"

The young man with the supple smooth body and moderately hairy chest flung up his head and gave Pyper the benefit of his frank blue eyes.

"We'll have no more of the kind of language in here if you don't mind! That African must leave! Now get him out of here!"

An angry murmur came from the other mineworkers. They were solidly behind the dynamic, thrustful and resourceful young Englishman. No kaffir government was going to dictate their club membership to them. This was one of their last havens along with the Dutch Deformed Church, the Jukskei Club and the British Empire Service League.

Matthias shrugged and fixed the young man with a look of dumb loathing, then headed for the stairs. Pforzheim and Crompton stopped him.

"Where are you going Matthias?" they asked in kindly tones.

"For some fresh air."

"There's air in here,"

"It's not worth the trouble."

Pforzheim brought Matthias back to the middle of his knot of friends. His spoilt features crinkled into a smile, a friendly smile.

"How long do you think it will be before they appoint you as chairman of the board of Mufunsi Mines Limited?" He enquired casually.

Matthias frowned and rubbed at his broad nose.

"Oh, about six months."

"Hmm, six months? So long?"

"What salary are you expecting?" Pyper squawked.

"Ten, twelve thousand, plus the usual perks."

"Any white women you fancy in particular? Just point them out and we'll lay it on for you."

"I'll lay it on for myself thanks John."

"Will you be a member of the Dutch Deformed Church Matthias," George Crompton asked. "They're a very evangelical group you know."

"I think I'll be their archbishop."

"There's a vacancy for a new captain of the darts team at the British Empire Service League," Albert Lewis said from the top of the stairs, his arms full of application-for-membership forms. "You should apply."

"Sounds just up my street. I'm number one man in the Open Pit

145

Assegai team anyway," Matthias shrugged expressively. "I'm the natural choice."

An old surveyor who had been sitting on a bar-stool near the one-armed bandit broke the terrible silence. With a groan he toppled off his perch and fell to the ground, quite dead. His blanched face and staring, horrified eyes triggered off shock reactions from all the other mineworkers. They staggered about holding their heads in aghast rage. They groped for red raving words to shout and exclaim their agonised disgust. Their minds were numbed by what they had seen. Two geologists were violently sick in an ice-bucket. A mine-captain knelt by the juke-box and prayed. A shift-boss tried to climb out of the window to commit suicide on the concrete car-park below. Above the uproar rose one voice: it had authority as well as adroitness and ambidexterity.

"All right! All right! Cool down! Don't let them see that they've upset you. You're just playing into their hands!"

"What about old Hendrik here?" raged a demented Cave-Scraper-man. "Look at the poor bugger! They've killed him. The filthy kaffir-loving bastards have killed the vice-president of the club!"

"Try proving that to the Zonkendawon police," Pforzheim said nastily. "Now settle down and we can get on with our game. We came to play squash not to get into political arguments."

"You think you're pretty damn good don't you?" said the tireless and thrustful young English hero. "I should think you play squash in about the same way as you behave. Ignorantly. Brutishly. And uncouthly."

Pforzheim tapped the tense strings of his racquet on his palm.

"I could take you apart any day you short-arsed cretin."

The young man smiled as his supporters began shouting for him to take the kaffir-boetie to the cleaners.

"Well? Want a game?" Pforzheim sneered. "You've got a big enough supporters club."

"Yes, I think we might manage that."

"I'll beat you. You'll look like a beginner."

"Will I?"

"I'm a shit-hot player. Watch my forehand. Wristy."

"We'll see."

"Want a bet Carruthers?"

"Why not? And my name isn't Carruthers."

"Twenty K? All right? What is your name then you bow-legged lounge lizard."

The young man slicked a quiff of blond hair from his forehead.

"Hurl Halfcock."

In the thunderous pause there were a few giggles from a couple of mineworkers who had not heard the name before.

"What did he say?" Albert whispered incredulously.

"I said Hurl Halfcock."

Mvhu steadied himself against the bar. Until the young man had announced his name, Mvhu had been suffering a resurgence of the eleven o'clock horrors, a sensation very close to the preliminaries of death. His gorge was full, his stomach in a queasy whirl, sweat pouring from his skin, and his hold on the real world had been very tenuous. When he heard the words that had crucified his spirit for so long coming from the mouth of their tormentor, it had been like a slap in the face. All the trembling subsided. His bones straightened.

"Where do you come from?" Mvhu asked stonily.

"Epsom originally."

"There are no Halfcocks in Epsom. It's a Liverpool family."

"Well, thereby hangs a tale old man. You see Hurl Halfcock has only been my name for a day."

A buzz of amazement rose from the Undesirables and the mineworkers.

"Why did you change your name to Hurl Halfcock?" Mvhu continued in his cold voice.

"It was a condition of employment."

"What is your employment?"

"I'm the Industrial Relations Officer of the Open Pit."

"Oh no, I'm the Industrial Relations Officer of the Open Pit."

The young man raised his eyebrows.

"Oh, so you're the one the Open Pit Manager is so anxious to get rid of? I think you'll find you're out of work old son."

"Don't call me old son."

"You must have made yourself pretty unpopular in a short space of time . . ."

"You know why Hammerkop made you change your name?"

"Because he had been forced to give an undertaking that Hurl Halfcock would be the Industrial Relations Officer of the Open Pit."

"That's right. You're a real gentleman aren't you? Is there anything you wouldn't do to get a job?"

"I wouldn't kiss an African's boots."

"But you'd kiss Hammerkop's arse."

Mvhu threw open the door that led down to the changing-rooms and pointed down the stairs with his racquet.

"Get down there Hurl Halfcock. You're playing me. And we'll change the bet."

"With pleasure," the young man said airily, "what would you like to stake on the outcome?"

"My life," Mvhu responded grimly, "my life!"

In white, white, between white walls, Mvhu and Hurl Halfcock thrashed the little black ball around in a surly, grudging warm-up. Both men were silent as they shuffled round the harshly white cube, sizing each other up, trying to spot a weakness or a blind spot. Mvhu noticed that Hurl Halfcock was quick on his feet and had a mastery of backhand and forehand. He could not help but be impressed with the young man's admirable physique, his own heaviness comparing unfavourably. After a minute of warm-up Mvhu found himself breathless but he knew that deep in the bowels of his anger there was a reservoir of power. He would burn up every ounce of energy in his big body and leave himself empty, or dead, rather than lose this match.

"Ready?" Hurl Halfcock lifted one side of his lip and twirled his racquet. "Rough or smooth?"

"Rough."

"Smooth it is. I serve."

Hurl Halfcock's first serve was an ace. It flew with rocketing force against the back wall then arched diagonally across court to Mvhu's corner where it struck the right-angle where the walls joined. Mvhu made a futile swipe at it and missed. Above him the mineworkers pounded the rail and roared with vicious laughter.

"Come on Halfcock! *Bulala* that lump of lard!"

"He's shagged already! Look at him heaving away! Christ man, there's no contest!"

Hurl Halfcock's next service whanged into the side wall and came into Mvhu's backhand. The ball lifted itself towards the red line above the tin but as soon as it struck, Hurl Halfcock was across to it, flicking it sideways into the opposite corner. Mvhu galloped across with his racquet held low to scoop it up but he was too late. The ball did a second bounce and Mvhu charged into the wall with his shoulder.

"Two love," sang Hurl Halfcock smugly.

"Christ! Come on Mvhu! You're stumbling about down there like Aunty Flo with her drawers on fire. Pull yourself together!"

148

Mvhu chased a high lob back into the corner. The ball bounced between his sprawling legs and rolled away.

"Three love!"

Another ace service flashed towards the back wall in a blur of hurtling rubber and rebounded to hit Mvhu full in the chest.

"Bit higher Halfcock and the dim bastard will swallow the next one!" shouted a comic among the mineworkers.

"Four love!"

Before Mvhu had time to rub the smart on his chest, the next serve shot past his backhand and rattled in the corner. Mvhu managed to get his racquet to it and return it to the back wall. Disdainfully Halfcock waited centre court and hammered a low shot on to the bottom line that hardly bounced up an inch and left Mvhu floundering again.

"Five love!"

Gasping for breath, near to vomiting, Mvhu lifted his eyes out of a red film. His heart was thudding in his chest. His knees felt woozy. He could hear the shouting from above and the rasp of his own breath. The ball zoomed towards him head-height. Vainly he struck at it and missed.

"Six love!"

He swallowed phlegm, gripped the towelling handle, brushed sweat out of his eyes and watched for that streaking ball. It came again, flying to the side wall. Drawing back his arm Mvhu sent it cracking back into the wall and shuffled across to command the centre. Hurl Halfcock took the rebound full-pitch and flicked it down into the corner, its velocity deadened. Mvhu lumbered forward again, but the shot was gone.

"Seven love!"

Then, with two more ace serves, Hurl Halfcock finished the first game and turned to his opponent. The big man was pale, his lips frothy with spittle, his eyes red and dull. He was dragging breath up out of his lungs while Hurl Halfocock was hardly breaking into his first sweat.

"Had enough?"

"Play on."

"You're out of condition."

"I said play on."

"You're making a fool of yourself, not that I mind. You're hardly giving me a decent game are you? You didn't win a point."

"Listen Halfcock, I'm going to beat you. Understand? I'm going to lay you low. I'm going to put you down once and for all! Now get on with the game!"

Hurl Halfcock tightened his lip and flexed his racquet.

"Well, you asked for it. You deserve everything you get after what you did up at the bar today. So damn you and all the others like you!"

His racquet flashed in a short arc and the next game began.

Mvhu missed the return by a foot.

Albert turned away. He could not watch any more. Pforzheim glared down the bar at the jubilant mineworkers, his fists balled. Matthias looked down in the mouth, aware of the comments that were directed at him from the enraged club members.

"Flog him jong! There's a black bastard up here who's breaking his heart! Get into him Pommy!"

"Now the kaffir isn't looking so cocky Halfcock! You're doing fine! We'll murder the coon when you've wrapped up his fat *chamware* down there!"

Crompton had been making practical use of the bar since the end of the first game. He could foretell the outcome with reasonable accuracy, he thought, and even though he had grown fond of Mvhu he had no intention of being involved in a punch-up on his behalf when the match had reached its inevitable conclusion. So George emptied a bottle of Scotch into a couple of pint glasses and swallowed them down, trying to bring on a bout of life-saving somnia. While the others were watching the match he spent his time dreaming about the wife of the metallurgist. If Pforzheim followed his natural love of violence there was a chance that the spoilt lad would get a severe drubbing at the hands of the mineworkers. This would keep him out of circulation for a while.

A rousing cheer came from the other Undesirables.

Mvhu had won his first point at eight points to Hurl Halfcock in the second game. But all it did was to stave off another whitewash. Hurl Halfcock took the next rally then put through an unstoppable serve to take the game at nine-one, leaving Mvhu a heaving beast, lathered in sweat and spit, leaning on his racquet. Matthias wrinkled up his nose.

"He's in bad shape, the old Mvhu."

"Christ, I reckon he's as clapped-out as the Anglican church," Pyper said regretfully. "He's losing hands down. What shall we do?"

"Let's knock a few of this lot about and piss off out of here," Pforzheim suggested. "There's no kudos to be collected here the way that obese bastard is playing."

Albert grabbed Pforzheim by the cuff and pointed.

Mvhu, feet planted securely in the centre of the court, had just swept up a forehand ball and sent it hurtling to the bottom line where it smacked into the wall with a noise like a pistol shot. Taking the serve he flailed the ball back along the red centre line, then powered Hurl Halfcock's return into the sidewall so it dropped away into the opposite corner.

Life was coming back into Mvhu.

The red mists were lifting from his eyes.

He was drawing on the burning lakes of indignation, pumping up the flaming oil.

He started to run rather than lumber, scurry rather than stumble.

"That's it Mvhu!" Albert yelled. "You've got all the shit out of your system now! Attaboy!"

Mvhu looked up. He could see the black bullet-head of Matthias behind the white rails and the beginnings of a smile on his face. His heart surged. With passion he clouted the ball into the back wall and saw it shoot through the air like a shell to explode in Hurl Halfcock's fumbled backhand. A muffed shot and the point was Mvhu's.

"Come on Mvhu! Now *vova* that clean-cut bastard until his arse is round his ankles!" shrieked Pyper. "You've got him on the run!"

"Mvhu! Mvhu!" boomed Matthias joyfully. "Get in there and win!"

"Better keep that kaffir quiet or he might get into trouble!"

Pforzheim smiled at the mineworker who had made the remark, noticing how the triumph had ebbed from the man's eyes to be replaced by a disappointed and churlish aggression. With a little luck, conditions were perfect for a splendid conclusion to the match.

The tension on the balcony mounted with each point. Mvhu took that game nine-four. Now he was completely drained of colour, his singlet sticking to his chest, his eyes manically bright. His first serve of the new game was fast and low, whipping off the back wall to kiss the side then ravel itself around Hurl Halfcock's legs. Miraculously he saved it, scooping it up in a high shot. Running forward Mvhu took it on the full-toss with an overarm smash that passed Hurl Halfcock without him seeing it.

Matthias roared with happiness and thumped the rails.

"Good old Mvhu! Give it plenty humpy!"

The mineworkers shifted a step closer to the delighted African.

A long rally followed, both men lunging around the court, white beasts panting and grunting in their white cage. Right, left, up, down flashed their racquets and the tiny ball flew in arc after arc, a black head battered, a black soul shot. They shuffled, countermoved, got in each other's way, playing the game, seeking the victory. Finally Mvhu lashed through a service that cannonaded off the back wall and hit Hurl Halfcock in the right eye. He screamed and dropped his racquet. Mvhu picked it up and thrust it back in his hand, pushed the wailing man into the opposite court and yelled "Ready?" while his opponent was still clutching at his injured eye. Clenching his teeth Hurl Halfcock tried for the ball but missed. It rolled back to Mvhu's feet and he jumped across to the other court and cracked through another service. Weeping with rage Hurl Halfcock slashed at it and hit the wood. Mvhu took an easy return and dropped a deadened ball into the corner. Hurl Halfcock wiped his eye and blinked. Mvhu could see blood on the eyeball. He smiled and belted his strongest service yet. It sang past Hurl Halfcock's ear and slapped against the wall, squashed nearly flat by the impact. Within two minutes the fourth game was over with Mvhu the winner.

It was even-stevens.

The gap between the two groups of spectators was now down to a yard. Only Pforzheim was aware of what was happening and he had no intention of warning his friends of the forthcoming battle as he feared they might run away. As Mvhu worked his way through the last game with an exhibition of wild bravura and dashing play, his voice roaring out the score, Pforzheim checked out the Undesirables. Crompton was re-charged, the Scotch and Mvhu's play having come together in an enthusiastic fusion of stimulants. Matthias was magnificently defiant, transported with victory and full of himself. Even Albert was strutting up and down the railings shaking his fist and yelling encouragement. With Pyper's nimbleness and expertise with the broken neck of a cane-for-pain bottle they stood a good chance of winning upstairs what was now being won downstairs.

The distance was down to a foot by the time Mvhu, the white monster, the hunter of the black ball, his breath harsh and deep like an express train, eyes crazed with beastly blood-lust, pounced, leapt, circled and skipped round the flagging Hurl Halfcock, his shots so hard that they were getting lost in the white fluorescent lighting. Six nil.

"Finish him off!" boomed Matthias. "Wrap him up Mvhu!"

"Hurry up Mvhu!" Pforzheim called sharply. "We've got the master-race waiting up here. They might run away."

"We won't run!" came the fierce answer. "You perverts are going to get what's coming to you win or lose."

"Who are you calling a pervert?" Pforzheim exclaimed with boyish delight. "Me?"

"And all your kaffir-loving friends!"

Pforzheim had waited patiently for this opportunity. If he had been prepared to hold on for another minute he would have seen Mvhu win the fifth match in great style, driving Hurl Halfcock to the ground. Instead this last match had to be played to the accompaniment of screams, groans, breaking glass and collapsing furniture. Albert was knocked senseless early in the fray and hung over the railings. Mvhu may even have been fired by the light in the printer's eyes as he urged himself on to his marvellous victory over himself; for glazed though the little Jew's eyes might be, they still held the answer to the mystery of love and why Man must ever defend himself against tyranny. Matthias became that black Caesar again, raised up like a black thunder-cloud over his enemies as he pounded the White Peril and laid them low. Crompton fought like a berserker, all hysteria and Scotch, his PR Man's white hands jabbing and cutting, unconscious of the blows rained upon him even though many of them were discolouring Hermione's living canvas. And within the protection of Crompton's dervish whirlings and dances danced Pyper, his familiar weapon in his hand, goosing, nailing, ripping.

In the thick, the Byronic boy, bursting with his arrogance, his righteous cause, and his spoilt boy's lust for war.

The match was over. Hurl Halfcock lay on the sprung floor of the court, his frank blue eyes desperate. Bloody, wheezing, wriggling, he tried to escape Mvhu's racquet as it flashed down again.

"No more! Please! For God's sake!"

Mvhu grinned wildly, his beast's heart big as a mountain.

"Can this be *Superman*?"

"Help! He'll murder me! Help!"

"Is this the African Aryan Uber Alles?"

"No! My father was in the Coldstream Guards!"

"Don't doubletalk me Halfcock! Take it like a Race Two with

153

trace elements of Race Three aspiring to be a Race One! Where's your stiff Upper House?"

He flogged Hurl Halfcock. The new IRO crawled away from the savage blows, dragging himself along like a wounded animal, whimpering piteously, looking up to the balcony for help. But the battle still raged. There was to be no help. Nothing. Only the big white madman pursuing him around the court, cutting and slashing.

Mvhu finally cornered Hurl Halfcock and beat him senseless. No mercy rose in his heart as the twitching, wealed body relaxed into the escape of unconsciousness. He had listened to the screams of his other self with fierce pleasure. It had been a bloody purging. Now he was in the clear.

With a final swipe at the inert loser, Mvhu sat down in the centre of the court, looked around the white cube that had contained his fight for self-knowledge, and sang with happy, deep-seated triumph.

FIFTEEN **REFLECTIONS ON THE WATER**

When the Undesirables returned to Pforzheim's house, Pyper phoned through his front-page story about racialism in sport. Pforzheim's bathroom was crowded with men trying to patch up their battered features and rubbing styptic pencil and salves on bruised knuckles in preparation for the inevitable celebrations that must follow Mvhu's victory. Pforzheim himself had reached a point of fulfilment which he had never reached before and lay on the crimson sheets of his nuptial bed while the wife of the metallurgist doctored his wounds and listened to his blow-for-blow account. Beside him lay George Crompton in the grip of a bout of somnia, his back bare except for a patch of grass and two dandelions which he had not been able to reach with the coarse towel.

"I reckon Dad would give me an extra allowance to install you here. He's a man of the world. He knows what it's like for a man to need a luxury. A mistress is almost a necessity for me. That's the kind of standard of living that I've been brought up to expect," he confided.

"What about your wife?" the wife of the metallurgist asked. "And

154

come to think of it, what about my husband?"

"Don't deliberately find problems sweetheart," Pforzheim sighed.
"Dad can fix it if I ask him."

Outside Mvhu was sitting with Matthias. Both of them were
curiously depressed in the aftermath of their triumph. It seemed to
have advanced nothing. Matthias was old enough to know that
alcoholic remorse was making its dark influence felt, backing up
the deflation. But Mvhu was struggling to understand how his nervous
system and his brain could be conspiring against him in such an
attack of satanic meanness. Surely he should feel lighter, freer, more
at home in the world? The alter-ego had been confronted and conquered.

"I don't trust myself any more Matthias. I don't understand my
own mind. I'm unpredictable, just a chemical mess. Come on, let's
get drunk."

"Ach, leave it. I'm tired of this town," Matthias grumbled. "It's
pointless to pretend that we're anything more than a gang of irresponsible piss-artists. Hammerkop lives. We get nowhere. What does
drink solve? As Doctor Mulombe says, choose! Drink and oblivion,
or me! Escape or reality! Look at the men I command. They are
poor, brainless, their mealie sacks are empty, their children pot-
bellied with malnutrition. Things stay the same. None of them try
to improve their standard of education. They do not attend Comm-
unity Development sessions. None of them are interested in the
co-operative started by Doctor Mulombe. None of them use the
voluntary savings scheme on the mine and they are forever seeking
cash-advances and unwarranted promotion to get more money for
doing less work. They have no concept of political adulthood, or
how to fully realise their rights as individuals, or the rights of their
unfortunate women and children. They are loafers and wasters,
fools, vandals and idiots. They are not worth anything. Sheer appetite.
How can Zonkendawo ever prosper with such a degenerate labour
force? We fight in the squash club to preserve their honour and their
status as free men in their own country and what do we find on our
return?"

He looked towards the nanny's *kaya* where the Bucket-Wheel
Excavator Gang could be heard shouting jovial vulgarities at each
other as the exhausted nanny was passed from hand to hand.

"Is that what we fought so gallantly for? That rubbish in there?
Where are our medals? Where is the gratitude? They were better

155

off when the bwanas had full power. At least their disgusting minds were understood. The bwanas knew them for what they were..."

"Be quiet Matthias," Mvhu urged with sudden heat.

"Why?"

"You don't mean a word of what you're saying."

"I do! The Zonkendawon working-class are drunks and bums. They don't belong in a civilised society!"

"You can't generalise like that."

"Who can't? I can! I've had to put up with them for long enough."

"You're starting to talk like Hammerkop."

"No I'm not. Hammerkop hates them because they're kaffirs. I hate them because I know what they really are. A waste of time!"

The door of the nanny's *kaya* opened and the ten members of the Bucket-Wheel Excavator Gang appeared, buttoning up their dirty overalls and laughing. Matthias watched them as they drifted across the lawn.

"See what I mean? Attila the Hun was a gentleman compared to this scum."

The Bucket-Wheel Excavator Gang greeted Matthias and gathered round him like children round the feet of a teacher. They quickly picked up the sourness of his mood and threw glances amongst themselves. They had seen their chief in this frame of mind before. As he glowered at them they smiled back, their red-freckled eyes gentle and loving. The outpouring of his silent scorn roused nothing more than stoical good humour.

"Ah Matthias, you have it on you!" one man said.

"Would you like to smoke a little magic?" asked Cumulus McCloud Molile. "You know you've got the Black Dogs again."

"Shut up!" roared Matthias. "Don't imagine you can understand me! We live in different worlds. You're all balls and taste-buds and I'm not. I care about the spirit! I care about the soul! I care about my country and its future!"

The Bucket-Wheel Excavator Gang sighed and shook their heads.

"Matthias, go to the bush. Go and meet the spirits of your ancestors. Relax. Forget us and forget Hammerkop. Have a day off with Mvhu, Albert, the Great Writer of Lies and the rest. Keep some cultured company and you'll feel better."

"What will happen?" Matthias smiled grimly. "You know as well as I do. You'll backslide. Hammerkop will use you, make fools of you."

156

Determinedly the Bucket-Wheel Excavator Gang gathered closer to their leader, their blue overalls stinking of millet-beer, their eyes gleaming through masks of grime. Cumulus McCloud Molile smiled wisely.

"Go well Matthias. You are cracking up."

"Have a break," they hummed fondly. "*Shali nippo mukwai!*"

Matthias frowned dubiously and looked around him.

"Why not?" he said eventually. "Round and round we go. If things don't improve in this sub-tropical whorehouse I can always use my Commonwealth status and emigrate to the United Kingdom."

"Oh Christ *mukwai*, what a thought!" the Bucket-Wheel Excavator Gang sang hoarsely as they shuffled off back to the nanny's *kaya* for some of her herb tea. "Our Matthias becoming a Pom bastard. No *ndita mukwai*! No thank you!"

So they shifted the celebrations into the bush.

As it was Pforzheim's birthday on the Sunday, he decided to ring up his father and ask for permission to use the family country cottage on the banks of the Kafue some thirty miles west of Mufunsi. His father agreed on the condition that his son put away the wife of the metallurgist. Pforzheim immediately agreed as she had already gone back to her husband for the day of rest. By mid-day two cars had been loaded with cool-boxes of beer, gin, brandy, whisky, rum, and Moses with cartons of food, and the Undesirables set off for The Shack, as Pforzheim called it.

When they arrived at The Shack, after a two hour journey over dirt road and bush track, they found a red-brick three-storey Georgian house in its own grounds. The white pillars of the front portico commanded the green river as it swung round in a deep bend. Pforzheim's father even had a fountain, using the silty water pumped up from the Kafue. It was a statue of a barrister in wig and gown and when the pump was turned on, foul-smelling fluid spouted from its mouth. As it was cast in copper, over the years it had oxidised until it was ambergris green. Mvhu stared at it, his subconscious recalling Chief Crazy Horse at the bottom of the river and Hammerkop's dreadful cry in his dream.

"This is what you call The Shack?" Crompton goggled.

"Dad likes to get away from it all now and then. Moses, take the *nyama* inside and put the booze in the refrigerators. And while you're at it you can take the covers off both billiard tables. We can have a game while you're making dinner."

The old servant curtsied and started untying the ropes on the roof-rack of the Jaguar while Pforzheim led his friends into The Shack. Crompton remained behind and helped Moses lug the heavy cool-boxes across to the house, muttering under his breath about the obscenity of unequal wealth.

After Moses had run all three baths, having started the oil-boiler and chased out the spiders, the Undesirables washed off the dust of the road. Then they went down to the huge billiard room where Pforzheim was chalking up the cues and placing the red balls in the wooden triangles in readiness for two games of snooker.

"Well George? You fancy yourself as a snooker player. I'll thrash you. You don't stand a chance. Want a bet?"

Crompton ran his PR Man's finger along the smooth baize. He was in an evil mood, disgusted with Pforzheim's flamboyant affluence and lack of social conscience.

"Jesus Pforzheim, you make me sick. Look at this place. You could get ten African families in here and feed the poor sods out of the garden. And it just stands here empty..."

"Don't give me that bullshit George. People in your line of business have no right to criticise money when they get paid for doing fuck all. Choose your weapon."

"You'll get your come-uppance one day you spoilt bastard!" Crompton raged as he snatched a cue from the rack.

"What's the bet George?"

"The winner gets a full week in the roster. No interference."

"Suits me."

"Let's get on with it then."

The two games of snooker started, Mvhu and Matthias playing on the other table while Pyper and Leonard ferried booze from the cocktail-bar in the corner. George Crompton was in good form. His first break was 10. His second was 14. He was potting reds like a demon, shooting in the colours like a human cannon. Pforzheim began to look worried, but he had no need. George was so angry and upset that he had ordered several pints of Scotch via Pyper and in-between shots he drank them down, oblivious of their inevitable effect. With the score at 47-6, George was lying along the side of the table, head over the cue, one leg raised to the cushion as it was a stretch-shot, when somnia struck again. His head fell forward on to the baize, his long body relaxed into sleep.

He was disqualified. After he had been rolled under the table, Pyper played a game with Pforzheim, the ivory balls clicking over Crompton's slumbering head and fiery breath until the black was potted and they all went through to dinner.

The big motor boat, its two Evinrude 70 horse-power engines bubbling quietly, purred through the grey-green murk of the Kafue crammed with human error. The fishing trip had been Pforzheim's idea but it had got off to a bad start. It was too early. The light dashed in their bleeding eyes. The stench off the water assaulted their palates. With the time at 7.45 on his watch Pyper levered the top off one of the cool-boxes and took the top off a bottle of lager.

"Anyone else want some breakfast?" he rasped.

Leonard reached across and took a bottle, his hands shaking.

"Pass one up here!" commanded the captain of the craft.

Leonard raised an eyebrow at Pforzheim who was standing at the wheel, his sailor's cap perched at a jaunty angle on his beautifully-barbered hair. When Pforzheim was given his lager he swallowed it down and clutched the empty bottle to his chest, drawing back the accelerator lever a fraction as the boat rounded a bend.

"Yah!" he shouted as the boat neared a mud-bank where two crocodiles were lying with their mouths open. "Yah! Yah!"

With an exultant whoop he watched the flying bottle bounce off the horny snout of one of the big reptiles. Grunting with rage it scuttled towards the boat to be met by two more unerringly thrown bottles which thudded into its prehistoric head. Pforzheim laughed gaily and swept the boat out of range of the enraged beast as it churned through the water after its persecutor.

"You're too slow you old moron!" the captain yelled. "You'll never catch me!"

The passengers, or crew as Pforzheim preferred to call them, groped for second bottles of lager, their trembling hands vibrating with increased intensity as they realised their plight. They were in the hands of a real Child of Nature and he was in his element. The whole river was just a skittle alley for his sporting instincts.

While they sat and tried to drink themselves into a state of reasonable self-assertion, Pforzheim continued on his destructive journey. He fetched a magnificent silhouette standing at the wheel of the boat, his paunch hanging over the front of his white shorts. Raised above them, in control, their only protection against the Wild, he affirmed his status as the expedition's leader. From childhood he had been brought up to love the wide open spaces and the *bundu*; to run with the sable and klipspringer, to hop with the jerboa rat. He could tell elephant-dung from the droppings of domestic cattle, the spoor of the crafty leopard from that of the wounded wart-hog. Now he showed them his place in the Scheme of Things; his power! Groping for his 12-bore shotgun, cocking it with one hand, he blasted grass-hoppers off long stalks as they rubbed their legs together; he blew holes in the wings of painted butterflies and soft-flying moths; he sent splattering hails of small-shot after water-beetles which scudded over the surface of the river; he shot birds of no special plumage or consequence into pitiable clouds of feathers as they passed overhead. His marksmanship was superb.

"Could you stop doing that Dave? Just for a while?"

Pforzheim looked down at Albert who had his fingers stuck in his ears.

"What's the matter Albert?"

"You're making my head ache more than it is already."

"You've got to be on your guard out here Albert, always on the alert."

"Can't we just chug along for a while until we feel better?"

Pforzheim stuck the shotgun beside the wheel and pulled back the accelerator, flogging a green spume up behind the boat.

"Fucking pansies," he muttered, "we'll see what you bastards are made of before the day's out."

So for a mile or so there was peace. Slowly the passengers came round and began to enjoy the sun as it came through the trees in green and gold, and the cool of the morning. Even the scents of the bush were losing their emetic qualities and becoming pleasurable. Sitting in the stern, Mvhu counted a row of sturdy *mubobo* trees, five serene giants of the bush, their pale green fruits hanging in the pale sun, light upon light. In this landscape with its host of unspeaking life he was beginning to feel secure, his new name merging with his mental awareness and his philosophical struggles.

"Spurwing!" Pforzheim shouted suddenly, grabbing the shotgun and prodding the passengers with its black reeking muzzles. "Look!"

He waved the gun at the sky and the passengers turned their sensi-tive eyes upwards as the big spurwing geese flew overhead and settled into an open dambo which was coming up on the left bank. Against the pale golds and leaf-shadows they had been strangely beautiful

160

and innocent, beating the new light with slow-easy wings.

"You're not going to shoot them are you Dave?" Albert asked nervously.

"Of course I'm going to shoot them!"

"You can't. They're protected!" Crompton growled.

"I've got a licence for birds. Are they birds George? Perhaps you thought they were a herd of flying bush-pigs? The D.T.s are coming your way George."

"You can't eat them," Leonard said calmly, trying to bring reason into the argument. "They're far too tough."

"The young ones aren't tough," Pforzheim muttered savagely as he broke the shotgun and thumbed two more cartridges into the breeches.

"How can you tell if they're young or old at this distance?" Crompton snorted. "Perhaps you could ask them to cruise over and fill in a form? Or hold up their hands if they're twenty-one?"

But Pforzheim was not to be stopped. True, he did have an unpleasant memory of a fire with a badly scorched carcase turning on it and himself tearing at the smouldering flesh with a pair of pliers after it had been roasting for seven and a half hours. Was that recollection to haunt all his goose-hunting days until he died? In any flock of geese there must be a distribution of ages – young, middle aged, and old. It was a gambler's chance.

Pforzheim throttled back the engines and brought the boat into a bank of reeds.

"You lot stay here. I won't be long," he instructed them as he shouldered the 12-bore.

"Dave, if we've got to shoot them, couldn't we have a go?" Albert asked, rubbing his inky palms together. "I've never been hunting."

"You'd miss Albert. You're half-blind with your glasses off."

"But Dave, I've got my glasses on."

"Look Albert, this is man's work. I've got to get out of the boat, wade through all kinds of mud and shit to get to firm ground, then crawl on my belly to where I can get a reasonable shot. It's no picnic."

"I wouldn't mind a go either," Leonard spoke up. "I'm quite a good shot."

"None of you are any good at bushcraft!" Pforzheim insisted.

"Come on Dave!" Pyper squawked. "Let your mates have a try. You've done it before. We haven't."

"Look man, there's only one gun. It's mine. And, in case you've

161

forgotten, it's my birthday."

"Christ you're spoilt!" Crompton hissed as he fumbled for the Scotch bottle in the bottom of the cool-box. "In fact you're despoilt!"

"I hope they attack you, you mean bastard!"

"I hope they peck your balls off!"

"I hope you shoot yourself!"

With these fervent messages in his ears, Pforzheim gave them all a stern look and, with his shotgun held high in one hand, vaulted athletically over the side of the boat and disappeared into twenty feet of water.

There was a long, luxurious silence and then Albert started singing *Happy Birthday*.

At this moment, Matthias woke up. He had fallen asleep under the benign influence of his breakfast and the dappling sun and all the old familiar smells of the bush. As he sat up he scratched at his groin and felt around. He was all there. It was not that he did not trust his friends but life in the village of his boyhood had taught him to always check out his equipment after a sleep in the bush. There were hungry hyenas, vultures, all the carnivores and carrion-eaters of Africa on the look-out for tasty morsels. So the habit of a quick visual check persisted. Pulling out the front of his shorts he peered down the right leg, the side he always dressed on, to see if everything was all right. It was. Purely out of interest he cast a glance down the left leg as well and saw Pforzheim surfacing.

"What's that silly bugger doing in there?" he demanded with irate concern. "Doesn't he know that it's dangerous? He could catch bilharzia."

Matthias's warning about the inimical activities of a minute water-snail which penetrates the skin and works a deadening poison into the bloodstream, was drowned by the bellowing, spitting captain who had grabbed hold of the gunwhale, having crashed the shotgun in on top of his passengers, and was now trying to haul himself aboard. The boat keeled over. The stern dipped. After some confusion and shouting, Pforzheim was firmly pushed out again as the boat was threatening to capsize.

"No sense in us all getting killed is there?" Albert called out in explanation. "Give us time to get ourselves organised. What do you think George?"

"Oh I think you're absolutely right Albert," Crompton nodded, an odd smile dimpling his cheek. "We need time to work this one out."

Roaring and spluttering, the captain tried once again to re-board his vessel. This time he grabbed the engine propeller shafts and hung there screaming blue murder. It was only when Leonard took the starting-strings and gave a short experimental pull that Pforzheim relinquished his hold and backstroked to a few feet away, screaming that they were all trying to assassinate him.

"Look, this is a question of balance. I reckon that if John comes here by me, Len goes in the middle and you Albert stand by the steering-wheel, we might be all right..."

But Mvhu had no time to finish his positioning of the crucial ballast. Already Pforzheim's fingers were clawing at the gunwhale and he was shrieking curses and threats, refusing to appreciate their technical difficulties. Matthias stretched out a beefy black arm, placed his broad palm on the skipper's wet head and pushed him under.

"Not yet Dave," he murmured, "patience *chamware*. We must have time."

"He's a noisy bastard isn't he?" Pyper complained. "You can always tell where Pforzheim is. Just follow the noise and you'll find him. If his Dad had disciplined him more as a child then he might not think that the whole world revolves around him. He gives my arse the headache at times."

"Only child," Leonard pointed out seriously, "wealthy father. He was brought up to believe he was something special. I suppose it's not all his fault."

"Here he comes again."

Albert prodded at Pforzheim's fingers with a short boat-hook as they slithered along the chromium cleated gunwhale of the bow. Anguished howls came from under the belly curve of the vessel, but the fingers remained, clamped tight to the metal trim.

"Albert..." Mvhu said quietly as the printer hammered at the digits with the flat side of the boat-hook.

"Yes Mvhu?"

"Are you ever going to let him get back in?"

"I think we should discuss it. It's not my decision, is it? I don't see why we should be jeopardised just for his sake. We didn't ask him to get out did we?"

Mvhu was looking back up the river the way they had come. About a hundred yards away he could see a foaming wake of green water and an armoured head cutting through the water like a destroyer. Vengeance was on its way. They had been followed.

"That crocodile is coming," Mvhu said gravely, "he's been tailing us."

"Did you know," Leonard began, "that when a crocodile kills it takes the carcase into a kind of den, generally in tree-roots, and sticks it there and lets it go rotten . . ."

Pforzheim was begging now. He trod water and pleaded with them for his life. Far down the river he could see the bow-waves of the *ngandu* as it churned towards him. Albert led the way into the stern, pushing the other passengers around until they were arranged to his satisfaction. Then he shouted to the hysterical captain to swim round to the bows and pull himself up. Pforzheim, gabbling frenziedly, obeyed. When he got to the bows he looked upward at the streaming keel which was now raised a yard out of the water due to all the weight being in the stern. He screamed that he could not reach. Albert and Matthias stepped forward to better hear what he was saying and the bows descended and struck Pforzheim on the head.

He sank again.

"What's he playing at?" Matthias grumbled as he looked over the side. "The bastard has disappeared."

"I sometimes wonder if he'll ever grow up," Crompton mused.

"It certainly doesn't help him to mature when his Dad bails him out of trouble all the time. He paid off two thousand K's worth of racing debts for him last week, as well as a year's hire-purchase on his hi-fi," Matthias said darkly. "In African society we also tend to be over-protective towards children once they've run the gauntlet of being born, early diseases and all that. But we never actually spoil our kids. They're brought up to live in the real world and to stand on their own two feet."

Pforzheim surfaced near the stern, blood streaming from a cut on his temple. He was gibbering with terror. Twenty yards away the destroyer became a torpedo as the crocodile scented the freshly-shed blood and charged for its sweet revenge.

"For Christ's sake, help me! Help!" Pforzheim implored.

"Will you let us have a go with the gun?" Albert asked firmly.

Pforzheim nodded frantically, casting glances over his shoulder at the boiling spume. Albert gave the signal and the Undesirables leaned out and grabbed Pforzheim's flailing hands and pulled him on board. A second later a thud was heard on the hull and the boat rocked as the disappointed crocodile snapped at the place where its prey had been and swam off into the deeps to brood.

Pforzheim lay on the bottom of the boat, his chest and paunch heaving. The weight of water in his shorts had dragged them down to his knees. Matthias eyed the captain speculatively and scratched his head.

"Does yours always shrink that much when you go in the water?" he murmured, not without compassion.

Pforzheim hoisted up his shorts with a snarl and groped for his shotgun.

"Come on, we can still get those spurwing."

He was right. In the dambo the geese still grazed. Pforzheim broke the gun and prised out the damp cartridges, then dried the chambers and barrel with a pull-through.

"Come on, bring the boat round and we'll find a better landing-place. Matthias and Leonard, you go over to those trees and then beat through to bring them up to the gun."

"What happens if they fly the other way?"

"They always fly back the way they've come."

"How do they get anywhere?"

"They're creatures of habit. Come on, bring her in on that little shore there."

As Pforzheim steered the boat close to the earth, Crompton suddenly snatched the gun out of Pforzheim's hands and shot off both barrels. From the dambo came a flurried honking in the echoing of the twin boom, and the geese took off northwards, thus contradicting Pforzheim's hypothesis since they had come from the south.

"Perhaps they're perverts?" Crompton smiled as he thrust the smoking gun into the well of the boat.

"Or perhaps Dave's talking out of his arse as usual," Pyper sniggered.

Pforzheim glared at his friends, thought about swinging a punch at Crompton, then slumped in a heap over the steering-wheel and cried his eyes out. They let him get his frustration out of his system while they opened more beers and smoked a contemplative cigarette.

"Nice here isn't it Mvhu?" Matthias said. "So peaceful."

> *Mulale kuni*
> *Pansi pali muswa*
> *Pali nyelee!*

Thus sang Matthias, his fishing rod held between his toes, his bullet-head held back as he watched the boughs and clouds slide past overhead while the boat slowly drifted back downstream. As he sang his free foot hammered the side of the boat.

"Christ, that's a beautiful number Matthias," Pyper giggled. "I'll just take up the rhythm with this Gilbeys gin bottle on George's head while he's dreaming about the General Manager's wife."

"How d'you know he's dreaming about her?"

"He keeps groaning and saying he wants a company car."

Matthias broke into his song again, drumming his heel against the metal hull.

"What does it mean Matthias?" Mvhu asked from his drowse. Long ago his hook had been snatched away by roots and the line hung uselessly from his rod like a spare prick at a wedding. But he did not care. Inside him were several bottles of lager, swallows of whisky, gin, rum, brandy. His was a golden bowl of dreams and delights. Here was true tranquillity.

"It's an old Angoni song I learned as a kid. All our music comes from the practical difficulties we had to face while living in the bush, not stuff like *loeuve* and heartbreak. That one means:

> Where will you sleep or lie
> as there are ants
> on the ground!

"Poetry Matthias," Albert smiled through the sparkling reflections on his glasses, "images from real life."

"You pseud bugger," the captain retorted, scowling from the helm. He had recovered from his tantrum a few hours ago and had immediately got his passengers organised as fishermen. Now they were all totally drunk, their rods hanging out of the boat at all angles with no interest in catching anything whatsover. Pforzheim looked at them with black disfavour. This was not his idea of a day out on the river.

"No wonder the Empire slipped out of our grasp," he seethed, "you phoneys gave it away because you didn't have the guts to keep on fighting."

Then George got a bite. His rod handle was clutched in his PR Man's soft hands but the end of it, including the reel, had been stuck under his belt by a considerate Albert. As the fish tugged at the line George was awakened by a severe constriction round his waist.

"No!" he yelled in his somnia. "Don't make me put that thing on again! Please Staff Officer! Not the Victorian truncheon!"

"What the hell is he talking about?" Leonard grinned. "Come

on George, you've got the first bite of the day."

"Bite!" George sat bolt upright, clutching at his groin. "Bite!"

"Look George, you've got one! Pull it in!"

Crompton cottoned on to what was happening and seized the rod and reel. Gritting his teeth he started to bring the fish in. As soon as it broke the surface in a burst of threshing silver, Pforzheim blew it to smithereens with his shotgun.

"Got the bastard!" he said with satisfaction.

George stared at his line. On his hook hung a tattered shred.

"What did you do that for?" he barked peevishly. "That was quite a big fish."

"It's my rod George. Don't forget that. My hook. My bait."

The Undesirables fell into a morose silence. They had thought that by fishing they could wean Pforzheim away from his gun and his lust for murder. All of them wanted peace and quiet and a chance to relax. The late afternoon was lazy, golden, full of the haze of the passing day. It was a time for contemplation and dreams, not for destruction.

"Ah Africa, poor Africa, poor old whore Africa..." sighed Matthias, trailing a hand in the water. "What a lot you have to put up with."

"Don't talk to me about Africa," Pforzheim said irascibly. "None of you bastards know the place or understand what it needs. I was born here! My family helped to build this country!"

"You mean you exploited it!" Crompton snapped.

"We built! We put brick on brick! We made it productive!"

"Are builders exploiters Albert?" Pyper asked impishly.

"Depends who is selling the bricks."

"And who lives in the house."

"And who irons the billiard-table."

Pforzheim turned away in disgust, his shotgun still in his hand. Matthias shook his head and started singing his song again. With a sudden jerk Pforzheim pulled back the accelerator lever and sent the boat surging forward on the broad bosom of the Kafue, tributary of the mighty Zambesi, queen of rivers. The bows climbed into the deeping blue air as the wash cut a swathe of foam across the slowly flowing currents. Matthias stopped singing, his voice drowned by the roar of the engines.

After making his point that he was still very much in charge of the expedition, Pforzheim throttled back and allowed the boat to drone on towards the oncoming darkness. Warm air billowed off the surface water. Above them the sun was flying slow red streamers through the trees and the moon was already visible, a faint light grey circle in the sky. In the bush the cicadas began their throbbing song. Egrets sailed in like ghosts and settled in the long grass. Africa began to grow smaller, curling up into the images available to their drunken eyes.

"Oh Africa," Matthias sighed again, "oh sweet Africa."

Mvhu saw a fish eagle sitting on the upper branches of one of the *mubobo* trees he had counted that morning, the whiteness of its breast glowing in the soft light. He remembered the crone's red eye and her name for the flighted hunter. Without thinking he pointed at the bird and called: *'Nkwazi.*

Pforzheim flung up his 12-bore and blew *'Nkwazi* off his perch. With a croak he fell into the river.

"That's our national bird," Matthias grumbled as the carcase floated past, talons still twitching. "What did you do that for?"

"Ruins the fishing," Pforzheim replied.

"You're making me sad today David," Matthias said in melancholy reproof. "I'm beginning to think that you might be a bit of a barbarian."

"Take no notice Matthias," Crompton assured the African. "One day he'll find out, when it's too late. He's only a kid."

"What's your national bird?" Matthias asked Mvhu with sudden interest. "The jenny wren?"

"No, the robin."

"Oh, the robin. A cheery fellow."

Pforzheim giggled at the wheel.

"Do Jews have a national bird Albert?"

Albert rubbed his chin for a moment and then said that he didn't think so.

"What about the magpie?" Pforzheim suggested. "Or the carrion crow?"

"The maribou stork is the ugliest bird in the world," Albert sniffed. "And that must be the United Arab Republic's national bird."

Matthias chuckled warmly, a bemused and affectionate smile on his face.

"Hmmm, the little robin redbreast. I like robins."

"You've never seen a fucking robin!" Pforzheim shouted, waving his gun round his head. "And don't pretend you have!"

"Of course I have!"

"For Christ's sake Matthias, there's no robins in Africa!" Pyper chirruped mirthfully. "You can't have seen one!"

"I have, plenty of times."

All the white men started to regard Matthias with chilly hostility. They were all fond of him as a man, but as an African he had no right to claim an acquaintance with the robin. That bird belonged to the cold winters of northern Europe. It was not a summer friend, a seasonal traitor, like the swift and the swallows. The robin belonged to the Old Country. It was a symbol in the dream. It was important that this fat black oaf should accept that there were limitations on his friendships.

"All right Matthias," Crompton said menacingly as he eased himself on to his feet. "When have you seen a robin?"

"I see them every year."

"Mixed up with the parrots?"

"No, no man. On the Christmas cards."

Crompton sat down again, crushed. All the white men fell into a depressed, moody silence. Matthias had played a trick on them. They all knew that there were no Christmas cards in Zonkendawo with fish-eagles on them. They were full of robins. Nor were there any Christmas cards in England with old 'Nkwazi up there on his tree. They were full of robins as well. Matthias had never seen snow or had his pipes burst.

He had no pipes.

"And I know all about an English spring as well," Matthias continued cheerfully, "oh yes. Lambs, catkins, daffodils. In fact I once spent a whole day in the bush looking for the birch tree bole which was in tiny leaf."

"Shut up Matthias," Crompton sighed. "We take your point."

"George, you don't understand. I like robins. I really like the little fellows. And bulldogs. And roses. Honest I do."

"Matthias," Crompton sighed as he groped for the last of the Scotch, "we all love 'Nkwazi as well. Well, nearly all of us."

The passengers or crew turned and looked at the captain, the spoilt young hero with his shotgun in the crook of his arm, and they tutted and murmured "Shame".

The boat cruised on.

Black and white in the dark.

When the boat reached a point half a mile upstream from The Shack, Pforzheim steered into the bank on an inside bend and peered through the first of the blue evening gloom.

"What are you looking for?" Leonard asked in a whisper as Pforzheim was crouched low over the wheel.

"Look!" Pforzheim pointed ahead.

In a broad stretch of water at the widest part of the bend a school of hippopotamuses blew, yawned and swam. Leonard immediately jammed his foot against the shotgun which Pforzheim was groping for. With an exasperated cry Pforzheim yanked back the throttle so the thundering engines bit deeper into the water, raising the bows into a flashing helm of steel.

"What are you doing, you fucking lunatic!" Pyper screamed as he fought for the wheel. "You hit one of those big buggers and we're dead!"

But it was too late. Although most of the beasts had quickly moved away, out of the path of the churning boat, one old bull refused to budge, his round back offered to the bucking keel like a slipway. With a sickening bump and bounce the boat struck him amidships and flew into the air.

"Jehovah save us!" Albert moaned, covering up his eyes and securing his spectacles.

The boat struck the water again with a huge splash, propellers whining wildly. Pforzheim throttled back and grinned.

"Got the old bastard. That'll teach him."

While he was chalking up another blow struck against the wilderness, his passengers were counting themselves. There was one missing. As the boat had collided with the old bull Mvhu had been sitting with his backside half over the stern. The impact had made him fall out. He was nowhere to be seen.

"Pforzheim!" Pyper chattered hysterically. "You've killed him! Now you've done it! You've killed old Mvhu!"

Pforzheim checked through passengers and tackle. No Mvhu. He only saw eyes mad with accusation and horror.

"He must be somewhere," he said lamely.

"Yes he is you murdering bastard! He's down there with those hippos. They've probably chomped the poor old Mvhu in half by now!"

"They don't eat meat..."

"Turn the boat round!"

"They'll come up under us!"

Crompton threw Pforzheim aside and took the wheel, steering the boat back to the pool. As he was as drunk as a lord he soon ran the boat aground.

"Oh shit!" he fumed. "Can't you do anything properly Pforzheim?"

Leonard jumped out of the boat and pushed it free, then clambered back on board. With the engine ticking over they searched the silty water for a sign of their lost friend.

Below the surface, in a green clime of swirling weeds and water, Mvhu felt strangely unafraid. This was a cool world, full of shadows, like the inner chambers of his dreaming mind. Shapes moved all around him and he could hear grunts and squeals through the natural sonar of the river. As his feet touched the bottom Mvhu was not even conscious that he was holding his breath. This environment had accepted him.

He knew that they were aware of his presence.

All he had to do was wait.

Soon, out of a patch of floating weed, emerged the old bull, bumping along on the river-bed like an astronaut on the moon. Where Pforzheim had used him as a launching-ramp was a deep gash with smoky trails of blood streaming from it. The old bull approached Mvhu and stared at him with curious piggy eyes.

"Mloof."

"Mloof," Mvhu replied in a stream of bubbles.

The old bull thrust his huge head forward and brushed Mvhu up and down with his enormous blunt mouth. Mvhu could see the pain in the herbivore's eyes. That wound would take months to heal in this disease-carrying river. It would fester, pulse, grow rotten, and may even cause the old bull's death. It was the mark of the Brotherhood of Pain, the terrible lord of Mankind, the true king of the Animal world.

Mvhu bent down and rested his head against the rough, bubbling muzzle of the great beast. He could think of nothing else to do. Then the old bull shook himself free in a shrug of irritation and stomped off, shaking his huge knobbly cranium while his short tufted pig's tail stirred the water in a frenzy of irritation.

Mvhu watched him go, saddened, yet elated.

There was a bond.

171

There was an almighty brother in animalhood!

Then the pressure in his lungs made itself felt and he thrust upwards into the light and air and blew so the river and the bush and the ears of his overjoyed friends were deafened by the overwhelming sound.

"Mvhu! Mvhu! MVHU!"

SIXTEEN ECHOES OF ENGLAND

"Ironheart," Mvhu whispered to Ironheart in bed that night, "I've had a marvellous experience."

"*Tcha*, that's nothing to what I can do when you're not tired out with too many beers," his manager sniffed from the pillow. "Why won't you listen to me? Keep away from Pyper and the others..."

"I didn't mean...that, though that was marvellous in its own way."

"You were half-asleep. You're nearly as bad as George Crompton."

"What do you know about George Crompton?"

There was a silence. Mvhu could sense that Ironheart was holding her breath.

"Have you been his manager as well?"

"No," she replied in a small voice. "Not his manager."

Mvhu raised himself up on the pillows and grinned in the darkness. When George was awake he was certainly a mover.

"Do you want me to tell you about my experience?"

Ironheart shrugged under the sheet.

"If you like."

"I'm asking you if *you* like."

"Is it about the Three Races Of Man?"

"No."

"Promise?"

"Yes."

"Go on then."

Drawing back the sheet, Mvhu ran his hand along Ironheart's body from top to toe. She lay still.

"Do you think you are an animal?" he asked softly.

"I know I'm not an animal," Ironheart whispered fiercely, "I'm a person. Don't you dare call me an animal."

"But you are. So am I."

"You sound like Hammerkop. He says we're baboons and should

172

live in the trees. Is that what you think?"

"What is this I am touching?"

He poked her flank.

"Me!"

Mvhu switched on the bedside light and looked down at the irate creature that was stuffing its head under the pillow.

"Ironheart," he insisted, pulling the pillow away, "we are animals. That's why we can take such pleasure in each other. We're in the same mould. Love is possible. Joy is possible. We work together."

"I thought you said it wasn't the Three Races Of Man thing you're always on about!" she complained, sitting up. "Now you're telling me lies."

"It's not."

"No, but it's the animal fathers thing isn't it? That's just the same!"

"Of course it isn't! They're completely different concepts!"

"They're the same to me. Stupid!"

"Ironheart, don't..."

"Why can't you be satisfied with what you've got? The rest of us have to be. What's so special about you? You've got a good job, a place to live, me...I suppose. Isn't that enough?"

Mvhu lapsed into a difficult silence. He had not told Ironheart about the way Hammerkop had managed to cheat him out of his job at the Open Pit. The time was not right to tell her. It might make her feel insecure when seen in conjunction with the more important news that he was becoming a hippopotamus.

"What I'm trying to say is that I'm becoming more and more conscious of my animalself..."

"So I've noticed."

"All right, all right..."

"Sex is human, isn't it? It has nothing to do with you being an animal. It is because you are a man."

"What is a man?"

"A nuisance who won't stop talking in the middle of the night."

"Ironheart, you've got to listen. This is important."

"And the washing, and the ironing, and the shopping and cleaning and cooking and everything else that I have to do?"

"Sometimes you sound like the woman I used to be married to. She had no imagination either."

"Thank you very much. An imagination would have never been much use to me. You can't eat it can you? Or can it cure hookworm?"

173

"Ironheart..."

"Go to sleep."

"Please listen."

"I am listening. How can I help but listen?"

"When I came out to Africa, I was looking for something."

"Most of you white people are when you come out here."

"I was looking for myself."

"Then you had a wasted journey, didn't you? What was it you had at home? Someone else?"

"Yes, in a way."

"Oh go to sleep and stop being stupid."

"Ironheart..."

"Yes?"

"One night, a few years ago, the woman who used to be my wife called me an animal."

"Then why did you get divorced? At least you agreed about something."

"It started me thinking, made me see everything in a new light. Now I know that she was right. What had made her able to see that I was animal was that she had forgotten that she was as well. She thought she was an individual."

"Good for her."

"Don't say nice things about the woman who used to be my wife. She was a pain in the arse."

"You must have liked her once."

"My artificially-created half liked her. Machines can like machines."

"Oh God."

"She was a manufactured article."

"Be quiet."

"Anyway, the thing is, I had this experience today and it's convinced me that my ideas were right, or partially right."

"I'm pleased for you. Now can we go to sleep?"

"Don't you want to know what the experience was?"

"No!"

Ironheart jumped off the bed and sat in a cane chair, wrapping a blanket round her. Her dark eyes stared angrily from the folds.

"I met an animal and we accepted each other as equals."

"What was it? A donkey?"

"A hippopotamus."

174

Ironheart raised her eyes to the ceiling and sighed with exasperation. "I'll kill that albino in the morning. So help me I will."

"It's not his fault."

"You're mad! Why do you white people always go mad when you come out here? Why must you start to behave like children? If it's not one thing it's another! You hate us Africans, or you hate yourselves. What's the matter with just treating Africa like everywhere else...like it was...Manchester?"

Mvhu frowned, shifting his glance away from that of his furious manager. He did not like the idea that Africa was Manchester.

"Because it's not. It's Africa. The oldest inhabited continent. The Cradle of Man."

"Rubbish!"

"It's not rubbish! You can feel it all around you! Here you can actually touch the real world."

"What is it you touch in England then?"

"Civilised nightmares."

"Oh all right! Stop it! I agree! I agree! You and the hippopotamus are brothers! Zonkendawo is perfect! It is Paradise!"

Ironheart stood up and swept round the end of the bed, the blanket clutched round her shoulders.

"Here there is no suffering! Everyone is happy! There is no illness! Good jobs for all! No bullying! No beatings! No Party card-sellers taking my wages off me! No Mulombe telling children to stand in the sun for four hours and wave flags that are worn out with waving. This is the Garden of Eden! My sister did not die of measles because my father was too drunk to cycle to the mission hospital for doctors. My babies are not fatherless because my boy-friends never had the sense or consideration to wear sheaths or something!"

"If they had you wouldn't have had any babies," Mvhu pointed out pedantically, "so that doesn't follow does it?"

"Oh shut up while I'm talking!" Ironheart screamed, her teeth chattering with fury. "It's my turn now! You listen to me for a change! This is not the best place in the world! Mulombe is one of those Race Ones you're always talking about. He's the biggest One of them all! Whose fault is that? You *musungus*! You came here and treated us like dirt and said you were very democratic. So what do you expect Mulombe to do? He knocks us about, says we want him to be president for life, says Zonkendawo is a natural one-party state, and at the same time says he believes in freedom like the bloody bwanas! No

175

wonder he's got it all wrong! And another thing, you big drunken fool!" Now she was trembling all over, tears in her big brown eyes. "Don't you forget that Mother Africa eats her children. We suffer and die here like nobody's business. The old sow eats her young! Good night!"

With a toss of the blanket Ironheart threw open the door and swept out of the bedroom. The door slammed behind her. That night he slept solo.

SEVENTEEN THE AWAY GAME

Mufunsi Blackpool had a fixture to play Elizabethville Extraordinaires away on the same week-end as Pyper had arranged to visit his friend Reg, the Chief of Security of the Haute-Katanga. As there was a crisis in the Congo at that time and all travellers had been advised to make up convoys at the border post at Mulengobeba, Pyper arranged for his friends to join the supporters' club and to get seats on the coach. When it set off from Mufunsi that Saturday morning Crompton, Albert, Pforzheim, Matthias and the Bucket-Wheel Excavator Gang were on board – but none of the women.

Ironheart was not there.

The Staff Officer was not there.

Even Margaret From The Tonga Bar was not there.

Pyper had said that taking them to Elizabethville was like taking coals to Newcastle. Mvhu had got into trouble with Ironheart over this ban. She knew Pyper. When he had been living with Ironheart there had been several occasions when the New Zealander had returned from Elizabethville in a depleted physical condition, wan, shrunken, feeble, only interested in crawling into bed and sleeping for three or four days.

"If you come home like that, then I'm leaving you. I will resign!" Ironheart said that morning from the balcony as Mvhu crossed Mulombe Square.

"Take no notice! Go your own way Mvhu!" shouted the albino from under the brown Christmas tree, hugging his bottle of Malawian Drambuie. "Stick up for yourself!"

Mvhu had argued that he could not miss the opportunity to go into the Congo which was the natural home of the most mysterious life-forces in Africa – the huge green heart, arteried by the Congo river. All the world was in Elizabethville, trying to help President Tshombe hold down the fractious giant of a land he was hoping to govern. Pyper was anxious to return with a large group of friends in order to prove to Reginald Mbwa, his friend in the regional government, that, as a journalist, he had faith in the country's future.

"Christ, when old Reg sees you lot on his doorstep he'll think the tourist trade is entering a period of boom. I reckon he'll tell me every state secret he knows," Pyper had said while encouraging Mvhu to ignore Ironheart's protests, "and don't forget that Hammerkop and the rugby XV are still after your blood."

As the coach bumped along the pot-holed road to the border, Albert told them all about his childhood in the Congo.

"They have a lot to forgive. The Belgians were not the best of colonial masters. It was only because my family had always been polite and courteous to everyone, especially the leaders of the underground movements and the obviously intelligent ones, that we were not molested at the time of the upheavals. Dad's tailor shop was never touched. They knew that he was a true sympathiser."

Pyper winked at Mvhu.

"The old en stroke ens can always tell a true friend Albert," he tinkled sharply, "someone who loves them for altruistic reasons."

The altruistic reason why Reg loved Pyper was something akin to the reason why Albert's family was held in such high regard by the Congolese rebels. The New Zealander had written an economic report on the Congo that had been syndicated in financial journals throughout the world. Basing his analysis on three days spent in the whorehouses and bars of Elizabethville with the genial police chief, and a drunken miscomprehension of the rate of exchange of the franc against the kwacha, Pyper had informed the stock markets of the Free World that the economy of Katanga was responding to the strong centralised government of President Tshombe and was entering a period of sustained growth. As a result, capital poured into the country from America, Belgium, France, Germany, Japan and Great Britain, only to be poured down the drain of a corrupt and irresponsible regime that had no idea what to do with it. As Reg had been in the drain at the time, he had developed a touching affection for the boyish charm of mon ami Pyper.

"I'm a personal friend of old Reg!" Pyper chirruped as he flashed a letter to the soldiers at the border road-block while handing over his

177

mandatory sliced loaf and packet of 200 Benson and Hedges cigarettes. The soldiers stood behind their wall of sliced bread and cartons (there were sixty people on the coach) and tried to read the letter, eventually handing it back with a shrug. It meant nothing to them.

"Christ, these bastards are illiterate!" Pyper fumed, folding up the letter. "Or perhaps old Reg has fallen from power. If he has then I'm really locked in the shithouse with the squitters and only two sheets of sandpaper."

At the next road-block, manned by unpaid gendarmes from the national army who had turned to banditry to make a living, all the passengers were rousted from the coach at gun-point and made to lie face-down at the side of the road. Pyper showed his letter to the wild-eyed robbers and blanched as it was promptly torn up and scattered to the wind. Nothing seemed to work with these men. Sliced bread failed. Benson and Hedges failed. The Bucket-Wheel Excavator Gang tried friendliness, a few cracks and jokes, a half-extended hand of friendship, but they received blows and curses for their pains.

The bandits wanted money.

And they wanted revenge.

When they had collected all the passports together, they found one issued by Her Majesty's Britannic government for a man called Hurl Halfcock. When they had stopped laughing they prodded the prone Englishmen with their automatic rifles and ribbed him about his name.

"That is a very unAfrican name sir."

"It is so unAfrican that we are going to shoot you."

"In a world like this is, a Halfcock is worse than no cock at all."

Dragging Hurl to his feet they stripped off his clothes and tied his wrists over the branch of a *muuti* tree. It was then that Mvhu found his voice. It had been hidden a long way down in his grovelling fear until then, but he realised that unless he spoke up the bandits would kill him there and then.

"That is not my real name," he quavered.

"What is your name then?"

"My name is Mvhu."

"Mvhu?"

"Yes."

"Then we are still going to shoot you."

"Why?"

"Mvhus are good eating. Cut into strips and dried in the sun they are nourishing and tasty."

Mvhu stared down the muzzles of the pointed rifles. He did not fully believe that he had been trapped in this situation. Other men were slaughtered on roadsides but not him, not the boy from Walton. What was he doing here?

The convoy of jeeps carrying Reg to meet his friend Pyper on the road to Elizabethville whirled round a sharp bend in the road just as Mvhu was picking out a final plea for his life in a fourth-form French that would have delighted his old language master, such was its power and colour. The bandits started running away but they were too late. While the coach-passengers covered their heads and whimpered, the bandits were shot down in mid-stride, their bodies spinning into the first fringe of bush as they ran. Reg's gendarmes went after them with bayonet and knife and while the passengers looked up for the first time, the cries of the wounded were stopped. Reg himself untied Mvhu from the *muuti* tree and held out his coat.

"On behalf of my government and myself may I offer you our deepest apologies. This is not the way we normally treat visitors."

Mvhu sank to his knees, crying his heart out.

It had been a near thing.

Out of the blue.

They had picked him out, just like the old Race Threes had always picked him out.

Why? Was this the proper end to his animalself? Sudden death from a stranger, a man with no cause to hate him? Mvhu fell weeping into the grass, dragging Reg's coat over his head.

Pyper looked down at the white body of his new friend and put an arm round Reg's shoulder.

"You'll have to forgive the poor old Pom showing you his arse like this Reg, he means no disrespect. He'll be all right in a minute. We'll get him dressed."

While the passengers re-distributed their belongings and got back on the bus, Pyper told Reg the story of the hold-up.

"Christ Reg, they wouldn't listen to reason. I even showed them your letter but they said they'd never heard of you and tore it up."

Reg's face went still. For a moment he appeared to be thinking. Then he snatched a sten-gun off one of his men and went along the road to where the bandits were piled in a bleeding heap. He emptied a full magazine into them, screaming unintelligibly through the smoke and gunfire, then returned to Pyper with a quiet smile.

"Well, they have heard of me now," he said. "I am introduced."

"You don't hang around do you Reg?" Pyper murmured. "I must remember to remain one of your closest buddies."

When Mvhu got back on to the coach Crompton refused to sit next to him and went to share a seat with Albert who was picking all his loose change out of the ash-tray in which he had stuffed his money when the bandits had first stopped the coach.

"Don't leave him by himself George," Albert whispered. "Have a heart man. Don't start one of your Guilty Liberal phases now."

"Those poor blighters!" George Crompton seethed. "They never had a a chance. They should have shot the stupid sod and stopped him messing about with his name. Who cares what he's called? He's a bloody parasite. He's like me! I'm just a bloody parasite! Who needs a Public Relations Man out here in the middle of nowhere? This whole business is a farce. What do I do with my life? I started getting pissed at half-past eight in the morning. By eleven I can't think straight. All I'm interested in is sensations and escape. Why didn't they shoot me? They should have shot both of us, a couple of bloody parasites!"

The leading jeep pulled off the road and into a clearing. Set among some *musense* trees was a low white building with a wooden board which said BAR in rough black letters. The passengers filed off the coach and into the hut, still chattering nervously about the hold-up and the executions. As soon as George Crompton got inside he ordered a bottle of whisky off the tall, statuesque African barmaid and asked if she was interested in laying on some *hlanganana* as he had reached a point of despair with the human condition and wanted to drown this murderous nihilism in orgasmic sensations.

"Wait until I've finished serving the customers," the barmaid said briskly as she ripped the tops off lines of litre bottles of Simba beer. "I've only got one pair of hands."

"My friend over there doesn't think much of your quick-fire justice Reg," Pyper grinned as he pointed at Crompton who was attacking the neck of the whisky bottle like a hungry babe at the breast. "He's very sensitive."

"Let him come and try to run the Congo," Reg smiled wearily, "and we'll see how long he stays that way."

180

In a dark corner the Bucket-Wheel Excavator Gang and Matthias crowded round Mvhu and tended his needs. They held his hand, wiped away the tears that still sprang from his eyes, listened to his trembling speech, gripped his shaking shoulders, gave him cigarettes, plied him with bottles of Simba beer, loved him, cared for him.

"Take no notice of George Crompton. He is like Albert when he becomes a Creeping Republican. It is all temporary. Tomorrow he will not be a Guilty Liberal, just old George the way we know him."

"Why me though?" Mvhu whimpered. "Why do they always pick on me?"

There was a commotion at the bar. Some of Reg's soldiery wanted drinks and the barmaid had been seen disappearing into the back room with Crompton. Reg left Pyper and went behind the bar, kicking open the door. Inside was Crompton heaving away between the thighs of the African woman, his whisky bottle still to his lips. Reg ordered him to stop, but not before one of the soldiers had erupted into an hysterical rage, claiming that Crompton was copulating with his mother, which was more than any man could bear.

"This woman is your mother?" Reg asked the jabbering soldier.

"As long as I live and breathe! Look at me Mother!"

Crompton looked at the crowd in the doorway and took the bottle from his lips. Pinning the barmaid against the wall he smoothed back his red hair.

"I say, would you chaps mind going away? Can't a fellow expect any privacy here?"

"Are you raping with that woman?" Reg demanded.

"Certainly not!"

"Are you this man's mother?" Reg asked the barmaid.

The barmaid gave an emphatic shake of her head.

Reg closed the door and slapped the soldier's face.

"We have enough disturbance of the Balance of Nature in our country without you adding to it. Serve the beers. Calm down, all of you. Everything is all right. Leave those two alone. They are harming nobody."

In the back room the Staff Officer was washing the make-up off her body and removing her wire-wool wig under Crompton's in- credulous eye.

"So you thought that you'd leave me behind eh? Well you've got another think coming!" the Staff Officer sniffed as she changed her clothes. "And another thing George, you're starting to get a

Whisky Wilt. Get it seen to before you come to dinner again, all right?"

When Crompton re-appeared in the bar with the Staff Officer on his arm the crowd went silent. Reg slapped the face of the soldier again and demoted him, then arrested the Staff Officer for impersonating a member of another race.

"That is a capital offence in my country."

"Christ Reg, this is the old Staff Officer. She meant no harm."

Mvhu stared at the Staff Officer, horror-struck. He felt as if he had been carried to a great height and forced to look down on the destruction of the knowable world. He knew nothing. The order which he had understood was gone and only chaos had replaced it. Faced by the dark accusing glances of the Staff Officer, and the memory of the black malignant eyes of the rifle muzzles, he suddenly wanted to surrender his mind, his new identity, and crawl into a hole and forget he was a thinking creature. There must be something he could hold on to.

There was.

Ironheart.

God how he needed her.

But they had left her behind.

"Look Reg, why don't you make the Staff Officer your own for the week-end. She's a good-hearted soul just naturally keen on travelling."

Reg looked at the Staff Officer, his eyes taking in the fine proportions of her Junoesque body and the width of her child-bearing hips. Her lips were parted in a life-saving smile. She slipped out half an inch of tongue.

"What's she like?" he asked abruptly.

"Better than the holes in the dingo fencing Reg."

Reg paused, brushing his lower lip.

"Hmm, I suppose we can arrange something to satisfy both the Law and ourselves. Take Mwape outside."

The soldier who had claimed that the Staff Officer was his mother was taken outside. In a patch of cleared ground Reg created the awesome atmosphere of a court-room. The afternoon sun beat down through the *musense* trees on the head of the man accused of impersonating the Staff Officer's son. While Mvhu lay curled up in the dust, scrabbling at the stones and grass with bleeding nails and sobbing for little Ironheart and her sense of organisation and manoeuvrable reality, Mwape was hanged with one of the jeep's tow-ropes. At the final moment, before the jeep was driven away to leave the soldier kicking, Mvhu crawled across the clearing and begged incoherently for the fellow's life. Reg smiled down at the dusty Englishman in his tears and grime, then shook his head.

"Sir, we are a free people now. When the Belgians were here right could not overcome wrong. Now there are no delays in having wrongs righted. We see them, pin-point them, then we act. You waste your time on what is unimportant. What is Mwape against the whole of this country? What is one ungovernable hysterical fool against an ungovernable state like the Congo?"

He had paused then, bending down to help Mvhu to his feet.

"What are your tears to me Englishman? It is better if you do not get involved in the affairs of this nation. We fight in our own way. We know what is it to die for nothing like Mwape. Did you hear him complain?"

It was true.

From the time when Reg had slapped him down to the moment when the noose tightened round his neck, the soldier had not said a word. His last emotion had been a mistaken affection for a mother not his own: a blackened white soul in a wilderness. What had made him cry out that the Staff Officer had borne him? Somewhere in the sediments of Africa such a woman's whitened bones were buried, sand and pebbles heaped in the pelvis through which Mwape's descendant life had been pushed. That woman had been an animal, but of what species? Would an ape have passed on the listless eye that Mwape had while being tried? Would any sane creature have just stood there like a stuffed dummy while his life was taken away from him by an autocrat's wild whim?

Even a hyena would have struggled, scattering its millions of ticks and fleas over its accusers, screeching with manic laughter.

A lion would have brought the sky down with its roaring.

A bee would have lodged its sting in the throat of its executioner then pulled itself away, leaving its entrails behind. A tiny humble bee. A Race Two worker bee.

Mwape had done none of these things.

He had just stood there and taken it all.

Where did that kind of mindless acceptance come from?

What animal? What creature would not defend itself?

Something had rotted in Mwape's soul.

183

His animalself.

If Reg had tried to get the Staff Officer up on the back of that jeep and tie that noose of coarse rope round her neck, she would have fought or fucked her way out.

Perhaps that is why Mwape called her Mother?

It could have been a cry for help.

EIGHTEEN **THE DANCE OF LIFE-IN-DEATH**

For the remainder of the journey to Elizabethville Mvhu travelled with Reg and Pyper in the jeep, unable to endure Crompton who had entered the worst and most vociferous phase of his Guilty Liberal agony, directly after the hanging of Mwape. Whenever Mvhu looked over his shoulder he could see Crompton stalking up and down the aisle of the coach, waving his arms, battering at his temples with clenched fists, or just staring at himself in the driver's rear-mirror and pulling faces of terrifying hatred, then breaking open his features like a dam-wall to expel the tears and sighs.

Mercifully for the other passengers the Guilty Liberal suffered from a bout of somnia just as the coach entered the suburbs of Elizabethville and when the convoy was stopped by three separate squads of United Nations Peacekeepers to check out the credentials of the visitors, Crompton was unable to inform them of the massacres that had taken place.

Outside the stadium Pyper told Mvhu that he was not really interested in watching the football match.

"I'll give you Reg's address on the back of my Press ticket and you can get a taxi when the match is over. For Christ's sake don't bring George or the Bucket-Wheel Excavator Gang with you or there'll be trouble. I want to find out what's going on with these old Simba rebels in the eastern province and I've got to keep Reg in a good mood. See you later."

Mvhu took the ticket and followed Pforzheim through the barrier. Ahead of them the Bucket-Wheel Excavator Gang were carrying Crompton on their shoulders while Albert shoved his way to the stand trying to look as though he had nothing to do with the Mufunsi Blackpool Supporters Club. As soon as the visitors arrived with their placards and copper green and black rosettes the Congolese crowd started hooting and jeering.

"Kaffirs have got no idea of sportsmanship!" Pforzheim muttered as he helped to prop Crompton up against a barrier rail. "Anyone would think we were from Brussels to listen to those bastards."

"And the risks we've taken to come here," Matthias grumbled. "No other team has had the guts to play the Extraordinaires at home since 1960 when the Belgians ran away. I hope the Blackpool beat them to pulp."

When Mufunsi Blackpool ran on to the field the armed guards along the touch-lines turned and moved a few steps closer to the crowd, obviously jittery as the barrage of cans and abuse came flying as accompaniment to an escalating roar of disgust. When the Extraordinaires ran out of the tunnel the soldiers were forced to fire shots in the air, such was the power of the crowd's rage and frustration.

"What's the matter with these bastards Albert?" Pforzheim shouted. "Why are they booing the home team?"

"Home?" Albert grimaced. "Home? At the moment there is no such word in the Congo. Listen to them! They've had enough of everything – the Belgians, the rebels, the mercenaries, the United Nations, the Americans, the whole world. They've got nothing to support. They're only here for the chance of a punch-up."

Mvhu watched the kick-off, gripping the crash-barrier with one hand and steadying Crompton with the other as he see-sawed on his midriff, fast asleep. Within thirty seconds there was a disputed free kick and three youths ran on to the pitch slashing at the players with sharpened telescopic car radio aerials. A whole touch-line of soldiers converged on them and the youths went down under a barrage of heels and rifle-butts. When the pitch was cleared the game continued.

"I don't feel well," Albert moaned, clutching his head. "This isn't like the old days."

The referee declared an Extraordinaire player off-side.

Without hesitation the captain walked off the field, calling to his men to follow him. From the safety of the wired-in tunnel he shouted back to the referee that the game would not proceed until the unfair decision was revoked. It was only when the Extraordinaires were marched back on to the pitch at gun-point that the captain relented, but only if the referee agreed to a bounce-up rather than a free-kick.

"I'm not standing here watching this rubbish!" Pforzheim declared, pushing his way through the crowd.

"What about George?" Mvhu shouted. "We can't leave him here!"

"He'll be all right with Matthias. Come on. Tell Albert we're going."

Mvhu passed on Pforzheim's message and Albert decided to come along as well. Two Blackpool players were presently involved in a kicking contest with the Extraordinares' centre line and the crowd had gone sullen, murmuring dangerously.

"We're better off out of this. We can have a drink, find somewhere to give us a good rate of exchange for our kwachas, pick up some cheap malachite," Albert said as he hurried Mvhu through the crowd. "What a waste of time. Vive le sport."

As the taxi carrying Mvhu, Albert and Pforzheim arrived at the address on the back of Pyper's Press ticket, Reg the Staff Officer and Pyper were just getting out of the police chief's Mercedes, having been first to the barracks to disembark the troops and make a report.

"Christ, that game didn't last long!" Pyper squawked jovially. "What happened? Did the bastards eat the fucking football?"

Pforzheim explained about the tasteless display of violence and poor sportsmanship which they had been forced to witness as Reg led them through the front garden. Reg nodded many times, shrugged, spread his hands, but said nothing. Mvhu noticed with alarm that a row of six concrete cherubs on a low balustrade had all been decapitated.

Reginald Mcwa's house lay in a western suburb of the city, a grand colonial mansion set in groves of jacaranda trees and a spacious ornamental garden. Leading to it was a long boulevard which ran back into the centre of Elizabethville. Whereas there were signs of war and destruction in the city's heart, buildings pockmarked by machine-gun fire and blasted by mortar shells, broken windows and petrol-bomb smears blackening the white and blue walls, here in Reg's suburb all was peace and quiet. Beneath the jacaranda trees, now in their light blue shadowy blossoms, was a corrugated-iron shed and five soldiers playing a game with pebbles. They were Reg's private bodyguard, provided by the state.

"So this is your new house Reg?" Pyper crowed admiringly. "Bloody beautiful isn't it?"

Reg smiled modestly.

"I have a flat in town as well, near to my headquarters. When the

186

pressure of work builds up I stay there overnight. Tonight you and your friends may sleep here with my wife while I take the Staff Officer to my flat for questioning. It will take a long time as she appears to be an interesting case of illegal entry."

Reg ushered them into the house.

The lounge was long and laid out with several suites of furniture like a show-room in a department store. On one of the five settees sat a tall African woman dressed in a long white toga. Printed on the material were pictures of King George the Sixth in profile.

"Christ, that's very complimentary isn't it Mvhu? Carrying round portraits of Her Majesty's Dad in a free and liberal republic like this. That's what I call holding out the hand of friendship." Pyper whistled admiringly as he shook the woman's hand. "And you look a beaut in it too Mrs. Reg, cross my heart you do."

Reg conducted the Staff Officer to a settee several yards away from Mrs. Mcwa whose handsome, rangy features had hardened as soon as the party had come through the door.

"I see you are admiring my wife's dress John," Reg smiled, "it is my favourite as well. Here in the Congo we hold President Kennedy in great respect. He is our first defence against Communism. My wife's under-garments are also imprinted with a similar likeness."

Pyper laughed and lost himself in a huge leather armchair.

"Reg, don't be having us on. You know that's a picture of the last king of England, old George the Sixth. You can't mistake that long-suffering expression. Wouldn't you look like that if you'd been number one totem-pole for the Poms for as long as he had?"

"That is President Kennedy," Reg said smoothly, "of that I am sure."

"No it's not sport. He looks nothing like that. Your old woman is wearing the Royal Family grandad or I'm the hair round the arse of an emu's egg."

Reg paused as he looked into the deep armchair and the unrelenting blue of the human cockatoo's eye, then turned away and put a record on the gramophone.

"If you'd asked me in the first place I'd have told you Reg. Just imagine the faux pas you might have made if you'd gone to a cocktail party with the British Consul and he'd commented favourably on your old woman's attire, Christ, there could have been a diplomatic incident! What a fool you'd have looked if you'd argued with him! And you only just started in the power-politics business Reg. You

187

don't want the whole world laughing up its sleeve at the Chef de Poste do you?"

Reg went into the kitchen without answering. Albert got out of his chair and started to edge towards the door.

"Are you trying to get us all killed?" he whined. "That kind of talk really upsets them John. He's probably gone to call his men in to shoot us."

"Not Reg, he knows I'm useful to him. I can teach him a thing or two. Once he's sorted out his priorities in the kitchen he'll come back smiling."

The Staff Officer gazed mournfully out of the window at the garden.

"I don't expect to get out of this alive. Why did I follow you here? God knows, there's plenty of life in Mufunsi if you care to look for it. I wish I was back in the office."

"Staff Officer, don't you worry. Old Reg is crazy about you. Once he's wandered up and down the valley a few times he'll be your slave for life."

Mrs. Mcwa drew herself up until her long head was craned to the ceiling. Mvhu watched her closely. In this room of raffish cheap furniture, cold deals of uncaring men, confusion and cruelty, she looked out of her medium. That slender black steeple of a neck, the dappling effect of the pictures of George the Sixth, dyed in yellow squares, along the length of her erect body, the set of her cloven-toed sandals on the parquet floor, even the angle of her head and the twin diamante knobbed pins in her turban; these were all reminiscent of someone more used to the open savanna.

Reg re-appeared with a copper tray full of bottles of Simba beer. He was smiling broadly, but there was little depth in his good humour. As he put the tray down on the table he rapidly instructed his wife to go and change into her President Kennedy outfit. Mrs. Mcwa craned her finely-sculptured head further into the leaves, pushing her soft muzzle towards the warming sun, and replied that she had no such dress in her wardrobe. Bowing to his guests and asking them to help themselves to the Simba, Reg seized his wife by her thin hocks and dragged her into the kitchen.

"She's in for it now!" Pyper cackled as he opened a bottle. "Old Reg doesn't go much for women's rights."

"But the poor woman hasn't got a President Kennedy outfit!" the Staff Officer protested, tears welling into her aluminium eyes. "He's using her to cover up his own ignorance. Listen to what the

188

beast is doing to her!"

From the kitchen came the sound of lashing, swishing followed by thwacks. No cries of pain followed. The blows increased. Crockery crashed. Feet stamped. Walls and doors were kicked by long spindly legs bucking.

Mvhu trapped his hands under his buttocks and bowed his forehead to touch his knees.

It was not the beast that was beating Mrs. Mcwa.

It was Mr. Mcwa who was beating the beast.

The tall, gentle, earnest lover of the upper leaves and the plains where she could run with strange cumbersome grace, outstripping the wild dogs, the lonely giraffe, was being flogged by a manself ruptured from its animalself.

The wild dogs would have eaten her if they had caught her.

But not beaten her.

When Reg came out of the kitchen leading the giraffe by the hand, the hippopotamus heaved himself to his feet and lumbered over to the window, grunts of disapproval rumbling in his throat. He could see the pain in the giraffe's deep dark eyes, the awkwardness in her gait, and the shame in the set of her soft velvet mouth. Across her squared brown and yellow coat lay black parallel lines, especially round her narrow withers and long thighs. Reg stood by her side, flipping a riding quirt against his calves while his chest rose and fell with his exertions.

"Drink up!" he called. "Then we dance! We dance all day and all night to celebrate!"

"That sounds like a good idea Reg!" Pyper chirped. "What are we celebrating?"

"The transformation of President Kennedy into King George the Sixth!"

Pyper laughed and squirmed in his armchair.

"Till dawn Reg! Christ, you're as imaginative as ever. No wonder you're breaking the back of the crime-wave!"

"Till dawn!" Reg echoed his friend joyfully. "What a night this is going to be! I know all the best places to go. And for you my friend, a woman. You must have a woman! What would you like? Innocence? Experience?"

Mvhu turned from the window and looked at the giraffe as she stood by the wall, her lips still trembling. She had closed her lovely

189

eyes and was resting her head against the wallpaper where a pattern of green leaves reminded her of better days. The hippopotamus heard the shrill voice of the heartless bird-man saying that he didn't go much on virgins. Reg was turning up the gramophone and starting to shuffle over the parquet floor, beating time with his quirt. With one chomp of his second-largest mouth in the world, Mvhu could have bitten him in half.

Was that what the giraffe really wanted?

Was there one vengeful bone in her seven great vertebrae that were still keeping that fine head proud and in the air?

Gently Mrs. Mcwa lowered herself into a chair and sat straight-backed, looking at the wall. Reg pulled the Staff Officer on to the floor. Pyper hopped up and down on the spot. Pforzheim and Albert stayed put, their eyes anxious.

"Dance" Reg shouted. "Dance or die!"

Pforzheim's nostrils pinched. His eyes shrank further into his head.

"Who with?"

"With your little friend!"

"I can't dance with Albert!"

Reg snatched the needle-arm off the record.

"You heard what I said? Dance or die. That is your choice. My friend Pyper is with me heart and soul, why can't you share my happiness? These are my good days. I will look back on them when I am older – if I ever get the chance – so relax and enjoy yourselves with me...and dance!"

Albert pressed himself into Pforzheim's chest.

"Do as he says Dave. You can lead. It's not worth arguing with him. I'll imagine you're the Irishwoman whose name I've forgotten and you can imagine I'm the wife of the metallurgist."

Pforzheim and Albert took the floor.

Reg smiled encouragingly at the big Englishman by the window.

"Will you dance with my wife sir?"

Mvhu fixed his small piggy eyes on the police chief and opened his nose-holes, releasing lungfulls of angry air. Plodding across to the seated woman he stood before her, feet firmly planted, and offered his arm.

"Come Louise!" Reg chuckled. "Here is a fitting partner for a woman of such good breeding as yourself. A gentleman if ever I saw one."

"I'm no fucking gentleman!" Mvhu roared suddenly. "Don't you call me names you decadent human offal!"

Reg stepped back, his quirt raised.

Mvhu braced himself for the blow.

With all his layers of fat, no amount of beating could get through.

Then Louise was standing by his side, her hoof in his.

She moved with infinite caution, a sway here, a sway there.

Mvhu could feel the shivers in her limbs. To move was hurting her but she nursed herself into Mvhu's arms and steered him away from her husband.

Reg lowered his quirt.

They were all dancing at last.

The puppets were working.

He put on his latest record, a Hully-Gully by Trini Lopez: "If I Had A Hammer."

As Mrs. Mcwa forced herself to catch the rhythm of the music she gasped and clutched at her back and thighs. Mvhu moved forward as if to shepherd her off the floor but she pushed him away. Her lips drew back with the smarting pain, agony flared her nostrils. Deep sighs of suffering eased from her narrow chest. But she danced; bending, dipping, wheeling, her body rolling from the hips like a loose ball-joint. Mvhu followed her, nervous of the mad brightening of her big soft eyes and the crashing canter of her shanks. She reached out for him and seized his neck, whirling his $4\frac{1}{2}$ tons round until they were stamping round in a great jig, driving the other dancers off the floor. Faster and faster she went, whimpering and laughing in turn, her mouth open, lips thrust forward towards Mvhu. They moved together, closer, closer, still spiralling, until the giraffe and the hippopotamus drove their mouths together. Their great tongues met, coiled and melted into a magnificent knot.

A great shout of triumph went up from the window. The soldiers had left their corrugated-iron billet and the blue shades of the jacaranda. All of them had loved Mrs. Mcwa for many a long, tedious month while they guarded her husband: now they all had a chance to see her as in their animal dreams as she stretched her long, knowing body through the barriers of pain, breaking into the frenzied clutch and kick of the dance of life-in-death.

NINETEEN PHÉNOMÈNE

"You really couldn't care less, could you?"

Albert's question was directed at Pyper. All Reg's visitors were standing in the ornamental garden by the beheaded cherubs while the Chef de Poste locked his wife in an upper bedroom and instructed the sentries. Reg had not been upset by the Englishman kissing his wife, in fact he had been strangely pleased as, he said, it proved that Louise was not as indifferent to herself as she had appeared to be since Reg had come to Elizabethville to serve Tshombe. The marriage had been over as far as sex was concerned for several years but Reg found Louise a boon at social functions and kept her on as an official wife while gratifying himself elsewhere. He needed to keep some glimmer of life in her big eyes.

"What are you talking about Albert?"

"He's saying your feathers are falling out," Mvhu said gruffly.

"You're a little shit. You're heartless."

Pyper lit a cigarette, his upper lip gleaming in the match-flame, still moist with Simba.

"You've got me arse-about-face Albert. News is what I'm basically interested in. News is change. Stories. But I don't start the change when I'm faced with a cold fish like Reg. He provides the action. On my own ground with Hammerkop I'll get things going, but not here. I want an undignified world Albert, but not undignified because I'm dead. Here I don't count. That's the way I want it. If I start counting then I'm in trouble like poor old Reg is. He's not here for long. He knows that. When Tshombe goes, Reg will go. You'll get your just punishment for old Reg in time. Just leave it to the Congo."

Reg came out of the house and beckoned his visitors to get in the Mercedes. He had booked a table at the Lido. Pforzheim, Albert and Mvhu had argued with Pyper about accepting the invitation but Reg had never bothered to extend it. He had merely instructed them to accompany him.

As Mvhu sat in the back seat with Albert and Pforzheim he thought about Louise and the long night she would spend in the furniture warehouse, guarded, alone, unhappy. In time would they have found each other's whole animalselves? Was her burst of passion just one hand reaching out between the bars of her prison? Would she spend the rest of her life as Reg's slave? A graceful carving of that noble, antique creature which looked down on the earth with

192

such gentle sorrow? Like the animal in Man, wasn't she an ornament on a psychic mantelshelf? Louise may have rejoined her animalself through loneliness, pushing her mind back through layer after layer of arid education, custom, habit. If she had always been aware of her origins she would never have married the mechanical maniac Reg. That would have been like the victim wedding the bullet.

"I received a telephone call while I was putting Louise away for the night. Someone by the name of Matthias. He is looking for you."

"Oh, don't worry about him Reg. . ." Pyper said dismissively.

"On the contrary John. Any friend of yours is a friend of mine. When he told me of the large numbers in his party I could not invite him to dinner with us, but I did tell him where we were going and suggested that he bring the others along for a swim and a few beers once they had found somewhere to eat."

Pyper looked apprehensive, pursing his cupidbow lips.

"Christ Reg, those bastards will come into the restaurant and spoil the evening. They're hungrier than the crematorium crows and not too sophisticated when it comes to wielding the old knife and fork."

"Don't worry John. They won't disturb us. I have ordered the maître d'hôtel to cancel all existing bookings for the evening – including one for the Canadian ambassador – and not to accept any further requests for tables. There's a hot-dog stand at the swimming-pool. They can feed there."

With Pyper still muttering about the dangers of inviting the Bucket-Wheel Excavator Gang anywhere after they had been on the beer for a while, Reg drove the Mercedes out of the city and on to an open road signposted to Leopoldville.

The restaurant that Reg had commandeered for the evening was part of a country club situated three miles outside Elizabethville. Reg drove into a deserted car-park and conducted his guests into the reception area where a bald, solemn European with tired eyes was waiting for them. He ushered the party into the restaurant, suggesting a table by the window so they could overlook the Olympic-size swimming-pool. Reg immediately ordered two bottles of champagne and some brandy.

"Wash away the taste of that beer. Freshen up the palate eh? Now John, ask your friends to look more cheerful please. Tonight we celebrate! No long faces!"

"You heard what the Chef de Poste says!" Pyper shrilled. "No long faces! Crack a smile or two for Christ's sake! Come on Staff Officer! Let's see your dimples!"

Pforzheim bared his teeth in a lupine grin.

Albert tried to give a nice friendly smile like his Dad had taught him to do whenever the rebels or intellectuals called in for a pair of trousers.

Mvhu crinkled up the corners of his eyes and showed his teeth.

The Staff Officer uncovered her tombstones.

But their hearts were not in it.

While the Belge poured out the champagne cocktails, Mvhu looked at the swimming-pool, enjoying the shimmering azure of the water and trying to forget how he would like to thrash Reg with his own quirt. Overhead a Congolese moon of luminous beauty spanned the night with pale sheets of silver while the cicadas and bush insects sang and chirruped in the distance. Without Reg it would have been a pleasant night out. Mvhu could have relaxed and had a few drinks with his friends. As it was he found himself angry, frustrated and impatient to leave. The sooner he got away from the brutal police chief the better. A pause began as conversation dried up again. Reg stared at his guests, about to command their cheerfulness.

Then came the sound of singing, mixed with the grumble of an engine.

> "*Luna lwaya lwaya lwaya ee lwaya*
> *Lwaya kwa liwate kwa upa musiale*
> *Mina mina ee mina*
> *Mina ba ba se banyandile.*"

Reg cocked his head to one side, then looked questioningly at Pyper.

"Your friends John?"

Pyper nodded gloomily.

"That's an old Lozi song they're singing. You know the Lozis came from the Congo years ago?" Reg said urbanely. "They're ex-Congolese actually."

"What does it mean?" Mvhu asked, intending to make some dialogue out of the arrival of the Bucket-Wheel Exacavator Gang as his contribution to the party, also irritated by Reg's claim on his friends' song.

Reg listened again. Many of the words were slurred or bawled so

194

rumbustiously that they were difficult to distinguish. Then he nodded and laid a hand on the table, beating time.

"We are going to the sea in the east,
You are remaining behind – farewell!"

Mvhu frowned, displeased that Reg should have found any association with men he had come to like. He preferred Reg as ignorant and cruel, like the man who had now turned to the maître d'hôtel and was cursing him for not having antelope *au poivre* on the menu. Reg had switched back to the attack, anger in his face. He would have continued with his attack on the Belge's incompetence as a caterer but the doors at the bottom end of the pool were suddenly thrown open and several waiters in red fezes were pushed through, followed by a crowd of rowdily drunken men carrying George Crompton.

"All right, then, what have you got?" Reg said sourly.

"Fillet steak. I am the only man in Elizabethville who has fillet steak. I will do it with a sauce made from cream, garlic..."

The Staff Officer smiled through the window as the Bucket-Wheel Excavator Gang eased George Crompton into a chair. Matthias smiled and waved. There was a continual uproar on the concrete surround of the pool as the supporters shouted their orders for beer at the waiters.

Pyper groaned.

"I'm sorry Reg."

"Sorry for what? One Congolese against sixty or seventy Zonkendawons! Aren't the odds on my side?" Reg laughed at his own joke and tipped another champagne cocktail down his throat. "Who is the European there? Is he ill?"

"No Reg. He's a Zombie. In fact George is the only white Zombie I know except for the New Zealand prime minister."

The arrival of the supporters' coach had enlivened the spirits of the dinner-guests and they now drank more freely. The Staff Officer began to glow and glitter, her skin dazzling white and perfumed beneath the silk dress which Reg had purloined from his wife's wardrobe. It was too small for the Staff Officer and she had a struggle to keep her splendid upper half covered while she drank from her glass and toyed with the hors d'oeuvres brought by the Belge. Conscious of Reg's eyes always on her, and the worshipping stares of the drunken horde now lying around the edge of the pool, the Staff Officer had begun to see opportunities in this outing that she had not perceived before. The steel was back in her eyes and her broad,

195

snowy shoulders spread as if the huge congress of hungry eyes were the caresses of lovers on her lionskin.

"To the best people in the world!" Reg tinkled his glass against Pyper's. "Tonight we will celebrate until you drop. I think you are beginning to thaw out now. A few rosy cheeks? Come on gentlemen! Don't disapprove of me. I am a child. We are all children! Be as your compatriots out there! Enjoy life!"

The Staff Officer could not take her eyes off the shining water. It was drawing her like a magnet. It was a mirror, a giant reflecting apparatus. Flying over it, her beauty would be magnified a thousand times and clearly visible to God, the aliens on the stars, the man in the moon, the astronauts in their sputniks, the great universal horn. She would be the swan of heaven, a white soaring splendour.

Pulling back the sliding window she stepped outside on to the pool surround, raising her hand as a roar of welcome went up from the crowd. Even George Crompton woke up.

"Hmmm!" Reg mused. "She must be some woman in her own country John. I wouldn't like to take her out to dinner every night with the speed she can empty glasses though. Will she be all right out there?"

"Reg, the old Staff Officer would have been all right doing a strip at the siege of Stalingrad. Don't worry about her. She's indestructible."

Standing by the side of the springboard, the Staff Officer shed her clothes. There was no attempt at titillation. They were just an encumbrance to be discarded as quickly as possible. Sensing that there were better things to come, the supporters hushed, waiting for her next move.

With a tripping run the Staff Officer reached the end of the springboard and jumped in the air. She sparkled bright in the beaming moon.

The crowd sighed softly.

When she came down on the board again she flexed her knees and jumped a bit higher. Her eyes flashed silver fire and her teeth dazzled.

The crowd moaned.

Soon she was leaping higher and higher, arms outstretched, hair tousled, skin on white fire with the moon, soft crooning sounds issuing from her parted lips as her feet slammed time after time on the rough matting. White, wonderful, the Staff Officer flung herself at the black night, challenging its darkness with her radiant flesh.

196

"Receive me!" she called. "Do not fight me!"

The crowd were hypnotised. They held on to chairs, plunged their heads in the water to convince themselves that this superb event was really happening in their lifetime, crawled over the concrete rubbing their hot lips over its roughness and drawing blood, clutched at their crutches, eyeballs and hair in ecstatic disbelief, shouted garbled pleas to the flying beauty which had invaded their most secret souls. The Staff Officer had taken them over. That night she could have the most crowded lionskin in the history of human relations.

Reg saw the shooting-star on the springboard, the dazzling white woman, and ground his teeth in madness. Responding to her erotic velocity, the thrusting, whooping, urging of her incandescent flesh as it shot higher and higher again, Reg swore that all that blaze should be his. He would wrap his manhood round it and snuff it out like a candle! But the Staff Officer was leaping beyond his reach! At each leap her body quivered upwards like a rocket at blast-off, silver fire bursting into the water below as she surged towards the sky. If he was ever to catch her, he would have to act quickly. Running out on to the pool surround he tried to step over the fallen supporters as they licked the backs of their hands and nestled into each other, whispering love-words. But they would not let him pass. He was grabbed and manhandled back to the window, angry, drugged eyes staring into his, curses falling on his head. How dare he try to hold the Staff Officer down? She was carrying all those masculine souls nearer to spiritual union with the Lord of all life at each fantastic bound.

"Get me a telephone!" Reg snarled at the gaping Belge.

While the crowd resumed its adoration of the throbbing woman, their hoarse voices echoing the musical thrum of the springboard, Reg made a call. For a minute he spoke urgently into the receiver, one palm battering at his thigh. Then he put the instrument down and, like a doomed man, turned his eyes back to the escaping dream.

The Staff Officer was soaring still but now she had introduced aerial acrobatics: twists, turns, somersaults. As she plummeted and streaked through the soft air her flesh seemed to attract even more lustre from the moon and the lapping water. Pirouetting to the drawn-out howls of tragic lust that were coming from deep in the tormented subconscious of her massed lovers, the Staff Officer rolled her beautiful belly, breast and thigh to educe even more from their sexual sources. Had any woman ever been so yearned for? she asked herself as the

197

board sang its deep note beneath her feet again. Was ever heart and soul so completely given by so many to one woman?

"Beg me to come down!" she cried throatily. "Beg me!"

The answering bellow was more than she could ever have hoped for. Bats clattered out of the trees deep inside the surrounding bush. Monkeys gibbered as the strange rutting cry went up into the Congolese night. Eyes of many small creatures were turned to the Lido and the flashing star that seemed to be shimmering high above it, appearing and disappearing in a rapid rhythm.

"More! More!" the Staff Officer shouted happily. "Grovel! Get on your knees and grovel!"

Albert jumped down from the table and ran on his hands and knees over the backs of weeping men who could take no more and had collapsed in orgasmic trances. Leaning against the filtration pipes he called up to the human comet that he had known all along she was Irish. Oh the swoop and whirl of creamy skin against the black velvet heavens, the diamond stars sparkling in the dark V of holy hair! Sinking to his knees again Albert crawled towards the springboard.

"Stay with me please! Don't go away! Remain on earth my love!"

Out of the corner of her eye the Staff Officer recognised Albert. Triumph rose in her breast. A few days ago that man had fought bitterly against her wish to have him love her on the lionskin. Now here he was, agog with desire, in flames! She laughed delightedly, throwing back her head and breathing happiness at the rejoicing moon.

"You see! He comes!"

"Oh, the voice of my beloved!" Albert howled. "Come to my bed! I cannot live without you!"

With superhuman energy the Staff Officer leapt even higher, her pleasure driving her upwards and clear of the roof until she could see all the lights of Elizabethville. It was all hers. To the lost horizons of the physical world, she was queen.

Had he been looking in the wrong place after all?

Mvhu inflamed, morose, uplifted, saw in the Staff Officer all the Greekishness and Gothicness of the civilisation he had tried to leave behind – the struggle to soar out of the earth and leave it far behind, arrowing into space where God waited, planets on his fingers, stars on his toes, his lap spread to catch Western Man as he keeled over at the top of his flight and fluttered down into the Holy Apron of the Lord. There she was, the essence of the thrust to get away from the animalself! A Corinthian column! A flying buttress! Obelisk! Post Office Tower! Nelson's Column! Statue of Liberty! Way, way up in the night she flew, the highest achievement of manself, escaping from the humbling earth. Why could he not join her? At least imagine himself transported to that zenith like the rest of the beseeching crowd? Was his whole quest only an admission of failure? A childish dream?

He seemed to be the only one who wanted to travel backwards rather than forwards.

Downwards rather than upwards.

Was he being left behind?

His animalself stirred defensively.

There was ecstasy and ecstasy. He would still seek for the joy he did not know, rather than the one he knew.

When she received Reg's telephone call Phénomène was packing in readiness for a visit to her lover General Duraantjji, the leader of the Simba rebels in the Marième province. As it was only through the serpentine influence of Reg that she could safely make these trips to see the old man, she grudgingly put off the time of her departure and took a taxi to the Lido.

She noticed that there were only two vehicles in the car-park – Reg's Mercedes and a coach with a ZK sticker on the rear. This was unusual for a Saturday night. Normally the Lido was packed. In fact she had been booked for an early dinner there with the Canadian ambassador but the appointment had been mysteriously cancelled. Once Phénomène got out of the taxi she heard the noise. Shouts, cheers, sobs, screams, frantic cries of joy, rose into the air as if a tremendous party was in full swing. Also, over the white flat roof of the restaurant, a brilliant white figure hurtled, slowed down at the apex of a great thrust upwards, then gracefully fell back to earth.

Pausing to go to the powder room, Phénomène wondered what was going on. Reg had many odd ideas. She only maintained her liaison with the dumpy bureaucrat in order to see her old man in the mountains, the barbaric general. Reg had never asked too much of her on previous occasions. Perhaps this was the night that the Chef de Poste went over the top? Shrugging as she adjusted her turban and the hang of her long silk dress on her pointed breasts, the powerfully-built courtesan glanced at herself in the mirror. No standard of beauty could be applied to the face that she saw reflected there. Phénomène was a standard on her own.

Under the emblazoned silk turban her small, slightly slanted eyes were black and quick, set high on her cheek-bones. Her complexion was smooth and dark, finely glossed. In her flat nose and big mouth was a brutal animal vigour that was also broadcast from every inch of her short, heavily-set body. When she moved, every atom of her being moved with her, communicating strength, pleasure and hunger. Her teeth were huge when she smiled but huge with welcome. When her mouth was closed there was only the rich fields of her purple lips and any man who saw them was drawn there.

She patted the earrings set in her small pricked ears.

Phénomène was ready for Reg, whatever his plans were.

Reg caught sight of her as she wended her way through the tables. "Quickly! Quickly!" he gasped. "You were never needed so!"

Phénomène studied the Chef de Poste. Sweat was dribbling down his cheeks. His hands were tightly knotted in his groin.

"Are you in pain Reg?" she asked in a low, heavy voice.

"Bring her down! Teach the white bitch a lesson! She's been up there for half-an-hour and won't come down! Beat her for me! I beg you!"

Phénomène stared out of the window and down the length of the swimming-pool. In the old days of colonial rule many strange things had happened at the Lido, many extravagant displays of love and madness, many perversions and forbidden delights. Black and white sybarites had given the city a reputation the length and breadth of Africa so that men had come from all parts of the world to see and enjoy sin and corruption, incredible decadence, blazing luxury and wealth, tortuously inventive malpractices.

None of them had seen what Phénomène could see now.

Anger drove her brows together.

Once the city had turned from the white moon. There had been blood in the streets on the nights when it was washed out of the Congolese sky. Now it had risen again, the pale bitch in whose service all dark men had been listed. At her feet roared a mass of slaves, begging for one touch of her divine finger-tip. Phénomène stormed down the length of the pool using the backs of these grovellers as paving-stones.

"My friends!" Reg shouted from the window, shielding his eyes from the Staff Officer. "I have brought you a competitor! Give her a chance! Please! Thank you..."

The Staff Officer reduced the aerial scope of her next series of leaps and held her hands together in contemplative mood as she watched the African woman walking towards the springboard. This was an unexpected intrusion. This was her territory.

"Now Staff Officer, we will have fair play!" Reg shouted from the window, eyes still averted. "We will see what you are made of!"

Shrugging her magnificent shoulders, the Staff Officer did a double back somersault which brought gasps of admiration from the crowd. Albert beat his head on the concrete and prayed to be struck dead, such was his overwhelming desire.

"Is this what you're worried about?" Phénomène boomed roughly, pointing up at the whirling white woman. "Is this what has set the Congo alight again? *Tcha!* She is an amateur!"

"What d'ya mean?" Pyper yelled, his girl's face shining with fanatical adoration. "She's a bloody miracle! She's the end of the world! Look at her go!"

Reg thrust his face across the table towards the shrieking New Zealander.

"Cool down John. You have seen nothing. Don't put any bets on it."

"Don't give me all that shit Reg!" Pyper retorted. "What's your girl wearing a bloody turban for? Is she bald or something?"

Slowly Phénomène began shifting her big feet about. At the same time two broad, stubby hands cunningly worked at unfastening her turban, winding its gold chain round and round her wrist. Slothfully the major contours of her squat body began to move.

"Aaaah!" Reg sighed encouragingly.

"Christ Reg!" Pyper screamed. "She's built like The Brown Bomber! I'd rather poke an overturned tramcar or a dead horse any day."

"Just give her time John," Reg said confidently, his eyes hidden from the soaring Staff Officer by a menu. "She will bring her down to earth."

"Not a chance!" Pforzheim yelled. "Anyone want a bet? I'll give twenty to one on the Staff Officer."

"Taken!" Reg said grimly, holding out his hand.

For Mvhu the night was getting darker as he watched Phénomène. As soon as she had entered the restaurant, he had felt her presence.

201

Now he saw her round, solid head, smooth and dark; now her short neck and strong shoulders; the fine curve of her arms. As he saw the dress fall away he could not bear to look – except at her feet. That was enough for a soul as troubled as his. To see her in all the burning darkness of her mighty body would be dangerous. It could break his heart out of his chest and leave it bleeding on the floor. The Staff Officer, unconscious of the fact that Phénomène had already upstaged her with one of her worshippers, continued to clatter up and down on the springboard.

"See what I mean?" Reg breathed. "See?"

Mvhu raised his eyes and promptly closed them again. Phénomène was the ultimate. One glimpse of the power in that round marvellous body was enough.

It was pure hippopotamagic.

"Whang! Whang!" went the springboard as the Staff Officer sensed some of the attention being diverted from her. Even now, tired as she was by her long sojourn in the air, she had other tricks. Tumbling upwards in a high arc she opened her legs and held on to her ankles, hurtling back to the springboard so her buttocks took the brunt of the descent. Like a phosphorous ball she flew upwards again, the imprint of the matting hatched across her dazzling rear.

"Did you see that?" Pyper screeched elatedly at Reg. "She's uncatchable! Take that heavyweight away! She can't be spoken of in the same breath as the Staff Officer! Look at her!"

"Let there be light!" Albert groaned, salivating over the tiles at the pool's edge. "Oh Jehovah save us!"

Reg did not reply. He was watching Phénomène. The sturdy beauty was standing, hands on hips, following the flight of the Staff Officer, her fleshy blue lips curled with contempt. Reg noticed that the big Englishman who had kissed his wife was affecting a dogged, ponderous regard for the black rival of the Staff Officer. His eyes had contracted. Deep, sensual grunts shook his rib-cage and his heavy loins squirmed in the chair.

"What do you think eh? That is woman as she should be. The black Genesis my friend. You cannot fathom that creature."

As Reg gave sly encouragement to Mvhu, Phénomène struck.

As the Staff Officer opened her legs again to repeat her arse-jarring rebound, Phénomène ran along the springboard and thrust herself upwards. The Staff Officer coming down met Phénomène coming up, the black adversary's neck and shoulders slamming straight into the Staff Officer's exposed crutch. Grabbing the Staff Officer's knees, Phénomène descended to the springboard again, gave a mighty heave which lifted her and her shrieking load upwards again, then dipped and hurled herself and the Staff Officer into the pool.

A terrible silence fell on the crowd. Their heat was suddenly extinguished, drowned. When the Staff Officer surfaced, cursing her opponent's unfair tactics, all she received was a cool sympathy. She was out of her element – whereas Phénomène was now completely immersed in hers. As the Staff Officer dragged her weary, pink body out of the water and lay gasping on the side, no eye sought her out. Every man in the wondering crowd was watching the underwater eroticism of Phénomène as she lazily swam, rolled and glided through the clear water, walked on the bottom, floated to the surface so her breasts sailed like two new basalt islands in a glittering ocean, sank again, blew water from her deep blue lips like a whale, sighed like an underwater volcano. Down there was the beginning of every shot sperm, every impregnated egg and every quickening embryo.

TWENTY THE TRIAL OF THE BEAST IN MAN

The Consul had been asked to keep a watching brief over British affairs and interests in the Democratic Republic of the Congo while his colleague returned to London for an operation. When Pyper got a message through to Myakajunji informing him of the arrest and pending trial of a British citizen in Elizabethville, the Consul thought it wise to fly up at once and check for himself on the circumstances of the case. There had recently been a number of embarrassing incidents involving British citizens who were recruits in the mercenary companies that had been raised by the Congolese government. One of them had been the son of a director of the Bank of England who had been arrested for black market offences while the other was the ex-husband of a fourth secretary in a Government ministry's third daughter who was urgently needed at home to feature in a divorce action. His colleague had managed to extricate both men from the hands of the Congolese police and get them back to England. It had cost the Foreign Service a lot of time and money but the government had reckoned both well spent.

The Consul thought that an opportunity to shine might be presented to him. He had suffered several days of harassing enquiries and accusations as a result of the article in the Zonkendawo Times alleging that he had planned to assassinate the Minister of Mines with a housebrick. Only yesterday had he managed to persuade the African government that the whole thing had been a ghastly mistake, mainly perpetrated by a Lost Englishman.

So the trip to Elizabethville was a welcome interlude.

The Consul was almost in holiday mood as he sat in the back of his taxi on the way to the prison in the northern suburbs.

Tonight he would dine with his old friend the Canadian ambassador, maybe play a few rubbers of bridge, talk, share a good bottle of wine. He would be able to forget the humiliation of recent events. All that was behind him now.

The Consul said a quiet prayer for the family connections of the prisoner, paid off the taxi and walked to the gate of the prison, his letter of authority to visit the British national snug in his inside pocket.

Such was his lightness of spirit, he whistled in between puffs on his cigarette.

"Have you brought the name-changing form?"

The Consul could not take his eyes off the bruised and bloody mess that was the face of his persecutor. The features of Hurl Halfcock had been crushed into a blue-black jelly from which two bloodshot eyes stared with gargoyle defiance. To frame a word took the prisoner several seconds as his mouth was askew and most of his front teeth were missing.

"I've decided what I want to change my name to."

The Consul dropped his eyes and looked at the table-top.

"Ah," he sighed, "oh holy God, why me? Why me of all people?"

"Will it take long to get it back from London?"

The Consul summoned up all his strength and looked into the puffy red eggs of the man he had come to save, his terrible animal eyes.

"Where is your passport?" he asked in a low, unsteady voice.

"Reg has it."

"Who is Reg?"

"He's the chief of police."

"Why do you call him Reg?"

"That's his name."

"Did he do this to you?"

"Not by himself. He had help."

"Where did it happen?"

"First at the Lido, then in the jeep, then at the police station, then in the cell. He's been to see me quite a lot."

"Are you going to say that you walked into a door?"

"No, I'm going to say that I walked into Reg."

"What did you do?"

The Consul chain-smoked while the prisoner told the story of the events of the previous night. It was an honest account, unvarnished and unembellished.

"Then you deserve everything you got Mr. Halfcock!" the Consul remarked bitterly.

"I didn't get anything. They all jumped in after me."

"You didn't actually..."

"No."

"So it was only an attempt?"

"I'm afraid so."

"Do you realise that if you had been successful it is more than likely that you would now be dead?"

The prisoner nodded.

"And you expect me to get you out of it?"

"No."

"Then why did you get me up here?"

"I didn't."

"Who did then?"

"One of the others."

"What others?"

The prisoner gave the Consul the names of his companions. When he reached Pyper the Consul held up his hand. He knew who had got him up there.

"Mr. Halfcock, you know what my natural inclination is?"

"I hope it brings you less trouble than mine," Mvhu replied sincerely.

"I feel like just walking out of here and letting you go through with this business alone. You have brought it on your own head. No one is going to believe that cock and bull story you've just told me."

Mvhu remained silent, deeply satisfied by the Consul's apposite

205

and sympathetic choice of phrase.

"But if I do, you know what will happen?"

"They'll put me in prison for ten years?"

"No, they'll more than likely take you to an out-of-the-way spot and shoot you. Personally I think that would be a good idea."

Mvhu leaned heavily over the table. He was unable to sit down because Reg and his aides had truncheoned his groin for twenty minutes the moment they had got him back to the police headquarters and their sound-proof room. His balls were three times their normal size and he had to walk with his legs wide apart.

"All right. I'm not holding you here. Let them get on with it."

"I can't do that," the Consul sighed again, with genuine regret.

"Why not?"

"Mr. Pyper."

"Pyper?"

"I have just spent a week getting myself out of the last load of trouble that congenital liar landed me in. If I refuse to help you then he will do it again. I will lose my position and be prematurely retired on a reduced pension. He will ruin my career."

"Then what are you going to do?"

"I will have to try and get you out of this mess, much as it goes against my better judgement. Firstly, have you made any statement to the police yet?"

"No. They haven't asked me for one. Whenever they come to see me it's only to beat me up."

"They haven't charged you with anything?"

"No."

"And you're sure that you were not successful, even in the confusion that there must have been with so many people in the water at the same time?"

"I wasn't. I wish I had been, then all this would have been worth while."

The Consul got to his feet.

"I will come back to see you tomorrow morning at the same time, all being well. Although it goes against the grain I will lodge a protest about the way you have been subjected to police brutality while in custody. You do realise that in my heart of hearts I would like to have wielded a truncheon myself?"

"Yes, I can understand that."

"Make no statements. Keep your mouth shut. Behave yourself."

206

"All right."

"And Mr. Halfcock, do me a favour."

"What's that?"

"Just be yourself for a while. If you try and use any of these aliases you keep going on about then I will have no chance to save you. Did you know that people who keep changing their names are either criminals or schizophrenics?"

"But when it is all over will you give me the form? I know what I want to be called now. No more doubts. I've decided."

"You know what I would like to call you, don't you?"

"Yes."

"And that if the Congolese take you into an out-of-the-way spot it doesn't matter what the hell you're called?"

"Yes, though I'd like this on my gravestone."

"I don't think they'll bother to mark the place."

Mvhu leaned over, put one mangled hand on the Consul's shoulder and whispered the name by which he wished to be known, should he survive. The Consul closed his eyes for a moment, sighed again, then left to begin his errand of mercy.

And until that name is made known, we must call him something transitory and anonymous.

Mr. X.

The Consul failed to prevent the trial.

Two days later he sat in the public gallery at No. 1, Central Court, his pamphlet on Roman-Dutch Law in his hands, and tried to follow the case. There were five judges, all African. From the beginning of the procedure, the ancient maxim that the accused in Roman-Dutch Law is guilty until proved innocent was studiously asserted. As soon as the prisoner was brought up to the court, the judges glowered at him as though he had abused each man's individual pride. When the court official read out the crime of which the Englishman was accused, the judges bit their lips with rage and stabbed their ball-point pens into the bench. The Consul gave the Canadian ambassador, who had agreed to accompany him to the trial, a sideways glance and shook his head.

"Who ever heard of a charge like that?" he whispered. "The whole thing is ludicrous."

For Mr. X had been accused of Rape Of The Fair Country and Insult To The National Pride, as well as Damage To The Flower Of

207

Congolese Womanhood.

The defence lawyer was a young African who had spent two years in Brussels at the Law faculty of the university, failed his legal practitioner's examinations, and had only been in business in Elizabethville for two months. Directly after the Consul's visit to his office, the young man had received a telephone call from Reg threatening his life if he did too good a job on the Englishman's case.

But the young lawyer had been unable to get his client to admit his guilt. When he rose to defend the accused there was a marked hesitation in his manner and his speech was halting. After a few sentences he started to shrug, twitch his gown and nibble at his papers.

The accused, he said, had been bewitched.

Was that the same as a plea of temporary insanity? asked a judge scornfully. For everyone knew that Englishmen did not get bewitched. Being bewitched was an African prerogative.

"No sir, for the accused has no intention of becoming unbewitched."

"You mean he is still bewitched?"

"Yes sir."

"Who has bewitched him?"

The lawyer held up his papers and only dared to peep over the top.

"I hardly find the courage to say it sir."

"Come on, we haven't got all day!"

"His animalself sir."

"His animalself?" the five judges chorused. "What is that?"

The lawyer explained as best he could, bringing in the fact that Mr. X had been bewitched by this inner demon into thinking that the woman in question – Phénomène – was a cow hippopotamus. When he made this point the bench of judges boiled over into tantrums of rage. All of them had knowledge of Phénomène. One thing they were all sure about. She was no cow hippopotamus but all woman from the tips of her cute little toes to the top of her stylish silk turban.

"If you will bear with me," the lawyer proceeded doggedly, "we will ask for the woman in question to be brought into court and the matter of animalself can be examined."

Reg leant across to the prosecutor and whispered something to him. The man, one of the few Belgians left in the department of Justice, rose to inform the judges that Phénomène had gone up-country to visit a sick uncle.

"Unnecessary anyway!" a judge shouted. "We don't need her!

This man is wasting our time with metaphysical nonsense!"

"Then may we call some of the accused's companions to witness the bewitching? They are all aware of his belief that he is entering the physical state of the animal under discussion."

Reg leant across again. The prosecutor rose.

"These aliens were all deported immediately after the riot at the Lido. The government wished to avoid a diplomatic incident and only arrested the chief offender, the prisoner."

"My client asserts, sirs, that he did not succeed in his apparent mission to acquire carnal knowledge of the woman. The power of the bewitching not only affected his mind, but also his aim and prowess."

The prosecutor rose again, this time of his own volition.

"Sirs, we have a sworn statement from the woman in question that she was penetrated and inseminated by the accused ten times in rapid succession."

The judges paused, their faces switching from irritation to intense speculation. The oldest, a rake-like man with a large nose and small gold wire spectacles leaned far over the bench, his hands knotted together.

"Mr. Prosecutor, when you say 'in rapid succession', what degree of rapidity are you talking about?" he asked.

The prosecutor consulted his papers.

"About the space of a minute sir."

"Ten times in about the space of a minute?" the old judge muttered incredulously. "Ten times in the space of a minute?"

"Ten times in the space of a minute?" said the next judge to the old man's right.

"Ten times in the space of a minute?" thought the court official who was watching a gecko lizard on the ceiling. "That's once every six seconds!"

He stood up, his face aglow.

"That's once every six seconds!" he told the bench.

"Once every six seconds?" said the senior judge sitting in the centre.

"Once in every six seconds!" shouted a policeman guarding the door. "By the bones of my father that's going some!"

"Once every six seconds?" whispered the Canadian ambassador to the Consul. "I don't believe it."

The Consul gave his friend a stony glance.

209

He believed it.

He believed that this Lost Englishman was capable of anything.

If the prosecutor had said that Mr. X had moved into the Congolese national at 186,000 feet per second he would have accepted it without qualm.

"Tell us more about this animalself," leered the senior judge winningly. "I'm really quite interested."

The prisoner shook his head and whispered to the defence counsel.

"He says that the court has got it all wrong sir," the young lawyer started to say. But the senior judge brought him up short.

"No, we have got it all right. What we wish to investigate is how he got it all right every six seconds. Let the man speak for himself. We want to know about this animalself, don't we?"

The other judges agreed strongly, smiling encouragingly at Mr. X. They were intrigued. In fact they had visibly warmed towards the big man who stood before them.

"Did he receive his injuries through this fantastic performance?" the oldest judge enquired solicitously. "Was it the vibrations?"

"No sir, the prisoner claims that he was beaten up by the authorities."

"What authorities?" the senior judge said indignantly. "Surely we would not treat a ten times in the space of a minute man with anything but the deepest respect?"

"Can't we get back to this animalself thing?" the old judge pleaded. "It seems to me to be the central issue."

Mr. X was asked to tell his story in his own words.

He started with his life in England and the life of mindless consumption. While he dwelt on this subject the judges became mildly bored but they did not interrupt as they were waiting for him to get to the important part of the story.

When he told them about his unhappy marriage they exchanged knowing glances and gave avuncular smiles. They had all been through this phase of development themselves. The oldest judge interrupted him to ask if he had been a ten times in the space of a minute man with his wife and was disappointed to learn that it had not been the case.

Then Mr. X got on to his Theory Of The Three Races Of Man.

At the end of the explanation the senior judge said that he thought it was as good an interpretation of the situation in Western Europe as he had heard, but did not the honourable prisoner realise that questions of race were necessarily different in Africa?

Mr. X agreed with the senior judge and proceeded to speak at length about the intellectual difficulties he had faced when trying to reconcile his theory with the various personalities which he had encountered in Africa so far, and how the whole structure of his theory had been undermined from shortly after the time when he had arrived, and then how it had completely collapsed under the strain of the Staff Officer, Pyper, Crompton and the Bucket-Wheel Excavator Gang, leaving the prisoner with only his search for an identity which he though must be contained in his animalself.

"Ah," said the old judge, rubbing his hands in anticipation, "this is the bit we have been waiting for. Take your time. Speak slowly so the court recorder can get all this down."

"The way I saw it," the prisoner began, "was this. I was essentially looking for my other half. In England I had only been conscious of my manself, the educated half, the processed half..."

"Do we have to go though all that again?" the senior judge begged gently. "We know what you mean. Get to the ten times in the space of a minute bit."

"Objection!" said the prosecutor jumping bravely to his feet. "The judge is leading the witness."

"Mr. Prosecutor."

"Yes sir."

"Shut up."

"Yes sir."

The senior judge nodded at Mr. X to continue.

"It's all very well for you!" Mr. X said with sudden spirit.

"What's all very well for us?" the old judge demanded. "I'd say that it was more all right for you than it is for us. None of us up here have ever been a ten times in the space of a minute man. Isn't that so?"

The other judges grudgingly agreed.

"What's he talking about?" one murmured enviously. "The lucky devil."

"No gratitude, not even any pride. I suppose this is the famous English sang-froid though I must say that ten times in the space of a minute hardly bears out that idea."

"You have lived here all your lives!" Mr. X banged the brass rail in front of him for emphasis. "I was brought up in a society of smug slaves..."

"Well, if all your friends at home were ten times in the space of a minuters then they'd got something to be smug about, hadn't they?"

"Did you know that the English haven't changed their rulers since 1660 when they brought King Charles the Second back from France?"

"I hear he was almost a ten times in the space of a minute man himself."

"While the rest of Europe was undergoing terrific changes in government, we just sat there, a nation of biddable dogs. The last revolution we had was in 1649 when we cut the king's head off, more than three hundred years ago. Things haven't changed since then. We're a nation always on its knees."

"I'm not surprised after ten times in the space of a minute, are you?"

"Even our socialist party prides itself on its conservatism. Our conservative party prides itself on its socialism. They spend all their time pissing in each other's pockets and grovelling to anyone who lets them get near enough. When you've been brought up in that kind of atmosphere what else do you expect a man to turn out like? One minute they tell you that you're the freest man in the world and the next they tell you to stop rocking the boat because we don't want any revolutions here like the Frogs had and the Russians and the Spaniards and the Chinese and the Irish and all the other unreliable people on Earth. Being born English is the most effective anaesthetic you can get. They can tear your internal organs out and you don't feel a thing. Is it any wonder that a man feels that he left half of himself behind in the womb?"

"And you've been trying ten times in the space of a minute to get back in there and retrieve it, haven't you lad?" chuckled the old judge, twisting his gold wired spectacles round in his hands.

Mr. X paused, his colour high, eyes flashing.

"I felt that I had been robbed of my physical self and, having spent three years studying a primitive language that was undergoing castration at the hands of the Christian Church I had no wish to be treated in the same way. What had happened to the Anglo-Saxons was not going to happen to me. I had to find out who I was in the first place, and then, from there, why I had developed into the over-schooled and subjugated person that my environment in England had created."

"You wanted to know where your bollocks came from?" suggested

212

a judge who had remained silent until now but was now clearly fired by the Englishman's tale.

"That's one way of putting it," the prisoner smiled warily.

"It's the only way of putting it!" the judge grinned and clapped his hands. "And that's how you came to be a ten times in the space of a minute person isn't it?"

Mr. X summoned up a second smile, but this time the strain showed.

"What I can't understand is why you're denying it!" the senior judge exclaimed good-naturedly. "With that kind of reputation a man could happily die and ask for no better testament."

"But it is not true," the prisoner insisted.

"Come on now. You admit it and we'll fine you one franc, then we can release the story to the newspapers. Where's the harm?"

"Why should Phénomène, who is an experienced woman as everyone on the bench will testify, say such a thing if it is not true? This is a matter in which she knows her onions."

"Look, I found my animalself. Then I recognised another animal-self which was the same as mine but the opposite sex. My natural instinct was to try and get her to join my herd...."

"You mean you have other women like this? Do you ten times in the space of a minute those as well?"

"No. Please try and treat what I'm saying seriously. This has been a tremendously important experience to me."

"And to us as well. You are the first ten times in the space of a minute rapist ever to appear before this court."

"It was not me," Mr. X insisted.

"Then who was it?"

Mr. X paused. His defence counsel had sat down, grey beneath his coal-black complexion. The Englishman might just as well be holding the gun to his own head. All he had to do was admit the crime and he would be a national hero but no...oh this passion for truth!

"Did I hear the prosecutor say before that all the other people from Zonkendawo had been sent back to their own country after the business at the Lido?" Mr. X asked.

"That is so," the prosecutor replied, "it was thought advisable in the national interest."

"What difference does that make to your case?" The oldest judge grinned. "As far as we're concerned you're still the culprit, and good luck to you young man. By the great king Christ I never managed that kind of recovery rate even in my best years. I take my hat off to you."

"I'll tell you who actually did it" Mr. X said. "I'll name the guilty party."

The senior judge scratched his head with his Biro and looked discomfited.

"You mean it really wasn't you?" he asked miserably.

"No."

"Oh all right then. Who was it?" the old judge shouted, deeply upset.

Mr. X betrayed his friends in a low, but clear voice:

> "Coronation Pork Mbaba
> Washable Trinket Muzozo
> Salvation Tuba Mkana
> Rose Powder Makulu
> Ginger Pencil Mulolo
> Rollyourown Mtine
> Cumulus McCloud Molile
> Zoom Mzlhovu
> Self-Raising Mnama
> Honey Balls Mukambo."

The bench of judges looked bitterly disappointed as Mr. X finished turning Queen's Evidence.

"Who are these men?" the senior judge asked. "And how do you know they are the real culprits?"

"They are the Bucket-Wheel Excavator Gang from Mufunsi Open Pit and they're the only people I know who can move that fast," Mr. X declared steadfastly.

The judges turned their gaze to the prosecutor.

"Who investigated this crime?"

"Monsieur Mcwa, the Chef..."

"Monsieur Mcwa, did you send these remarkable men back to their own country without fully investigating this matter?"

Reg stood up, his shoulders caved, his eyes numb with defeat. He nodded.

"Are you aware that you have deprived me and my colleagues of a really fascinating piece of legal work, the like of which will not come our way again as we are all oldish fellows?"

Reg nodded again.

"And are you aware that you have fallen from power Monsieur

Mcwa and are going to be sent to manage a small border post on the disputed frontier with Ruanda-Urundi where the average life-expectation of our officials is four and a half hours?"

Reg nodded for the last time.

"The case against this Englishman, a Race Three by his own reckoning if ever I saw one, is dismissed. The court is adjourned until tomorrow. Long live the President and God help those who get paid to judge right from wrong as it is a most frustrating business."

As the court adjourned and Mr. X was taken down, the Consul turned to the Canadian ambassador with an acid smile.

"You see how it is Jeff? If that had been someone worth while they would have hanged, drawn and quartered him. As it is this idiot gets off scot-free. There's no justice, you know that don't you? No justice anywhere."

"That looks like how it is," his companion shook his head, sharing the Consul's melancholy. "I suppose all we can do is just do the job we're paid for. All I'm thankful for is that the Limey punk isn't a Canadian who thinks he's a grizzly bear."

TWENTY ONE **MALADIE D'AMOUR**

The Consul accompanied Mr. X all the way back to Mufunsi. At the door of the flat over the Greek supermarket he relieved the Lost Englishman of his passport, explaining that he would need it as part of the application for the name-changing. When the Consul had gone, Mr. X let himself in with the key left under the mat. Even in that familiar room he felt strange – he was now innominate, the no-name, the unidentified. He was as free as the motes of dust in the still air.

Going to the bathroom he tried to tidy up his face. He was still in bad shape. Even the albino had tetched compassionately to himself as he saw the battered features looking over the concrete side of the stairs. Poor Mvhu looked worse thah he did. The beggar decided to call on the IRO to offer him some Malawian Drambuie, it being a salve for those afflicted with loathsome ugliness.

"What do you want?" Mr. X demanded churlishly, holding the door half-shut.

"Have a drink with me?" The albino hold out the bottle. "It won't make you feel worse. Forget your face for a while."

"Where's Ironheart?"

"Ah, Ironheart."

"Well, where is she?"

"She has gone home."

"But this is her home!" Mr. X opened the door wide, his voice raised. "She lives here."

"She has gone to the northern province to her people. When your friends came back from the Congo and told her what had happened, that was when she left you. If I know the ways of women, she will have left you a note."

Mr. X grabbed the albino's bottle and pulled the awful child inside. The first thing that he saw while scanning the room was a letter propped up on the mantelpiece behind the travelling-clock.

"Drink, then read," the albino advised softly.

Mr. X took a long draught of the sweet, heavy liqueur, then opened the letter. The writing was neat, the spelling absolutely correct. Ironheart had obviously paid the township scribe to pen her farewell. It read:

> My dear man,   Sunday.
>   You are a fool to destroy the life God the Great Christ gave you. You will never be satisfied with me. If they do not take your life in the Congo, there will be other ways for you to find to throw it away. This world is not beers. It is not all Congolese women. Why don't you grow up? I am up to here with you and what you are doing to yourself so from now on I will be completely unobtainable at the house of my father. c/o P.O. Box 3, Mwalanda Village, Lundazi District, N. Province. Signed by your friend, IRONHEART.

Mr. X sat down, letting the letter fall to the floor.

Suddenly he had had enough.

All the way back from Elizabethville he had endured the hostility and cynicism of the Consul secure in the knowledge that Ironheart would be waiting at the flat to comfort him. He had dreamed of her hands, of the squares on her head, of her voice. She was the one sane anchor in this ocean of wild currents and winds called Africa. He had refused to ask himself the question as to whether he loved her.

Besides his hunt for himself the emotions which he experienced could only be pointers or guides, hopefully towards the great discovery of the animal fathers. Ironheart might have held more secrets in her dainty head then he could have imagined. Now she was gone, far into the north.

The beatings were back in his head.

His body ached. The truncheons thundered on his life again.

Sweat started on his forehead, then sprang from every pore in his body.

A black, treacherous faint struggled up from his lungs.

Fighting it back Mr. X cried out to the albino, Help me! Help me!

The albino took the bottle of Malawian Drambuie and stared at it.

In ten years of drinking it he had never seen it produce such reactions. The man of Ironheart appeared to be sinking into a deathly coma, his limbs twitching, sweat streaming down his battered face. In his voice was the desperate plea of the dying to be saved from death.

Mr. X collapsed, struck down by a dose of cerebral malaria.

During the night of his first awareness of his hippopotamorphosis when he had slept in the bush after Mrs. W. T. Franks's party, Mr. X had been assaulted by a female Anopheles mosquito, herself an ancient and fiercely independent life-form. She had driven her sharp proboscis into Mr. X's skin and pumped an animal of the phylum Protozoa, in the genus Plasmodium, into his blood stream. This busy parasite, in an asexual free-swimming form of sporozoite had not checked with Mr. X's philosophical mind-cells before deciding to get to work on its host. It immediately burrowed into a red blood cell, developed a ringlike shape, and blew itself into a greater size called a schizoni. This schizoni then divided up into forms called merozoites and they started the really serious business of rupturing Mr. X's blood-cells. Just as he received Ironheart's good-bye letter, the merozoites made their first major break-through in the battle, ably assisted by the thrashings administered upon their host's body by Reg's men and the callous unkindness of the Consul, now winging his way towards Myakajunji.

Animalself in its lowest form had truly entered into Mr. X, but by the back door. As he lay on the floor shuddering with the malarial chill and projectile vomiting clean across the room, he dreamed a dream.

He was at last in his looked-for land. Mr. X was home and dry. Oh things were different there.

It was Animal Paradise.

Bloody, battered and buggered by insects from without, parasites from within, men from outside and women from inside, he was in a fit state to perceive the great truths which lie at the heart of the mystery. He was a life-hero, one who had fought and fallen in his finest hour. In the war of self-discovery he was the victor, bringing all parts of his divided soul back together into one Wholecock.

There was the Serpent.

Round and round the slave-tree it was wound.

What a sad song it was singing while its scales blazed with all the colours beyond each end of the seen spectrum!

Fee-fi-fo-fum!

I smell the blood of an Englishman!

"G'day!" it squawked with the voice of Pyper. "Have you seen Margaret From The Iron Bar?"

Mr. X wandered in the shade of the tree, a few *mupundukaina* leaves discreetly covering his genitals.

"G'day!" came the identical squawk from under the cluster of *mupundukaina* leaves. "Seen anything of The Staff Heart?"

Mr. X lifted the leaves and there was Pyper with a ruff of red and gold feathers sitting on a nest of Mr. X's pubic hair. He had two tufts of frail purple on the crown of his delicate head and a silver beak with tiny nostrils in the shape of stars.

Hanging across one of the branches of the tree was George Crompton. He was covered with moss. Hermione was in the branches above him dropping leaves on to the moss to make a beautiful pattern. Her red hair tumbled all the way down to the ground and monkeys hid in it gnawing berries. One of them was a nursing mother and she had two felt-pens for teats. As the baby sucked at her it developed an intricate drawing over its small hairy body.

It was a human heart inside a human heart inside a human heart inside a human heart.

TWENTY-TWO **JOURNEY TO THE END**

Mr. X lay in his hospital bed on the first day that he was allowed to receive visitors and watched the door of the ward as the bell rang.

The matron, who had not been particularly tender to him during his illness as he consistently changed the name on his temperature chart from H. Halfcock to Mr. X, had told him that only two visitors were allowed at a time. People had enquired after his health, one or two, she said. Someone might come.

Mr. X hoped they would.

He did not like the hospital.

Being the only patient in a ward of fourteen beds was a tedious business.

The nurses were all tough, hard-eyed women who treated him as if he were a lump of dirt in their clean, scrubbed ward.

Even the African cleaning-women had caught this professional attitude from their superiors and brushed and polished around Mr. X's bed as if he was a mountain of steaming horse manure in a glaciated landscape. They did not want to listen to his stories. They refused to bring him beer. When Mr. X had asked how the fight against Hammerkop was going, the women had looked at him as if he was mad. They were cleaners of the fee-paying hospital, the building where the bwanas were born, suffered and died. What could they know of the fight against Hammerkop? When they were transferred for disciplinary reasons to the teeming non-fee-paying hospital in the township where there were twenty-eight patients in a ward for fourteen, then they might know.

Mr. X heard a shouting in the corridors.

His heart lifted.

Above the bass rumbling of men's voices he could hear the matron screaming hysterically. Then the note of her complaint changed to a new alarm sound. Her person had been interfered with.

Before they burst through the ward door, boots flying, flies agape, millet-beer in their hair and up their noses, copies of Playboy clutched in their hands, he knew that it could only be the Bucket-Wheel Excavator Gang who had come to see him.

"Oh dear," they muttered in distress as they looked at the pale, shrunken shadow of his former self, "is this what IROing does to a man? It is all our fault."

Mr. X laughed and dismissed their guilty condolences. He had never been so glad to see anyone in his life before. While the Bucket-Wheel Excavator Gang filled his bedside cabinet, his pee-bottle and his bed with dumpies of lager, he asked them for news. What was happening in Mufunsi? How was Pyper, Albert, Pforzheim?

And where was Matthias?

The Bucket-Wheel Excavator Gang fell silent.

"Well, where is he?"

Cumulus McCloud Molile lay on the next bed, his hands folded on his chest.

"Ah, if only you knew," he said sadly. "The shame of it!"

"What's he done?"

"He has joined the bwanas. In fact he has been bwanad much as you were debwanad."

"Matthias? I don't believe it!" Mr. X gasped.

"Hammerkop has made him night-shift mine-captain. He is to get £220 a month and a new bungalow near the sporting amenities, and he is to be allowed to join the Mine Club, the Dutch Reformed Church and the British Empire Service League!" Cumulus McCloud Molile intoned. "It is the end!"

"No! No!" Mr. X got out of bed, such was his agitation. "Not Matthias!"

"And I, of all people, am to be the next supervisor of the Bucket-Wheel Excavator Gang," Cumulus McCloud Molile sighed. "I will not live long with that burden. Like you, my friend, I think I will take refuge in fantasies instead."

Mr. X sat down on the edge of the bed, his knees woolly and weak. The Bucket-Wheel Excavator Gang, seeing what little colour left in his face had drained away, rolled him back into bed and tucked him up.

"You must speak to him for us. We have all failed. Pyper has gone down on his knees to him. But Matthias says no. He is disgusted with us, his work-mates, for what we did to that *umfazi* in the pool. We even had a collection to bribe him but he would not accept it. Only you can change his mind, O mighty dreamer. He blames us for his despair. He says we are hopeless rubbish."

The matron arrived at that point with four male ward orderlies and a mine policeman. She was surprised when the Bucket-Wheel Excavator Gang retreated without a murmur, shuffling off down the corridor like a crowd of old, defeated men.

"Nice friends you've got!" the matron hissed as she dug all the beer bottles out of the bed and the cabinet. "If I was you sonny I'd start thinking about how I could improve my social standing instead of consorting with those people. I'll have to fumigate this ward now."

Half-way through visiting-time Mr. X had another visitor.

He hardly recognised her as she came through the door.

It was Gladys.

She had changed.

There was a new roughness in her face, blended with a vigour that had not been there before. Her body had a jaunty awkwardness as if it was propelled by forces which she was not quite able to control or understand. Her clothes were older, less ordered in the way they hung upon her body. Even her shoes were scuffed.

"Hiya!" she chortled and plonked herself down on the bed, leaning over him to plant a big wet kiss on his mouth. "Mmmm! You look like something the cat brought in."

Mr. X was amazed.

Where was the Dresden china? Who had burgled the display cabinet?

"Gladys... I hardly recognised you," he murmured unintelligibly.

"Eh?" Gladys screwed a finger-tip into her ear. "What was that? You look as though you need livening up a bit."

Mr. X stared in astonishment as Gladys scratched at her left breast which had nearly fallen out of her blouse.

"What's happened to you?" he managed to say in a faint voice.

"Hormones. The doctors said it was those leaves. They stimulated the ovaries and the ovaries stimulated the uterus and the uterus stimulated the vagina and where else could I go from there?"

She crinkled up her dancing blue eyes and nudged the patient with a playful elbow.

"Frank had to take a few days off work. I ran him into the ground. He never knew what hit him."

"I'm glad everything worked out all right," Mr. X smiled, already feeling much better. "Frank thinks a lot of you. I think you'd be better off back in South Africa now, don't you?"

Gladys's eyes contracted into shrewish blue burn.

"Now don't you start that. Frank is bad enough. He's been trying to get me to agree to frolic around with all those stuck-up half-dead walking shithouses he calls the Board. Well I'm not interested in being bored by the Board. I want men, not a bevy of broken-down armchair fuckers like that lot. Which is one of the reasons why I came to see you."

She leaned forward, a mischievous grin on her unpainted rosebud.

"Have you any idea how I can find a feller called The Old Man Of The Woods?"

"The Old Man Of The Woods?" Mr. X repeated stupidly.

"That's right. I've heard he's fantastic."

"Who told you that?"

"Some of the girls."

"Which girls?"

"Never you mind you horny bugger. Come on, cough up. Do you know where I can find him?"

Mr. X blinked up at the lively, lecherous face of the statue that had come to life. He saw her blonde wispy hair hanging round her face like summer grass, her once-pinched nostrils now flared, sniffing up his smells and the scents of the wallflowers in the bed outside. In his heart he wanted to give her directions to find Mushikishi and his charcoal-beds but he shuddered to think what Hammerkop would do to her if he ever found out.

"Gladys, I think The Old Man Of The Woods is just a story. He doesn't exist," he said hesitantly.

"He does!" Gladys hissed, leaning closer. "I've talked to women who've been with him."

"Why won't they tell you?"

"Because The Old Man Of The Woods made them promise not to. He said that he was getting too many visitors. But I reckon that once I get out there and find him he won't mind one extra. I'll give him the time of his life."

"Gladys, why don't you stick to Frank..."

"Oh don't be silly. You know he's only a start. Christ man, I'm thirty-five and I know nothing! I've been wasting time up till now. Please tell me how to find The Old Man Of The Woods..."

"Gladys! What are you doing?"

"Please...come on, make room!"

"Gladys, I'm still very weak!"

"The hell you are! You've been lying here having erotic fantasies about me haven't you?"

"That sounds a bit more like the old Gladys. Ouch!"

The matron returned and hauled Gladys out of Mr. X's bed, then ran her through the ward doors by the scruff of her neck. When she came back there was a new hardness in her eyes and round her down-curving mouth.

"Come on, out! On your bike! I don't care what the doc says, you're out! Off you go! You go and ruin your health like you're obviously determined to do at the first opportunity. On your feet

222

soldier! I want you dressed and out of here in five minutes. And if you're dying at any time, don't come running to me for sympathy. Stay in the gutter where you belong!"

The matron gave Mr. X a plastic bag to put his belongings in and conducted him to the gate, watching him slowly walk down the avenue towards the town centre before she was satisfied that he had really gone away. Mr. X did not find the walking easy as he was weaker than he thought. After half a mile he sat down on the kerb for a rest. While he was sitting there Pyper drove up in his car.

"Hop in you Pom hasbeen. You look like last night's french letter hanging on a barbed-wire fence. Come on, I'll take you out for a bite of lunch."

Mr. X was glad to see the human parakeet.

But he could see that things were not the same.

There was an unspoken moroseness in the hang of his comb and the sheen on his feathers.

"Matthias?"

"Don't talk to me about that black bastard!" Pyper screeched.

"The Bucket-Wheel Excavator Gang came to see me."

"I know. I told them to!"

"I still can't believe it."

"Listen Pom, since you went down with malaria everything has gone Hammerkop's way. He struck upon this ruse with Matthias – he'd never thought of buying the fat bastard off before – and Gladys has suddenly come across. Everyone loves Hammerkop. The board of directors are up here from Johannesburg by the minute to stay overnight at his mansion. Productivity has gone up. He's on the pig's back. I reckon if he started shitting gold nuggets it would cause him neither pain nor surprise."

Sitting in a booth at the British Empire Service League the New Zealander tried to explain to Mr. X why Matthias had suddenly switched his allegiances.

"The oldest answer. Cash. Admittedly he's never had a penny to bless himself with but that's no reason to sell your friends down the river."

Mr. X thought for a while before pointing out that a streak of similar expediency ran through Pyper's nature, witness his attitude to Reg. Where was Pyper on that fateful night at the Lido when Reg's men were beating the living daylights out of Mvhu?

"That was the Congo Pom. I can't care about the whole of Africa. This place is my concern. If Matthias goes then I'm on my own. The rest of you bastards are only in it for what you can get out of it. When the good Doctor deports me there'll be no one to carry on the work. You'll be grovelling around somewhere thinking you're a Venus Fly Trap, Pforzheim will be kissing his father's arse, Albert will be negotiating a government contract to print parking tickets... oh what's the fucking use!"

Pyper's shoulders sagged and into his merciless blue eye crept a strange thing: a tear.

"The Bucket-Wheel Excavator Gang said he might listen to me," Mr. X said hesitantly. "I'll give it a try if you think it's worth while."

"Why should he listen to you? I've told him often enough that you're as intellectually developed as a gnu's nudger. No man, that fat slob can see the light at the end of the tunnel. He's selling out while he's got the chance. Can you blame him? Hammerkop's offered him ten times his wages to become a bwana. Christ, money washes whiter you know. What a bloody world!"

After the seventh course of the lunch, a gin 'n lemon, Pyper became aggressively critical of his environment and started to pick a fight with two Portuguese cable-layers off the pylon gangs working for the Kariba Dam project. Mr. X decided to leave him to it, knowing that he would be of little use in a fight and besides, Pyper deserved to be deserted once in a while.

The flat over the Greek supermarket was empty.

Dusty. Dirty.

Dishes lay in the kitchen sink, encrusted with egg-yolk.

Mr. X crawled on to the bed and fell into a deep sleep.

He dreamed no dream for the time for dreams was over.

That night he walked the long road to the Open Pit and sat in the dark in what used to be his office, watching the big trucks toiling up out of the chasm to be handed over to the night-shift drivers. When they were all drawn up in lines on the giant park outside the offices Mr. X walked along the verandah to the mine-captain's office. There was Matthias checking the time-sheets, his bullet-head bowed over his work.

"Hello Matthias," Mr. X said quietly.

Matthias looked up, startled.

"Well, it's you! I thought you were in hospital!" he exclaimed, half-rising out of his chair.

"No, I have just got out of hospital – but you will shortly be going into hospital," Mr. X said steadily.

"Me? Why should I be going into hospital?"

"Because I am going to attack you with this geological hammer."

"Come on man, be reasonable..."

As Matthias pushed back his chair and tried to get to his feet Mr. X struck him behind the ear with the flat end of the sampling hammer. Checking the verandah first he then dragged his unconscious friend along to the European management showers, dumped him under the sprinkler with the taps off, and ran back to his office. A moment later he was reporting to the Mine Police that an African employee was using Hammerkop's shower.

Once again he sat in the dark and waited.

He did not have long to wait.

Within two minutes a Mine Police Land-Rover roared down the Open Pit road, followed by Hammerkop's green Dodge. Mr. X sprinted round to the showers, tore off Matthias's overalls, rubbed soap into his hair, and turned on the water. He was only just in time. As he ran out of the door and back down the verandah he heard the crash of boots and blowing of whistles as the Mine Police baton-charged the showers, Hammerkop shrieking encouragement from behind. Not long after, the naked form of Matthias was dragged out of the showers, handcuffed and chained at the ankles, and heaved into the back of the Land-Rover.

Mr. X sat in his office, a grim smile on his lips.

He could hear Hammerkop in his office.

He was talking to the General Manager on the telephone.

"Christ you stupid Pom bastard you really had me fooled with your sophisticated ideas! Promote the kaffir you said! Buy him out! What did I say then? I said that once a kaffir always a kaffir! He'll let us down! Why don't you get back to that shithouse in Surrey where you were dragged up by a lesbian nanny and the local national assistance officer you Pom creep? What d'you mean what's the matter? Didn't I say he'd start taking liberties? Give them an inch and they'll take a mile! What?...Christ Almighty, anyone would think it was me who'd done something wrong! Well I'll be...you *rooinek*...*sauty*...Pom...bastard..."

Hammerkop put the telephone down, unemployed.

225

The celebrations that followed the defeat of Hammerkop and his discharge from the service of Mufunsi Mines Ltd. went on for three days. The hero of the hour was Mr. X. By a masterstroke of IROing, knowing his basic human psychology and using his natural intelligence, he had manoeuvred the Open Pit Manager out of office. His lickspittle, the new Hurl Halfcock, had been pushed aside in this battle. He sat somewhere in a toady silence, still nursing his wounds. And Matthias had been saved from becoming the first black bwana. So there was a lot to celebrate. The Undesirables swept through all the 234 bars in Mufunsi carrying George Crompton and wherever they went became a scene of extravagant drunken wildness. They handed themselves over to the little gods of the body and danced.

On the last night, when Mr. X was exhaustedly drunk, still debilitated by his bout of cerebral malaria, Pyper did the only decent thing.

He agreed to let Mr. X *hlanganana* Margaret From The Tonga Bar.

When Pyper made the announcement Mr. X was lying in a corner with George Crompton and Pforzheim, singing one of the old songs that Matthias had been teaching them:

Muuna kulima
Musali uitulezi
Weyaya weyaya
Kangyana kambuwa
Kupuu!

which means: Men are cultivating
                                but the women are loafing.

in the Lozi language of the south. As the three men droned away in the corner, Pyper made his generous offer, a curious grin on his beautiful bird-man's face.

"Well come on then Mr. X, what are you waiting for?"

Mr. X looked up from the floor and shook himself free of George Crompton's dormant grip.

"Christ, you're a big-hearted bastard John," he mumbled. "There's not many people would make that kind of sacrifice, even for a good friend."

"Well, Pom, it's the least I can do for the man who got rid of Hammerkop for us. I've told Margaret From The Tonga Bar. She's upstairs waiting for you."

With a roar of delight, the Bucket-Wheel Excavator Gang picked

Mr. X up off the floor and carried him up the well-worn stairs, their hoarse voices raised in a great chorus of triumph:

> *Tilonjele imfumu yawela*
> *Welu, welu,*
> *Sabata acita ubecha*
> *Onani asungwana*
> *Oyee, oyee!*

which means:
Let us welcome
the chief
who has come!

in the Tumbuka language of the north-east. Spreadeagled on their stretcher of willing hands Mr. X heard their coarse harmonising and the translation bellowed from the bottom of the stairs by a radiant, overwhelmingly happy Matthias. It could be, he thought to himself, a little previous. He knew that he was astoundingly drunk again and though his soul was at peace in a harbour of alcoholic shelter, he was uncertain about his physical powers.

"This makes us feel less guilty about what we did in the pool in Elizabethville," Cumulus McCloud Molile whispered to Mr. X. "Now all your sufferings are going to be worth while."

Matthias shouldered his way through the Bucket-Wheel Excavator Gang and hammered on the door, his ringing baritone pealing out yet another traditional song as his size 11 desert boots started to stamp and kick in a thunderous rhythm.

> *Okacembele kozwa*
> *Oomo munhanda*
> *Koteelela!*
> *Nobaza bwiimba*
> *Teelela mubateelele*
> *Basika mbaabo balombe*
> *Bawoonda mulimo!*

Around him and down in the Tonga Bar the song was repeated until it was a giant of sound. The windows shook in their frames. Glasses jigged on tables and the stairs shivered. Mr. X closed his eyes as Matthias thrust his head next to his and hissed the translation:

> Woman who will one day be old
> Come out of that room
> And listen to the singing
> Of the triumphant men!

"Matthias, don't you think I've had enough of a build-up?"

227

Mr. X whimpered, his confidence on the ebb. The boastings of the song and the dance were outstripping what reserves of strength he felt that he had.

"Mr. X, this is a big night in your life!" Matthias shouted boisterously. "We can't let it pass without a murmur."

"Christ Mr. X, you getting cold feet old sport?" Pyper shrieked above the din. "Perhaps you'd like me to nip out and get you a bag of cement."

The door opened.

A hush descended on the riotous crowd.

Mr. X trembled in the arms of the Bucket-Wheel Excavator Gang. Was there anything in the world to match this marvellous work of a generous life-giving God? Oh where was his strength? Sapped by booze and lack of sleep he lay like an old man looking on beauty with only his eyes, his body unable to respond.

"Let him stand by himself," Margaret From The Tonga Bar said.

Gently the Bucket-Wheel Excavator Gang set him down. He felt his knees buckle. Oh no! Animalself be with me now! Don't fail me! he thought desperately, feeling for the wall. Help me old fathers! Be with me in this hour! Give me your power!

Margaret From The Tonga Bar took his hand and led him into the room. As she closed the door prolonged cheering rose from the stairs and bar and Matthias struck up another song. Leading Mr. X across to the bed, Margaret From The Tonga Bar helped him to sit down.

"I have a question to ask you," she said with a loving smile. But there was a touch of seriousness in her throaty, welcoming, warm voice.

"Oh Christ . . ." Mr. X started to moan, "please don't torment me."

"I'm not tormenting you," Margaret From The Tonga Bar assured him as she stripped off his shirt. "All I want to ask is a fair question."

"Margaret From The Tonga Bar," Mr. X cried, desire miraculously starting to clamber up his exhausted limbs like fire up a dead tree. "Ask a thousand questions and I will look for the answer!"

"What am I?"

Mr. X looked up at her black, open-hearted, undignified beauty. Far away in the rich brown earth of her eyes he saw a movement. A twinkle. An eye within another eye. Many eyes! His strength quickened in its streaming back into his aroused blood. So that's where they'd been hiding, the crafty old ancients! The old devils!

See where they peered at him from! They had always been there, camouflaged! Tumultuous thrills shuddered through his limbs as he saw those squinting, cunning, cheerful eyes relaying backwards, backwards, proliferating into their thousands of millions. Through those two windows in the African whore's eyes he saw the countless herd of the animal fathers stretched over the great plains of history. With a wild whoop of joy and recognition he knelt up on the bed and threw his arms wide.

"Father!"

"Eh?" Margaret From The Tonga Bar said in bewilderment, backing away.

"Oh Father! Father! Father!" Mr. X cried in a deep mysterious voice which reverberated with his wonderful discovery. "Oh Almighty Dad!"

Seizing hold of Margaret From The Tonga Bar's hands he stared fanatically through the peep-holes of her loving pupils, bathed in the proud fatherly expressions of the great herd of the old heavens. Their leery, ancient eyes bore the freckled green of the spring leaf, the yellow of the butterfly, the purple of the sea-shell's blood. Now they shouted to him! Roughly, across oceans of time they bellowed, holding up their scarred hands and waving excitedly. Hello, mighty dreamer! Hello son! From the dreaming land of the dead they cried out thunderous greetings and in the background he could hear their warm chuckles and snorts of pleasure. Please! they roared. Carry on! Don't stop hunting son, keep looking and ye shall find! Never give up!

Mr. X knew their meaning. Once the philosophers of the senses died, natural doctors of the earth like Mushikishi, then the animal fathers would be swept from those starry plains like dust before the brawling broom of the wind. Men would forget the wild old ones, rationalise them out of existence in the same way as they abolished the flat world. The *beginning* would be lost, then the middle, and then the end. Man would drift away from himself, a leaking ship that had slipped her anchor.

Mr. X sat back on his haunches, still holding Margaret From The Tonga Bar's hands. Tears streamed down his cheeks. Happiness blossomed in his body and head like a soft red flower, powerful in perfume. Oh they had come so far to talk to *him*! So far through space and time! Was he worthy of the vision? Could he live with such a revelation constantly beating at his brain to be enacted again? Who

229

could he tell? Was this naked, half-blind, inefficient creature in the bedroom of a genial strumpet the true carrier of that awful responsibility? Should he have been given that insight, or did it rightly belong to someone else who had more sense?

"Well," Margaret From The Tonga Bar asked, "what am I?"

"You're a woman," Mr. X confessed humbly.

"Yet you called me your father."

"Yes," Mr. X nodded, "I did."

"What does that make me then?"

"A womanimal?"

Margaret From The Tonga Bar smiled.

"You were hearing voices *musungu*?"

"And seeing faces."

"You are a big dreamer. Where is it going to get you?"

Mr. X lay back on the bed. He could have answered that his dreams and his quests would make him old before his time, or they might provide him with the secret of eternal youth. He might die, grey headed and broken, but still with the mind and heart of a child. There were many possibilities and he was grateful for them. Whoever he was, Hurl Halfcock, war-chief of the Oglala Sioux, *y*, George Robinson, the new IRO, Mvhu, or Mr. X, he was alive and he now knew what it was to be alive right through to the last molecule of tissue. Africa had pushed him deep into the vessel of himself until every nook and cranny was filled with being.

Margaret From The Tonga Bar turned out all the lights except one blue bulb. While Mr. X waited doubts and glories filled the theatre of his mind, chasing each other on and off, fighting a brilliant pantomime war of confidence and fear. Who would win in the end? Looking upwards he saw the enormous mirror that spanned the ceiling in its carved golden frame of goats' heads, vine-leaves and children. In the blue sea of light he saw shadows of black and white swimming together through teeming oceans, the blue men and the grey women, the fish and flesh, the dried-up driftwood and the springing green branch torn off by the inland hurricane, the old and new, the dead and the living. The glass was full of images of early life and they whorled into pools of eyes and feet, hair and flanks as he stared upwards: they evoked sensations of agelessness and freedom from death. Every hour that he had spent in Africa was stretched to a hundred years and he reached backwards to his first landing, the journey, the arrival in Mufunsi, Mushikishi. Then one dark figure

reached him. That black, rich womanimal drawing him upwards.
Was it Phénomène, his natural mate?
Ironheart, his manager?
Or the timeless Mother of God, Father of Man?
No, it was none of these.
It was Margaret From The Tonga Bar.
And she did not find him wanting.

AN EPILOGUE **WHICH BRINGS SOME OF THE FIRST TO BE LAST WHICH IS ALSO OFTEN THE AFRICAN WAY**

The next morning Mr. X rose early, leaving Margaret From The Tonga Bar asleep. As he looked down at her he was conscious of the proof of her promise: he did feel a better man. Man and animal had integrated. He was whole. Now the important thing was to get out to Mushikishi, his fellow philosopher, and to tell him the answers he had found.

Sadly he was already too late. While Mr. X had been in the arms of Margaret From The Tonga Bar, pillowed on the bounty of a generous and loving God, Mushikishi had received some visitors. At the time the African Socrates had been lying between two of his smouldering charcoal-beds with Arabella Parkinson, responding to her voluntary charity work. During the next half hour, the Predikant of the Dutch Deformed Church, the ·underground manager of South Orebody, and Mr Viljoen, the manager of the crematorium and florist's shop on 14th Avenue, solved for the old *penseur* the riddle of the bwanas.

They tied a rope around his ankles, threw the end over an overhanging tree, and suspended the philosopher over his own charcoal fire.

"Why take out your own failures on me?" Mushikishi had pleaded as his frizzy hair began to singe. "Why don't you sort yourselves out instead of blaming us for your inadequacies?"

"Shut up kaffir and fry!" the Predikant had snarled, giving Mushikishi a boot in the ear that set him swinging like a pendulum.

"By the great king Christ you bwanas are pathetic creatures," the old charcoal-burner persisted as he swung through the smoke, his hoarse voice heavy with grief. "Look at the way you are behaving now. It leads me to think that although we, the black people, evolved here in Africa, you white bwanas start devolving as soon as you come here. Hnm, if you could only see your faces. What a picture you make. What I can't understand is why, or how, you ever got the idea that you were superior? It cannot be because of your behaviour, or the bigness of your hearts, for your hearts are as tight as a crab's arse and that is water-tight."

"So this is the Old Man Of The Woods," the underground manager of South Orebody sneered as he took a brand out of the fire and tried to set light to Mushikishi's vest. "This kaffir filth!"

With another kick he sent Mushikishi swinging in an even greater arc.

"Don't you understand, you ignorant men? Because we invented Man here, we also had to invent forgiveness. Otherwise how would he ever have survived in this world? How would we get by with all the murder in our bones and the hatred in our hearts? We kaffirs had to invent forgiveness and try to teach you *musungus* how to use it! But we failed. Oh, how we failed! We should have kept you out of Africa! Passed immigration laws! Then the concept of the bwana would never have been born!

A wind ran through the bush. As it blew through the undergrowth Mr. Viljoen grabbed the rope and steadied the upside-down old man over the fire. The whole business was taking too long. Soon the fire was leaping up at the twisting head.

Arabella Parkinson ran off towards the road, trying to rub the finger-marks off her creamy skin.

Behind her she heard explosions.

"God," she thought, "they're shooting him to make sure."

But it was not gunshots, but Mushikishi's eyes. They exploded from their sockets like whirling silver stars. Then his ear-drums burst like twin thunder. Tongues of flame poured from his mouth. Showers of sparks shot from his nostrils. His balls detonated like a thousand deep-throated bells. His navel blew off and roared away into the darkness like a flying saucer. Finally his whole body erupted with a deafening bang and the philosophical soul of Mushikishi rose in a column of beautiful red smoke to join the Cloud of Unknowing where all true thinkers have their final resting-place.

When Mr. X arrived next morning there was nothing left, only a charred rope and a dead fire. He sat around for two hours, hoping his old friend would return. When he could wait no longer he scribbled a note and left it stuck on a twig where Mushikishi could find it.

> Have scrapped Three Races of Man but definitely confirmed
> continued existence of animal fathers through contemporary
> human agencies. Dying to tell you all about it. As for the
> mystery of the bwanas, I think Dignity is one key. The only
> real riddle is why they failed as animals. I think it must be
> because they wandered away from Africa. Can you forgive
> them? Or must I say US? I'll call again and we can have a
> long talk. Yours, your *disciple*.

Sorry to have missed his master, Mr. X walked back to Mufunsi
and the flat over the Greek supermarket. As he entered, a shadow
settled over his feeling of resolution and wholeness. Something was
missing. Something that Margaret From The Tonga Bar, the old
animal fathers, his brothers above and below water, could not offer
him.

Care.

The manself love.

Now he had found himself, this was what he needed. It would
bind him together. Keep him in one piece and strong against all the
apostles of disintegration.

He went out on to the balcony.

It was a bright morning. The brown Christmas tree stood in the
square, sturdy and reassuring relic of a season past and a season
to come.

Under its branches he saw a ghastly pink and brown hand raised.

He waved back, then went into the kitchen to make some coffee.

It was while he was brushing his teeth in the bathroom that he
heard it, the singing.

Poking his head round the bathroom door he saw the slight figure
on its knees as a blurr in the frosted glass. With his toothbrush still
in his mouth he ran down thé corridor and flung open the door.

"Ironheart!" he foamed. "Oh ayanblurmph!"

She got to her feet and held the delirious man at bay as he tried to
take her into his arms. He smiled through the dentifrice like a child
covered in ice-cream, his green eyes greener with joy as he spat the
toothbrush out and plastered her soft black cheek with white bubbly
kisses.

"Ironheart! You've come back!" he murmured delightedly.
"You're back!"

233

"Am I?" she sniffed. "Only because you asked me to."

Mr X paused.

It had been on his mind to look for the letter which Ironheart had left for him on the mantelpiece. Perhaps he had really done it sometime during the last few days when he had been drunk? What did it matter? She was back, standing there, as pigeon-toed as ever. He hugged her, kissing every square on her head.

"Why did you wait so long before sending me the telegram?" she asked critically. "I was stuck up there for days."

"I don't know," Mr. X answered truthfully — for he could not remember sending a telegram at all. In his mind he blessed himself for having had the good sense to do so, if he had. That was a time when the thinking powers of his manself had done him a good turn. Perhaps he had more brains than he suspected?

Outside, under the brown Christmas tree, the albino beggar sat without his bottle of Malawian Drambuie. He had seen Ironheart arrive and that had helped to allay the pangs in his stomach. Today he had suffered, but it was worth it. If he worked hard tomorrow he might make up the deficit that his visit to the telegram counter at the Post Office had caused.

As he watched the steps to the flat he also saw the Consul arrive in a big black Ford with two Zonkendawon immigration officers. He could only guess at what their business might be with the happy couple.

In the Consul's brief-case there was a brand-new passport issued by Her Britannic Majesty's Foreign Office.

The holder had been born in Walton, Liverpool.

He was twenty-five years old.

And his name was Crazy River Horse.

On its first stamp page was a deportation order signed by Doctor Mulombe himself, to take immediate effect.

Resting next to the passport was an aeroplane ticket paid for out of Foreign Office funds for the repatriation of a Lost Englishman.

There are but a few seconds left to Crazy River Horse and Ironheart before the nicotine-stained thumb of the Consul presses the electric bell of the flat over the Greek supermarket.

Let us leave them to it.